FABLES, FOLKLORE & ANCIENT STORIES

VIKING

FOLK & FAIRY TALES

FLAME TREE PUBLISHING
6 Melbray Mews, Fulham,
London SW6 3NS, United Kingdom
www.flametreepublishing.com

First published and copyright © 2022
Flame Tree Publishing Ltd

22 24 26 25 23
1 3 5 7 9 10 8 6 4 2

ISBN: 978-1-80417-230-8

Cover and pattern art was created by Flame Tree Studio, with elements
courtesy of Shutterstock.com/Bourbon-88. Inside decorations courtesy of
Shutterstock.com/robin.ph/ttd1387.

Judith John (Glossary) is a writer and editor specializing in literature and history. A former
secondary school English Language and Literature teacher, she has subsequently worked
as an editor on major educational projects, including *English A: Literature* for the Pearson
International Baccalaureate series. Judith's major research interests include Romantic and
Gothic literature, and Renaissance drama.

Original compilers, authors, editors and translators for the stories in this book include:
Hans Christian Andersen, Peter Christen Asbjørnsen/Jørgen Engebretsen Moe, G. W.
Dasent, Jacob and Wilhelm Grimm/Margaret Hunt, Thomas Wentworth Higginson,
Andrew Lang, Clara Stroebe/Frederick H. Martens, Charles John Tibbits.

A copy of the CIP data for this book is available
from the British Library.

Designed and created in the UK | Printed and bound in China

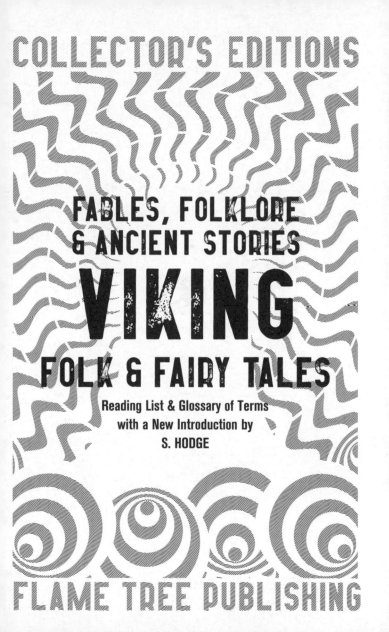

COLLECTOR'S EDITIONS

FABLES, FOLKLORE
& ANCIENT STORIES

VIKING

FOLK & FAIRY TALES

Reading List & Glossary of Terms
with a New Introduction by
S. HODGE

FLAME TREE PUBLISHING

CONTENTS

5

FABLES, FOLKLORE & ANCIENT STORIES

VIKING

FOLK & FAIRY TALES

SERIES FOREWORD

Stretching back to the oral traditions of thousands of years ago, tales of heroes and disaster, creation and conquest have been told by many different civilizations in many different ways. Their impact sits deep within our culture even though the detail in the tales themselves are a loose mix of historical record, transformed narrative and the distortions of hundreds of storytellers.

Today the language of mythology lives with us: our mood is jovial, our countenance is saturnine, we are narcissistic and our modern life is hermetically sealed from others. The nuances of myths and legends form part of our daily routines and help us navigate the world around us, with its half truths and biased reported facts.

The nature of a myth is that its story is already known by most of those who hear it, or read it. Every generation brings a new emphasis, but the fundamentals remain the same: a desire to understand and describe the events and relationships of the world. Many of the great stories are archetypes that help us find our own place, equipping us with tools for self-understanding, both individually and as part of a broader culture.

For Western societies it is Greek mythology that speaks to us most clearly. It greatly influenced the mythological heritage of the ancient Roman civilization and is the lens through which we still see the Celts, the Norse and many of the other great peoples and religions. The Greeks themselves learned much from their neighbours, the Egyptians, an older culture that became weak with age and incestuous leadership.

It is important to understand that what we perceive now as mythology had its own origins in perceptions of the divine and the rituals of the sacred. The earliest civilizations, in the crucible of the Middle East, in the Sumer of the third millennium BC, are the source to which many of the mythic archetypes can be traced. As humankind collected together in cities for the first time, developed writing and industrial scale agriculture, started to irrigate the rivers and attempted to control rather than be at the mercy of its environment, humanity began to write down its tentative explanations of natural events, of floods and plagues, of disease.

Early stories tell of Gods (or god-like animals in the case of tribal societies such as African, Native American or Aboriginal cultures) who are crafty and use their wits to survive, and it is reasonable to suggest that these were the first rulers of the gathering peoples of the earth, later elevated to god-like status with the distance of time. Such tales became more political as cities vied with each other for supremacy, creating new Gods, new hierarchies for their pantheons. The older Gods took on primordial roles and became the preserve of creation and destruction, leaving the new gods to deal with more current, everyday affairs. Empires rose and fell, with Babylon assuming the mantle from Sumeria in the 1800s BC, then in turn to be swept away by the Assyrians of the 1200s BC; then the Assyrians and the Egyptians were subjugated by the Greeks, the Greeks by the Romans and so on, leading to the spread and assimilation of common themes, ideas and stories throughout the world.

The survival of history is dependent on the telling of good tales, but each one must have the 'feeling' of truth, otherwise it will be ignored. Around the firesides, or embedded in a book or a computer, the myths and legends of the past are still the living materials of retold myth, not restricted to an exploration of origins. Now we have devices and global communications that give us unparalleled access to a diversity of traditions. We can find out about Native American, Indian, Chinese and tribal African mythology in a way that was denied to our ancestors, we can find connections, match the archaeology, religion and the mythologies of the world to build a comprehensive image of the human experience that is endlessly fascinating.

The stories in this book provide an introduction to the themes and concerns of the myths and legends of their respective cultures, with a short introduction to provide a linguistic, geographic and political context. This is where the myths have arrived today, but undoubtedly over the next millennia, they will transform again whilst retaining their essential truths and signs.

Jake Jackson
General Editor

FABLES, FOLKLORE & ANCIENT STORIES

VIKING

FOLK & FAIRY TALES

INTRODUCTION
& FURTHER READING

A NEW INTRODUCTION TO
VIKING FOLK & FAIRY TALES

Some stories are centuries old. From their first narrations over camp fires, many have drifted on the breeze of time until they reach and envelop us, carrying us back to their own faraway pasts. For their magical, extraordinary characters, their breathtaking settings, and their inventive actions and conclusions, these stories can still capture and absorb us.

The stories and legends in this book were first told verbally over a thousand years ago, but they were not written down until the thirteenth century. They are Viking – or Norse – folklore, and they include heroic sagas, accounts of some of the earliest seafarers, magic, fantastic creatures, fables, histories and myths of adventure and daring. They are exciting and thought-provoking, alarming and inspiring. They explain the world and they add mystery to it. Originally, they were recited as people sat together around camp fires, each staring into the flickering tongues of flame, individually forming their own imaginative images. Deep into the night, the stories came to their conclusions as the glowing embers died away into the darkness. Later, poets recounted them in shadowy halls after great feasts, as the guests sat back to listen and dream, and later still, parents told the tales to their children as they gathered around crackling hearths on cold winter nights. They are grand tales of magic, love, treachery, conquest and defeat. Many explained religious beliefs for their original listeners, but they remain eternal and universal human stories that continue to have resonance for us all.

The Norsemen spoke Old Norse, which they called *dönsk tunga* (the Danish tongue). With minor variations, this language was spoken throughout the Norse lands during the Viking period. The Vikings did not develop a written culture, but used runes to record short works, and long works were remembered using poetry. In its vehemence to implement Christianity in Europe, the Church did not authorize the recording of Viking myths, so once the Vikings had integrated with Christian society, most of the stories were either not written down, or were recorded by Christian priests who kept historical records, but lacked understanding of their original meanings. This meant that much of our knowledge of the Viking people has come from scant or obscure sources.

The Vikings and Norse people were strong, energetic and resourceful, originally from Norway, Sweden and Denmark, who existed from approximately 790 to 1100. They were originally traders, farmers, craftworkers and seafarers who took to the seas to raid, trade or explore, while Norsemen (Northmen) were traders and seafarers, but not fighters or warriors. Norse also refers to the language spoken by the Vikings and Norse people. By the eleventh century, many Vikings and Norsemen had settled across Northern and Western Europe and were becoming assimilated into those cultures.

FORWARD-THINKING

For about 300 years, the Vikings and Norsemen travelled to Europe, and they hugely influenced the cultures they settled amongst, particularly those in parts of Scotland, England, France and Ireland. Some founded Dublin, colonized Normandy in France, formed the area of the Danelaw in Britain, and became established in various communities throughout Scotland. Some settled in Iceland and Greenland and others travelled to North America. In the late 980s, the explorer Erik 'the Red' (c. 950– c. 1003) set up the first Viking settlement in Greenland. In c. 1000, his son, Leif 'the Lucky' (c. 970–c. 1020) arrived in North America. Influences went two ways, as eventually, Christianity was adopted by many of the Scandinavian settlers.

Although Vikings are now perceived to have been solely fierce warriors who undertook violent and deadly raids in their quests for treasure and slaves, they were also a highly developed civilization, who greatly valued the arts – including storytelling. They farmed and traded, created elaborate craftwork and they undertook daring voyages of discovery. Their society was divided into three classes; the Jarls (aristocracy), the Karls (lower classes) and the Thralls (slaves). However, rather than being ferocious and filthy as popular history suggests, in general, Vikings addressed their personal hygiene and their appearance. They braided their hair and the Jarls in particular wore fine cloaks, often silk robes, and intricately crafted jewellery. Women were usually treated with greater equality and respect than in many other contemporary cultures. They could inherit property, represent themselves in legal cases, own their own businesses and, if they were unmarried, choose where to live.

THE NORSE UNIVERSE

Viking religious beliefs included a universe that was full of gods, goddesses, spirits and supernatural energies. Like other pagan religions, each god or goddess had his or her own personality, abilities and specialisms, each explained aspects of the mysteries of the world, made things happen and generally helped mortals. However, each god also had his or her own failings and faults.

There were different types of gods. The Aesir gods represented power and combat. In maintaining order in the cosmos, they fought the Frost Giants – who represented darkness and confusion. These Frost Giants – called jötunns – were not necessarily huge. They had magical powers, and while some were ugly, others were beautiful. Although they were the enemies of the gods, they were also sometimes their lovers or spouses. The Aesir gods included Baldr, Bragi, Idun, Odin, Sif and Thor. The Vanir gods were gentler. They could see into the future and were associated with such benefits as health, fertility, nature and knowledge. They included Freya, Loki, Njord, Vili and Ve.

Several of these gods have become famous beyond the folklore, such as the hammer-wielding thunder-god Thor and one-eyed Odin, who carried his spear and pursued knowledge. In an act of self-sacrifice, Odin hanged himself upside-down for nine days and nights to gain knowledge of the runic alphabet, which he passed on to humanity. He was associated closely with death, wisdom and poetry; Loki was 'the author of all fraud and mischief,' and beautiful, sensual Freyja wore a feathered cloak and rode into battles to look for her missing husband Óðr. Her brother Freyr was associated with the weather, royalty, human sexuality and agriculture, and he brought peace and pleasure to humanity. Some women, known as Volva, could hear and understand the gods' language and they translated it for other mortals. With their origins in the Germanic gods of Northern Europe, Norse gods were believed to bestow life, and so it was up to every human to prove him or herself worthy of such a gift.

Four of our days of the week are named after these gods. They are: Tuesday – from Tyr, the bravest god of war and the lawgiver; Wednesday – from Odin (known in Old English as Wōden) who was married to Frigg; Thursday – from Thor, Odin's son, the god of thunder among many other attributes; and Friday – from Frigg, the goddess of marriage, families and motherhood, married to Odin and stepmother to Thor.

The Norse creation story explains that before the world began there was only the world of Muspelheim, that was a world of fire. Ages passed and then Niflheim was made; a world of ice – although Niflheim translates as 'World of Fog.' Between the two worlds was the void of Ginnungagap. Eventually, life emerged in Ginnungagap – a giant named Ymir – and soon he was joined by a cow called Audhumla. Audhumla fed Ymir milk from her udders. Meanwhile, she also licked the ice and this freed the trapped god Búri, who then produced a son, Borr. Borr married Bestla, the daughter of Bolthorn, a Frost Giant, and Bestla gave birth to the gods Odin, Vili and Ve. Together, these three gods killed Ymir and used his body to create the world – a sacred tree called Yggdrasil. Ymir's bones became rocks, his skull, the sky. The first humans to live in part of Yggdrasil were Ask and Embla, who had neither spirit nor form until Odin breathed life into them, and other gods gave them reason and passion. Because of Ymir's murder, all giants were a constant threat to both humans and gods.

CREATION AND DESTRUCTION

Before the creation of the cosmos, the freezing winds and ice of Niflheim met with the searing heat and fire from Muspelheim.

Sparks flew and the gods, led by Odin, made the world from Ymir's body. This world was an enormous ash tree called Yggdrasil that had nine planes of existence. These planes were Midgard (Middle Earth – where mortals live), Asgard (where the Aesir gods live), Vanaheim (home to the Vanir gods), Jotunheim (land of the giants – the arch enemies of the gods), Alfheim (home to the fair elves), Svartalfaheim (home to the dark elves) and Nidavellir (where the dwarfs live and work). Niflheim was situated in the north, Muspelheim in the south. Women who died in childbirth went to the Hall of Frigg in Asgard, where they lived for eternity with Odin's wife, while men who died heroically in battle went to Odin's Hall of Valhalla.

Yggdrasil was nourished by three wells; the Well of Urd (the meeting place of the gods), the Well of Mimir (that gives wisdom to anyone who drinks from it) and the Well of Hvergelmir (where snakes and dragons live). Also living on and around Yggdrasil were several creatures; a wise eagle, a hawk called Veðrfölnir, four stags, a dragon, and a squirrel called Ratatosk. Sol drove the golden sun's chariot across the sky, pursued by the wolf Sköll. Sol's brother Mani drove the silver moon's chariot, chased by the wolf Hati. Jörð was the goddess of the Earth, Dagr was the god of day and Nótt was a jötunn of night.

Midgard was surrounded by water, where the World Serpent lived, and it was connected to Asgard by the Rainbow Bridge. Meanwhile, the whole of Yggdrasil was cared for by the Norns; three wise women who made mud with water from the Well of Urd each day and smeared it on to the tree's bark to keep it strong. Without the Norns, Yggdrasil would die. Travel between the worlds happens often in the myths, and the gods and other beings interact directly with humanity.

FACT AND FICTION INTERTWINED

Feared across Northern Europe, the Vikings undertook sudden raids on ordinary people, killing many, stealing goods and treasures and capturing people as slaves. With spears, axes, bows, knives and hammers, they fought to the death. Their captives were put to work on farms or in Viking fortified towns called ring forts.

The Viking beliefs underpinned their lives. For example, men, women and children all worked hard – a fact that was echoed in some of the stories, such as *The Mead of Poetry*, in which Odin works the fields. Viking craftworkers included weavers, metalworkers, carvers and blacksmiths, and dwarfs of their beliefs were the best craftworkers, alleged to have made, among other things, Thor's hammer, Mjölnir and Odin's spear, Gungnir. The legend of the dragon-slaying hero Sigurd includes real historical figures.

The Vikings believed in two opposite ways of living: innangard, meaning 'within the enclosure', and utangard, meaning 'outside the enclosure.' Humans and civilized gods lived innangard, while the dark elves, dwarfs, trolls and giants lived utangard. The giants were the greatest adversaries of the Norse gods and goddesses. Unlike giants in other tales, Viking giants were not slow-witted, nor even huge. Like the gods, the giants had positive and negative aspects to their personalities. Some were beautiful or capable of kindnesses. Some were clever, astute or sporty, and some were cunning, vicious and full of malice. They included Ymir, the first giant; Surtr, the savage leader of the Fire Giants who brandished a blazing sword; and Aegir and Rán, who lived under the sea with their nine children. Giant animals include the serpent Jörmungandr (who encircled Midgard and who especially hated Thor), the malevolent serpent-dragon Nidhogg, the wolf Fenrir

– who would ravage Yggdrasil during Ragnarök – and the Kraken, a giant squid-like creature that was said to measure more than a mile long and that lay in wait in deep waters, rising up only when disturbed by boats. Sailors often mistook the Kraken for land and headed straight for it, only realizing their mistake when they were pulled down to the bottom of the sea.

Other strange and supernatural beings existed, who, while not as powerful as the gods or giants, were capable of changing events or outcomes, usually working surreptitiously. These included dwarfs, elves, trolls and spirits. Some were kind and helpful, but most were not. For instance, in their underground maze of tunnels in Svartalfheim, dwarfs created Sif's golden hair, Odin's magical ring Draupnir and Freyr's ship, as well as other wonderful treasures. Elves could similarly be good or bad – the good elves helped the Vanir gods, and like the dwarfs, the dark elves lived underground. Closely related to the giants, the trolls were ugly and evil and they lurked in dark places. Additionally, the Vikings believed that unseen spirits hovered over them during many important moments of life and just after death, such as on battlefields, at every child's birth and on distant voyages. Spirits were often female and generally protective. They included the Norns, who as well as caring for Yggdrasil, were present at every baby's birth; the landvættir who protected nature, and the Valkyries, who flew over battlefields and carried valorous fallen warriors to Valhalla. Animal spirits included the eight-legged horse Sleipnir, and two ravens owned by Odin: Hugin (or Huginn), who oversaw thoughts, and Munin (or Muninn), who oversaw memory. Odin used them to keep an eye on his people and to gain wisdom.

As with most religions, life after death was important to the Vikings. Warriors were told that if they fell bravely, they would be taken to Valhalla by Valkyries. This was a vast hall, owned by Odin, with a roof made of shields, wolves guarding its 540 doors, and eagles encircling the roof. Hel, Loki's daughter, ruled Niflheim, where many of the dead were believed to go, or they might be chosen by the goddess Freyja to live in her field Fólkvangr. The goddess Rán claimed those who died at sea.

FROM BELIEF TO BOOK

Although these beliefs were well-established in Viking lore, and for years, most Vikings viewed Christianity with suspicion and scepticism, by 1100, Christianity had almost completely eclipsed Norse philosophies. For a while, many Vikings observed the two religions concurrently. For instance, some prayed to both Jesus and Thor, while others perceived Odin as being interchangeable with Jesus. Niflheim became exchanged with Heaven, and Muspelheim became assimilated with Hell. Gradually, Viking beliefs were disregarded. Some aspects of some of the tales had been carved on to stone and wood in runes, such as the story of Sigurd and the Dragon that was carved into a church doorway in Norway, but there were few written records or reliable sources.

Christianity eventually pushed away Viking paganism, old gods and deities were discarded – but they still appeared in tales, as fantastic characters and magical creatures. Christianity fitted with their outlook; Norse morality was based on personal accountability, and there was a sense of social responsibility, which is often apparent in the stories. Most of these are now known from two books: The Poetic Edda and The Prose Edda. The Poetic Edda was a collection of Old Norse poems that revealed information about the gods and heroes of pre-Christian Vikings and Norse people, their unique vision of the beginning and end of the world and more. The Poetic Edda includes eddic verse that includes stories of the gods, and skaldic verse, a form of bloodthirsty heroic poetry that was popular in the Viking Age. The Poetic Edda comes from an Icelandic medieval manuscript known as the Codex Regius, which contains thirty-one poems, and many later poets and writers have acknowledged their debt to them, including, for instance, English writer, poet and academic, J.R.R. Tolkien (1892–1973). Although the Codex Regius was written during the thirteenth century, it remained in obscurity until 1643, when it came into the possession of the Bishop of Skálholt. He sent it to the Danish king as a gift and for centuries it was stored in the Royal Library in Copenhagen. In 1971, it was returned to Iceland.

During the early thirteenth century, the Icelandic historian, chieftain and poet Snorri Sturluson (1179–1241) was concerned that the tradition of composing poetry to commemorate stories and events was dying, and he researched Norse mythology – including The Poetic Edda. He wrote The Prose Edda, a four-part book that includes both prose and poetry. While most of Snorri's sources are unknown, he aimed for The Prose Edda to be a handbook for composing skaldic verse. He also sought to represent the stories unambiguously and impartially, but his perspective was quite male-oriented and although much is written about the importance of gods, there is less about the goddesses. There are some, for example, Frigg, the goddess of marriage, motherhood and the sky, who knows everyone's destiny; the merciless skiing goddess Skaði; Iðunn, who keeps apples that grant eternal youth; and Sif, the golden-haired goddess of the Earth, crops, fertility and farming. However, it is likely that there were more tales about the females than we now know.

The stories in this book focus on the fairy and folk tales. Some are old, but some are relatively modern, yet they grew from older oral traditions, or borrowed narrative elements from the ancient myths. Since the seventeenth century, many of them have attracted the attention of European scholars, and during the Romantic period (approximately 1800–50), a revival of interest in much of the subject matter increased. Later still, these stories were copied, edited, translated and reinterpreted, and with their widespread publication, the stories spread into European literary culture. Many remain timeless and compelling, and aspects have been retold by others, such as the Danish children's author Hans Christian Andersen (1805–75) and the Norwegian authors Peter Christen Asbjørnsen (1812–55) and Jørgen Moe (1813–82). Several of these and those by other writers feature in this book.

Among the tales here are 'Why the Sea Is Salt', a Norwegian fairy tale collected by Asbjørnsen and Moe about a poor man and his rich brother. Ultimately, in strong fairy tale tradition, the story gives an imaginative reason why the sea became salty. 'The Little Match Seller' by Hans Christian Andersen tells of a poor little girl in the bitter winter, dreaming of warmth and food as she tries to earn money for her family. The moral of the tale is to behave charitably towards those who are less fortunate. 'The Seven Foals' is another story collected by Asbjørnsen and Moe, reminiscent of 'Cinderella', but about a boy known as Cinder-lad, while also by them is 'East of the Sun and West of the Moon', in which a young girl breaks her promise and has to travel east of the sun and west of the moon.

The folk-tales contained here have not only stood the test of time, but have shown an understanding of and empathy with the natural world and human nature. Although the Vikings were commonly perceived as heathens, their stories have been endlessly reinvented, instilling moral values while retaining their original brilliance and vitality.

S. Hodge

FURTHER READING

Asbjørnsen, Peter Christen; Moe, Jørgen; Nunnally, Tiina, trans., *The Complete and Original Norwegian Folktales of Asbjørnsen and Moe* (University of Minnesota Press, 2019)

Bartlett, W.B., *Vikings: A History of the Northmen* (Amberley Publishing, 2021)

Byock, Jesse, *The Prose Edda: Tales from Norse Mythology* (Penguin Classics, 2005)

Crossley-Holland, Kevin, *Norse Myths: Tales of Odin, Thor and Loki* (Walker Studio, 2017)

Eiriksson, Leifur, *Egil's Saga* (Penguin Classics, 2004)

Gaiman, Neil, *Norse Mythology* (Bloomsbury Publishing, 2018)

Guerber, Helen A., *Tales of Norse Mythology* (Barnes & Noble Books, 2017)

Haywood, John, *The Penguin Historical Atlas of the Vikings* (Penguin Books, 1995)

Larrington, Caroline, *The Poetic Edda* (Oxford World's Classics, 2014)

Lundbergh, Holger, trans., *Swedish Folk Tales* (Floris Press, 2004)

Philip, Neil, *Myths of the Vikings* (Anness Publishing, 2018)

Roesdahl, Else, *The Vikings* (Penguin Books, 1992)

Stefánsson, Hjörleifur Helgi, *Icelandic Folk Tales* (The History Press, 2020)

Stevenson, Peter, *Boggarts, Trolls and Tylwyth Teg: Folk Tales of Hidden People & Lost Lands* (The History Press, 2021)

Sturluson, Snorri, *The Prose Edda* (Benediction Classics, 2015)

Sturluson, Snorri, *Heimskringla: History of the Kings of Norway* (University of Texas Press, 1991)

Thynell, Ulla, *Nordic Tales: Folktales from Norway, Sweden, Finland, Iceland, and Denmark* (Chronicle Books, 2019)

S. Hodge is an author, historian and artist with over 80 books published, mainly on art and history, spanning from the Knights Templar to World War Two. She also writes articles, web resources for museums and galleries, and gives workshops and lectures at schools, universities, museums, galleries, businesses and societies. She has taught in schools and colleges and contributes to radio and TV documentaries.

TALES OF BRAVERY

The sight of the legendary warrior Holger Danske is an inspiring one. 'Clad in iron and steel', he sleeps – down endless centuries – in a deep, dark dungeon. In Denmark's hour of need, we're told, he'll rouse himself to save his people. It's an unsettling image too, however, hinting as it does at the existence of another dimension, an underworld of fears we feel can't quite fathom – and certainly aren't equipped to deal with all that well.

His destiny as his country's sleeping guardian clearly recalls that of King Arthur's as protector of Britain (another story being constantly retold at this point in the nineteenth century). This only underlines the extent to which Holger Danske was seen, not specifically as a soldier but as a defender against the more universal anxieties of the age. How were ancient qualities to be retooled for the modern world? What did Viking virtues of loyalty and valour have to offer in a here and now beset by very different challenges and problems?

Heroism has been harder to define since the age of the warrior ended. Perhaps it has been harder to attain as well.

HOLGER DANSKE

In Denmark there stands an old castle named Kronenburg, close by the Sound of Elsinore, where large ships, both English, Russian, and

Prussian, pass by hundreds every day. And they salute the old castle with cannons, "Boom, boom," which is as if they said, "Good-day." And the cannons of the old castle answer "Boom," which means "Many thanks." In winter no ships sail by, for the whole Sound is covered with ice as far as the Swedish coast, and has quite the appearance of a high-road. The Danish and the Swedish flags wave, and Danes and Swedes say, "Good-day," and "Thank you" to each other, not with cannons, but with a friendly shake of the hand; and they exchange white bread and biscuits with each other, because foreign articles taste the best.

But the most beautiful sight of all is the old castle of Kronenburg, where Holger Danske sits in the deep, dark cellar, into which no one goes. He is clad in iron and steel, and rests his head on his strong arm; his long beard hangs down upon the marble table, into which it has become firmly rooted; he sleeps and dreams, but in his dreams he sees everything that happens in Denmark. On each Christmas Eve an angel comes to him and tells him that all he has dreamed is true, and that he may go to sleep again in peace, as Denmark is not yet in any real danger; but should danger ever come, then Holger Danske will rouse himself, and the table will burst asunder as he draws out his beard. Then he will come forth in his strength, and strike a blow that shall sound in all the countries of the world.

An old grandfather sat and told his little grandson all this about Holger Danske, and the boy knew that what his grandfather told him must be true. As the old man related this story, he was carving an image in wood to represent Holger Danske, to be fastened to the prow of a ship; for the old grandfather was a carver in wood, that is, one who carved figures for the heads of ships, according to the names given to them. And now he had carved Holger Danske, who stood there erect and proud, with his long beard, holding in one hand his broad battle-axe, while with the other he leaned on the Danish arms. The old grandfather told the little boy a great deal about Danish men and women who had distinguished themselves in olden times, so that he fancied he knew as much even as Holger Danske himself, who, after all, could only dream; and when the little fellow went to bed, he thought so much about it that he actually pressed his chin against the counterpane, and imagined that he had a long beard which had become rooted to it. But the old grandfather remained sitting at his work and carving away at the last part of it, which was the Danish arms. And when he had finished he looked at the whole figure, and thought of all he had heard and read, and what he had that evening related to his little grandson. Then he nodded his head, wiped his spectacles and put them on, and said, "Ah, yes; Holger Danske will not appear in my lifetime, but the boy who is in bed there may very likely live to see him when the event really comes to pass." And the old grandfather nodded again; and the more he looked at Holger Danske, the more satisfied he felt that he had carved a good image of him. It seemed to glow with the color of life; the armor glittered like iron and steel. The hearts in the Danish arms grew more and more red; while the lions, with gold crowns on their heads, were leaping up. "That is the most beautiful coat of arms in the world," said the old man. "The lions represent strength; and the hearts, gentleness and love." And as he gazed on the uppermost lion, he thought of King Canute, who chained great England to Denmark's throne; and he looked at the second lion, and thought of Waldemar, who untied Denmark and conquered the Vandals. The third lion reminded him of Margaret, who united Denmark, Sweden, and Norway. But when he gazed at the red hearts, their colors glowed more deeply, even as flames, and his memory followed each in turn. The first led him to a dark, narrow prison, in which sat a prisoner, a beautiful woman, daughter of Christian the Fourth, Eleanor Ulfeld, and the flame became a rose on her bosom, and its blossoms were not more pure than the heart of this noblest and best of all Danish women. "Ah, yes; that is indeed a noble heart in the Danish arms," said the grandfather, and his spirit followed the second flame, which carried him out to sea, where cannons roared and the ships lay shrouded in smoke, and the flaming heart attached itself to the breast of Hvitfeldt in the form of the ribbon of an order, as he blew himself and his ship into the air in order to save the fleet. And the third flame led him to Greenland's wretched huts, where the preacher, Hans Egede, ruled with love in every word and action. The flame was as a star on his breast, and added another heart to the Danish arms. And as the old grandfather's spirit followed the next hovering flame, he knew whither it would lead him. In a peasant woman's humble room stood Frederick the Sixth, writing his name with chalk on the beam. The flame trembled on his breast and in his heart, and it was in the peasant's room that his heart became one for the Danish arms. The old grandfather wiped his eyes, for he had known King Frederick, with his silvery locks and his honest blue eyes, and had lived for him, and he folded his hands and remained for some time silent. Then his daughter came to him and said it was getting late, that he ought to rest for a while, and that the supper was on the table.

"What you have been carving is very beautiful, grandfather," said she. "Holger Danske and the old coat of arms; it seems to me as if I have seen the face somewhere."

"No, that is impossible," replied the old grandfather; "but I have seen it, and I have tried to carve it in wood, as I have retained it in my memory. It was a long time ago, while the English fleet lay in the roads, on the second of April, when we showed that we were true, ancient Danes. I was on board the Denmark, in Steene Bille's squadron; I had a man by my side whom even the cannon balls seemed to fear. He sung old songs in a merry voice, and fired and fought as if he were something more than a man. I still remember his face, but from whence he came, or whither he went, I know not; no one knows. I have often thought it might have been Holger Danske himself, who had swam down to us from Kronenburg to help us in the hour of danger. That was my idea, and there stands his likeness."

The wooden figure threw a gigantic shadow on the wall, and even on part of the ceiling; it seemed as if the real Holger Danske stood behind it, for the shadow moved; but this was no doubt caused by the flame of the lamp not burning steadily. Then the daughter-in-law kissed the old grandfather, and led him to a large arm-chair by the table; and she, and her husband, who was the son of the old man and the father of the little boy who lay in bed, sat down to supper with him. And the old grandfather talked of the Danish lions and the Danish hearts, emblems of strength and gentleness, and explained quite clearly that there is another strength than that which lies in a sword, and he pointed to a shelf where lay a number of old books, and amongst them a collection of Holberg's plays, which are much read and are so clever and amusing that it is easy to fancy we have known the people of those days, who are described in them.

"He knew how to fight also," said the old man; "for he lashed the follies and prejudices of people during his whole life."

Then the grandfather nodded to a place above the looking-glass, where hung an almanac, with a representation of the Round Tower upon it, and said "Tycho Brahe was another of those who used a sword, but not one to cut into the flesh and bone, but to make the way of the stars of heaven clear, and plain to be understood. And then he whose father belonged to my calling, – yes, he, the son of the old image-carver, he whom we ourselves have seen, with his silvery locks and his broad shoulders, whose name is known in all lands; – yes, he was a sculptor, while I am only a carver. Holger Danske can appear in marble, so that people in all countries of the world may hear of the strength of Denmark. Now let us drink the health of Bertel."

But the little boy in bed saw plainly the old castle of Kronenburg, and the Sound of Elsinore, and Holger Danske, far down in the cellar, with his beard rooted to the table, and dreaming of everything that was passing above him.

And Holger Danske did dream of the little humble room in which the image-carver sat; he heard all that had been said, and he nodded in his dream, saying, "Ah, yes, remember me, you Danish people, keep me in your memory, I will come to you in the hour of need."

The bright morning light shone over Kronenburg, and the wind brought the sound of the hunting-horn across from the neighboring shores. The ships sailed by and saluted the castle with the boom of the cannon, and Kronenburg returned the salute, "Boom, boom." But the roaring cannons did not awake Holger Danske, for they meant only "Good morning," and "Thank you." They must fire in another fashion before he awakes; but wake he will, for there is energy yet in Holger Danske.

THE LEGEND OF THORGUNNA

A **ship** from Iceland chanced to winter in a haven near Helgafels. Among the passengers was a woman named Thorgunna, a native of the Hebrides, who was reported by the sailors to possess garments and household furniture of a fashion far surpassing those used in Iceland. Thurida, sister of the pontiff Snorro, and wife of Thorodd, a woman of a vain and covetous disposition, attracted by these reports, made a visit to the stranger, but could not prevail upon her to display her treasures. Persisting, however, in her inquiries, she pressed Thorgunna to take up her abode at the house of Thorodd. The Hebridean reluctantly assented, but added, that as she could labour at every usual kind of domestic industry, she trusted in that manner to discharge the obligation she might lie under to the family, without giving any part of her property in recompense of her lodging. As Thurida continued to urge her request, Thorgunna accompanied her to Froda, the house of Thorodd, where the seamen deposited a huge chest and cabinet, containing the property of her new guest, which Thurida viewed with curious and covetous eyes. So soon as they had pointed out to Thorgunna the place assigned for her bed, she opened the chest, and took forth such an embroidered bed coverlid, and such a splendid and complete set of tapestry hangings, and bed furniture of English linen, interwoven with silk, as had never been seen in Iceland.

"Sell to me," said the covetous matron, "this fair bed furniture."

"Believe me," answered Thorgunna, "I will not lie upon straw in order to feed thy pomp and vanity;" an answer which so greatly displeased Thurida that she never again repeated her request. Thorgunna, to whose character subsequent events added something of a mystical solemnity, is described as being a woman of a tall and stately appearance, of a dark complexion, and having a profusion of black hair. She was advanced in age; assiduous in the labours of the field and of the loom; a faithful attendant upon divine worship; grave, silent, and solemn in domestic society. She had little intercourse with the household of Thorodd, and showed particular dislike to two of its inmates. These were Thorer, who, having lost a leg in the skirmish between Thorbiorn and Thorarin the Black, was called Thorer-Widlegr (wooden-leg), from the substitute he had adopted; and his wife, Thorgrima, called Galldra-Kinna (wicked sorceress), from her supposed skill in enchantments. Kiartan, the son of Thurida, a boy of excellent promise, was the only person of the household to whom Thorgunna showed much affection; and she was much vexed at times when the childish petulance of the boy made an indifferent return to her kindness.

After this mysterious stranger had dwelt at Froda for some time, and while she was labouring in the hay-field with other members of the family, a sudden cloud from the northern mountain led Thorodd to anticipate a heavy shower. He instantly commanded the hay-workers to pile up in ricks the quantity which each had been engaged in turning to the wind. It was afterwards remembered that Thorgunna did not pile up her portion, but left it spread on the field. The cloud approached with great celerity, and sank so heavily around the farm, that it was scarce possible to see beyond the limits of the field. A heavy shower next descended, and so soon as the clouds broke away and the sun shone forth it was observed that it had rained blood. That which fell upon the ricks of the other labourers soon dried up, but what Thorgunna had wrought upon remained wet with gore. The unfortunate Hebridean, appalled at the omen, betook herself to her bed, and was seized with a mortal illness. On the approach of death she summoned Thorodd, her landlord, and intrusted to him the disposition of her property and effects.

"Let my body," said she, "be transported to Skalholt, for my mind presages that in that place shall be founded the most distinguished church in this island. Let my golden ring be given to the priests who shall celebrate my obsequies, and do thou indemnify thyself for the funeral charges out of my remaining effects. To thy wife I bequeath my purple mantle, in order that, by this sacrifice to her avarice, I may secure the right of disposing of the rest of my effects at my own pleasure. But for my bed, with its coverings, hangings, and furniture, I entreat they may be all consigned to the flames. I do not desire this because I envy any one the possession of these things after my death, but because I wish those evils to be avoided which I plainly foresee will happen if my will be altered in the slightest particular."

Thorodd promised faithfully to execute this extraordinary testament in the most exact manner. Accordingly, so soon as Thorgunna was dead, her faithful executor prepared a pile for burning her splendid bed. Thurida entered, and learned with anger and astonishment the purpose of these preparations. To the remonstrances of her husband she answered that the menaces of future danger were only caused by Thorgunna's selfish envy, who did not wish any one should enjoy her treasures after her decease. Then, finding Thorodd inaccessible to argument, she had recourse to caresses and blandishments, and at length extorted permission to separate from the rest of the bed-furniture the tapestried curtains and coverlid; the rest was consigned to the flames, in obedience to the will of the testator. The body of Thorgunna, being wrapped in new linen and placed in a coffin, was next to be transported through the precipices and morasses of Iceland to the distant district she had assigned for her place of sepulture. A remarkable incident occurred on the way. The transporters of the body arrived at evening, late, weary, and drenched with rain, in a house called Nether-Ness, where the niggard hospitality of the proprietor only afforded them house-room, without any supply of food or fuel. But, so soon as they entered, an unwonted noise was heard in the kitchen of the mansion, and the figure of a woman, soon recognised to be the deceased Thorgunna, was seen busily employed in preparing victuals. Their inhospitable landlord, being made acquainted with this frightful circumstance, readily agreed to supply every refreshment which was necessary, on which the vision instantly disappeared. The apparition having become public, they had no reason to ask twice for hospitality as they proceeded on their journey, and they came to Skalholt, where Thorgunna, with all due ceremonies of religion, was deposited quietly in the grave. But the consequences of the breach of her testament were felt severely at Froda.

The dwelling at Froda was a simple and patriarchal structure, built according to the fashion used by the wealthy among the Icelanders. The apartments were very large, and a part boarded off contained the beds of the family. On either side was a sort of store-room, one of which contained meal, the other dried fish. Every evening large fires were lighted in this apartment for dressing the victuals; and the domestics of the family usually sat around them for a considerable time, until supper was prepared. On the night when the conductors of Thorgunna's funeral returned to Froda, there appeared, visible to all who were present, a meteor, or spectral appearance, resembling a half-moon, which glided around the boarded walls of the mansion in an opposite direction to the course of the sun, and continued to perform its revolutions until the domestics retired to rest. This apparition was renewed every night during a whole week, and was pronounced by Thorer with the wooden leg to presage pestilence or mortality. Shortly after a herdsman showed signs of mental alienation, and gave various indications of having sustained the persecution of evil demons. This man was found dead in his bed one morning, and then commenced a scene of ghost-seeing unheard of in the annals of superstition. The first victim was Thorer, who had presaged the calamity. Going out of doors one evening, he was grappled by the spectre of the deceased shepherd as he attempted to re-enter the house. His wooden leg stood him in poor stead in such an encounter; he was hurled to the earth, and so fearfully beaten, that he died in consequence of the bruises. Thorer was no sooner dead than his ghost associated itself to that of the herdsman, and joined him in pursuing and assaulting the inhabitants of Froda. Meantime an infectious disorder spread fast among them, and several of the bondsmen died one after the other. Strange portents were seen within-doors, the meal was displaced and mingled, and the dried fish flung about in a most alarming manner, without any visible agent. At length, while the servants were forming their evening circle round the fire, a spectre, resembling the head of a seal-fish, was seen to emerge out of the pavement of the room, bending its round black eyes full on the tapestried bed-curtains of Thorgunna. Some of the domestics ventured to strike at this figure, but, far from giving way, it rather erected itself further from the floor, until Kiartan, who seemed to have a natural predominance over these supernatural prodigies, seizing a huge forge-hammer, struck the seal repeatedly on the head, and compelled it to disappear, forcing it down into the floor, as if he had driven a stake into the earth. This prodigy was found to intimate a new calamity. Thorodd, the master of the family, had some time before set forth on a voyage to bring home a cargo of dried fish; but in crossing the river Enna the skiff was lost and he perished with the servants who attended him. A solemn funeral feast was held at Froda, in memory of the deceased, when, to the astonishment of the guests, the apparition of Thorodd and his followers seemed to enter the apartment dripping with water. Yet this vision excited less horror than might have been expected, for the Icelanders, though nominally Christians, retained, among other pagan superstitions, a belief that the spectres of such drowned persons as had been favourably received by the goddess Rana were wont to show themselves at their funeral feast. They saw, therefore, with some composure, Thorodd and his dripping attendants plant themselves by the fire, from which all mortal guests retreated to make room for them. It was supposed this apparition would not be renewed after the conclusion of the festival. But so far were their hopes disappointed, that, so soon as the mourning guests had departed, the fires being lighted, Thorodd and his comrades marched in on one side, drenched as before with water; on the other entered Thorer, heading all those who had died in the pestilence, and who appeared covered with dust. Both parties seized the seats by the fire, while the half-frozen and terrified domestics spent the night without either light or warmth. The same phenomenon took place the next night, though the fires had been lighted in a separate house, and at length Kiartan was obliged to compound matters with the spectres by kindling a large fire for them in the principal apartment, and one for the family and domestics in a separate hut. This prodigy continued during the whole feast of Jol. Other portents also happened to appal this devoted family: the contagious disease again broke forth, and when any one fell a sacrifice to it his spectre was sure to join the troop of persecutors, who had now almost full possession of the mansion of Froda. Thorgrima Galldrakinna, wife of Thorer, was one of these victims, and, in short, of thirty servants belonging to the household, eighteen died, and five fled for fear of the apparitions, so that only seven remained in the service of Kiartan.

Kiartan had now recourse to the advice of his maternal uncle Snorro, in consequence of whose counsel, which will perhaps appear surprising to the reader, judicial measures were instituted against the spectres. A Christian priest was, however, associated with Thordo Kausa, son of Snorro, and with Kiartan, to superintend and sanctify the proceedings. The inhabitants were regularly summoned to attend upon the inquest, as in a cause between man and man, and the assembly was constituted before the gate of the mansion, just as the spectres had assumed their wonted station by the fire. Kiartan boldly ventured to approach them, and, snatching a brand from the fire, he commanded the tapestry belonging to Thorgunna to be carried out of doors, set fire to it, and reduced it to ashes with all the other ornaments of her bed, which had been so inconsiderately preserved at the request of Thurida. A tribunal being then constituted with the usual legal solemnities, a charge was preferred by Kiartan against Thorer with the wooden leg, by Thordo Kausa against Thorodd, and by others chosen as accusers against the individual spectres present, accusing them of molesting the mansion, and introducing death and disease among its inhabitants. All the solemn rites of judicial procedure were observed on this singular occasion; evidence was adduced, charges given, and the cause formally decided. It does not appear that the ghosts put themselves on their defence, so that sentence of ejectment was pronounced against them individually in due and legal form. When Thorer heard the judgment, he arose, and saying –

"I have sat while it was lawful for me to do so," left the apartment by the door opposite to that at which the judicial assembly was constituted. Each of the spectres, as it heard its individual sentence, left the place, saying something which indicated its unwillingness to depart, until Thorodd himself was solemnly called on to leave.

"We have here no longer," said he, "a peaceful dwelling, therefore will we remove."

Kiartan then entered the hall with his followers, and the priest, with holy water, and celebration of a solemn mass, completed the conquest over the goblins, which had been commenced by the power and authority of the Icelandic law.

TALES FROM THE PROSE EDDA

The Gods and the Wolf

Among the Æsir, or gods, is reckoned one named Loki or Loptur. By many he is called the reviler of the gods, the author of all fraud and mischief, and the shame of gods and men alike. He is the son of the giant Farbauti, his mother being Laufey or Nal, and his brothers Byleist and Helblindi. He is of a goodly appearance and elegant form, but his mood is changeable, and he is inclined to all wickedness. In cunning and perfidy he excels every one, and many a time has he placed the gods in great danger, and often has he saved them again by his cunning. He has a wife named Siguna, and their son is called Nari.

Loki had three children by Angurbodi, a giantess of Jotunheim (the giants' home). The first of these was Fenris, the wolf; the second was Jörmungand, the Midgard serpent; and the third was

Hela, death. Very soon did the gods become aware of this evil progeny which was being reared in Jotunheim, and by divination they discovered that they must receive great injury from them. That they had such a mother spoke bad for them, but their coming of such a sire was a still worse presage. All-father therefore despatched certain of the gods to bring the children to him, and when they were brought before him he cast the serpent down into the ocean which surrounds the world. There the monster waxed so large that he wound himself round the whole globe, and that with such ease that he can with his mouth lay hold of his tail. Hela All-father cast into Niflheim, where she rules over nine worlds. Into these she distributes all those who are sent to her, – that is to say, all who die through sickness or old age. She has there an abode with very thick walls, and fenced with strong gates. Her hall is Elvidnir; her table is Hunger; her knife, Starvation; her man-servant, Delay; her maid-servant, Sloth; her threshold, Precipice; her bed, Care; and her curtains, Anguish of Soul. The one half of her body is livid, the other half is flesh-colour. She has a terrible look, so that she can be easily known.

As to the wolf, Fenris, the gods let him grow up among themselves, Tyr being the only one of them who dare give him his food. When, however, they perceived how he every day increased prodigiously in size, and that the oracles warned them that he would one day prove fatal to them, they determined to make very strong iron fetters for him which they called Loeding. These they presented to the wolf, and desired him to put them on to show his strength by endeavouring to break them. The wolf saw that it would not be difficult for him to burst them, so he let the gods put the fetters on him, then violently stretching himself he broke the fetters asunder, and set himself free.

Having seen this, the gods went to work, and prepared a second set of fetters, called Dromi, half as strong again as the former, and these they persuaded the wolf to put on, assuring him that if he broke them he would then furnish them with an undeniable proof of his power. The wolf saw well enough that it would not be easy to break this set, but he considered that he had himself increased in strength since he broke the others, and he knew that without running some risk he could never become celebrated. He therefore allowed the gods to place the fetters on him. Then Fenris shook himself, stretched his limbs, rolled on the ground, and at length burst the fetters, which he made fly in all directions. Thus did he free himself the second time from his chains, and from this has arisen the saying, "To get free from Loeding, or to burst from Dromi," meaning to perform something by strong exertion.

The gods now despaired of ever being able to secure the wolf with any chain of their own making. All-father, however, sent Skirnir, the messenger of the god Frey, into the country of the Black Elves, to the dwarfs, to ask them to make a chain to bind Fenris with. This chain was composed of six things – the noise made by the fall of a cat's foot, the hair of a woman's beard, the roots of stones, the nerves of bears, the breath of fish, and the spittle of birds.

The fetters were as smooth and as soft as silk, and yet, as you will presently see, of great strength. The gods were very thankful for them when they were brought to them, and returned many thanks to him who brought them. Then they took the wolf with them on to the island Lyngvi, which is in the lake Amsvartnir, and there they showed him the chain, desiring him to try his strength in breaking it. At the same time they told him that it was a good deal stronger than it looked. They took it in their own hands and pulled at it, attempting in vain to break it, and then they said to Fenris –

"No one else but you, Fenris, can break it."

"I don't see," replied the wolf, "that I shall gain any glory by breaking such a slight string, but if any artifice has been employed in the making of it, you may be sure, though it looks so fragile, it shall never touch foot of mine."

The gods told him he would easily break so slight a bandage, since he had already broken asunder shackles of iron of the most solid make.

"But," said they, "if you should not be able to break the chain, you are too feeble to cause us any anxiety, and we shall not hesitate to loose you again."

"I very much fear," replied the wolf, "that if you once tie me up so fast that I cannot release myself, you will be in no haste to unloose me. I am, therefore, unwilling to have this cord wound around me; but to show you I am no coward, I will agree to it, but one of you must put his hand in my mouth, as a pledge that you intend me no deceit."

The gods looked on one another wistfully, for they found themselves in an embarrassing position.

Then Tyr stepped forward and bravely put his right hand in the monster's mouth. The gods then tied up the wolf, who forcibly stretched himself, as he had formerly done, and exerted all his powers to disengage himself; but the more efforts he made the tighter he drew the chain about him, and then all the gods, except Tyr, who lost his hand, burst out into laughter at the sight. Seeing that he was so fast tied that he would never be able to get loose again, they took one end of the chain, which was called Gelgja, and having drilled a hole for it, drew it through the middle of a large broad rock, which they sank very deep in the earth. Afterwards, to make all still more secure, they tied the end of the chain, which came through the rock to a great stone called Keviti, which they sank still deeper. The wolf used his utmost power to free himself, and, opening his mouth, tried to bite them. When the gods saw that they took a sword and thrust it into his mouth, so that it entered his under jaw right up to the hilt, and the point reached his palate. He howled in the most terrible manner, and since then the foam has poured from his mouth in such abundance that it forms the river called Von. So the wolf must remain until Ragnarök.

Such a wicked race has Loki begot. The gods would not put the wolf to death because they respected the sanctity of the place, which forbade blood being shed there.

Thor's Journey to the Land of the Giants

One day the god Thor set out with Loki in his chariot drawn by two he-goats. Night coming on they were obliged to put up at a peasant's cottage, when Thor slew his goats, and having skinned them, had them put into the pot. When this had been done he sat down to supper and invited the peasant and his children to take part in the feast. The peasant had a son named Thjalfi, and a daughter, Röska. Thor told them to throw the bones into the goatskins, which were spread out near the hearth, but young Thjalfi, in order to get at the marrow, broke one of the shank bones with his knife. Having passed the night in this place, Thor rose early in the morning, and having dressed himself, held up his hammer, Mjolnir, and thus consecrating the goatskins; he had no sooner done it than the two goats took again their usual form, only one of them was now lame in one of its hind-legs. When Thor saw this he at once knew that the peasant or one of his family had handled the bones of the goat too roughly, for one was broken. They were terribly afraid when Thor knit his brows, rolled his eyes, seized his hammer, and grasped it with such force that the very joints of his fingers were white again. The peasant, trembling, and fearful that he would be struck down by the looks of the god, begged with his family for pardon, offering whatever they possessed to repair the damage they might have done. Thor allowed them to appease him, and contented himself with taking with him Thjalfi and Röska, who became his servants, and have since followed him.

Leaving his goats at that place, Thor set out to the east, to the country of the giants. At length they came to the shore of a wide and deep sea which Thor, with Loki, Thjalfi, and Röska passed over. Then they came to a strange country, and entered an immense forest in which they journeyed all day. Thjalfi was unexcelled by any man as a runner, and he carried Thor's bag, but in the forest they could find nothing eatable to put in it. As night came on they searched on all sides for a place where they might sleep, and at last they came to what appeared to be a large hall, the gate of which was so large that it took up the whole of one side of the building. Here they lay down to sleep, but about the middle of the night they were alarmed by what seemed to be an earthquake which shook the whole of the building. Thor, rising, called his companions to seek with him some safer place. Leaving the apartment they were in, they found on their right hand an adjoining chamber into which they entered, but while the others, trembling with fear, crept to the farthest corner of their retreat, Thor, armed with his mace, remained at the entrance ready to defend himself, happen what might. Throughout the night they heard a terrible groaning, and when the morning came, Thor, going out, observed a man of enormous size, lying near, asleep and snoring heavily. Then Thor knew that this was the noise he had heard during the night. He immediately girded on his belt of prowess which had the virtue of increasing his strength. The giant awoke and stood up, and it is said that for once Thor was too frightened to use his hammer, and he therefore contented himself with inquiring the giant's name.

"My name," replied the giant, "is Skrymir. As for you it is not necessary I should ask your name. You are the god Thor. Tell me, what have you done with my glove?"

Then Skrymir stretched out his hand and took it up, and Thor saw that what he and his companions had taken for a hall in which they had passed the night, was the giant's glove, the chamber into which they had retreated being only the thumb.

Skrymir asked whether they might not be friends, and Thor agreeing, the giant opened his bag and took out something to eat. Thor and his companions also made their morning meal, but eat in another place. Then Skrymir, proposing that they should put their provisions together, and Thor assenting to it, put all into one bag, and laying it on his shoulder marched before them, with huge strides, during the whole day. At night he found a place where Thor and his companions might rest under an oak. There, he said, he would lie down and sleep.

"You take the bag," said he, "and make your supper."

He was soon asleep, and, strange as it may seem, when Thor tried to open the bag he could not untie a single knot nor loose the string. Enraged at this he seized his hammer, swayed it in both his hands, took a step forward, and hurled it at the giant's head. This awoke the giant, who asked him if a leaf had not fallen on his head, and whether they had finished their supper. Thor said they were just about to lie down to sleep, and went to lie under another oak tree. About midnight, observing that Skrymir was snoring so loudly that the forest re-echoed the din, Thor grasped his hammer and hurled it with such force at him that it sank up to the handle in his head.

"What is the matter?" asked he, awakening. "Did an acorn fall on my head? How are you going on, Thor?"

Thor departed at once, saying that it was only midnight and that he hoped to get some more sleep yet. He resolved, however, to have a third blow at the giant, hoping that with this he might settle everything. Seizing his hammer, he, with all his force, threw it at the giant's cheek, into which it buried itself up to the handle. Skrymir, awaking, put his hand to his cheek, and said –

"Are there any birds perched on this tree? I thought some moss fell upon me. How! art thou awake, Thor? It is time, is it not, for us to get up and dress ourselves? You have not far, however, to go before you arrive at the city Utgard. I have heard you whispering together that I am a very tall fellow, but there you will see many larger than me. Let me advise you then when you get there not to take too much upon yourselves, for the men of Utgard-Loki will not bear much from such little folk as you. I believe your best way would even be to turn back again, but if you are determined to proceed take the road that goes towards the east, as for me mine now lies to the north."

After he had said this, he put his bag upon his shoulder and turned away into a forest; and I could never hear that Thor wished him a good journey.

Proceeding on his way with his companions, Thor saw towards noon a city situated in the middle of a vast plain. The wall of the city was so lofty that one could not look up to the top of it without throwing one's head quite back upon the shoulder. On coming to the wall, they found the gateway closed with bars, which

Thor never could have opened, but he and his companions crept in between them, and thus entered the place. Before them was a large palace, and as the door of it was open, they entered and found a number of men of enormous size, seated on benches. Going on they came into the presence of the king, Utgard-Loki, whom they saluted with great respect, but he, looking upon them for a time, at length cast a scornful glance at them, and burst into laughter.

"It would take up too much time," said he, "to ask you concerning the long journey you have made, but if I am not mistaken that little man there is Aku-Thor. You may," said he to Thor, "be bigger than you seem to be. What are you and your companions skilled in that we may see what they can do, for no one may remain here unless he understands some art and excels in it all other men?"

"I," said Loki, "can eat quicker than any one else, and of that I am ready to give proof if there is here any one who will compete with me."

"It must, indeed, be owned," replied the king, "that you are not wanting in dexterity, if you are able to do what you say. Come, let us test it."

Then he ordered one of his followers who was sitting at the further end of the bench, and whose name was Logi (Flame) to come forward, and try his skill with Loki. A great tub or trough full of flesh meat was placed in the hall, and Loki having placed himself at one end of the trough, and Logi having set himself at the other end, the two commenced to eat. Presently they met in the middle of the trough, but Loki had only devoured the flesh of his portion, whereas the other had devoured both flesh and bones. All the company therefore decided that Loki was beaten.

Then Utgard-Loki asked what the young man could do who accompanied Thor. Thjalfi said that in running he would compete with any one. The king admitted that skill in running was something very good, but he thought Thjalfi must exert himself to the utmost to win in the contest. He rose and, accompanied by all the company, went to a plain where there was a good place for the match, and then calling a young man named Hugi (Spirit or Thought), he ordered him to run with Thjalfi. In the first race Hugi ran so fast away from Thjalfi that on his returning to the starting-place he met him not far from it. Then said the king –

"If you are to win, Thjalfi, you must run faster, though I must own no man has ever come here who was swifter of foot."

In the second trial, Thjalfi was a full bow-shot from the boundary when Hugi arrived at it.

"Very well do you run, Thjalfi," said Utgard-Loki; "but I do not think you will gain the prize. However, the third trial will decide."

They ran a third time, but Hugi had already reached the goal before Thjalfi had got halfway. Then all present cried out that there had been a sufficient trial of skill in that exercise.

Then Utgard-Loki asked Thor in what manner he would choose to give them a proof of the dexterity for which he was so famous. Thor replied that he would contest the prize for drinking with any one in the court. Utgard-Loki consented to the match, and going into the palace, ordered his cup-bearer to bring the large horn out of which his followers were obliged to drink when they had trespassed in any way against the customs of the court. The cup-bearer presented this to Thor, and Utgard-Loki said –

"Whoever is a good drinker will empty that horn at a draught. Some men make two draughts of it, but the most puny drinker of all can empty it in three."

Thor looked at the horn, which seemed very long, but was otherwise of no extraordinary size. He put it to his mouth, and, without drawing breath, pulled as long and as deeply as he could, that he might not be obliged to make a second draught of it. When, however, he set the horn down and looked in it he could scarcely perceive that any of the liquor was gone.

"You have drunk well," said Utgard-Loki; "but you need not boast. Had it been told me that Asu-Thor could only drink so little, I should not have credited it. No doubt you will do better at the second pull."

Without a word, Thor again set the horn to his lips and exerted himself to the utmost. When he looked in it seemed to him that he had not drunk quite so much as before, but the horn could now be carried without danger of spilling the liquor. Then Utgard-Loki said –

"Well, Thor, you should not spare yourself more than befits you in such drinking. If now you mean to drink off the horn the third time it seems to me you must drink more than you have done. You will never be reckoned so great a man amongst us as the Æsir make you out to be if you cannot do better in other games than it appears to me you will do in this."

Thor, angry, put the horn to his mouth and drank the best he could and as long as he was able, but when he looked into the horn the liquor was only a little lower. Then he gave the horn to the cup-bearer, and would drink no more.

Then said Utgard-Loki –

"It is plain that you are not so mighty as we imagined. Will you try another game? It seems to me there is little chance of your taking a prize hence."

"I will try more contests yet," answered Thor. "Such draughts as I have drunk would not have seemed small to the Æsir. But what new game have you?"

Utgard-Loki answered –

"The lads here do a thing which is not much. They lift my cat up from the ground. I should not have thought of proposing such a feat to Asu-Thor, had I not first seen that he is less by far than we took him to be."

As he spoke there sprang upon the hall floor a very large grey cat. Thor went up to it and put his hand under its middle and tried to lift it from the floor. The cat bent its back as Thor raised his hands, and when Thor had exerted himself to the utmost the cat had only one foot off the floor. Then Thor would make no further trial.

"I thought this game would go so," said Utgard-Loki. "The cat is large and Thor is little when compared with our men."

"Little as you call me," answered Thor, "let any one come here and wrestle with me, for now I am angry."

Utgard-Loki looked along the benches, and said –

"I see no man here who would not think it absurd to wrestle with you, but let some one call here the old woman, my nurse, Elli, and let Thor wrestle with her, if he will. She has cast to the ground many a man who seemed to me to be as strong as Thor."

Then came into the hall a toothless old woman, and Utgard-Loki told her to wrestle with Asu-Thor. The story is not a long one. The harder Thor tightened his hold, the firmer the old woman stood. Then she began to exert herself, Thor tottered, and at last, after a violent tussle, he fell on one knee. On this Utgard-Loki told them to stop, adding that Thor could not desire any one else to wrestle with him in the hall, and the night had closed in. He showed Thor and his companions to seats, and they passed the night, faring well.

At daybreak the next morning, Thor and his companions rose, dressed themselves, and prepared to leave at once. Then

Utgard-Loki came to them and ordered a table to be set for them having on it plenty of meat and drink. Afterwards he led them out of the city, and on parting asked Thor how he thought his journey had prospered, and whether he had met with any stronger than himself. Thor said he must own he had been much shamed.

"And," said he, "I know you will call me a man of little might, and I can badly bear that."

"Shall I tell you the truth?" said Utgard-Loki. "We are now out of the city, and while I live and have my own way, you will never again enter it. By my word you had never come in had I known before you had been so strong and would bring us so near to great misfortune. I have deluded thee with vain shows; first in the forest, where I met you, and where you were unable to untie the wallet because I had bound it with iron-thread so that you could not discover where the knot could be loosened. After that you gave me three blows with your hammer. The first blow, though the lightest, would have killed me had it fallen on me, but I put a rock in my place which you did not see. In that rocky mountain you will find three dales, one of which is very deep, those are the dints made by your hammer. In the other games, I have deceived you with illusions. The first one was the match with Loki. He was hungry and eat fast, but Logi was Flame, and he consumed not only the flesh but the trough with it. When Thjalfi contended with Hugi in running, Hugi was my thought, and it was not possible for Thjalfi to excel that in swiftness. When you drank of the horn and the liquor seemed to get lower so slowly, you did, indeed, so well that had I not seen it, I should never have believed it. You did not see that one end of the horn was in the sea, but when you come to the shore you will see how much the sea has shrunk in consequence of your draughts, which have caused what is called the ebb. Nor did you do a less wondrous thing when you lifted up the cat, and I can assure you all were afraid when you raised one of its paws off the ground. The cat was the great Midgard serpent which lies stretched round the whole earth, and when you raised it so high then did its length barely suffice to enclose the earth between its head and tail. Your wrestling match with Elli was, too, a great feat, for no one has there been yet, and no one shall there be whom old age does not come and trip up, if he but await her coming. Now we must part, and let me say that it will be better for both of us if you never more come to seek me, for I shall always defend my city with tricks, so that you will never overcome me."

When Thor heard that he grasped his mace in a rage, and raised it to hurl it at Utgard-Loki, but he had disappeared. Then Thor wanted to return to the city, but he could see nothing but a wide fair plain. So he turned, and went on his way till he came to Thrudvang, resolving if he had an opportunity to attack the Midgard serpent.

The Death of Baldur

Baldur the Good had dreams which forewarned him that his life was in danger, and he told the gods of them. The gods took counsel together what should be done, and it was agreed that they should conjure away all danger that might threaten him. Frigga took an oath of fire, water, iron, and all other metals, stones, earth, trees, sicknesses, beasts, birds, poisons, and worms, that these would none of them hurt Baldur. When this had been done the gods used to divert themselves, Baldur standing up in the assembly, and all the others throwing at him, hewing at him, and smiting him with stones, for, do all they would, he received no hurt, and in this sport all enjoyed themselves.

Loki, however, looked on with envy when he saw that Baldur was not hurt. So he assumed the form of a woman, and set out to Fensalir to Frigga. Frigga asked if the stranger knew what the gods did when they met. He answered that they all shot at Baldur and he was not hurt.

"No weapon, nor tree may hurt Baldur," answers Frigga, "I have taken an oath of them all not to do so."

"What," said the pretended woman, "have all things then sworn to spare Baldur?"

"There is only one little twig which grows to the east of Valhalla, which is called the mistletoe. Of that I took no oath, for it seemed to me too young and feeble to do any hurt."

Then the strange woman departed, and Loki having found the mistletoe, cut it off, and went to the assembly. There he found Hodur standing apart by himself, for he was blind. Then said Loki to him –

"Why do you not throw at Baldur?"

"Because," said he, "I am blind and cannot see him, and besides I have nothing to throw."

"Do as the others," said Loki, "and honour Baldur as the rest do. I will direct your aim. Throw this shaft at him."

Hodur took the mistletoe and, Loki directing him, aimed at Baldur. The aim was good. The shaft pierced him through, and Baldur fell dead upon the earth. Surely never was there a greater misfortune either among gods or men.

When the gods saw that Baldur was dead then they were silent, aghast, and stood motionless. They looked on one another, and were all agreed as to what he deserved who had done the deed, but out of respect to the place none dared avenge Baldur's death. They broke the silence at length with wailing, words failing them with which to express their sorrow. Odin, as was right, was more sorrowful than any of the others, for he best knew what a loss the gods had sustained.

At last when the gods had recovered themselves, Frigga asked –

"Who is there among the gods who will win my love and good-will? That shall he have if he will ride to Hel, and seek Baldur, and offer Hela a reward if she will let Baldur come home to Asgard."

Hermod the nimble, Odin's lad, said he would make the journey. So he mounted Odin's horse, Sleipner, and went his way.

The gods took Baldur's body down to the sea-shore, where stood Hringhorn, Baldur's vessel, the biggest in the world. When the gods tried to launch it into the water, in order to make on it a funeral fire for Baldur, the ship would not stir. Then they despatched one to Jotunheim for the sorceress called Hyrrokin, who came riding on a wolf with twisted serpents by way of reins. Odin called for four Berserkir to hold the horse, but they could not secure it till they had thrown it to the ground. Then Hyrrokin went to the stem of the ship, and set it afloat with a single touch, the vessel going so fast that fire sprang from the rollers, and the earth trembled. Then Thor was so angry that he took his hammer and wanted to cast it at the woman's head, but the gods pleaded for her and appeased him. The body of Baldur being placed on the ship, Nanna, the daughter of Nep, Baldur's wife, seeing it, died of a broken heart, so she was borne to the pile and thrown into the fire.

Thor stood up and consecrated the pile with Mjolnir. A little dwarf, called Litur, ran before his feet, and Thor gave him a push, and threw him into the fire, and he was burnt. Many kinds of people came to this ceremony. With Odin came Frigga and the

Valkyrjor with his ravens. Frey drove in a car drawn by the boar, Gullinbursti or Slidrugtanni. Heimdall rode the horse Gulltopp, and Freyja drove her cats. There were also many of the forest-giants and mountain-giants there. On the pile Odin laid the gold ring called Draupnir, giving it the property that every ninth night it produces eight rings of equal weight. In the same pile was also consumed Baldur's horse.

For nine nights and days Hermod rode through deep valleys, so dark that he could see nothing. Then he came to the river Gjöll which he crossed by the bridge which is covered with shining gold. The maid who keeps the bridge is called Modgudur. She asked Hermod his name and family, and told him that on the former day there had ridden over the bridge five bands of dead men.

"They did not make my bridge ring as you do, and you have not the hue of the dead. Why ride you thus on the way to Hel?"

He said –

"I ride to Hel to find Baldur. Have you seen him on his way to that place?"

"Baldur," answered she, "has passed over the bridge, but the way to Hel is below to the north."

Hermod rode on till he came to the entrance of Hel, which was guarded by a grate. He dismounted, looked to the girths of his saddle, mounted, and clapping his spurs into the horse, cleared the grate easily. Then he rode on to the hall and, dismounting, entered it. There he saw his brother, Baldur, seated in the first place, and there Hermod stopped the night.

In the morning he saw Hela, and begged her to let Baldur ride home with him, telling her how much the gods had sorrowed over his death. Hela told him she would test whether it were true that Baldur was so much loved.

"If," said she, "all things weep for him, then he shall return to the gods, but if any speak against him or refuse to weep, then he shall remain in Hel."

Then Hermod rose to go, and Baldur, leading him out of the hall, gave him the ring, Draupnir, which he wished Odin to have as a keepsake. Nanna also sent Frigga a present, and a ring to Fulla.

Hermod rode back, and coming to Asgard related all he had seen and heard. Then the gods sent messengers over all the world seeking to get Baldur brought back again by weeping. All wept, men and living things, earth, stones, trees, and metals, all weeping as they do when they are subjected to heat after frost. Then the messengers came back again, thinking they had done their errand well. On their way they came to a cave wherein sat a hag named Thaukt. The messengers prayed her to assist in weeping Baldur out of Hel.

"I will weep dry tears," answered she, "over Baldur's pyre. What gain I by the son of man, be he live or dead? Let Hela hold what she has."

It was thought that this must have been Loki, Laufey's son, he who has ever wrought such harm to the gods.

The Punishment of Loki

The gods were so angry with Loki that he had to run away and hide himself in the mountains, and there he built a house which had four doors, so that he could see around him on every side. He would often in the day-time change himself into a salmon and hide in the water called Franangursfors, and he thought over what trick the gods might devise to capture him there. One day while he sat in his house, he took flax and yarn, and with it made meshes like those of a net, a fire burning in front of him. Then he became aware that the gods were near at hand, for Odin had seen out of Hlidskjalf where he was. Loki sprang up, threw his work into the fire, and went to the river. When the gods came to the house, the first that entered was Kvasir, who was the most acute of them all. In the hot embers he saw the ashes of a net, such as is used in fishing, and he told the gods of it, and they made a net like that which they saw in the ashes. When it was ready they went to the river and cast the net in, Thor holding one end and the rest of the gods the other, and so they drew it. Loki travelled in front of it and lay down between two stones so that the net went over him, but the gods felt that something living had been against the net. Then they cast the net a second time, binding up in it a weight so that nothing could pass under it. Loki travelled before it till he saw the sea in front of him. Then he leapt over the top of the net and again made his way up the stream. The gods saw this, so they once more dragged the stream, while Thor waded in the middle of it. So they went to the sea.

Then Loki saw in what a dangerous situation he was. He must risk his life if he swam out to sea. The only other alternative was to leap over the net. That he did, jumping as quickly as he could over the top cord.

Thor snatched at him, and tried to hold him, but he slipped through his hand, and would have escaped, but for his tail, and this is the reason why salmon have their tails so thin.

Loki being captured, they took him to a certain cavern, and they took three rocks, through each of which they bored a hole. Then they took Loki's sons Vali and Nari, and having changed Vali into a wolf, he tore his brother Nari into pieces. Then the gods took his intestines and bound Loki with them to the three stones, and they changed the cord into bands of iron. Skadi then took a serpent and suspended it over Loki's head so that the venom drops from it on to his face. Siguna, Loki's wife, stands near him, and holds a dish receiving the venom as it falls, and when the dish is full she goes out and pours its contents away. While she is doing this, however, the venom falls on Loki, and causes him such intense pain that he writhes so that the earth is shaken as if by an earthquake.

There he lies till Ragnarök (the twilight of the gods).

HARALD THE VIKING

Erik the Red, the most famous of all Vikings, had three sons, and once when they were children the king came to visit Erik and passed through the playground where the boys were playing. Leif and Biorn, the two oldest, were building little houses and barns and were making believe that they were full of cattle and sheep, while Harald, who was only four years old, was sailing chips of wood in a pool. The king asked Harald what they were, and he said, "Ships of war." King Olaf laughed and said, "The time may come when you will command ships, my little friend." Then he asked Biorn what he would like best to have. "Corn-land," he said; "ten farms." "That would yield much corn," the king replied. Then he asked Leif the same question, and he answered, "Cows." "How many?" "So many that when they went to the lake to be watered, they would stand close round the edge, so that not another could pass." "That would be a large housekeeping," said the king, and he asked the same question of Harald. "What would you like best to have?" "Servants and followers," said the child, stoutly. "How many would you like?" "Enough," said the child, "to eat up all the cows and crops of my brothers at a single meal." Then the king laughed, and said to the mother of the children, "You are bringing up a king."

As the boys grew, Leif and Harald were ever fond of roaming, while Biorn wished to live on the farm at peace. Their sister Freydis went with the older boys and urged them on. She was not gentle and amiable, but full of energy and courage: she was also quarrelsome and vindictive. People said of her that even if her brothers were all killed, yet the race of Erik the Red would not end while she lived; that "she practised more of shooting and the handling of sword and shield than of sewing or embroidering, and that as she was able, she did evil oftener than good; and that when she was hindered she ran into the woods and slew men to get their property." She was always urging her brothers to deeds of daring and adventure. One day they had been hawking, and when they let slip the falcons, Harald's falcon killed two blackcocks in one flight and three in another. The dogs ran and brought the birds, and he said proudly to the others, "It will be long before most of you have any such success," and they all agreed to this. He rode home in high spirits and showed his birds to his sister Freydis. "Did any king," he asked, "ever make so great a capture in so short a time?" "It is, indeed," she said, "a good morning's hunting to have got five blackcocks, but it was still better when in one morning a king of Norway took five kings and subdued all their kingdoms." Then Harald went away very humble and besought his father to let him go and serve on the Varangian Guard of King Otho at Constantinople, that he might learn to be a warrior.

So Harald was brought from his Norwegian home by his father Erik the Red, in his galley called the *Sea-serpent*, and sailed with him through the Mediterranean Sea, and was at last made a member of the Emperor Otho's Varangian Guard at Constantinople. This guard will be well remembered by the readers of Scott's novel, "Count Robert of Paris," and was maintained by successive emperors and drawn largely from the Scandinavian races. Erik the Red had no hesitation in leaving his son among them, as the young man was stout and strong, very self-willed, and quite able to defend himself. The father knew also that the Varangian Guard, though hated by the people, held to one another like a band of brothers; and that any one brought up among them would be sure of plenty of fighting and plenty of gold, – the two things most prized by early Norsemen. For ordinary life, Harald's chief duties would be to lounge about the palace, keeping guard, wearing helmet and buckler and bearskin, with purple underclothes and golden clasped hose; and bearing as armor a mighty battle-axe and a small scimitar. Such was the life led by Harald, till one day he had a message from his father, through a new recruit, calling him home to join an expedition to the western seas. "I hear, my son," the message said, "that your good emperor, whom may the gods preserve, is sorely ill and may die any day. When he is dead, be prompt in getting your share of the plunder of the palace and come back to me."

The emperor died, and the order was fulfilled. It was the custom of the Varangians to reward themselves in this way for their faithful services of protection; and the result is that, to this day, Greek and Arabic gold crosses and chains are to be found in the houses of Norwegian peasants and may be seen in the museums of Christiania and Copenhagen. No one was esteemed the less for this love of spoil, if he was only generous in giving. The Norsemen spoke contemptuously of gold as "the serpent's bed," and called a generous man "a hater of the serpent's bed," because such a man parts with gold as with a thing he hates.

When the youth came to his father, he found Erik the Red directing the building of one of the great Norse galleys, nearly eighty feet long and seventeen wide and only six feet deep. The boat had twenty ribs, and the frame was fastened together by withes made of roots, while the oaken planks were held by iron rivets. The oars were twenty feet long, and were put through oar holes, and the rudder, shaped like a large oar, was not at the end, but was attached to a projecting beam on the starboard (originally steer-board) side. The ship was to be called a Dragon, and was to be painted so as to look like one, having a gilded dragon's head at the bow and a gilded tail on the stern; while the moving oars would look like legs, and the row of red and white shields, hung along the side of the boat, would resemble the scales of a dragon, and the great square sails, red and blue, would look like wings. This was the vessel which young Harald was to command.

He had already made trips in just such vessels with his father; had learned to attack the enemy with arrow and spear; also with stones thrown down from above, and with grappling-irons to clutch opposing boats. He had learned to swim, from early childhood, even in the icy northern waters, and he had been trained in swimming to hide his head beneath his floating shield, so that it could not be seen. He had learned also to carry tinder in a walnut shell, enclosed in wax, so that no matter how long he had been in the water he could strike a light on reaching shore. He had also learned from his father acts of escape as well as attack. Thus he had once sailed on a return trip from Denmark after plundering a town; the ships had been lying at anchor all night in a fog, and at sunlight in the morning lights seemed burning on the sea. But Erik the Red said, "It is a fleet of Danish ships, and the sun strikes on the gilded dragon crests; furl the sail and take to the oars." They rowed their best, yet the Danish ships were overtaking them, when Erik the Red ordered his men to throw wood overboard and cover it with Danish plunder. This made some delay, as the Danes stopped to pick it up, and in the same way Erik the Red dropped his provisions, and finally his prisoners; and in the delay thus caused he got away with his own men.

But now Harald was not to go to Denmark, but to the new western world, the Wonderstrands which Leif had sought and had left without sufficient exploration. First, however, he was to call at Greenland, which his father had first discovered. It was the custom of the Viking explorers, when they reached a new country, to throw overboard their "seat posts," or *setstokka*, – the curved part of their doorways, – and then to land where they floated ashore. But Erik the Red had lent his to a friend and could not get them back, so that he sailed in search of them, and came to a new land which he called Greenland, because, as he said, people would be attracted thither if it had a good name. Then he established a colony there, and then Leif the Lucky, as he was called, sailed still farther, and came to the Wonderstrand, or Magic Shores. These he called Vinland or Wine-land, and now a rich man named Karlsefne was to send a colony thither from Greenland, and the young Harald was to go with it and take command of it.

Now as Harald was to be presented to the rich Karlsefne, he thought he must be gorgeously arrayed. So he wore a helmet on his head, a red shield richly inlaid with gold and iron, and a sharp sword with an ivory handle wound with golden thread. He had also a short spear, and wore over his coat a red silk short cloak on which was embroidered, both before and behind, a yellow lion. We may well believe that the sixty men and five women who composed the expedition were ready to look on him with admiration, especially as one of the women was his own sister, Freydis, now left to his peculiar care, since Erik the Red had died. The sturdy old hero had died still a heathen, and it was only just after his death that

Christianity was introduced into Greenland, and those numerous churches were built there whose ruins yet remain, even in regions from which all population has gone.

So the party of colonists sailed for Vinland, and Freydis, with the four older women, came in Harald's boat, and Freydis took easily the lead among them for strength, though not always, it must be admitted, for amiability.

The boats of the expedition having left Greenland soon after the year 1000, coasted the shore as far as they could, rarely venturing into open sea. At last, amidst fog and chilly weather, they made land at a point where a river ran through a lake into the sea, and they could not enter from the sea except at high tide. It was once believed that this was Narragansett Bay in Rhode Island, but this is no longer believed. Here they landed and called the place Hóp, from the Icelandic word *hópa*, meaning an inlet from the ocean. Here they found grapevines growing and fields of wild wheat; there were fish in the lake and wild animals in the woods. Here they landed the cattle and the provisions which they had brought with them; and here they built their huts. They went in the spring, and during that summer the natives came in boats of skin to trade with them – men described as black, and ill favored, with large eyes and broad cheeks and with coarse hair on their heads. These, it is thought, may have been the Esquimaux. The first time they came, these visitors held up a white shield as a sign of peace, and were so frightened by the bellowing of the bull that they ran away. Then returning, they brought furs to sell and wished to buy weapons, but Harald tried another plan: he bade the women bring out milk, butter, and cheese from their dairies, and when the Skraelings saw that, they wished for nothing else, and, the legend says, "the Skraelings carried away their wares in their stomachs, but the

Norsemen had the skins they had purchased." This happened yet again, but at the second visit one of the Skraelings was accidentally killed or injured.

The next time the Skraelings came they were armed with slings, and raised upon a pole a great blue ball and attacked the Norsemen so furiously that they were running away when Erik's sister, Freydis, came out before them with bare arms, and took up a sword, saying, "Why do you run, strong men as you are, from these miserable dwarfs whom I thought you would knock down like cattle? Give me weapons, and I will fight better than any of you." Then the rest took courage and began to fight, and the Skraelings were driven back. Once more the strangers came, and one of them took up an axe, a thing which he had not before seen, and struck at one of his companions, killing him. Then the leader took the axe and threw it into the water, after which the Skraelings retreated, and were not seen again.

The winter was a mild one, and while it lasted, the Norsemen worked busily at felling wood and house-building. They had also many amusements, in most of which Harald excelled. They used to swim in all weathers. One of their feats was to catch seals and sit on them while swimming; another was to pull one another down and remain as long as possible under water. Harald could swim for a mile or more with his armor on, or with a companion on his shoulder. Indoors they used to play the tug of war, dragging each other by a walrus hide across the fire. Harald was good at this, and was also the best archer, sometimes aiming at something placed on a boy's head, the boy having a cloth tied around his head, and held by two men, that he might not move at all on hearing the whistling of the arrow. In this way Harald could even shoot an arrow under a nut placed on the head, so that the nut would roll down and the head not be hurt. He could plant a spear in the ground and then shoot an arrow upward so skilfully that it would turn in the air and fall with the point in the end of the spear-shaft. He could also shoot a blunt arrow through the thickest ox-hide from a cross-bow. He could change weapons from one hand to the other during a fencing match, or fence with either hand, or throw two spears at the same time, or catch a spear in motion. He could run so fast that no horse could overtake him, and play the rough games with bat and ball, using a ball of the hardest wood. He could race on snowshoes, or wrestle when bound by a belt to his antagonist. Then when he and his companions wished a rest, they amused themselves with harp-playing or riddles or chess. The Norsemen even played chess on board their vessels, and there are still to be seen, on some of these, the little holes that were formerly used for the sharp ends of the chessmen, so that they should not be displaced.

They could not find that any European had ever visited this place; but some of the Skraelings told them of a place farther south, which they called "the Land of the Whiteman," or "Great Ireland." They said that in that place there were white men who clothed themselves in long white garments, carried before them poles to which white cloths were hung, and called with a loud voice. These, it was thought by the Norsemen, must be Christian processions, in which banners were borne and hymns were chanted. It has been thought from this that some expedition from Ireland – that of St. Brandan, for instance – may have left a settlement there, long before, but this has never been confirmed. The Skraelings and the Northmen were good friends for a time; until at last one of Erik's own warriors killed a Skraeling by accident, and then all harmony was at an end.

They saw no hope of making a lasting settlement there, and, moreover, Freydis who was very grasping, tried to deceive the other settlers and get more than her share of everything, so that Harald himself lost patience with her and threatened her. It happened that one of the men of the party, Olaf, was Harald's foster-brother. They had once had a fight, and after the battle had agreed that they would be friends for life and always share the same danger. For this vow they were to walk under the turf; that is, a strip of turf was cut and held above their heads, and they stood beneath and let their blood flow upon the ground whence the turf had been cut. After this they were to own everything by halves and either must avenge the other's death. This was their brotherhood; but Freydis did not like it; so she threatened Olaf, and tried to induce men to kill him, for she did not wish to bring upon herself the revenge that must come if she slew him.

This was the reason why the whole enterprise failed, and why Olaf persuaded Harald, for the sake of peace, to return to Greenland in the spring and take a load of valuable timber to sell there, including one stick of what was called massur-wood, which was as valuable as mahogany, and may have been at some time borne by ocean currents to the beach. It is hardly possible that, as some have thought, the colonists established a regular trade in this wood for no such wood grows on the northern Atlantic shores. However this may be, the party soon returned, after one winter in Vinland the Good; and on the way back Harald did one thing which made him especially dear to his men.

A favorite feat of the Norsemen was to toss three swords in the air and catch each by the handle as it came down. This was called the *handsax* game. The young men used also to try the feat of running along the oar-blades of the rowers as they were in motion, passing around the bow of the vessel with a spring and coming round to the stern over the oars on the other side. Few could accomplish this, but no one but Harald could do it and play the *handsax* game as he ran; and when he did it, they all said that he was the most skilful man at *idrottie* ever seen. That was their word for an athletic feat. But presently came a time when not only his courage but his fairness and justice were to be tried.

It happened in this way. There was nothing of which the Norsemen were more afraid than of the *teredo*, or shipworm, which gnaws the wood of ships. It was observed in Greenland and Iceland that pieces of wood often floated on shore which were filled with holes made by this animal, and they thought that in certain places the seas were full of this worm, so that a ship would be bored and sunk in a little while. It is said that on this return voyage Harald's vessel entered a worm-sea and presently began to sink. They had, however, provided a smaller boat smeared with sea-oil, which the worms would not attack. They went into the boat, but found that it would not hold more than half of them all. Then Harald said, "We will divide by lots, without regard to the rank; each taking his chance with the rest." This they thought, the Norse legend says, "a high-minded offer." They drew lots, and Harald was among those assigned to the safer boat. He stepped in, and when he was there a man called from the other boat and said, "Dost thou intend, Harald, to separate from me here?" Harald answered, "So it turns out," and the man said, "Very different was thy promise to my father when we came from Greenland, for the promise was that we should share the same fate."

Then Harald said, "It shall not be thus. Go into the boat, and I will go back into the ship, since thou art so anxious to live." Then Harald went back to the ship, while the man took his place in the boat, and after that Harald was never heard of more.

THE DWARF-SWORD TIRFING

Euaforlami, the second in descent from Odin, was king over Gardarike (Russia). One day he rode a-hunting, and sought long after a hart, but could not find one the whole day. When the sun was setting, he found himself plunged so deep in the forest that he knew not where he was. On his right hand he saw a hill, and before it he saw two dwarfs. He drew his sword against them, and cut off their retreat by getting between them and the rock. They offered him ransom for their lives, and he asked them their names, and they said that one of them was called Dyren and the other Dualin. Then he knew that they were the most ingenious and the most expert of all the dwarfs, and he therefore demanded that they should make for him a sword, the best that they could form. Its hilt was to be of gold, and its belt of the same metal. He moreover commanded that the sword should never miss a blow, should never rust, that it should cut through iron and stone as through a garment, and that it should always be victorious in war and in single combat. On these conditions he granted the dwarfs their lives.

At the time appointed he came, and the dwarfs appearing, they gave him the sword. When Dualin stood at the door, he said –

"This sword shall be the bane of a man every time it is drawn, and with it shall be perpetrated three of the greatest atrocities, and it will also prove thy bane."

Suaforlami, when he heard that, struck at the dwarf, so that the blade of the sword penetrated the solid rock. Thus Suaforlami became possessed of this sword, and he called it Tirfing. He bore it in war and in single combat, and with it he slew the giant Thiasse, whose daughter Fridur he took.

Suaforlami was soon after slain by the Berserker Andgrim, who then became master of the sword. When the twelve sons of

Andgrim were to fight with Hialmar and Oddur for Ingaborg, the beautiful daughter of King Inges, Angantyr bore the dangerous Tirfing, but all the brethren were slain in the combat, and were buried with their arms.

Angantyr left an only daughter, Hervor, who, when she grew up, dressed herself in man's attire, and took the name of Hervardar, and joined a party of Vikinger, or pirates. Knowing that Tirfing lay buried with her father, she determined to awaken the dead, and obtain the charmed blade. She landed alone, in the evening, on the Island of Sams, where her father and uncles lay in their sepulchral mounds, and ascending by night to their tombs, that were enveloped in flame, she, by the force of entreaty, obtained from the reluctant Angantyr the formidable Tirfing.

Hervor proceeded to the court of King Gudmund, and there one day, as she was playing at tables with the king, one of the servants chanced to take up and draw Tirfing, which shone like a sunbeam. But Tirfing was never to see the light but for the bane of men, and Hervor, by a sudden impulse, sprang from her seat, snatched the sword, and struck off the head of the unfortunate man.

After this she returned to the house of her grandfather, Jarl Biartmar, where she resumed her female attire, and was married to Haufud, the son of King Gudmund. She bore him two sons, Angantyr and Heidreker; the former of a mild and gentle disposition, the latter violent and fierce. Haufud would not permit Heidreker to remain at his court, and as he was departing, his mother, among other gifts, presented him with Tirfing.

His brother accompanied him out of the castle. Before they parted, Heidreker drew out his sword to look at and admire it, but scarcely did the rays of light fall on the magic blade, when the Berserker rage came on its owner, and he slew his gentle brother.

After this he joined a body of Vikinger, and became so distinguished that King Harold, for the aid he lent him, gave him his daughter Helga in marriage. But it was the destiny of Tirfing to commit crime, and Harold fell by the sword of his son-in-law. Heidreker was afterwards in Russia, and the son of the king was his foster-son. One day as they were out hunting, Heidreker and his foster-son happened to be separated from the rest of the party, when a wild boar appeared before them.

Heidreker ran at him with his spear, but the beast caught it in his mouth and broke it across. Then he alighted and drew Tirfing, and killed the boar. On looking round him, he saw no one but his foster-son, and Tirfing could only be appeased with warm human blood, so Heidreker slew the poor youth.

In the end Heidreker was murdered in his bed by his Scottish slaves, who carried off Tirfing. His son Angantyr, who succeeded him, discovered the thieves and put them to death, and recovered the magic blade. He made great slaughter in battle against the Huns, but among the slain was discovered his own brother, Landur.

So ends the history of the Dwarf-Sword Tirfing.

THE PRINCESS AND THE GLASS MOUNTAIN

Once upon a time there was a king who took such a joy in the chase, that he knew no greater pleasure than hunting wild beasts. Early and late he camped in the forest with hawk and hound, and good fortune always followed his hunting. But it chanced one day that he could rouse no game, although he had tried in every direction since morning. And then, when evening was coming on, and he was about to ride home, he saw a dwarf or wild man running through the forest before him. The king at once spurred on his horse, rode after the dwarf, seized him and he was surprised at his strange appearance; for he was small and ugly, like a troll, and his hair was as stiff as bean-straw. But no matter what the king said to him, he would return no answer, nor say a single word one way or another. This angered the king, who was already out of sorts because of his ill-success at the hunt, and he ordered his people to seize the wild man and guard him carefully lest he escape. Then the king rode home.

Now his people said to him: "You should keep the wild man a captive here at your court, in order that the whole country may talk of what a mighty huntsman you are. Only you should guard him so that he does not escape; because he is of a sly and treacherous disposition." When the king had listened to them he said nothing for a long time. Then he replied: "I will do as you say, and if the wild man escape, it shall be no fault of mine. But I vow that whoever lets him go shall die without mercy, and though he were my own son!"

The following morning, as soon as the king awoke, he remembered his vow.

He at once sent for wood and beams, and had a small house or cage built quite close to the castle. The small house was built of great timbers, and protected by strong locks and bolts, so that none could break in; and a peephole was left in the middle of the wall through which food might be thrust.

When everything was completed the king had the wild man led up, placed in the small house, and he himself took and kept the key. There the dwarf had to sit a prisoner, day and night, and the people came afoot and a-horseback to gaze at him. Yet no one ever heard him complain, or so much as utter a single word.

Thus matters went for some time. Then a war broke out in the land, and the king had to take the field. At parting he said to the queen: "You must rule the kingdom now in my stead, and I leave land and people in your care. But there is one thing you must promise me you will do: that you will guard the wild man securely so that he does not escape while I am away." The queen promised to do her best in all respects, and the king gave her the key to the cage. Thereupon he had his long galleys, his "sea-wolves," push out from the shore, hoisted sail, and took his course far, far away to the other country.

The king and queen had only one child, a prince who was still small; yet great in promise. Now when the king had gone, it chanced one day that the little fellow was wandering about the royal courtyard, and came to the wild man's cage. And he began to play with an apple of gold he had. And while he was playing with it, it happened that suddenly the apple fell through the window in the wall of the cage. The wild man at once appeared and threw back the apple. This seemed a merry game to the little fellow: he threw the apple in again, and the wild man threw it out again, and thus they played for a long time. Yet for all the game had been so pleasant, it turned to sorrow in the end: for the wild man kept the apple of gold, and would not give it back again. And when all was of no avail, neither threats nor prayers, the little fellow at last began to weep. Then the wild man said: "Your father did ill to capture me, and you will never get your apple of gold again, unless you let me out." The little fellow answered: "And how can I let you out? Just you give me back my apple again, my apple of gold!" Then the wild man said: "You must do what I now tell you. Go up to your mother, the queen, and beg her to comb your hair. Then see to it that you take the key from her girdle, and come down and unlock the door. After that you can return the key in the same way, without any one knowing anything about it."

After the wild man had talked to the boy in this way, he finally did as he said, went up to his mother, begged her to comb his hair, and took the key from her girdle. Then he ran down to the cage and opened the door. And when they parted, the dwarf said: "Here is your apple of gold, that I promised to give back to you, and I thank you for setting me free. And another time when you have need of me, I will help you in turn." And with that he ran off on his own way. But the prince went back to his mother, and returned the key in the same way he had taken it.

When they learned at the king's court that the wild man had broken out, there was great commotion, and the queen sent people over hill and dale to look for him. But he was gone and he stayed gone. Thus matters went for a while and the queen grew more and more unhappy; for she expected her husband to return every day. And when he did reach shore his first question was whether the wild man had been well guarded. Then the queen had to confess how matters stood, and told him how everything had happened. But the king was enraged beyond measure, and said he would punish the malefactor, no matter who he might be. And he ordered a great investigation at his court, and every human being in it had to testify. But no one knew anything. At last the little prince also had to come forward. And as he stood before the king he said: "I know that I have deserved my father's anger; yet I cannot hide the truth; for I let out the wild man." Then the queen turned white, and the others as well, for there was not one who was not fond of the prince. At last the king spoke: "Never shall it be said of me that I was false to my vow, even for the sake of my own flesh and blood! No, you must die the death you have deserved." And with that he gave the order to take the prince to the forest and kill him. And they were to bring back the boy's heart as a sign that his command had been obeyed.

Now sorrow unheard of reigned among the people, and all pleaded for the little prince. But the king's word could not be recalled. His serving-men did not dare disobey, took the boy in their midst, and set forth. And when they had gone a long way into the forest, they saw a swine-herd tending his pigs. Then one said to another: "It does not seem right to me to lay hand on the king's son; let us buy a pig instead and take its heart, then all will believe it is the heart of the prince." The other serving-men thought that he spoke wisely, so they bought a pig from the swine-herd, led it into the wood, butchered it and took its heart. Then they told the prince to go his way and never return. They themselves went back to the king's castle, and it is easy to imagine what grief they caused when they told of the prince's death.

The king's son did what the serving-men had told him. He kept on wandering as far as he could, and never had any other food than the nuts and wild berries that grow in the forest. And when he had wandered far and long, he came to a mountain upon whose very top stood a fir tree. Said he to himself: "After all, I might as well climb the fir tree and see whether I can find a path anywhere." No sooner said than done: he climbed the tree. And as he sat in the very top of its crown, and looked about on every side, he saw a large and splendid royal castle rising in the distance, and gleaming in the sun. Then he grew very happy and at once set forth in that direction. On the way he met a farm-hand who was ploughing, and begged him to change clothes with him, which he did. Thus fitted out he at last reached the king's castle, went in, asked for a place, and was taken on as a herdsman, to tend the king's cattle. Now he went to the forest early and late, and in the course of time forgot his grief, grew up, and became so tall and brave that his equal could not be found.

And now our story turns to the king who was reigning at the splendid castle. He had been married, and he had an only daughter. She was lovelier by far than other maidens, and had so kind and cheerful a disposition that whoever could some day take her to his home might well consider himself fortunate. Now when the princess had completed her fifteenth year, a quite unheard of swarm of suitors made their appearance, as may well be imagined; and for all that she said no to all of them, they only increased in number. At last the princess said: "None other shall win me save he who can ride up the high Glass Mountain in full armor!" The king thought this a good suggestion. He approved of his daughter's wish, and had proclaimed throughout the kingdom that none other should have the princess save he who could ride up the Glass Mountain.

And when the day set by the king had arrived, the princess was led up the Glass Mountain. There she sat on its highest peak, with a golden crown on her head, and a golden apple in her hand, and she looked so immeasurably lovely that there was no one who would not have liked to risk his life for her. Just below the foot of the hill all the suitors assembled with splendid horses and glittering armor, that shone like fire in the sun, and from round about the people flocked together in great crowds to watch their tilting. And when everything was ready, the signal was given by horns and trumpets, and then the suitors, one after another, raced up the mountain with all their might. But the mountain was high, as slippery as ice, and besides it was steep beyond all measure. Not one of the suitors rode up more than a little way, before he tumbled down again, head over heels, and it might well happen that arms and legs were broken in the process. This made so great a noise, together with the neighing of the horses, the shouting of the people, and the clash of arms, that the tumult and the shouting could be heard far away.

And while all this was going on, the king's son was rambling about with his oxen, deep in the wood. But when he heard the tumult and the clashing of arms, he sat down on a stone, leaned his cheek on his hand, and became lost in thought. For it had occurred to him how gladly he would have fared forth with the rest. Suddenly he heard footsteps and when he looked up, the wild man was standing before him. "Thank you for the last time!" said he, "and why do you sit here so lonely and full of sorrow?" "Well," said the prince, "I have no choice but to be sad and joyless. Because of you I am a fugitive from the land of my father, and now I have not even a horse and armor to ride up the Glass Mountain and fight for the princess." "Ah," said the wild man, "if that be all you want, then I can help you! You helped me once before and now I will help you in turn." Then he took the prince by the hand, led him deep down into the earth into his cave, and behold, there hung a suit of armor forged out of the hardest steel, and so bright that a blue gleam played all around it. Right beside it stood a splendid steed, saddled and bridled, pawing the earth with his steel hoofs, and champing his bit till the white foam dropped to the ground. The wild man said: "Now get quickly into your armor, ride out and try your luck! In the meantime I will tend your oxen." The prince did not wait to be told a second time; but put on helmet and armor, buckled on his spurs, hung his sword at his side, and felt as light in his steel armor as a bird in the air. Then he leaped into the saddle so that every clasp and buckle rang, laid his reins on the neck of his steed, and rode hastily toward the mountain.

The princess's suitors were about to give up the contest, for none of them had won the prize, though each had done his best. And while they stood there thinking it over, and saying that perhaps fortune would favor them another time, they suddenly saw a youth ride out of the wood straight toward the mountain. He was clad in steel from head to foot, with helmet on head, sword in belt and shield on arm, and he sat his horse with such knightly grace that it was a pleasure to look at him. At once all eyes were turned to the strange knight, and all asked who he might be; for none had ever seen him before. Yet they had had but little time to talk and question, for no sooner had he cleared the wood, than he rose in his stirrups, gave his horse the spurs, and shot forward like an arrow straight up the Glass Mountain. Yet he did not ride up all the way; but when he had reached the middle of the steep ascent, he suddenly flung around his steed and rode down again, so that the sparks flew from his horse's hoofs. Then he disappeared in the wood like a bird in flight. One may imagine the excitement which now seized upon all the people, and there was not one who did not admire the strange knight. All agreed they had never seen a braver knight.

Time passed, and the princess's suitors decided to try their luck a second time. The king's daughter was once more led up the Glass Mountain, with great pomp and richly gowned, and was seated on its topmost peak, with the golden crown on her head, and a golden apple in her hand. At the foot of the hill gathered all the suitors with handsome horses and splendid armor, and round about stood all the people to watch the contest. When all was ready the signal was given by horns and trumpets, and at the same moment the suitors, one after another, darted up the mountain with all their might. But all took place as at the first time. The mountain was high, and as slippery as ice, and besides, it was steep beyond all measure; not one rode up more than a little way before tumbling down again head over heels. Meanwhile there was much noise, and the horses neighed, and the people shouted, and the armor clashed, so that the tumult and the shouting sounded far into the deep wood.

And while all this was going on, the young prince was tending his oxen, which was his duty. But when he heard the tumult and the clashing of arms, he sat down on a stone, leaned his cheek on his hand, and wept; for he thought of the king's beautiful daughter, and it occurred to him how much he would like to take part and ride with the rest. That very moment he heard footsteps and when he looked up, the wild man was standing before him. "Good-day!" said the wild man, "and why do you sit here so lonely and full of sorrow?" Thereupon the prince replied: "I have no choice but to be sad and joyless. Because of you I am a fugitive from the land of my father, and now I have not even a horse and armor to ride up the mountain and fight for the princess!" "Ah," said the wild man, "if that be all you want, then I can help you! You helped me once before, and now I will help you in turn." Then he took the prince by the hand, led him deep down in the earth into his cave, and there on the wall hung a suit of armor altogether forged of the clearest silver, and so bright that it shone afar. Right beside it stood a snow-white steed, saddled and bridled, pawing the earth with his silver hoofs, and champing his bit till the foam dropped to the ground. The wild man said: "Now get quickly into your armor, ride out and try your luck! In the meantime I will tend your oxen." The prince did not wait to be told a second time; but put on his helmet and armor in all haste, securely buckled on his spurs, hung his sword at his side, and felt as light in his silver armor as a bird in the air. Then he leaped into the saddle so that every clasp and buckle rang, laid his reins on the neck of his steed, and rode hastily toward the Glass Mountain.

The princess's suitors were about to give over the contest, for none of them had won the prize, though each had played a man's part. And while they stood there thinking it over, and saying that perhaps fortune would favor them the next time, they suddenly saw a youth ride out of the wood, straight toward the mountain. He was clad in silver from head to foot, with helmet on head, shield on arm, and sword at side, and he sat his horse with such knightly grace that a braver-looking youth had probably never been seen. At once all eyes were turned toward him, and the people noticed that he was the same knight who had appeared before. But the prince did not leave them much time for wonderment; for no sooner had he reached the plain, than he rose in his stirrups, spurred on his horse, and rode like fire straight up the steep mountain. Yet he did not ride quite up to the top; but when he had come to its crest, he greeted the princess with great courtesy, flung about his steed, and rode down the mountain again till the sparks flew about his horse's hoofs. Then he disappeared into the wood as the storm flies. As one may imagine, the people's excitement was even greater than the first time, and there was not one who did not admire the strange knight. And all were agreed that a more splendid steed or a handsomer youth were nowhere to be found.

Time passed, and the king set a day when his daughter's suitors were to make a third trial. The princess was now once more led to the Glass Mountain, and seated herself on its highest peak, with the golden crown and the golden apple, as she had before. At the foot of the mountain gathered the whole swarm of suitors, with splendid horses and polished armor, handsome beyond anything seen thus far, and round about the people flocked together to watch the contest. When all was ready the suitors, one after another, darted up the mountain with all their might. The mountain was as smooth as ice, and besides, it was steep beyond all measure; so that not one rode up more than a little way, before tumbling down again, head over heels. This made a great noise, the horses neighed, the people shouted, and the armor clashed, till the tumult and the shouting echoed far into the wood.

While this was all taking place the king's son was busy tending his oxen as usual. And when he once more heard the noise and the clash of arms, he sat down on a stone, leaned his cheek on his hand, and wept bitterly. Then he thought of the lovely princess, and would gladly have ventured his life to win her. That very moment the wild man was standing before him: "Good-day!" said the wild man, "And why do you sit here so lonely and full of sorrow?" "I have no choice but to be sad and joyless," said the prince. "Because of you I am a fugitive from the land of my father, and now I have not even a sword and armor to ride up the mountain and fight for the princess!" "Ah," said the wild man, "if that be all that troubles you I can help you! You helped me once before, and now I will help you in turn." With that he took the prince by the hand, led him into his cave deep down under the earth, and showed him a suit of armor all forged of the purest gold, and gleaming so brightly that its golden glow shone far and wide. Beside it stood a magnificent steed, saddled and bridled, pawing the earth with its golden hoofs, and champing its bit until the foam fell to the ground. The wild man said: "Now get quickly into your armor, ride out and try your luck! In the meantime I will tend your oxen." And to tell the truth, the prince was not lazy; but put on his helmet and armor, buckled on his golden spurs, hung his sword at his side, and felt as light in his golden armor as a bird in the air. Then he leaped into the saddle, so that every clasp and buckle rang, laid his reins on the neck of his steed, and rode hastily toward the mountain.

The princess's suitors were about to give up the contest; for none of them had won the prize, though each had done his best. And while they stood there thinking over what was to be done, they suddenly saw a youth come riding out of the wood, straight toward the mountain. He was clad in gold from head to foot, with the golden helmet on his head, the golden shield on his arm, and the golden sword at his side, and so knightly was his bearing that a bolder warrior could not have been met with in all the wide world. At once all eyes were turned toward him, and one could see that he was the same youth who had already appeared at different times. But the prince gave them but little time to question and wonder; for no sooner had he reached the plain than he gave his horse the spurs, and shot up the steep mountain like a flash of lightning. When he had reached its highest peak, he greeted the beautiful princess with great courtesy, kneeled before her, and received the golden apple from her hand. Then he flung about his steed, and rode down the Glass Mountain again, so that the sparks flew about the golden hoofs of his horse, and a long ribbon of golden light gleamed behind him. At last he disappeared in the wood like a star. What a commotion now reigned about the mountain! The people broke forth into cheers that could be heard far away, horns sounded, trumpets called, horses neighed, arms clashed, and the king had proclaimed far and near that the unknown golden knight had won the prize.

Now all that was wanting was some information about the golden knight; for no one knew him; and all the people expected that he would at once make his appearance at the castle. But he did not come. This caused great surprise, and the princess grew pale and ill. But the king was put out, and the suitors murmured and found fault day by day. And at length, when they were all at their wits' end, the king had a great meeting announced at his castle, which every man, high and low, was to attend; so that the princess might choose among them herself. There was no one who was not glad to go for the princess's sake, and also because it was a royal command, and a countless number of people gathered together. And when they had all assembled, the princess came out of the castle with great pomp, and followed by her maids, passed through the entire multitude. But no matter how much she looked about her on every side, she did not find the one for whom she was looking. When she reached the last row she saw a man who stood quite hidden by the crowd. He had a flat cap and a wide gray mantle such as shepherds wear; but its hood was drawn up so that his face could not be seen. At once the princess ran up to him, drew down his hood, fell upon his neck and cried: "Here he is! Here he is!" Then all the people laughed; for they saw that it was the king's herdsman, and the king himself called out: "May God console me for the son-in-law who is to be my portion!" The man, however, was not at all abashed, but replied: "O, you need not worry about that at all! I am just as much a king's son as you are a king!"

With that he flung aside his wide mantle. And there were none left to laugh; for instead of the grey herdsman, there stood a handsome prince, clad in gold from head to foot, and holding the princess's golden apple in his hand. And all could see that it was the same youth who had ridden up the Glass Mountain.

Then they prepared a feast whose like had never before been seen, and the prince received the king's daughter, and with her half of the kingdom. Thenceforward they lived happily in their kingdom, and if they have not died they are living there still. But nothing more was ever heard of the wild man. And that is the end.

THE MASTER-MAID

Once upon a time there was a king who had many sons. I do not exactly know how many there were, but the youngest of them could not stay quietly at home, and was determined to go out into the world and try his luck, and after a long time the King was forced to give him leave to go. When he had traveled about for several days, he came to a giant's house, and hired himself to the giant as a servant. In the morning the giant had to go out to pasture his goats, and as he was leaving the house he told the King's son that he must clean out the stable. "And after you have done that," he said, "you need not do any more work today, for you have come to a kind master, and that you shall find. But what I set you to do must be done both well and thoroughly, and you must on no account go into any of the rooms which lead out of the room in which you slept last night. If you do, I will take your life."

"Well to be sure, he is an easy master!" said the Prince to himself as he walked up and down the room humming and singing, for he thought there would be plenty of time left to clean out the stable; "but it would be amusing to steal a glance into his other rooms as well," thought the Prince, "for there must be something that he is afraid of my seeing, as I am not allowed to enter them." So he went into the first room. A cauldron was hanging from the walls; it was boiling, but the Prince could see no fire under it. "I wonder what is inside it," he thought, and dipped a lock of his hair in, and the hair became just as if it were all made of copper. "That's a nice kind of soup. If anyone were to taste that his throat would be gilded," said the youth, and then he went into the next chamber. There, too, a cauldron was hanging from the wall, bubbling and boiling, but there was no fire under this either. "I will just try what this is like too," said the Prince, thrusting another lock of his hair into it, and it came out silvered over. "Such costly soup is not to be had in my father's palace," said the Prince; "but everything depends on how it tastes," and then he went into the third room. There, too, a cauldron was hanging from the wall, boiling, exactly the same as in the two other rooms, and the Prince took pleasure in trying this also, so he dipped a lock of hair in, and it came out so brightly gilded that it shone again. "Some talk about going from bad to worse," said the Prince; "but this is better and better. If he boils gold here, what can he boil in there?" He was determined to see, and went through the door into the fourth room. No cauldron was to be seen there, but on a bench someone was seated who was like a king's daughter, but, whosoever she was, she was so beautiful that never in the Prince's life had he seen her equal.

"Oh! in heaven's name what are you doing here?" said she who sat upon the bench.

"I took the place of servant here yesterday," said the Prince.

"May you soon have a better place, if you have come to serve here!" said she.

"Oh, but I think I have got a kind master," said the Prince. "He has not given me hard work to do today. When I have cleaned out the stable I shall be done."

"Yes, but how will you be able to do that?" she asked again. "If you clean it out as other people do, ten pitchforksful will come in for every one you throw out. But I will teach you how to do it; you must turn your pitchfork upside down, and work with the handle, and then all will fly out of its own accord."

"Yes, I will attend to that," said the Prince, and stayed sitting where he was the whole day, for it was soon settled between them that they would marry each other, he and the King's daughter; so the first day of his service with the giant did not seem long to him. But when evening was drawing near she said that it would now be better for him to clean out the stable before the giant came home. When he got there he had a fancy to try if what she had said were true, so he began to work in the same way that he had seen the stable-boys doing in his father's stables, but he soon saw that he must give up that, for when he had worked a very short time he had scarcely any room left to stand. So he did what the Princess had taught him, turned the pitchfork round, and worked with the handle, and in the twinkling of an eye the stable was as clean as if it had been scoured. When he had done that, he went back again into the room in which the giant had given him leave to stay, and there he walked backward and forward on the floor, and began to hum and sing.

Then came the giant home with the goats. "Have you cleaned the stable?" asked the giant.

"Yes, now it is clean and sweet, master," said the King's son.

"I shall see about that," said the giant, and went round to the stable, but it was just as the Prince had said.

"You have certainly been talking to my Master-maid, for you never got that out of your own head," said the giant.

"Master-maid! What kind of a thing is that, master?" said the Prince, making himself look as stupid as an ass; "I should like to see that."

"Well, you will see her quite soon enough," said the giant.

On the second morning the giant had again to go out with his goats, so he told the Prince that on that day he was to fetch home his horse, which was out on the mountain-side, and when he had done that he might rest himself for the remainder of the day, "for you have come to a kind master, and that you shall find," said the giant once more. "But do not go into any of the rooms that I spoke of yesterday, or I will wring your head off," said he, and then went away with his flock of goats.

"Yes, indeed, you are a kind master," said the Prince; "but I will go in and talk to the Master-maid again; perhaps before long she may like better to be mine than yours."

So he went to her. Then she asked him what he had to do that day.

"Oh! not very dangerous work, I fancy," said the King's son. "I have only to go up the mountain-side after his horse."

"Well, how do you mean to set about it?" asked the Master-maid.

"Oh! there is no great art in riding a horse home," said the King's son. "I think I must have ridden friskier horses before now."

"Yes, but it is not so easy a thing as you think to ride the horse home," said the Master-maid; "but I will teach you what to do. When you go near it, fire will burst out of its nostrils like flames from a pine torch; but be very careful, and take the bridle which is hanging by the door there, and fling the bit straight into his jaws, and then it will become so tame that you will be able to do what you like with it." He said he would bear this in mind, and then he again sat in there the whole day by the Master-maid, and they chatted and talked of one thing and another, but the first thing and the last now was, how happy and delightful it would be if they could but marry each other, and get safely away from the giant; and the Prince would have forgotten both the mountain-side and the horse if the Master-maid had not reminded him of them as evening drew near, and said that now it would be better if he went to fetch the horse before the giant came. So he did this, and took the bridle which was hanging on a crook, and strode up the mountain-side, and it was not long before he met with the horse, and fire and red flames streamed forth out of its nostrils. But the youth carefully watched his opportunity, and just as it was rushing at him with open jaws he threw the bit straight into its mouth, and the horse stood as quiet as a young lamb, and there was no difficulty at all in getting it home to the stable. Then the Prince went back into his room again, and began to hum and to sing.

Toward evening the giant came home. "Have you fetched the horse back from the mountain-side?" he asked.

"That I have, master; it was an amusing horse to ride, but I rode him straight home, and put him in the stable too," said the Prince.

"I will see about that," said the giant, and went out to the stable, but the horse was standing there just as the Prince had said. "You have certainly been talking with my Master-maid, for you never got that out of your own head," said the giant again.

"Yesterday, master, you talked about this Master-maid, and today you are talking about her; ah, heaven bless you, master, why will you not show me the thing? for it would be a real pleasure to me to see it," said the Prince, who again pretended to be silly and stupid.

"Oh! you will see her quite soon enough," said the giant.

On the morning of the third day the giant again had to go into the wood with the goats. "Today you must go underground and fetch my taxes," he said to the Prince. "When you have done this, you may rest for the remainder of the day, for you shall see what an easy master you have come to," and then he went away.

"Well, however easy a master you may be, you set me very hard work to do," thought the Prince; "but I will see if I cannot find your Master-maid; you say she is yours, but for all that she may be able to tell me what to do now," and he went back to her. So, when the Master-maid asked him what the giant had set him to do that day, he told her that he was to go underground and get the taxes.

"And how will you set about that?" said the Master-maid.

"Oh! you must tell me how to do it," said the Prince, "for I have never yet been underground, and even if I knew the way I do not know how much I am to demand."

"Oh! yes, I will soon tell you that; you must go to the rock there under the mountain-ridge, and take the club that is there, and knock on the rocky wall," said the Master-maid. "Then someone will come out who will sparkle with fire; you shall tell him your errand, and when he asks you how much you want to have you are to say: 'As much as I can carry.'"

"Yes, I will keep that in mind," said he, and then he sat there with the Master-maid the whole day, until night drew near, and he would gladly have stayed there till now if the Master-maid had not reminded him that it was time to be off to fetch the taxes before the giant came.

So he set out on his way, and did exactly what the Master-maid had told him. He went to the rocky wall, and took the club, and knocked on it. Then came one so full of sparks that they flew both out of his eyes and his nose. "What do you want?" said he.

"I was to come here for the giant, and demand the tax for him," said the King's son.

"How much are you to have then?" said the other.

"I ask for no more than I am able to carry with me," said the Prince.

"It is well for you that you have not asked for a horse-load," said he who had come out of the rock. "But now come in with me."

This the Prince did, and what a quantity of gold and silver he saw! It was lying inside the mountain like heaps of stones in a waste place, and he got a load that was as large as he was able to carry, and with that he went his way. So in the evening, when the giant came home with the goats, the Prince went into the chamber and hummed and sang again as he had done on the other two evenings.

"Have you been for the tax?" said the giant.

"Yes, that I have, master," said the Prince.

"Where have you put it then?" said the giant again.

"The bag of gold is standing there on the bench," said the Prince.

"I will see about that," said the giant, and went away to the bench, but the bag was standing there, and it was so full that gold and silver dropped out when the giant untied the string.

"You have certainly been talking with my Master-maid!" said the giant, "and if you have I will wring your neck."

"Master-maid?" said the Prince; "yesterday my master talked about this Master-maid, and today he is talking about her again, and the first day of all it was talk of the same kind. I do wish I could see the thing myself," said he.

"Yes, yes, wait till tomorrow," said the giant, "and then I myself will take you to her."

"Ah! master, I thank you – but you are only mocking me," said the King's son.

Next day the giant took him to the Master-maid. "Now you shall kill him, and boil him in the great big cauldron you know of, and when you have got the broth ready give me a call," said the giant; then he lay down on the bench to sleep, and almost immediately began to snore so that it sounded like thunder among the hills.

So the Master-maid took a knife, and cut the Prince's little finger, and dropped three drops of blood upon a wooden stool; then she took all the old rags, and shoe-soles, and all the rubbish she could lay hands on, and put them in the cauldron; and then she filled a chest with gold dust, and a lump of salt, and a water-flask which was hanging by the door, and she also took with her a golden apple, and two gold chickens; and then she and the Prince went away with all the speed they could, and when they had gone a little way they came to the sea, and then they sailed, but where they got the ship from I have never been able to learn.

Now, when the giant had slept a good long time, he began to stretch himself on the bench on which he was lying. "Will it soon boil?" said he.

"It is just beginning," said the first drop of blood on the stool.

So the giant lay down to sleep again, and slept for a long, long time. Then he began to move about a little again. "Will it soon be ready now?" said he, but he did not look up this time any more than he had done the first time, for he was still half asleep.

"Half done!" said the second drop of blood, and the giant believed it was the Master-maid again, and turned himself on the bench, and lay down to sleep once more. When he had slept again for many hours, he began to move and stretch himself. "Is it not done yet?" said he.

"It is quite ready," said the third drop of blood. Then the giant began to sit up and rub his eyes, but he could not see who it was who had spoken to him, so he asked for the Master-maid, and called her. But there was no one to give him an answer.

"Ah! well, she has just stolen out for a little," thought the giant, and he took a spoon, and went off to the cauldron to have a taste; but there was nothing in it but shoe-soles, and rags, and such trumpery as that, and all was boiled up together, so that he could not tell whether it was porridge or milk pottage. When he saw this, he understood what had happened, and fell into such a rage that he hardly knew what he was doing. Away he went after the Prince and the Master-maid so fast that the wind whistled behind him, and it was not long before he came to the water, but he could not get over it. "Well, well, I will soon find a cure for that; I have only to call my river-sucker," said the giant, and he did call him. So his river-sucker came and lay down, and drank one, two, three draughts, and with that the water in the sea fell so low that the giant saw the

Master-maid and the Prince out on the sea in their ship. "Now you must throw out the lump of salt," said the Master-maid, and the Prince did so, and it grew up into such a great high mountain right across the sea that the giant could not come over it, and the river-sucker could not drink any more water. "Well, well, I will soon find a cure for that," said the giant, so he called to his hill-borer to come and bore through the mountain so that the river-sucker might be able to drink up the water again. But just as the hole was made, and the river-sucker was beginning to drink, the Master-maid told the Prince to throw one or two drops out of the flask, and when he did this the sea instantly became full of water again, and before the river-sucker could take one drink they reached the land and were in safety. So they determined to go home to the Prince's father, but the Prince would on no account permit the Master-maid to walk there, for he thought that it was unbecoming either for her or for him to go on foot.

"Wait here the least little bit of time, while I go home for the seven horses which stand in my father's stable," said he; "it is not far off, and I shall not be long away, but I will not let my betrothed bride go on foot to the palace."

"Oh! no, do not go, for if you go home to the King's palace you will forget me, I foresee that."

"How could I forget you? We have suffered so much evil together, and love each other so much," said the Prince; and he insisted on going home for the coach with the seven horses, and she was to wait for him there, by the sea-shore. So at last the Master-maid had to yield, for he was so absolutely determined to do it. "But when you get there you must not even give yourself time to greet anyone, but go straight into the stable, and take the horses, and put them in the coach, and drive back as quickly as you can. For they will all come round about you; but you must behave just as if you did not see them, and on no account must you taste anything, for if you do it will cause great misery both to you and to me," said she; and this he promised.

But when he got home to the King's palace one of his brothers was just going to be married, and the bride and all her kith and kin had come to the palace; so they all thronged round him, and questioned him about this and that, and wanted him to go in with them; but he behaved as if he did not see them, and went straight to the stable, and got out the horses and began to harness them. When they saw that they could not by any means prevail on him to go in with them, they came out to him with meat and drink, and the best of everything that they had prepared for the wedding; but the Prince refused to touch anything, and would do nothing but put the horses in as quickly as he could. At last, however, the bride's sister rolled an apple across the yard to him, and said: "As you won't eat anything else, you may like to take a bite of that, for you must be both hungry and thirsty after your long journey." And he took up the apple and bit a piece out of it. But no sooner had he got the piece of apple in his mouth than he forgot the Master-maid and that he was to go back in the coach to fetch her.

"I think I must be mad! what do I want with this coach and horses?" said he; and then he put the horses back into the stable, and went into the King's palace, and there it was settled that he should marry the bride's sister, who had rolled the apple to him.

The Master-maid sat by the sea-shore for a long, long time, waiting for the Prince, but no Prince came. So she went away, and when she had walked a short distance she came to a little hut which stood all alone in a small wood, hard by the King's palace. She entered it and asked if she might be allowed to stay there. The hut belonged to an old crone, who was also an ill-tempered and malicious troll. At first she would not let the Master-maid remain with her; but at last, after a long time, by means of good words and good payment, she obtained leave. But the hut was as dirty and black inside as a pigsty, so the Master-maid said that she would smarten it up a little, that it might look a little more like what other people's houses looked inside. The old crone did not like this either. She scowled, and was very cross, but the Master-maid did not trouble herself about that. She took out her chest of gold, and flung a handful of it or so into the fire, and the gold boiled up and poured out over the whole of the hut, until every part of it both inside and out was gilded. But when the gold began to bubble up the old hag grew so terrified that she fled as if the Evil One himself were pursuing her, and she did not remember to stoop down as she went through the doorway, and so she split her head and died. Next morning the sheriff came traveling by there. He was greatly astonished when he saw the gold hut shining and glittering there in the copse, and he was still more astonished when he went in and caught sight of the beautiful young maiden who was sitting there; he fell in love with her at once, and straightway on the spot he begged her, both prettily and kindly, to marry him.

"Well, but have you a great deal of money?" said the Master-maid.

"Oh! yes; so far as that is concerned, I am not ill off," said the sheriff. So now he had to go home to get the money, and in the evening he came back, bringing with him a bag with two bushels in it, which he set down on the bench. Well, as he had such a fine lot of money, the Master-maid said she would have him, so they sat down to talk.

But scarcely had they sat down together before the Master-maid wanted to jump up again. "I have forgotten to see to the fire," she said.

"Why should you jump up to do that?" said the sheriff; "I will do that!" So he jumped up, and went to the chimney in one bound.

"Just tell me when you have got hold of the shovel," said the Master-maid.

"Well, I have hold of it now," said the sheriff.

"Then you may hold the shovel, and the shovel you, and pour red-hot coals over you, till day dawns," said the Master-maid. So the sheriff had to stand there the whole night and pour red-hot coals over himself, and, no matter how much he cried and begged and entreated, the red-hot coals did not grow the colder for that. When the day began to dawn, and he had power to throw down the shovel, he did not stay long where he was, but ran away as fast as he possibly could; and everyone who met him stared and looked after him, for he was flying as if he were mad, and he could not have looked worse if he had been both flayed and tanned, and everyone wondered where he had been, but for very shame he would tell nothing.

The next day the attorney came riding by the place where the Master-maid dwelt. He saw how brightly the hut shone and gleamed through the wood, and he too went into it to see who lived there, and when he entered and saw the beautiful young maiden he fell even more in love with her than the sheriff had done, and began to woo her at once. So the Master-maid asked him, as she had asked the sheriff, if he had a great deal of money, and the attorney said he was not ill off for that, and would at once go home to get it; and at night he came with a great big sack of money – this time it was a four-bushel sack – and set it on the bench by the Master-maid. So she promised to have him, and he sat down on the bench by her to arrange about it, but suddenly she said that she had forgotten to lock the door of the porch that night, and must do it.

"Why should you do that?" said the attorney; "sit still, I will do it."

So he was on his feet in a moment, and out in the porch.

"Tell me when you have got hold of the door-latch," said the Master-maid.

"I have hold of it now," cried the attorney.

"Then you may hold the door, and the door you, and may you go between wall and wall till day dawns."

What a dance the attorney had that night! He had never had such a waltz before, and he never wished to have such a dance again. Sometimes he was in front of the door, and sometimes the door was in front of him, and it went from one side of the porch to the other, till the attorney was well-nigh beaten to death. At first he began to abuse the Master-maid, and then to beg and pray, but the door did not care for anything but keeping him where he was till break of day.

As soon as the door let go its hold of him, off went the attorney. He forgot who ought to be paid off for what he had suffered, he forgot both his sack of money and his wooing, for he was so afraid lest the house-door should come dancing after him. Everyone who met him stared and looked after him, for he was flying like a madman, and he could not have looked worse if a herd of rams had been butting at him all night long.

On the third day the bailiff came by, and he too saw the gold house in the little wood, and he too felt that he must go and see who lived there; and when he caught sight of the Master-maid he became so much in love with her that he wooed her almost before he greeted her.

The Master-maid answered him as she had answered the other two, that if he had a great deal of money, she would have him. "So far as that is concerned, I am not ill off," said the bailiff; so he was at once told to go home and fetch it, and this he did. At night he came back, and he had a still larger sack of money with him than the attorney had brought; it must have been at least six bushels, and he set it down on the bench. So it was settled that he was to have the Master-maid. But hardly had they sat down together before she said that she had forgotten to bring in the calf, and must go out to put it in the byre.

"No, indeed, you shall not do that," said the bailiff; "I am the one to do that." And, big and fat as he was, he went out as briskly as a boy.

"Tell me when you have got hold of the calf's tail," said the Master-maid.

"I have hold of it now," cried the bailiff.

"Then may you hold the calf's tail, and the calf's tail hold you, and may you go round the world together till day dawns!" said the Master-maid. So the bailiff had to bestir himself, for the calf went over rough and smooth, over hill and dale, and, the more the bailiff cried and screamed, the faster the calf went. When daylight began to appear, the bailiff was half dead; and so glad was he to leave loose of the calf's tail, that he forgot the sack of money and all else. He walked now slowly – more slowly than the sheriff and the attorney had done, but, the slower he went, the more time had everyone to stare and look at him; and they used it too, and no one can imagine how tired out and ragged he looked after his dance with the calf.

On the following day the wedding was to take place in the King's palace, and the elder brother was to drive to church with his bride, and the brother who had been with the giant with her sister. But when they had seated themselves in the coach and were about to drive off from the palace one of the trace-pins broke, and, though they made one, two, and three to put in its place, that did not help them, for each broke in turn, no matter what kind of wood they used to make them of. This went on for a long time, and they could not get away from the palace, so they were all in great trouble. Then the sheriff said (for he too had been bidden to the wedding at Court): "Yonder away in the thicket dwells a maiden, and if you can get her to lend you the handle of the shovel that she uses to make up her fire I know very well that it will hold fast." So they sent off a messenger to the thicket, and begged so prettily that they might have the loan of her shovel-handle of which the sheriff had spoken that they were not refused; so now they had a trace-pin which would not snap in two.

But all at once, just as they were starting, the bottom of the coach fell in pieces. They made a new bottom as fast as they could, but, no matter how they nailed it together, or what kind of wood they used, no sooner had they got the new bottom into the coach and were about to drive off than it broke again, so that they were still worse off than when they had broken the trace-pin. Then the attorney said, for he too was at the wedding in the palace: "Away there in the thicket dwells a maiden, and if you could but get her to lend you one-half of her porch-door I am certain that it will hold together." So they again sent a messenger to the thicket, and begged so prettily for the loan of the gilded porch-door of which the attorney had told them that they got it at once. They were just setting out again, but now the horses were not able to draw the coach. They had six horses already, and now they put in eight, and then ten, and then twelve, but the more they put in, and the more the coachman whipped them, the less good it did; and the coach never stirred from the spot. It was already beginning to be late in the day, and to church they must and would go, so everyone who was in the palace was in a state of distress. Then the bailiff spoke up and said: "Out there in the gilded cottage in the thicket dwells a girl, and if you could but get her to lend you her calf I know it could draw the coach, even if it were as heavy as a mountain." They all thought that it was ridiculous to be drawn to church by a calf, but there was nothing else for it but to send a messenger once more, and beg as prettily as they could, on behalf of the King, that she would let them have the loan of the calf that the bailiff had told them about. The Master-maid let them have it immediately – this time also she would not say "no."

Then they harnessed the calf to see if the coach would move; and away it went, over rough and smooth, over stock and stone, so that they could scarcely breathe, and sometimes they were on the ground, and sometimes up in the air; and when they came to the church the coach began to go round and round like a spinning-wheel, and it was with the utmost difficulty and danger that they were able to get out of the coach and into the church. And when they went back again the coach went quicker still, so that most of them did not know how they got back to the palace at all.

When they had seated themselves at the table the Prince who had been in service with the giant said that he thought they ought to have invited the maiden who had lent them the shovel-handle, and the porch-door, and the calf up to the palace, "for," said he, "if we had not got these three things, we should never have got away from the palace."

The King also thought that this was both just and proper, so he sent five of his best men down to the gilded hut, to greet the maiden courteously from the King, and to beg her to be so good as to come up to the palace to dinner at mid-day.

"Greet the King, and tell him that, if he is too good to come to me, I am too good to come to him," replied the Master-maid.

So the King had to go himself, and the Master-maid went with him immediately, and, as the King believed that she was more than she appeared to be, he seated her in the place of honor by the youngest bridegroom. When they had sat at the table for a short time, the Master-maid took out the cock, and the hen, and the golden apple which she had brought away with her from the giant's house, and set them on the table in front of her, and instantly the cock and the hen began to fight with each other for the golden apple.

"Oh! look how those two there are fighting for the golden apple," said the King's son.

"Yes, and so did we two fight to get out that time when we were in the mountain," said the Master-maid.

So the Prince knew her again, and you may imagine how delighted he was. He ordered the troll-witch who had rolled the apple to him to be torn in pieces between four-and-twenty horses, so that not a bit of her was left, and then for the first time they began really to keep the wedding, and, weary as they were, the sheriff, the attorney, and the bailiff kept it up too.

TALES OF BEASTS & ANIMALS

In 'Dapplegrim', a dapple-grey foal asks a young man to sacrifice twelve other foals for three years in a row so that their mares can nurse him. In the process, he grows into a giant, gleaming steed like no other, and guides the young man as they undertake several perilous trials to free a princess from a troll and win her hand in marriage.

This story is one of many tales collected by Peter Christen Asbjørnsen and Jørgen Engebretsen Moe, and reminiscent of many tales found throughout the Eddas and Sagas, in which the hero shares a deep, even sacred, bond with his trusted steed.

The reality is that birds and animals speak to us in so many different ways, even if we don't literally understand the words they say. Living amongst thick forests at home; pursued by the plaintive seagull's cry as they made their way along the 'whale's road', the early Vikings had learned this lesson very well. Wildlife figures prominently in the mythological legacy they left behind: Nature speaks very clearly in these stories.

DAPPLEGRIM

There was once upon a time a couple of rich folks who had twelve sons, and when the youngest was grown up he would not stay at home any longer, but would go out into the world and seek his fortune. His father and mother said that they thought he was very well off at home, and that he was welcome to stay with them; but he could not rest, and said that he must and would go, so at last they had to give him leave. When he had walked a long way, he came to a King's palace. There he asked for a place and got it.

Now the daughter of the King of that country had been carried off into the mountains by a Troll, and the King had no other children, and for this cause both he and all his people were full of sorrow and affliction, and the King had promised the Princess and half his kingdom to anyone who could set her free; but there was no one who could do it, though a great number had tried. So when the youth had been there for the space of a year or so, he wanted to go home again to pay his parents a visit; but when he got there his father and mother were dead, and his brothers had divided everything that their parents possessed between themselves, so that there was nothing at all left for him.

"Shall I, then, receive nothing at all of my inheritance?" asked the youth.

"Who could know that you were still alive – you who have been a wanderer so long?" answered the brothers. "However, there are twelve mares upon the hills which we have not yet divided among us, and if you would like to have them for your share, you may take them."

So the youth, well pleased with this, thanked them, and at once set off to the hill where the twelve mares were at pasture. When he got up there and found them, each mare had her foal, and by the side of one of them was a big dapple-grey foal as well, which was so sleek that it shone again.

"Well, my little foal, you are a fine fellow!" said the youth.

"Yes, but if you will kill all the other little foals so that I can suck all the mares for a year, you shall see how big and handsome I shall be then!" said the Foal.

So the youth did this – he killed all the twelve foals, and then went back again.

Next year, when he came home again to look after his mares and the foal, it was as fat as it could be, and its coat shone with brightness, and it was so big that the lad had the greatest difficulty in getting on its back, and each of the mares had another foal.

"Well, it's very evident that I have lost nothing by letting you suck all my mares," said the lad to the yearling; "but now you are quite big enough, and must come away with me."

"No," said the Colt, "I must stay here another year; kill the twelve little foals, and then I can suck all the mares this year also, and you shall see how big and handsome I shall be by summer."

So the youth did it again, and when he went up on the hill next year to look after his colt and the mares, each of the mares had her foal again; but the dappled colt was so big that when the lad wanted to feel its neck to see how fat it was, he could not reach up to it, it was so high? and it was so bright that the light glanced off its coat.

"Big and handsome you were last year, my colt, but this year you are ever so much handsomer," said the youth; "in all the King's court no such horse is to be found. But now you shall come away with me."

"No," said the dappled Colt once more; "here I must stay for another year. Just kill the twelve little foals again, so that I can suck the mares this year also, and then come and look at me in the summer."

So the youth did it – he killed all the little foals, and then went home again.

But next year, when he returned to look after the dappled colt and the mares, he was quite appalled. He had never imagined that any horse could become so big and overgrown, for the dappled horse had to lie down on all fours before the youth could get on his back, and it was very hard to do that even when it was lying down, and it was so plump that its coat shone and glistened just as if it had been a looking-glass. This time the dappled horse was not unwilling to go away with the youth, so he mounted it, and when he came riding home to his brothers they all smote their hands together and crossed themselves, for never in their lives had they either seen or heard tell of such a horse as that.

"If you will procure me the best shoes for my horse, and the most magnificent saddle and bridle that can be found," said the youth, "you may have all my twelve mares just as they are standing out on the hill, and their twelve foals into the bargain." For this year also each mare had her foal. The brothers were quite willing to do this; so the lad got such shoes for his horse that the sticks and stones flew high up into the air as he rode away over the hills, and such a gold saddle and such a gold bridle that they could be seen glittering and glancing from afar.

"And now we will go to the King's palace," said Dapplegrim – that was the horse's name, "but bear in mind that you must ask the King for a good stable and excellent fodder for me."

So the lad promised not to forget to do that. He rode to the palace, and it will be easily understood that with such a horse as he had he was not long on the way.

When he arrived there, the King was standing out on the steps, and how he did stare at the man who came riding up!

"Nay," said he, "never in my whole life have I seen such a man and such a horse."

And when the youth inquired if he could have a place in the King's palace, the King was so delighted that he could have danced on the steps where he was standing, and there and then the lad was told that he should have a place.

"Yes; but I must have a good stable and most excellent fodder for my horse," said he.

So they told him that he should have sweet hay and oats, and as much of them as the dappled horse chose to have, and all the other riders had to take their horses out of the stable that Dapplegrim might stand alone and really have plenty of room.

But this did not last long, for the other people in the King's Court became envious of the lad, and there was no bad thing that they would not have done to him if they had but dared. At last they bethought themselves of telling the King that the youth had said that, if he chose, he was quite able to rescue the Princess who had been carried off into the mountain a long time ago by the Troll.

The King immediately summoned the lad into his presence, and said that he had been informed that he had said that it was in his power to rescue the Princess, so he was now to do it. If he succeeded in this, he no doubt knew that the King had promised his daughter and half the kingdom to anyone who set her free, which promise should be faithfully and honourably kept, but if he failed he should be put to death. The youth denied that he had said this, but all to no purpose, for the King was deaf to all his words; so there was nothing to be done but say that he would make the attempt.

He went down into the stable, and very sad and full of care he was. Then Dapplegrim inquired why he was so troubled, and the youth told him, and said that he did not know what to do, "for as to setting the Princess free, that was downright impossible."

"Oh, but it might be done," said Dapplegrim. "I will help you; but you must first have me well shod. You must ask for ten pounds of iron and twelve pounds of steel for the shoeing, and one smith to hammer and one to hold."

So the youth did this, and no one said him nay. He got both the iron and the steel, and the smiths, and thus was Dapplegrim shod strongly and well, and when the youth went out of the King's palace a cloud of dust rose up behind him. But when he came to the mountain into which the Princess had been carried, the difficulty was to ascend the precipitous wall of rock by which he was to get on to the mountain beyond, for the rock stood right up on end, as steep as a house side and as smooth as a sheet of glass. The first time the youth rode at it he got a little way up the precipice, but then both Dapplegrim's fore legs slipped, and down came horse and rider with a sound like thunder among the mountains. The next time that he rode at it he got a little farther up, but then one of Dapplegrim's fore legs slipped, and down they went with the sound of a landslip. But the third time Dapplegrim said: "Now we must show what we can do," and went at it once more till the stones sprang up sky high, and thus they got up. Then the lad rode into the mountain cleft at full gallop and caught up the Princess on his saddle-bow, and then out again before the Troll even had time to stand up, and thus the Princess was set free.

When the youth returned to the palace the King was both happy and delighted to get his daughter back again, as may easily be believed, but somehow or other the people about the Court had so worked on him that he was angry with the lad too. "Thou shalt have my thanks for setting my Princess free," he said, when the youth came into the palace with her, and was then about to go away.

"She ought to be just as much my Princess as she is yours now, for you are a man of your word," said the youth.

"Yes, yes," said the King. "Have her thou shalt, as I have said it; but first of all thou must make the sun shine into my palace here."

For there was a large and high hill outside the windows which overshadowed the palace so much that the sun could not shine in.

"That was no part of our bargain," answered the youth. "But as nothing that I can say will move you, I suppose I shall have to try to do my best, for the Princess I will have."

So he went down to Dapplegrim again and told him what the King desired, and Dapplegrim thought that it might easily be done; but first of all he must have new shoes, and ten pounds of iron and twelve pounds of steel must go to the making of them, and two smiths were also necessary, one to hammer and one to hold, and then it would be very easy to make the sun shine into the King's palace.

The lad asked for these things and obtained them instantly, for the King thought that for very shame he could not refuse to give them, and so Dapplegrim got new shoes, and they were good ones. The youth seated himself on him, and once more they went their way, and for each hop that Dapplegrim made, down went the hill fifteen ells into the earth, and so they went on until there was no hill left for the King to see.

When the youth came down again to the King's palace he asked the King if the Princess should not at last be his, for now no one could say that the sun was not shining into the palace. But the other people in the palace had again stirred up the King, and he answered that the youth should have her, and that he had never intended that he should not; but first of all he must get her quite as good a horse to ride to the wedding on as that which he had himself. The youth said that the King had never told him he was to do that, and it seemed to him that he had now really earned the Princess; but the King stuck to what he had said, and if the youth were unable to do it he was to lose his life, the King said. The youth went down to the stable again, and very sad and sorrowful he was, as anyone may well imagine. Then he told Dapplegrim that the King had now required that he should get the Princess as good a bridal horse as that which the bridegroom had, or he should lose his life. "But that will be no easy thing to do," said he, "for your equal is not to be found in all the world."

"Oh yes, there is one to match me," said Dapplegrim. "But it will not be easy to get him, for he is underground. However, we will try. Now you must go up to the King and ask for new shoes for me, and for them we must again have ten pounds of iron, twelve pounds of steel, and two smiths, one to hammer and one to hold, but be very particular to see that the hooks are very sharp. And you must also ask for twelve barrels of rye, and twelve slaughtered oxen must we have with us, and all the twelve ox-hides with twelve hundred spikes set in each of them; all these things must we have, likewise a barrel of tar with twelve tons of tar in it. The youth went to the King and asked for all the things that Dapplegrim had named, and once more, as the King thought that it would be disgraceful to refuse them to him, he obtained them all.

So he mounted Dapplegrim and rode away from the Court, and when he had ridden for a long, long time over hills and moors, Dapplegrim asked: "Do you hear anything?"

"Yes; there is such a dreadful whistling up above in the air that I think I am growing alarmed," said the youth.

"That is all the wild birds in the forest flying about; they are sent to stop us," said Dapplegrim. "But just cut a hole in the corn sacks, and then they will be so busy with the corn that they will forget us."

The youth did it. He cut holes in the corn sacks so that barley and rye ran out on every side, and all the wild birds that were in the forest came in such numbers that they darkened the sun. But when they caught sight of the corn they could not refrain from it, but flew down and began to scratch and pick at the corn and rye, and at last they began to fight among themselves, and forgot all about the youth and Dapplegrim, and did them no harm.

And now the youth rode onwards for a long, long time, over hill and dale, over rocky places and morasses, and then Dapplegrim began to listen again, and asked the youth if he heard anything now.

"Yes; now I hear such a dreadful crackling and crashing in the forest on every side that I think I shall be really afraid," said the youth.

"That is all the wild beasts in the forest," said Dapplegrim; "they are sent out to stop us. But just throw out the twelve carcasses of the oxen, and they will be so much occupied with them that they will quite forget us." So the youth threw out the carcasses of the oxen, and then all the wild beasts in the forest, both bears and wolves, and lions, and grim beasts of all kinds, came. But when they caught sight of the carcasses of the oxen they began to fight for them till the blood flowed, and they entirely forgot Dapplegrim and the youth.

So the youth rode onwards again, and many and many were the new scenes they saw, for travelling on Dapplegrim's back was not travelling slowly, as may be imagined, and then Dapplegrim neighed.

"Do you hear anything?" he said.

"Yes; I heard something like a foal neighing quite plainly a long, long way off," answered the youth.

"That's a full-grown colt," said Dapplegrim, "if you hear it so plainly when it is so far away from us."

So they travelled onwards a long time, and saw one new scene after another once more. Then Dapplegrim neighed again.

"Do you hear anything now?" said he.

"Yes; now I heard it quite distinctly, and it neighed like a full-grown horse," answered the youth.

"Yes, and you will hear it again very soon," said Dapplegrim; "and then you will hear what a voice it has." So they travelled on through many more different kinds of country, and then Dapplegrim neighed for the third time; but before he could ask the youth if he heard anything, there was such a neighing on the other side of the heath that the youth thought that hills and rocks would be rent in pieces.

"Now he is here!" said Dapplegrim. "Be quick, and fling over me the ox-hides that have the spikes in them, throw the twelve tons of tar over the field, and climb up into that great spruce fir tree. When he comes, fire will spurt out of both his nostrils, and then the tar will catch fire. Now mark what I say – if the flame ascends I conquer, and if it sinks I fail; but if you see that I am winning, fling the bridle, which you must take off me, over his head, and then he will become quite gentle."

Just as the youth had flung all the hides with the spikes over Dapplegrim, and the tar over the field, and had got safely up into the spruce fir, a horse came with flame spouting from his nostrils, and the tar caught fire in a moment; and Dapplegrim and the horse began to fight until the stones leapt up to the sky. They bit, and they fought with their fore legs and their hind legs, and sometimes the youth looked at them. And sometimes he looked at the tar, but at last the flames began to rise, for wheresoever the strange horse bit or wheresoever he kicked he hit upon the spikes in the hides, and at length he had to yield. When the youth saw that, he was not long in getting down from the tree and flinging the bridle over the horse's head, and then he became so tame that he might have been led by a thin string.

This horse was dappled too, and so like Dapplegrim that no one could distinguish the one from the other. The youth seated himself on the dappled horse which he had captured, and rode home again to the King's palace, and Dapplegrim ran loose by his side. When he got there, the King was standing outside in the courtyard.

"Can you tell me which is the horse I have caught, and which is the one I had before?" said the youth. "If you can"t, I think your daughter is mine."

The King went and looked at both the dappled horses; he looked high and he looked low, he looked before and he looked behind, but there was not a hair's difference between the two.

"No," said the King; "that I cannot tell thee, and as thou hast procured such a splendid bridal horse for my daughter thou shalt have her; but first we must have one more trial, just to see if thou art fated to have her. She shall hide herself twice, and then thou shalt hide thyself twice. If thou canst find her each time that she hides herself, and if she cannot find thee in thy hiding-places, then it is fated, and thou shalt have the Princess."

"That, too, was not in our bargain," said the youth. "But we will make this trial since it must be so."

So the King's daughter was to hide herself first.

Then she changed herself into a duck, and lay swimming in a lake that was just outside the palace. But the youth went down into the stable and asked Dapplegrim what she had done with herself.

"Oh, all that you have to do is to take your gun, and go down to the water and aim at the duck which is swimming about there, and she will soon discover herself," said Dapplegrim.

The youth snatched up his gun and ran to the lake. "I will just have a shot at that duck," said he, and began to aim at it.

"Oh, no, dear friend, don't shoot! It is I," said the Princess. So he had found her once.

The second time the Princess changed herself into a loaf, and laid herself on the table among four other loaves; and she was so like the other loaves that no one could see any difference between them.

But the youth again went down to the stable to Dapplegrim, and told him that the Princess had hidden herself again, and that he had not the least idea what had become of her.

"Oh, just take a very large bread-knife, sharpen it, and pretend that you are going to cut straight through the third of the four loaves which are lying on the kitchen table in the King's palace – count them from right to left – and you will soon find her," said Dapplegrim.

So the youth went up to the kitchen, and began to sharpen the largest bread-knife that he could find; then he caught hold of the third loaf on the left-hand side, and put the knife to it as if he meant to cut it straight in two. "I will have a bit of this bread for myself," said he.

"No, dear friend, don't cut, it is I!" said the Princess again; so he had found her the second time.

And now it was his turn to go and hide himself; but Dapplegrim had given him such good instructions that it was not easy to find him. First he turned himself into a horse-fly, and hid himself in Dapplegrim's left nostril. The Princess went poking about and searching everywhere, high and low, and wanted to go into Dapplegrim's stall too, but he began to bite and kick about so that she was afraid to go there, and could not find the youth. "Well," said she, "as I am unable to find you, you must show yourself; "whereupon the youth immediately appeared standing there on the stable floor.

Dapplegrim told him what he was to do the second time, and he turned himself into a lump of earth, and stuck himself between the hoof and the shoe on Dapplegrim's left fore foot. Once more the King's daughter went and sought everywhere, inside and outside, until at last she came into the stable, and wanted to go into the stall beside Dapplegrim. So this time he allowed her to go into it, and she peered about high and low, but she could not look under his hoofs, for he stood much too firmly on his legs for that, and she could not find the youth.

"Well, you will just have to show where you are yourself, for I can't find you," said the Princess, and in an instant the youth was standing by her side on the floor of the stable.

"Now you are mine!" said he to the Princess.

"Now you can see that it is fated that she should be mine," he said to the King.

"Yes, fated it is," said the King. "So what must be, must."

Then everything was made ready for the wedding with great splendour and promptitude, and the youth rode to church on Dapplegrim, and the King's daughter on the other horse. So everyone must see that they could not be long on their way thither.

PRINCE LINDWORM

Once upon a time, there was a fine young King who was married to the loveliest of Queens. They were exceedingly happy, all but for one thing – they had no children. And this often made them both sad, because the Queen wanted a dear little child to play with, and the King wanted an heir to the kingdom.

One day the Queen went out for a walk by herself, and she met an ugly old woman. The old woman was just like a witch: but she was a nice kind of witch, not the cantankerous sort. She said, "Why do you look so doleful, pretty lady?" "It's no use my telling you," answered the Queen, "nobody in the world can help me." "Oh, you never know," said the old woman. "Just you let me hear what your trouble is, and maybe I can put things right."

"My dear woman, how can you?" said the Queen: and she told her, "The King and I have no children: that's why I am so distressed." "Well, you needn't be," said the old witch. "I can set that right in a twinkling, if only you will do exactly as I tell you. Listen. Tonight, at sunset, take a little drinking-cup with two ears" (that is, handles), "and put it bottom upwards on the ground in the northwest corner of your garden. Then go and lift it up tomorrow morning at sunrise, and you will find two roses underneath it, one red and one white. If you eat the red rose, a little boy will be born to you: if you eat the white rose, a little girl will be sent. But, whatever you do, you mustn't eat *both* the roses, or you'll be sorry, – that I warn you! Only one: remember that!" "Thank you a thousand times," said the Queen, "this is good news indeed!" And she wanted to give the old woman her gold ring; but the old woman wouldn't take it.

So the Queen went home and did as she had been told: and next morning at sunrise she stole out into the garden and lifted up the little drinking-cup. She was surprised, for indeed she had hardly expected to see anything. But there were the two roses underneath it, one red and one white. And now she was dreadfully puzzled, for she did not know which to choose. "If I choose the red one," she thought, "and I have a little boy, he may grow up and go to the wars and get killed. But if I choose the white one, and have a little girl, she will stay at home awhile with us, but later on she will get married and go away and leave us. So, whichever it is, we may be left with no child after all."

However, at last she decided on the white rose, and she ate it. And it tasted so sweet, that she took and ate the red one too: without ever remembering the old woman's solemn warning.

Some time after this, the King went away to the wars: and while he was still away, the Queen became the mother of twins. One was a lovely baby boy, and the other was a Lindworm, or Serpent. She was terribly frightened when she saw the Lindworm, but he wriggled away out of the room, and nobody seemed to have seen him but herself: so that she thought it must have been a dream. The baby Prince was so beautiful and so healthy, the Queen was full of joy: and likewise, as you may suppose, was the King when he came home and found his son and heir. Not a word was said by anyone about the Lindworm: only the Queen thought about it now and then.

Many days and years passed by, and the baby grew up into a handsome young Prince, and it was time that he got married. The King sent him off to visit foreign kingdoms, in the Royal coach, with six white horses, to look for a Princess grand enough to be his wife. But at the very first crossroads, the way was stopped by an enormous Lindworm, enough to frighten the bravest. He lay in the middle of the road with a great wide open mouth, and cried, "A bride for me before a bride for you!" Then the Prince made the coach turn round and try another road: but it was all no use. For, at the first cross-ways, there lay the Lindworm again, crying out, "A bride for me before a bride for you!" So the Prince had to turn back home again to the Castle, and give up his visits to the foreign kingdoms. And his mother, the Queen, had to confess that what the Lindworm said was true. For he was really the eldest of her twins: and so he ought to have a wedding first.

There seemed nothing for it but to find a bride for the Lindworm, if his younger brother, the Prince, were to be married at all. So the King wrote to a distant country, and asked for a Princess to marry his son (but, of course, he didn't say which son), and presently a Princess arrived. But she wasn't allowed to see her bridegroom until he stood by her side in the great hall and was married to her, and then, of course, it was too late for her to say she wouldn't have him. But next morning the Princess had disappeared. The Lindworm lay sleeping all alone: and it was quite plain that he had eaten her.

A little while after, the Prince decided that he might now go journeying again in search of a Princess. And off he drove in the Royal chariot with the six white horses. But at the first cross-ways, there lay the Lindworm, crying with his great wide open mouth, "A bride for me before a bride for you!" So the carriage tried another road, and the same thing happened, and they had to turn back again this time, just as formerly. And the King wrote to several foreign countries, to know if anyone would marry his son. At last another Princess arrived, this time from a very far distant land. And, of course, she was not allowed to see her future husband before the wedding took place, – and then, lo and behold! it was the Lindworm who stood at her side. And next morning the

Princess had disappeared: and the Lindworm lay sleeping all alone; and it was quite clear that he had eaten her.

By and by the Prince started on his quest for the third time: and at the first crossroads there lay the Lindworm with his great wide open mouth, demanding a bride as before. And the Prince went straight back to the castle, and told the King: "You must find another bride for my elder brother."

"I don't know where I am to find her," said the King, "I have already made enemies of two great Kings who sent their daughters here as brides: and I have no notion how I can obtain a third lady. People are beginning to say strange things, and I am sure no Princess will dare to come."

Now, down in a little cottage near a wood, there lived the King's shepherd, an old man with his only daughter. And the King came one day and said to him, "Will you give me your daughter to marry my son the Lindworm? And I will make you rich for the rest of your life." – "No, sire," said the shepherd, "that I cannot do. She is my only child, and I want her to take care of me when I am old. Besides, if the Lindworm would not spare two beautiful Princesses, he won't spare her either. He will just gobble her up: and she is much too good for such a fate."

But the King wouldn't take "No" for an answer: and at last the old man had to give in.

Well, when the old shepherd told his daughter that she was to be Prince Lindworm's bride, she was utterly in despair. She went out into the woods, crying and wringing her hands and bewailing her hard fate. And while she wandered to and fro, an old witch-woman suddenly appeared out of a big hollow oak tree, and asked her, "Why do you look so doleful, pretty lass?" The shepherd-girl said, "It's no use my telling you, for nobody in the world can help me." – "Oh, you never know," said the old woman. "Just you let me hear what your trouble is, and maybe I can put things right." – "Ah, how can you?" said the girl, "For I am to be married to the King's eldest son, who is a Lindworm. He has already married two beautiful Princesses, and devoured them: and he will eat me too! No wonder I am distressed."

"Well, you needn't be," said the witch-woman. "All that can be set right in a twinkling: if only you will do exactly as I tell you." So the girl said she would.

"Listen, then," said the old woman. "After the marriage ceremony is over, and when it is time for you to retire to rest, you must ask to be dressed in ten snow-white shifts. And you must then ask for a tub full of lye," (that is, washing water prepared with wood-ashes) "and a tub full of fresh milk, and as many whips as a boy can carry in his arms, – and have all these brought into your bed-chamber. Then, when the Lindworm tells you to shed a shift, do you bid him slough a skin. And when all his skins are off, you must dip the whips in the lye and whip him; next, you must wash him in the fresh milk; and, lastly, you must take him and hold him in your arms, if it's only for one moment."

"The last is the worst notion – ugh!" said the shepherd's daughter, and she shuddered at the thought of holding the cold, slimy, scaly Lindworm.

"Do just as I have said, and all will go well," said the old woman. Then she disappeared again in the oak tree.

When the wedding-day arrived, the girl was fetched in the Royal chariot with the six white horses, and taken to the castle to be decked as a bride. And she asked for ten snow-white shifts to be brought her, and the tub of lye, and the tub of milk, and as many whips as a boy could carry in his arms. The ladies and courtiers in the castle thought, of course, that this was some bit of peasant superstition, all rubbish and nonsense. But the King said, "Let her have whatever she asks for." She was then arrayed in the most wonderful robes, and looked the loveliest of brides. She was led to the hall where the wedding ceremony was to take place, and she saw the Lindworm for the first time as he came in and stood by her side. So they were married, and a great wedding-feast was held, a banquet fit for the son of a king.

When the feast was over, the bridegroom and bride were conducted to their apartment, with music, and torches, and a great procession. As soon as the door was shut, the Lindworm turned to her and said, "Fair maiden, shed a shift!" The shepherd's daughter answered him, "Prince Lindworm, slough a skin!" – "No one has ever dared tell me to do that before!" said he. – "But I command you to do it now!" said she. Then he began to moan and wriggle: and in a few minutes a long snake-skin lay upon the floor beside him. The girl drew off her first shift, and spread it on top of the skin.

The Lindworm said again to her, "Fair maiden, shed a shift."

The shepherd's daughter answered him, "Prince Lindworm, slough a skin."

"No one has ever dared tell me to do that before," said he. – "But I command you to do it now," said she. Then with groans and moans he cast off the second skin: and she covered it with her second shift. The Lindworm said for the third time, "Fair maiden, shed a shift." The shepherd's daughter answered him again, "Prince Lindworm, slough a skin." – "No one has ever dared tell me to do that before," said he, and his little eyes rolled furiously. But the girl was not afraid, and once more she commanded him to do as she bade.

And so this went on until nine Lindworm skins were lying on the floor, each of them covered with a snow-white shift. And there was nothing left of the Lindworm but a huge thick mass, most horrible to see. Then the girl seized the whips, dipped them in the lye, and whipped him as hard as ever she could. Next, she bathed him all over in the fresh milk. Lastly, she dragged him on to the bed and put her arms round him. And she fell fast asleep that very moment.

Next morning very early, the King and the courtiers came and peeped in through the keyhole. They wanted to know what had become of the girl, but none of them dared enter the room. However, in the end, growing bolder, they opened the door a tiny bit. And there they saw the girl, all fresh and rosy, and beside her lay – no Lindworm, but the handsomest prince that any one could wish to see.

The King ran out and fetched the Queen: and after that, there were such rejoicings in the castle as never were known before or since. The wedding took place all over again, much finer than the first, with festivals and banquets and merrymakings for days and weeks. No bride was ever so beloved by a King and Queen as this peasant maid from the shepherd's cottage. There was no end to their love and their kindness towards her: because, by her sense and her calmness and her courage, she had saved their son, Prince Lindworm.

THE SEVEN FOALS

There was once upon a time a couple of poor folks who lived in a wretched hut, far away from everyone else, in a wood. They only just managed to live from hand to mouth, and had great difficulty in doing even so much as that, but they had three sons, and the youngest of them was called Cinderlad, for he did nothing else but lie and poke about among the ashes.

One day the eldest lad said that he would go out to earn his living; he soon got leave to do that, and set out on his way into the world. He walked on and on for the whole day, and when night was beginning to fall he came to a royal palace. The King was standing outside on the steps, and asked where he was going.

"Oh, I am going about seeking a place, my father," said the youth.

"Wilt thou serve me, and watch my seven foals?" asked the King. "If thou canst watch them for a whole day and tell me at night what they eat and drink, thou shalt have the Princess and half my kingdom, but if thou canst not, I will cut three red stripes on thy back."

The youth thought that it was very easy work to watch the foals, and that he could do it well enough.

Next morning, when day was beginning to dawn, the King's Master of the Horse let out the seven foals; and they ran away, and the youth after them just as it chanced, over hill and dale, through woods end bogs. When the youth had run thus for a long time he began to be tired, and when he had held on a little longer he was heartily weary of watching at all, and at the same moment he came to a cleft in a rock where an old woman was sitting spinning with her distaff in her hand.

As soon as she caught sight of the youth, who was running after the foals till the perspiration streamed down his face, she cried:

"Come hither, come hither, my handsome son, and let me comb your hair for you."

The lad was willing enough, so he sat down in the cleft of the rock beside the old hag, and laid his head on her knees, and she combed his hair all day while he lay there and gave himself up to idleness.

When evening was drawing near, the youth wanted to go.

"I may just as well go straight home again," said he, "for it is no use to go to the King's palace."

"Wait till it is dusk," said the old hag, "and then the King's foals will pass by this place again, and you can run home with them; no one will ever know that you have been lying here all day instead of watching the foals."

So when they came she gave the lad a bottle of water and a bit of moss, and told him to show these to the King and say that this was what his seven foals ate and drank.

"Hast thou watched faithfully and well the whole day long?" said the King, when the lad came into his presence in the evening.

"Yes, that I have!" said the youth.

"Then you are able to tell me what it is that my seven foals eat and drink," said the King.

So the youth produced the bottle of water and the bit of moss which he had got from the old woman, saying:

"Here you see their meat, and here you see their drink."

Then the King knew how his watching had been done, and fell into such a rage that he ordered his people to chase the youth back to his own home at once; but first they were to cut three red stripes in his back, and rub salt into them.

When the youth reached home again, anyone can imagine what a state of mind he was in. He had gone out once to seek a place, he said, but never would he do such a thing again.

Next day the second son said that he would now go out into the world to seek his fortune. His father and mother said "No," and bade him look at his brother's back, but the youth would not give up his design, and stuck to it, and after a long, long time he got leave to go, and set forth on his way. When he had walked all day he too came to the King's palace, and the King was standing outside on the steps, and asked where he was going; and when the youth replied that he was going about in search of a place, the King said that he might enter into his service and watch his seven foals. Then the King promised him the same punishment and the same reward that he had promised his brother.

The youth at once consented to this and entered into the King's service, for he thought he could easily watch the foals and inform the King what they ate and drank.

In the grey light of dawn the Master of the Horse let out the seven foals, and off they went again over hill and dale, and off went the lad after them. But all went with him as it had gone with his brother. When he had run after the foals for a long, long time and was hot and tired, he passed by a cleft in the rock where an old woman was sitting spinning with a distaff, and she called to him:

"Come hither, come hither, my handsome son, and let me comb your hair."

The youth liked the thought of this, let the foals run where they chose, and seated himself in the cleft of the rock by the side of the old hag. So there he sat with his head on her lap, taking his ease the livelong day.

The foals came back in the evening, and then he too got a bit of moss and a bottle of water from the old hag, which things he was to show to the King. But when the King asked the youth: "Canst thou tell me what my seven foals eat and drink?" and the youth showed him the bit of moss and the bottle of water, and said: "Yes here may yōu behold their meat, and here their drink," the King once more became wroth, and commanded that three red stripes should be cut on the lad's back, that salt should be strewn upon them, and that he should then be instantly chased back to his own home. So when the youth got home again he too related all that had happened to him, and he too said that he had gone out in search of a place once, but that never would he do it again.

On the third day Cinderlad wanted to set out. He had a fancy to try to watch the seven foals himself, he said.

The two others laughed at him, and mocked him. "What! when all went so ill with us, do you suppose that you are going to succeed? You look like succeeding – you who have never done anything else but lie and poke about among the ashes!" said they.

"Yes, I will go too," said Cinderlad, "for I have taken it into my head."

The two brothers laughed at him, and his father and mother begged him not to go, but all to no purpose, and Cinderlad set out on his way. So when he had walked the whole day, he too came to the King's palace as darkness began to fall.

There stood the King outside on the steps, and he asked whither he was bound.

"I am walking about in search of a place," said Cinderlad.

"From whence do you come, then?" inquired the King, for by this time he wanted to know a little more about the men before he took any of them into his service.

So Cinderlad told him whence he came, and that he was brother to the two who had watched the seven foals for the King, and then he inquired if he might be allowed to try to watch them on the following day.

"Oh, shame on them!" said the King, for it enraged him even to think of them. "If thou art brother to those two, thou too art not good for much. I have had enough of such fellows."

"Well, but as I have come here, you might just give me leave to make the attempt," said Cinderlad.

"Oh, very well, if thou art absolutely determined to have thy back flayed, thou may'st have thine own way if thou wilt," said the King.

"I would much rather have the Princess," said Cinderlad.

Next morning, in the grey light of dawn, the Master of the Horse let out the seven foals again, and off they set over hill and dale, through woods and bogs, and off went Cinderlad after them. When he had run thus for a long time, he too came to the cleft in the rock. There the old hag was once more sitting spinning from her distaff, and she cried to Cinderlad;

"Come hither, come hither, my handsome son, and let me comb your hair for you."

"Come to me, then; come to me!" said Cinderlad, as he passed by jumping and running, and keeping tight hold of one of the foals' tails.

When he had got safely past the cleft in the rock, the youngest foal said:

"Get on my back, for we have still a long way to go." So the lad did this.

And thus they journeyed onwards a long, long way.

"Dost thou see anything now?" said the Foal.

"No," said Cinderlad.

So they journeyed onwards a good bit farther.

"Dost thou see anything now?" asked the Foal.

"Oh, no," said the lad.

When they had gone thus for a long, long way, the Foal again asked:

"Dost thou see anything now?"

"Yes, now I see something that is white," said Cinderlad. "It looks like the trunk of a great thick birch tree."

"Yes, that is where we are to go in," said the Foal.

When they got to the trunk, the eldest foal broke it down on one side, and then they saw a door where the trunk had been standing, and inside this there was a small room, and in the room there was scarcely anything but a small fireplace and a couple of benches, but behind the door hung a great rusty sword and a small pitcher.

"Canst thou wield that sword?" asked the Foal.

Cinderlad tried, but could not do it; so he had to take a draught from the pitcher, and then one more, and after that still another, and then he was able to wield the sword with perfect ease.

"Good," said the Foal; "and now thou must take the sword away with thee, and with it shalt thou cut off the heads of all seven of us on thy wedding-day, and then we shall become princes again as we were before. For we are brothers of the Princess whom thou art to have when thou canst tell the King what we eat and drink, but there is a mighty Troll who has cast a spell over us. When thou hast cut off our heads, thou must take the greatest care to lay each head at the tail of the body to which it belonged before, and then the spell which the Troll has cast upon us will lose all its power."

Cinderlad promised to do this, and then they went on farther.

When they had travelled a long, long way, the Foal said:

"Dost thou see anything?"

"No," said Cinderlad.

So they went on a great distance farther.

"And now?" inquired the Foal, "seest thou nothing now?"

"Alas! no," said Cinderlad.

So they travelled onwards again, for many and many a mile, over hill and dale.

"Now, then," said the Foal, "dost thou not see anything now?"

"Yes," said Cinderlad; "now I see something like a bluish streak, far, far away."

"That is a river," said the Foal, "and we have to cross it."

There was a long, handsome bridge over the river, and when they had got to the other side of it they again travelled on a long, long way, and then once more the Foal inquired if Cinderlad saw anything. Yes, this time he saw something that looked black, far, far away, and was rather like a church tower.

"Yes," said the Foal, "we shall go into that."

When the Foals got into the churchyard they turned into men and looked like the sons of a king, and their clothes were so magnificent that they shone with splendour, and they went into the church and received bread and wine from the priest, who was standing before the altar, and Cinderlad went in too. But when the priest had laid his hands on the princes and read the blessing, they went out of the church again, and Cinderlad went out too, but he took with him a flask of wine and some consecrated bread. No sooner had the seven princes come out into the churchyard than they became foals again, and Cinderlad got upon the back of the youngest, and they returned by the way they had come, only they went much, much faster.

First they went over the bridge, and then past the trunk of the birch tree, and then past the old hag who sat in the cleft of the rock spinning, and they went by so fast that Cinderlad could not hear what the old hag screeched after him, but just heard enough to understand that she was terribly enraged.

It was all but dark when they got back to the King at nightfall, and he himself was standing in the courtyard waiting for them.

"Hast thou watched well and faithfully the whole day?" said the King to Cinderlad.

"I have done my best," replied Cinderlad.

"Then thou canst tell me what my seven foals eat and drink?" asked the King.

So Cinderlad pulled out the consecrated bread and the flask of wine, and showed them to the King. "Here may you behold their meat, and here their drink," said he.

"Yes, diligently and faithfully hast thou watched," said the King, "and thou shalt have the Princess and half the kingdom."

So all was made ready for the wedding, and the King said that it was to be so stately and magnificent that everyone should hear of it, and everyone inquire about it.

But when they sat down to the marriage-feast, the bridegroom arose and went down to the stable, for he said that he had forgotten something which he must go and look to. When he got there, he did what the foals had bidden him, and cut off the heads of all the seven. First the eldest, and then the second, and so on according to their age, and he was extremely careful to lay each head at the tail of the foal to which it had belonged, and when that was done, all the foals became princes again. When he returned to the marriage-feast with the seven princes, the King was so joyful that he both kissed Cinderlad and clapped him on the back, and his bride was still more delighted with him than she had been before.

"Half my kingdom is thine already," said the King, "and the other half shall be thine after my death, for my sons can get countries and kingdoms for themselves now that they have become princes again."

Therefore, as all may well believe, there was joy and merriment at that wedding.

THE FIR TREE

Far down in the forest, where the warm sun and the fresh air made a sweet resting-place, grew a pretty little fir tree; and yet it was not happy, it wished so much to be tall like its companions – the pines and firs which grew around it. The sun shone, and the soft air fluttered its leaves, and the little peasant children passed by, prattling merrily, but the fir tree heeded them not. Sometimes the children would bring a large basket of raspberries or strawberries, wreathed on a straw, and seat themselves near the fir tree, and say, "Is it not a pretty little tree?" which made it feel more unhappy than before. And yet all this while the tree grew a notch or joint taller every year; for by the number of joints in the stem of a fir tree we can discover its age. Still, as it grew, it complained, "Oh! how I wish I were as tall as the other trees, then I would spread out my branches on every side, and my top would over-look the wide world. I should have the birds building their nests on my boughs, and when the wind blew, I should bow with stately dignity like my tall companions." The tree was so discontented, that it took no pleasure in the warm sunshine, the birds, or the rosy clouds that floated over it morning and evening. Sometimes, in winter, when the snow lay white and glittering on the ground, a hare would come springing along, and jump right over the little tree; and then how mortified it would feel! Two winters passed, and when the third arrived, the tree had grown so tall that the hare was obliged to run round it. Yet it remained unsatisfied, and would exclaim, "Oh, if I could but keep on growing tall and old! There is nothing else worth caring for in the world!" In the autumn, as usual, the wood-cutters came and cut down several of the tallest trees, and the young fir tree, which was now grown to its full height, shuddered as the noble trees fell to the earth with a crash. After the branches were lopped off, the trunks looked so slender and bare, that they could scarcely be recognized. Then they were placed upon wagons, and drawn by horses out of the forest. "Where were they going? What would become of them?" The young fir tree wished very much to know; so in the spring, when the swallows and the storks came, it asked, "Do you know where those trees were taken? Did you meet them?"

The swallows knew nothing, but the stork, after a little reflection, nodded his head, and said, "Yes, I think I do. I met several new ships when I flew from Egypt, and they had fine masts that smelt like fir. I think these must have been the trees; I assure you they were stately, very stately."

"Oh, how I wish I were tall enough to go on the sea," said the fir tree. "What is the sea, and what does it look like?"

"It would take too much time to explain," said the stork, flying quickly away.

"Rejoice in thy youth," said the sunbeam; "rejoice in thy fresh growth, and the young life that is in thee."

And the wind kissed the tree, and the dew watered it with tears; but the fir tree regarded them not.

Christmas-time drew near, and many young trees were cut down, some even smaller and younger than the fir tree who enjoyed neither rest nor peace with longing to leave its forest home. These young trees, which were chosen for their beauty, kept their branches, and were also laid on wagons and drawn by horses out of the forest.

"Where are they going?" asked the fir tree. "They are not taller than I am: indeed, one is much less; and why are the branches not cut off? Where are they going?"

"We know, we know," sang the sparrows; "we have looked in at the windows of the houses in the town, and we know what is done with them. They are dressed up in the most splendid manner. We have seen them standing in the middle of a warm room, and adorned with all sorts of beautiful things, – honey cakes, gilded apples, playthings, and many hundreds of wax tapers."

"And then," asked the fir tree, trembling through all its branches, "and then what happens?"

"We did not see any more," said the sparrows; "but this was enough for us."

"I wonder whether anything so brilliant will ever happen to me," thought the fir tree. "It would be much better than crossing the sea. I long for it almost with pain. Oh! when will Christmas be here? I am now as tall and well grown as those which were taken away last year. Oh! that I were now laid on the wagon, or standing in the warm room, with all that brightness and splendor around me! Something better and more beautiful is to come after, or the trees would not be so decked out. Yes, what follows will be grander and more splendid. What can it be? I am weary with longing. I scarcely know how I feel."

"Rejoice with us," said the air and the sunlight. "Enjoy thine own bright life in the fresh air."

But the tree would not rejoice, though it grew taller every day; and, winter and summer, its dark-green foliage might be seen in the forest, while passers by would say, "What a beautiful tree!"

A short time before Christmas, the discontented fir tree was the first to fall. As the axe cut through the stem, and divided the pith, the tree fell with a groan to the earth, conscious of pain and faintness, and forgetting all its anticipations of happiness, in sorrow at leaving its home in the forest. It knew that it should never again see its dear old companions, the trees, nor the little bushes and many-colored flowers that had grown by its side; perhaps not even the birds. Neither was the journey at all pleasant. The tree first recovered itself while being unpacked in the courtyard of a house, with several other trees; and it heard a man say, "We only want one, and this is the prettiest."

Then came two servants in grand livery, and carried the fir tree into a large and beautiful apartment. On the walls hung pictures, and near the great stove stood great china vases, with lions on the lids. There were rocking chairs, silken sofas, large tables, covered with pictures, books, and playthings, worth a great deal of money, – at least, the children said so. Then the fir tree was placed in a large tub, full of sand; but green baize hung all around it, so that no one could see it was a tub, and it stood on a very handsome carpet. How the fir tree trembled! "What was going to happen to him now?" Some young ladies came, and the servants helped them to adorn the tree. On one branch they hung little bags cut out of colored paper, and each bag was filled with sweetmeats; from other branches hung gilded apples and walnuts, as if they had grown there; and above, and all round, were hundreds of red, blue, and white tapers, which were fastened on the branches. Dolls, exactly like real babies, were placed under the green leaves, – the tree had never seen such things before, – and at the very top was fastened a glittering star, made of tinsel. Oh, it was very beautiful!

"This evening," they all exclaimed, "how bright it will be!" "Oh, that the evening were come," thought the tree, "and the tapers lighted! then I shall know what else is going to happen. Will the trees of the forest come to see me? I wonder if the sparrows will peep in at the windows as they fly? shall I grow faster here, and keep on all these ornaments summer and winter?" But guessing was of very little use; it made his bark ache, and this pain is as bad for a slender fir tree, as headache is for us. At last the tapers were lighted, and then what a glistening blaze of light the tree presented! It trembled so with joy in all its branches, that one of the candles fell among the green leaves and burnt some of them. "Help! help!" exclaimed the young ladies, but there was no danger, for they quickly extinguished the fire. After this, the tree tried not to tremble at all, though the fire frightened him; he was so anxious not to hurt any of the beautiful ornaments, even while their brilliancy dazzled him. And now the folding doors were thrown open, and a troop of children rushed in as if they intended to upset the tree; they were followed more silently by their elders. For a moment the little ones stood silent with astonishment, and then they shouted for joy, till the room rang, and they danced merrily round the tree, while one present after another was taken from it.

"What are they doing? What will happen next?" thought the fir. At last the candles burnt down to the branches and were put out. Then the children received permission to plunder the tree.

Oh, how they rushed upon it, till the branches cracked, and had it not been fastened with the glistening star to the ceiling, it must have been thrown down. The children then danced about with their pretty toys, and no one noticed the tree, except the children's maid who came and peeped among the branches to see if an apple or a fig had been forgotten.

"A story, a story," cried the children, pulling a little fat man towards the tree.

"Now we shall be in the green shade," said the man, as he seated himself under it, "and the tree will have the pleasure of hearing also, but I shall only relate one story; what shall it be? Ivede-Avede, or Humpty Dumpty, who fell down stairs, but soon got up again, and at last married a princess."

"Ivede-Avede," cried some. "Humpty Dumpty," cried others, and there was a fine shouting and crying out. But the fir tree remained quite still, and thought to himself, "Shall I have anything to do with all this?" but he had already amused them as much as they wished. Then the old man told them the story of Humpty Dumpty, how he fell down stairs, and was raised up again, and married a princess. And the children clapped their hands and cried, "Tell another, tell another," for they wanted to hear the story of "Ivede-Avede;" but they only had "Humpty Dumpty." After this the fir tree became quite silent and thoughtful; never had the birds in the forest told such tales as "Humpty Dumpty," who fell down stairs, and yet married a princess.

"Ah! yes, so it happens in the world," thought the fir tree; he believed it all, because it was related by such a nice man. "Ah! well," he thought, "who knows? perhaps I may fall down too, and marry a princess;" and he looked forward joyfully to the next evening, expecting to be again decked out with lights and playthings, gold and fruit. "Tomorrow I will not tremble," thought he; "I will enjoy all my splendor, and I shall hear the story of Humpty Dumpty again, and perhaps Ivede-Avede." And the tree remained quiet and thoughtful all night. In the morning the servants and the housemaid came in. "Now," thought the fir, "all my splendor is going to begin again." But they dragged him out of the room and up stairs to the garret, and threw him on the floor, in a dark corner, where no daylight shone, and there they left him. "What does this mean?" thought the tree, "what am I to do here? I can hear nothing in a place like this," and he had time enough to think, for days and nights passed and no one came near him, and when at last somebody did come, it was only to put away large boxes in a corner. So the tree was completely hidden from sight as if it had never existed. "It is winter now," thought the tree, "the ground is hard and covered with snow, so that people cannot plant me. I shall be sheltered here, I dare say, until spring comes. How thoughtful and kind everybody is to me! Still I wish this place were not so dark, as well as lonely, with not even a little hare to look at. How pleasant it was out in the forest while the snow lay on the ground, when the hare would run by, yes, and jump over me too, although I did not like it then. Oh! it is terrible lonely here."

"Squeak, squeak," said a little mouse, creeping cautiously towards the tree; then came another; and they both sniffed at the fir tree and crept between the branches.

"Oh, it is very cold," said the little mouse, "or else we should be so comfortable here, shouldn't we, you old fir tree?"

"I am not old," said the fir tree, "there are many who are older than I am."

"Where do you come from? and what do you know?" asked the mice, who were full of curiosity. "Have you seen the most beautiful places in the world, and can you tell us all about them? and have you been in the storeroom, where cheeses lie on the shelf, and hams hang from the ceiling? One can run about on tallow candles there, and go in thin and come out fat."

"I know nothing of that place," said the fir tree, "but I know the wood where the sun shines and the birds sing." And then the tree told the little mice all about its youth. They had never heard such an account in their lives; and after they had listened to it attentively, they said, "What a number of things you have seen? you must have been very happy."

"Happy!" exclaimed the fir tree, and then as he reflected upon what he had been telling them, he said, "Ah, yes! after all those were happy days." But when he went on and related all about Christmas Eve, and how he had been dressed up with cakes and lights, the mice said, "How happy you must have been, you old fir tree."

"I am not old at all," replied the tree, "I only came from the forest this winter, I am now checked in my growth."

"What splendid stories you can relate," said the little mice. And the next night four other mice came with them to hear what the tree had to tell. The more he talked the more he remembered, and then he thought to himself, "Those were happy days, but they may come again. Humpty Dumpty fell down stairs, and yet he married the princess; perhaps I may marry a princess too." And the fir tree thought of the pretty little birch tree that grew in the forest, which was to him a real beautiful princess.

"Who is Humpty Dumpty?" asked the little mice. And then the tree related the whole story; he could remember every single word, and the little mice was so delighted with it, that they were ready to jump to the top of the tree. The next night a great many more mice made their appearance, and on Sunday two rats came with them; but they said, it was not a pretty story at all, and the little mice were very sorry, for it made them also think less of it.

"Do you know only one story?" asked the rats.

"Only one," replied the fir tree; "I heard it on the happiest evening of my life; but I did not know I was so happy at the time."

"We think it is a very miserable story," said the rats. "Don't you know any story about bacon, or tallow in the storeroom."

"No," replied the tree.

"Many thanks to you then," replied the rats, and they marched off.

The little mice also kept away after this, and the tree sighed, and said, "It was very pleasant when the merry little mice sat round me and listened while I talked. Now that is all passed too. However, I shall consider myself happy when some one comes to take me out of this place." But would this ever happen? Yes; one morning people came to clear out the garret, the boxes were packed away, and the tree was pulled out of the corner, and thrown roughly on the garret floor; then the servant dragged it out upon the staircase where the daylight shone. "Now life is beginning again," said the tree, rejoicing in the sunshine and fresh air. Then it was carried down stairs and taken into the courtyard so quickly, that it forgot to think of itself, and could only look about, there was so much to be seen. The court was close to a garden, where everything looked blooming. Fresh and fragrant roses hung over the little palings. The linden trees were in blossom; while the swallows flew here and there, crying, "Twit, twit, twit, my mate is coming," – but it was not the fir tree they meant. "Now I shall live," cried the tree, joyfully spreading out its branches; but alas! they were all withered and yellow, and it lay in a corner amongst weeds and nettles. The star of gold paper still stuck in the top of the tree and glittered in the sunshine. In the same courtyard two of the merry children were playing who had danced round the tree at Christmas, and had been so happy. The youngest saw the gilded star, and ran and pulled it off the tree. "Look what is sticking to the ugly old fir tree," said the child, treading on the branches till they crackled under his boots. And the tree saw all the fresh bright flowers in the garden, and then looked at itself, and wished it had remained in the dark corner of the garret. It thought of its fresh youth in the forest, of the merry Christmas evening, and of the little mice who had listened to the story of "Humpty Dumpty." "Past! past!" said the old tree; "Oh, had I but enjoyed myself while I could have done so! but now it is too late." Then a lad came and chopped the tree into small pieces, till a large bundle lay in a heap on the ground. The pieces were placed in a fire under the copper, and they quickly blazed up brightly, while the tree sighed so deeply that each sigh was like a pistol-shot. Then the children, who were at play, came and seated themselves in front of the fire, and looked at it and cried, "Pop, pop." But at each "pop," which was a deep sigh, the tree was thinking of a summer day in the forest; and of Christmas evening, and of "Humpty Dumpty," the only story it had ever heard or knew how to relate, till at last it was consumed. The boys still played in the garden, and the youngest wore the golden star on his breast, with which the tree had been adorned during the happiest evening of its existence. Now all was past; the tree's life was past, and the story also, – for all stories must come to an end at last

THE TINDERBOX

A soldier came marching along the high road: "Left, right – left, right." He had his knapsack on his back, and a sword at his side; he had been to the wars, and was now returning home.

As he walked on, he met a very frightful-looking old witch in the road. Her under-lip hung quite down on her breast, and she stopped and said, "Good evening, soldier; you have a very fine sword, and a large knapsack, and you are a real soldier; so you shall have as much money as ever you like."

"Thank you, old witch," said the soldier.

"Do you see that large tree," said the witch, pointing to a tree which stood beside them. "Well, it is quite hollow inside, and you must climb to the top, when you will see a hole, through which you can let yourself down into the tree to a great depth. I will tie a rope round your body, so that I can pull you up again when you call out to me."

"But what am I to do, down there in the tree?" asked the soldier.

"Get money," she replied; "for you must know that when you reach the ground under the tree, you will find yourself in a large hall, lighted up by three hundred lamps; you will then see three doors, which can be easily opened, for the keys are in all the locks. On entering the first of the chambers, to which these doors lead, you will see a large chest, standing in the middle of the floor, and upon it a dog seated, with a pair of eyes as large as teacups. But you need not be at all afraid of him; I will give you my blue checked apron, which you must spread upon the floor, and then boldly seize hold of the dog, and place him upon it. You can then open the chest, and take from it as many pence as you please, they are only copper pence; but if you would rather have silver money, you must go into the second chamber. Here you will find another dog, with eyes as big as mill-wheels; but do not let that trouble you. Place him upon my apron, and then take what money you please. If, however, you like gold best, enter the third chamber, where there is another chest full of it. The dog who sits on this chest is very dreadful; his eyes are as big as a tower, but do not mind him. If he also is placed upon my apron, he cannot hurt you, and you may take from the chest what gold you will."

"This is not a bad story," said the soldier; "but what am I to give you, you old witch? for, of course, you do not mean to tell me all this for nothing."

"No," said the witch; "but I do not ask for a single penny. Only promise to bring me an old tinder-box, which my grandmother left behind the last time she went down there."

"Very well; I promise. Now tie the rope round my body."

"Here it is," replied the witch; "and here is my blue checked apron."

As soon as the rope was tied, the soldier climbed up the tree, and let himself down through the hollow to the ground beneath; and here he found, as the witch had told him, a large hall, in which many hundred lamps were all burning. Then he opened the first door. "Ah!" there sat the dog, with the eyes as large as teacups, staring at him.

"You're a pretty fellow," said the soldier, seizing him, and placing him on the witch's apron, while he filled his pockets from the chest with as many pieces as they would hold. Then he closed the lid, seated the dog upon it again, and walked into another chamber, And, sure enough, there sat the dog with eyes as big as mill-wheels.

"You had better not look at me in that way," said the soldier; "you will make your eyes water;" and then he seated him also upon the apron, and opened the chest. But when he saw what a quantity of silver money it contained, he very quickly threw away all the coppers he had taken, and filled his pockets and his knapsack with nothing but silver.

Then he went into the third room, and there the dog was really hideous; his eyes were, truly, as big as towers, and they turned round and round in his head like wheels.

"Good morning," said the soldier, touching his cap, for he had never seen such a dog in his life. But after looking at him more closely, he thought he had been civil enough, so he placed him on the floor, and opened the chest. Good gracious, what a quantity of gold there was! enough to buy all the sugar-sticks of the sweet-stuff women; all the tin soldiers, whips, and rocking-horses in the world, or even the whole town itself There was, indeed, an immense quantity. So the soldier now threw away all the silver money he had taken, and filled his pockets and his knapsack with gold instead; and not only his pockets and his knapsack, but even his cap and boots, so that he could scarcely walk.

He was really rich now; so he replaced the dog on the chest, closed the door, and called up through the tree, "Now pull me out, you old witch."

"Have you got the tinder-box?" asked the witch.

"No; I declare I quite forgot it." So he went back and fetched the tinderbox, and then the witch drew him up out of the tree, and he stood again in the high road, with his pockets, his knapsack, his cap, and his boots full of gold.

"What are you going to do with the tinder-box?" asked the soldier.

"That is nothing to you," replied the witch; "you have the money, now give me the tinder-box."

"I tell you what," said the soldier, "if you don't tell me what you are going to do with it, I will draw my sword and cut off your head."

"No," said the witch.

The soldier immediately cut off her head, and there she lay on the ground. Then he tied up all his money in her apron, and slung it on his back like a bundle, put the tinderbox in his pocket, and walked off to the nearest town. It was a very nice town, and he put up at the best inn, and ordered a dinner of all his favorite dishes, for now he was rich and had plenty of money.

The servant, who cleaned his boots, thought they certainly were a shabby pair to be worn by such a rich gentleman, for he had not yet bought any new ones. The next day, however, he procured some good clothes and proper boots, so that our soldier soon became known as a fine gentleman, and the people visited him, and told him all the wonders that were to be seen in the town, and of the king's beautiful daughter, the princess.

"Where can I see her?" asked the soldier.

"She is not to be seen at all," they said; "she lives in a large copper castle, surrounded by walls and towers. No one but the king himself can pass in or out, for there has been a prophecy that she will marry a common soldier, and the king cannot bear to think of such a marriage."

"I should like very much to see her," thought the soldier; but he could not obtain permission to do so. However, he passed a very pleasant time; went to the theatre, drove in the king's garden, and gave a great deal of money to the poor, which was very good of him; he remembered what it had been in olden times to be without a shilling. Now he was rich, had fine clothes, and many friends, who all declared he was a fine fellow and a real gentleman, and all this gratified him exceedingly. But his money would not last forever; and as he spent and gave away a great deal daily, and received none, he found himself at last with only two shillings left. So he was obliged to leave his elegant rooms, and live in a little garret under the roof, where he had to clean his own boots, and even mend them with a large needle. None of his friends came to see him, there were too many stairs to mount up. One dark evening, he had not even a penny to buy a candle; then all at once he remembered that there was a piece of candle stuck in the tinder-box, which he had brought from the old tree, into which the witch had helped him.

He found the tinder-box, but no sooner had he struck a few sparks from the flint and steel, than the door flew open and the dog with eyes as big as teacups, whom he had seen while down in the tree, stood before him, and said, "What orders, master?"

"Hallo," said the soldier; "well this is a pleasant tinderbox, if it brings me all I wish for."

"Bring me some money," said he to the dog.

He was gone in a moment, and presently returned, carrying a large bag of coppers in his month. The soldier very soon discovered after this the value of the tinder-box. If he struck the flint once, the dog who sat on the chest of copper money made his appearance; if twice, the dog came from the chest of silver; and if three times, the dog with eyes like towers, who watched over the gold. The soldier had now plenty of money; he returned to his elegant rooms, and reappeared in his fine clothes, so that his friends knew him again directly, and made as much of him as before.

After a while he began to think it was very strange that no one could get a look at the princess. "Every one says she is very beautiful," thought he to himself; "but what is the use of that if she is to be shut up in a copper castle surrounded by so many towers. Can I by any means get to see her. Stop! where is my tinder-box?" Then he struck a light, and in a moment the dog, with eyes as big as teacups, stood before him.

"It is midnight," said the soldier, "yet I should very much like to see the princess, if only for a moment."

The dog disappeared instantly, and before the soldier could even look round, he returned with the princess. She was lying on the dog's back asleep, and looked so lovely, that every one who saw her would know she was a real princess. The soldier could not help kissing her, true soldier as he was. Then the dog ran back with the princess; but in the morning, while at breakfast with the king and queen, she told them what a singular dream she had had during the night, of a dog and a soldier, that she had ridden on the dog's back, and been kissed by the soldier.

"That is a very pretty story, indeed," said the queen. So the next night one of the old ladies of the court was set to watch by the princess's bed, to discover whether it really was a dream, or what else it might be.

The soldier longed very much to see the princess once more, so he sent for the dog again in the night to fetch her, and to run with her as fast as ever he could. But the old lady put on water boots, and ran after him as quickly as he did, and found that he carried the princess into a large house. She thought it would help her to remember the place if she made a large cross on the door with a piece of chalk. Then she went home to bed, and the dog presently returned with the princess. But when he saw that a cross had been made on the door of the house, where the soldier lived, he took another piece of chalk and made crosses on all the doors in the town, so that the lady-in-waiting might not be able to find out the right door.

Early the next morning the king and queen accompanied the lady and all the officers of the household, to see where the princess had been.

"Here it is," said the king, when they came to the first door with a cross on it.

"No, my dear husband, it must be that one," said the queen, pointing to a second door having a cross also.

"And here is one, and there is another!" they all exclaimed; for there were crosses on all the doors in every direction.

So they felt it would be useless to search any farther. But the queen was a very clever woman; she could do a great deal more than merely ride in a carriage. She took her large gold scissors, cut a piece of silk into squares, and made a neat little bag. This bag she filled with buckwheat flour, and tied it round the princess's neck;

and then she cut a small hole in the bag, so that the flour might be scattered on the ground as the princess went along. During the night, the dog came again and carried the princess on his back, and ran with her to the soldier, who loved her very much, and wished that he had been a prince, so that he might have her for a wife. The dog did not observe how the flour ran out of the bag all the way from the castle wall to the soldier's house, and even up to the window, where he had climbed with the princess. Therefore in the morning the king and queen found out where their daughter had been, and the soldier was taken up and put in prison. Oh, how dark and disagreeable it was as he sat there, and the people said to him, "Tomorrow you will be hanged." It was not very pleasant news, and besides, he had left the tinder-box at the inn. In the morning he could see through the iron grating of the little window how the people were hastening out of the town to see him hanged; he heard the drums beating, and saw the soldiers marching. Every one ran out to look at them, and a shoemaker's boy, with a leather apron and slippers on, galloped by so fast, that one of his slippers flew off and struck against the wall where the soldier sat looking through the iron grating. "Hallo, you shoemaker's boy, you need not be in such a hurry," cried the soldier to him. "There will be nothing to see till I come; but if you will run to the house where I have been living, and bring me my tinder-box, you shall have four shillings, but you must put your best foot foremost."

The shoemaker's boy liked the idea of getting the four shillings, so he ran very fast and fetched the tinder-box, and gave it to the soldier. And now we shall see what happened. Outside the town a large gibbet had been erected, round which stood the soldiers and several thousands of people. The king and the queen sat on splendid thrones opposite to the judges and the whole council.

The soldier already stood on the ladder; but as they were about to place the rope around his neck, he said that an innocent request was often granted to a poor criminal before he suffered death. He wished very much to smoke a pipe, as it would be the last pipe he should ever smoke in the world. The king could not refuse this request, so the soldier took his tinder-box, and struck fire, once, twice, thrice, – and there in a moment stood all the dogs; – the one with eyes as big as teacups, the one with eyes as large as mill-wheels, and the third, whose eyes were like towers. "Help me now, that I may not be hanged," cried the soldier.

And the dogs fell upon the judges and all the councillors; seized one by the legs, and another by the nose, and tossed them many feet high in the air, so that they fell down and were dashed to pieces.

"I will not be touched," said the king. But the largest dog seized him, as well as the queen, and threw them after the others. Then the soldiers and all the people were afraid, and cried, "Good soldier, you shall be our king, and you shall marry the beautiful princess."

So they placed the soldier in the king's carriage, and the three dogs ran on in front and cried "Hurrah!" and the little boys whistled through their fingers, and the soldiers presented arms. The princess came out of the copper castle, and became queen, which was very pleasing to her. The wedding festivities lasted a whole week, and the dogs sat at the table, and stared with all their eyes.

TALES OF TRANSFORMATION & TRICKERY

In 'The Wonderful Birch', a girl's mother is transformed into a black sheep by a wicked witch, who subsequently slaughters her to make a soup. But her daughter lovingly gathers up her bones and buries them. She springs up out of the ground renewed, a living tree.

Mythic transformation can be for good or ill; it can be done in malevolence or spite, in a spirit of revenge or punishment, or kindly, to help someone out of a tight spot. It can hint ominously that the apparently benign may not be all it seems or reassure us that bad situations might yet end well. For better or worse, in other words, things can always change. At a still deeper level, tales of transformation exemplify the magical power of literature itself, the ability of metaphor to make one thing into another.

Trickery transforms situations. It makes appearances even more deceptive than they already were and finds solutions where there seem to be only problems. In so doing, it reminds us of the power of human ingenuity and resourcefulness. Our ability to make things better than they are.

THE WONDERFUL BIRCH

Once upon a time there were a man and a woman, who had an only daughter. Now it happened that one of their sheep went astray, and they set out to look for it, and searched and searched, each in a different part of the wood. Then the good wife met a witch, who said to her:

"If you spit, you miserable creature, if you spit into the sheath of my knife, or if you run between my legs, I shall change you into a black sheep."

The woman neither spat, nor did she run between her legs, but yet the witch changed her into a sheep. Then she made herself look exactly like the woman, and called out to the good man:

"Ho, old man, halloa! I have found the sheep already!"

The man thought the witch was really his wife, and he did not know that his wife was the sheep; so he went home with her, glad at heart because his sheep was found. When they were safe at home the witch said to the man:

"Look here, old man, we must really kill that sheep lest it run away to the wood again."

The man, who was a peaceable quiet sort of fellow, made no objections, but simply said:

"Good, let us do so."

The daughter, however, had overheard their talk, and she ran to the flock and lamented aloud:

"Oh, dear little mother, they are going to slaughter you!"

"Well, then, if they do slaughter me," was the black sheep's answer, "eat you neither the meat nor the broth that is made of me, but gather all my bones, and bury them by the edge of the field."

Shortly after this they took the black sheep from the flock and slaughtered it. The witch made pease-soup of it, and set it before the daughter. But the girl remembered her mother's warning. She did not touch the soup, but she carried the bones to the edge of the field and buried them there; and there sprang up on the spot a birch tree – a very lovely birch tree.

Some time had passed away – who can tell how long they might have been living there? – when the witch, to whom a child had been born in the meantime, began to take an ill-will to the man's daughter, and to torment her in all sorts of ways.

Now it happened that a great festival was to be held at the palace, and the King had commanded that all the people should be invited, and that this proclamation should be made:

> "Come, people all!
> Poor and wretched, one and all!
> Blind and crippled though ye be,
> Mount your steeds or come by sea."

And so they drove into the King's feast all the outcasts, and the maimed, and the halt, and the blind. In the good man's house, too, preparations were made to go to the palace. The witch said to the man:

"Go you on in front, old man, with our youngest; I will give the elder girl work to keep her from being dull in our absence."

So the man took the child and set out. But the witch kindled a fire on the hearth, threw a potful of barleycorns among the cinders, and said to the girl:

"If you have not picked the barley out of the ashes, and put it all back in the pot before nightfall, I shall eat you up!"

Then she hastened after the others, and the poor girl stayed at home and wept. She tried to be sure to pick up the grains of barley, but she soon saw how useless her labour was; and so she went in her sore trouble to the birch tree on her mother's grave, and cried and cried, because her mother lay dead beneath the sod and could help her no longer. In the midst of her grief she suddenly heard her mother's voice speak from the grave, and say to her:

"Why do you weep, little daughter?"

"The witch has scattered barleycorns on the hearth, and bid me pick them out of the ashes," said the girl; "that is why I weep, dear little mother."

"Do not weep," said her mother consolingly. "Break off one of my branches, and strike the hearth with it crosswise, and all will be put right." The girl did so. She struck the hearth with the birchen branch, and lo! the barleycorns flew into the pot, and the hearth was clean. Then she went back to the birch tree and laid the branch upon the grave. Then her mother bade her bathe on one side of the stem, dry herself on another, and dress on the third. When the girl had done all that, she had grown so lovely that no one on earth could rival her. Splendid clothing was given to her, and a horse, with hair partly of gold, partly of silver, and partly of something more precious still. The girl sprang into the saddle, and rode as swift as an arrow to the palace. As she turned into the courtyard of the castle the King's son came out to meet her, tied her steed to a pillar, and led her in. He never left her side as they passed through the castle rooms; and all the people gazed at her, and wondered who the lovely maiden was, and from what castle she came; but no one knew her – no one knew anything about her. At the banquet the Prince invited her to sit next him in the place of honour; but the witch's daughter gnawed the bones under the table. The Prince did not see her, and thinking it was a dog, he gave her such a push with his foot that her arm was broken. Are you not sorry for the witch's daughter? It was not her fault that her mother was a witch.

Towards evening the good man's daughter thought it was time to go home; but as she went, her ring caught on the latch of the door, for the King's son had had it smeared with tar. She did not take time to pull it off, but, hastily unfastening her horse from the pillar, she rode away beyond the castle walls as swift as an arrow. Arrived at home, she took off her clothes by the birch tree, left her horse standing there, and hastened to her place behind the stove. In a short time the man and the woman came home again too, and the witch said to the girl:

"Ah! you poor thing, there you are to be sure! You don't know what fine times we have had at the palace! The King's son carried my daughter about, but the poor thing fell and broke her arm."

The girl knew well how matters really stood, but she pretended to know nothing about it, and sat dumb behind the stove.

The next day they were invited again to the King's banquet.

"Hey! old man," said the witch, "get on your clothes as quick as you can; we are bidden to the feast. Take you the child; I will give the other one work, lest she weary."

She kindled the fire, threw a potful of hemp seed among the ashes, and said to the girl:

"If you do not get this sorted, and all the seed back into the pot, I shall kill you!"

The girl wept bitterly; then she went to the birch tree, washed herself on one side of it and dried herself on the other; and this time still finer clothes were given to her, and a very beautiful steed. She broke off a branch of the birch tree, struck the hearth with it, so that the seeds flew into the pot, and then hastened to the castle.

Again the King's son came out to meet her, tied her horse to a pillar, and led her into the banqueting hall. At the feast the girl sat next him in the place of honour, as she had done the day before. But the witch's daughter gnawed bones under the table, and the Prince gave her a push by mistake, which broke her leg – he had never noticed her crawling about among the people's feet. She was VERY unlucky!

The good man's daughter hastened home again betimes, but the King's son had smeared the door-posts with tar, and the girl's golden circlet stuck to it. She had not time to look for it, but sprang to the saddle and rode like an arrow to the birch tree. There she left her horse and her fine clothes, and said to her mother:

"I have lost my circlet at the castle; the door-post was tarred, and it stuck fast."

"And even had you lost two of them," answered her mother, "I would give you finer ones."

Then the girl hastened home, and when her father came home from the feast with the witch, she was in her usual place behind the stove. Then the witch said to her:

"You poor thing! what is there to see here compared with what WE have seen at the palace? The King's son carried my daughter from one room to another; he let her fall, 'tis true, and my child's foot was broken.'

The man's daughter held her peace all the time, and busied herself about the hearth.

The night passed, and when the day began to dawn, the witch awakened her husband, crying:

"Hi! get up, old man! We are bidden to the royal banquet."

So the old man got up. Then the witch gave him the child, saying:

"Take you the little one; I will give the other girl work to do, else she will weary at home alone."

She did as usual. This time it was a dish of milk she poured upon the ashes, saying:

"If you do not get all the milk into the dish again before I come home, you will suffer for it."

How frightened the girl was this time! She ran to the birch tree, and by its magic power her task was accomplished; and then she rode away to the palace as before. When she got to the courtyard she found the Prince waiting for her. He led her into the hall, where she was highly honoured; but the witch's daughter sucked the bones under the table, and crouching at the people's feet she got an eye knocked out, poor thing! Now no one knew any more than before about the good man's daughter, no one knew whence she came; but the Prince had had the threshold smeared with tar, and as she fled her gold slippers stuck to it. She reached the birch tree, and laying aside her finery, she said:

"Alas I dear little mother, I have lost my gold slippers!"

"Let them be," was her mother's reply; "if you need them I shall give you finer ones."

Scarcely was she in her usual place behind the stove when her father came home with the witch. Immediately the witch began to mock her, saying:

"Ah! you poor thing, there is nothing for you to see here, and WE—ah: what great things we have seen at the palace! My little girl was carried about again, but had the ill-luck to fall and get her eye knocked out. You stupid thing, you, what do you know about anything?"

"Yes, indeed, what can I know?" replied the girl; "I had enough to do to get the hearth clean."

Now the Prince had kept all the things the girl had lost, and he soon set about finding the owner of them. For this purpose a great banquet was given on the fourth day, and all the people were invited to the palace. The witch got ready to go too. She tied a wooden beetle on where her child's foot should have been, a log of wood instead of an arm, and stuck a bit of dirt in the empty socket for an eye, and took the child with her to the castle. When all the people were gathered together, the King's son stepped in among the crowd and cried:

"The maiden whose finger this ring slips over, whose head this golden hoop encircles, and whose foot this shoe fits, shall be my bride."

What a great trying on there was now among them all! The things would fit no one, however.

"The cinder wench is not here," said the Prince at last; "go and fetch her, and let her try on the things."

So the girl was fetched, and the Prince was just going to hand the ornaments to her, when the witch held him back, saying:

"Don't give them to her; she soils everything with cinders; give them to my daughter rather."

Well, then the Prince gave the witch's daughter the ring, and the woman filed and pared away at her daughter's finger till the ring fitted. It was the same with the circlet and the shoes of gold. The witch would not allow them to be handed to the cinder wench; she worked at her own daughter's head and feet till she got the things forced on. What was to be done now? The Prince had to take the witch's daughter for his bride whether he would or no; he sneaked away to her father's house with her, however, for he was ashamed to hold the wedding festivities at the palace with so strange a bride. Some days passed, and at last he had to take his bride home to the palace, and he got ready to do so. Just as they were taking leave, the kitchen wench sprang down from her place by the stove, on the pretext of fetching something from the cowhouse, and in going by she whispered in the Prince's ear as he stood in the yard:

"Alas! dear Prince, do not rob me of my silver and my gold."

Thereupon the King's son recognised the cinder wench; so he took both the girls with him, and set out. After they had gone some little way they came to the bank of a river, and the Prince threw the witch's daughter across to serve as a bridge, and so got over with the cinder wench. There lay the witch's daughter then, like a bridge over the river, and could not stir, though her heart was consumed with grief. No help was near, so she cried at last in her anguish:

"May there grow a golden hemlock out of my body! perhaps my mother will know me by that token."

Scarcely had she spoken when a golden hemlock sprang up from her, and stood upon the bridge.

Now, as soon as the Prince had got rid of the witch's daughter he greeted the cinder wench as his bride, and they wandered together to the birch tree which grew upon the mother's grave. There they received all sorts of treasures and riches, three sacks full of gold, and as much silver, and a splendid steed, which bore them home to the palace. There they lived a long time together, and the young wife bore a son to the Prince. Immediately word was brought to the witch that her daughter had borne a son – for they all believed the young King's wife to be the witch's daughter.

"So, so," said the witch to herself; "I had better away with my gift for the infant, then."

And so saying she set out. Thus it happened that she came to the bank of the river, and there she saw the beautiful golden hemlock growing in the middle of the bridge, and when she began to cut it down to take to her grandchild, she heard a voice moaning:

"Alas! dear mother, do not cut me so!"

"Are you here?" demanded the witch.

"Indeed I am, dear little mother," answered the daughter "They threw me across the river to make a bridge of me."

In a moment the witch had the bridge shivered to atoms, and then she hastened away to the palace. Stepping up to the young Queen's bed, she began to try her magic arts upon her, saying:

"Spit, you wretch, on the blade of my knife; bewitch my knife's blade for me, and I shall change you into a reindeer of the forest."

"Are you there again to bring trouble upon me?" said the young woman.

She neither spat nor did anything else, but still the witch changed her into a reindeer, and smuggled her own daughter into her place as the Prince's wife. But now the child grew restless and cried, because it missed its mother's care. They took it to the court, and tried to pacify it in every conceivable way, but its crying never ceased.

"What makes the child so restless?" asked the Prince, and he went to a wise widow woman to ask her advice.

"Ay, ay, your own wife is not at home," said the widow woman; "she is living like a reindeer in the wood; you have the witch's daughter for a wife now, and the witch herself for a mother-in-law."

"Is there any way of getting my own wife back from the wood again?" asked the Prince.

"Give me the child," answered the widow woman. "I'll take it with me tomorrow when I go to drive the cows to the wood. I'll make a rustling among the birch leaves and a trembling among the aspens – perhaps the boy will grow quiet when he hears it."

"Yes, take the child away, take it to the wood with you to quiet it," said the Prince, and led the widow woman into the castle.

"How now? you are going to send the child away to the wood?" said the witch in a suspicious tone, and tried to interfere.

But the King's son stood firm by what he had commanded, and said:

"Carry the child about the wood; perhaps that will pacify it."

So the widow woman took the child to the wood. She came to the edge of a marsh, and seeing a herd of reindeer there, she began all at once to sing –

> "Little Bright-eyes, little Redskin,
> Come nurse the child you bore!
> That bloodthirsty monster,
> That man-eater grim,
> Shall nurse him, shall tend him no more.
> They may threaten and force as they will,
> He turns from her, shrinks from her still,"

and immediately the reindeer drew near, and nursed and tended the child the whole day long; but at nightfall it had to follow the herd, and said to the widow woman:

"Bring me the child tomorrow, and again the following day; after that I must wander with the herd far away to other lands."

The following morning the widow woman went back to the castle to fetch the child. The witch interfered, of course, but the Prince said:

"Take it, and carry it about in the open air; the boy is quieter at night, to be sure, when he has been in the wood all day."

So the widow took the child in her arms, and carried it to the marsh in the forest. There she sang as on the preceding day –

> *"Little Bright-eyes, little Redskin,*
> *Come nurse the child you bore!*
> *That bloodthirsty monster,*
> *That man-eater grim,*
> *Shall nurse him, shall tend him no more.*
> *They may threaten and force as they will,*
> *He turns from her, shrinks from her still,"*

and immediately the reindeer left the herd and came to the child, and tended it as on the day before. And so it was that the child throve, till not a finer boy was to be seen anywhere. But the King's son had been pondering over all these things, and he said to the widow woman:

"Is there no way of changing the reindeer into a human being again?"

"I don't rightly know," was her answer. "Come to the wood with me, however; when the woman puts off her reindeer skin I shall comb her head for her; whilst I am doing so you must burn the skin."

Thereupon they both went to the wood with the child; scarcely were they there when the reindeer appeared and nursed the child as before. Then the widow woman said to the reindeer:

"Since you are going far away tomorrow, and I shall not see you again, let me comb your head for the last time, as a remembrance of you."

Good; the young woman stript off the reindeer skin, and let the widow woman do as she wished. In the meantime the King's son threw the reindeer skin into the fire unobserved.

"What smells of singeing here?" asked the young woman, and looking round she saw her own husband. "Woe is me! you have burnt my skin. Why did you do that?"

"To give you back your human form again."

"Alack-a-day! I have nothing to cover me now, poor creature that I am!" cried the young woman, and transformed herself first into a distaff, then into a wooden beetle, then into a spindle, and into all imaginable shapes. But all these shapes the King's son went on destroying till she stood before him in human form again.

"Alas! wherefore take me home with you again," cried the young woman, "since the witch is sure to eat me up?"

"She will not eat you up," answered her husband; and they started for home with the child.

But when the witch wife saw them she ran away with her daughter, and if she has not stopped she is running still, though at a great age. And the Prince, and his wife, and the baby lived happy ever afterwards.

KATIE WOODENCLOAK

Once on a time there was a King who had become a widower. By his Queen he had one daughter, who was so clever and lovely, there wasn't a cleverer or lovelier Princess in all the world. So the King went on a long time sorrowing for the Queen, whom he had loved so much, but at last he got weary of living alone, and married another Queen, who was a widow, and had, too, an only daughter; but this daughter was just as bad and ugly as the other was kind, and clever, and lovely, The stepmother and her daughter were jealous of the Princess, because she was so lovely; but so long as the King was at home, they daredn't do her any harm, he was so fond of her.

Well, after a time, he fell into war with another King, and went out to battle with his host, and then the stepmother thought she might do as she pleased; and so she both starved and beat the Princess, and was after her in every hole and corner of the house. At last she thought everything too good for her, and turned her out to herd cattle. So there she went about with the cattle, and herded them in the woods and on the fells. As for food, she got little or none, and she grew thin and wan, and was always sobbing and sorrowful. Now in the herd there was a great dun bull, which always kept himself so neat and sleek, and often and often he came up to the Princess, and let her pat him. So one day when she sat there, sad, and sobbing, and sorrowful, he came up to her and asked her outright why she was always in such grief. She answered nothing, but went on weeping.

"Ah!" said the Bull, "I know all about it quite well, though you won't tell me; you weep because the Queen is bad to you, and because she is ready to starve you to death. But food you've no need to fret about, for in my left ear lies a cloth, and when you take and spread it out, you may have as many dishes as you please."

So she did that, took the cloth and spread it out on the grass, and lo! it served up the nicest dishes one could wish to have; there was wine too, and mead, and sweet cake. Well, she soon got up her flesh again, and grew so plump, and rosy, and white, that the Queen and her scrawny chip of a daughter turned blue and yellow for spite. The Queen couldn't at all make out how her stepdaughter got to look so well on such bad fare, so she told one of her maids to go after her in the wood, and watch and see how it all was, for she thought some of the servants in the house must give her food. So the maid went after her, and watched in the wood, and then she saw how the stepdaughter took the cloth out of the Bull's ear, and spread it out, and how it served up the nicest dishes, which the stepdaughter ate and made good cheer over. All this the maid told the Queen when she went home.

And now the King came home from war, and had won the fight against the other king with whom he went out to battle. So there was great joy throughout the palace, and no one was gladder than the King's daughter. But the Queen shammed sick, and took to her bed, and paid the doctor a great fee to get him to say she could never be well again unless she had some of the Dun Bull's flesh to eat. Both the king's daughter and the folk in the palace asked the doctor if nothing else would help her, and prayed hard for the Bull, for every one was fond of him, and they all said there wasn't that Bull's match in all the land. But, no; he must and should be slaughtered, nothing else would do. When the king's daughter heard that, she got very sorrowful, and went down into the byre to the Bull. There, too, he stood and hung down his head, and looked so downcast that she began to weep over him.

"What are you weeping for?" asked the Bull.

So she told him how the King had come home again, and how the Queen had shammed sick and got the doctor to say she could never be well and sound again unless she got some of the Dun Bull's flesh to eat, and so now he was to be slaughtered.

"If they get me killed first", said the Bull, "they'll soon take your life too. Now, if you're of my mind, we'll just start off, and go away tonight."

Well, the Princess thought it bad, you may be sure, to go and leave her father, but she thought it still worse to be in the house with the Queen; and so she gave her word to the Bull to come to him.

At night, when all had gone to bed, the Princess stole down to the byre to the Bull, and so he took her on his back, and set off from the homestead as fast as ever he could. And when the folk got up at cockcrow next morning to slaughter the Bull, why, he was gone; and when the King got up and asked for his daughter, she was gone too. He sent out messengers on all sides to hunt for them, and gave them out in all the parish churches; but there was no one who had caught a glimpse of them. Meanwhile, the Bull went through many lands with the King's daughter on his back, and so one day they came to a great copper-wood, where both the trees, and branches, and leaves, and flowers, and everything, were nothing but copper.

But before they went into the wood, the Bull said to the King's daughter:

"Now, when we get into this wood, mind you take care not to touch even a leaf of it, else it's all over both with me and you, for here dwells a Troll with three heads who owns this wood."

No, bless her, she'd be sure to take care not to touch anything. Well, she was very careful, and leant this way and that to miss the boughs, and put them gently aside with her hands; but it was such a thick wood, 'twas scarce possible to get through; and so, with all her pains, somehow or other she tore off a leaf, which she held in her hand.

"AU! AU! what have you done now?" said the Bull; "there's nothing for it now but to fight for life or death; but mind you keep the leaf safe."

Soon after they got to the end of the wood, and a Troll with three heads came running up:

"Who is this that touches my wood?" said the Troll.

"It's just as much mine as yours", said the Bull.

"Ah!" roared the Troll, "we'll try a fall about that."

"As you choose", said the Bull.

So they rushed at one another, and fought; and the Bull he butted, and gored, and kicked with all his might and main; but the Troll gave him as good as he brought, and it lasted the whole day before the Bull got the mastery; and then he was so full of wounds, and so worn out, he could scarce lift a leg. Then they were forced to stay there a day to rest, and then the Bull bade the King's daughter to take the horn of ointment which hung at the Troll's belt, and rub him with it. Then he came to himself again, and the day after they trudged on again. So they travelled many, many days, until, after a long long time, they came to a silver wood, where both the trees, and branches, and leaves, and flowers, and everything, were silvern.

Before the Bull went into the wood, he said to the King's daughter:

"Now, when we get into this wood, for heaven's sake mind you take good care; you mustn't touch anything, and not pluck off so much as one leaf, else it is all over both with me and you; for here is a Troll with six heads who owns it, and him I don't think I should be able to master."

"No", said the King's daughter; "I'll take good care and not touch anything you don't wish me to touch."

But when they got into the wood, it was so close and thick, they could scarce get along. She was as careful as careful could be, and leant to this side and that to miss the boughs, and put them on one side with her hands, but every minute the branches struck her across the eyes, and in spite of all her pains, it so happened she tore off a leaf.

"AU! AU! what have you done now?" said the Bull. "There's nothing for it now but to fight for life and death, for this Troll has six heads, and is twice as strong as the other, but mind you keep the leaf safe, and don't lose it."

Just as he said that, up came the Troll:

"Who is this", he said, "that touches my wood?"

"It's as much mine as yours", said the Bull.

"That we'll try a fall about", roared the Troll.

"As you choose", said the Bull, and rushed at the Troll, and gored out his eyes, and drove his horns right through his body, so that the entrails gushed out; but the Troll was almost a match for him, and it lasted three whole days before the Bull got the life gored out of him. But then he, too, was so weak and wretched, it was as much as he could do to stir a limb, and so full of wounds, that the blood streamed from him. So he said to the King's daughter she must take the horn of ointment that hung at the Troll's belt, and rub him with it. Then she did that, and he came to himself; but they were forced to stay there a week to rest before the Bull had strength enough to go on.

At last they set off again, but the Bull was still poorly, and they went rather slowly at first. So, to spare time, the King's daughter said, as she was young and light of foot, she could very well walk, but she couldn't get leave to do that. No; she must seat herself up on his back again. So on they travelled through many lands a long time, and the King's daughter did not know in the least whither they went; but after a long, long time they came to a gold wood. It was so grand, the gold dropped from every twig, and all the trees, and boughs, and flowers, and leaves, were of pure gold. Here, too, the same thing happened as had happened in the silver wood and copper wood. The Bull told the King's daughter she mustn't touch it for anything, for there was a Troll with nine heads who owned it, and he was much bigger and stouter than both the others put together; and he didn't think he could get the better of him. No; she'd be sure to take heed not to touch it; that he might know very well. But when they got into the wood, it was far thicker and closer than the silver wood, and the deeper they went into it, the worse it got. The wood went on, getting thicker and thicker, and closer and closer; and at last she thought there was no way at all to get through it. She was in such an awful fright of plucking off anything, that she sat, and twisted, and turned herself this way and that, and hither and thither, to keep clear of the boughs, and she put them on one side with her hands; but every moment the branches struck her across the eyes, so that she couldn't see what she was clutching at; and lo! before she knew how it came about, she had a gold apple in her hand. Then she was so bitterly sorry, she burst into tears, and wanted to throw it away; but the Bull said, she must keep it safe and watch it well, and comforted her as well as he could; but he thought it would be a hard tussle, and he doubted how it would go.

Just then up came the Troll with the nine heads, and he was so ugly, the King's daughter scarcely dared to look at him.

"WHO IS THIS THAT TOUCHES MY WOOD?" he roared.

"It's just as much mine as yours", said the Bull.

"That we'll try a fall about", roared the Troll again.

"Just as you choose", said the Bull; and so they rushed at one another, and fought, and it was such a dreadful sight, the King's daughter was ready to swoon away. The Bull gored out the Troll's eyes, and drove his horns through and through his body, till the entrails came tumbling out; but the Troll fought bravely; and when the Bull got one head gored to death, the rest breathed life into it again, and so it lasted a whole week before the Bull was able to get the life out of them all. But then he was utterly worn out and wretched. He couldn't stir a foot, and his body was all one wound. He couldn't so much as ask the King's daughter to take the horn of ointment which hung at the Troll's belt, and rub it over him. But she did it all the same, and then he came to himself by little and little; but they had to lie there and rest three weeks before he was fit to go on again.

Then they set off at a snail's pace, for the Bull said they had still a little further to go, and so they crossed over many high hills and thick woods. So after awhile they got upon the fells.

"Do you see anything?" asked the Bull.

"No, I see nothing but the sky, and the wild fell", said the King's daughter.

So when they clomb higher up, the fell got smoother, and they could see further off.

"Do you see anything now?" asked the Bull.

"Yes, I see a little castle far, far away", said the Princess.

"That's not so little though", said the Bull.

After a long, long time, they came to a great cairn, where there was a spur of the fell that stood sheer across the way.

"Do you see anything now?" asked the Bull.

"Yes, now I see the castle close by", said the King's daughter, "and now it is much, much bigger."

"Thither you're to go", said the Bull. "Right underneath the castle is a pig-sty, where you are to dwell. When you come thither you'll find a wooden cloak, all made of strips of lath; that you must put on, and go up to the castle and say your name is 'Katie Woodencloak', and ask for a place. But before you go, you must take your penknife and cut my head off, and then you must flay me, and roll up the hide, and lay it under the wall of rock yonder, and under the hide you must lay the copper leaf, and the silver leaf, and the golden apple. Yonder, up against the rock, stands a stick; and when you want anything, you've only got to knock on the wall of rock with that stick."

At first she wouldn't do anything of the kind; but when the Bull said it was the only thanks he would have for what he had done for her, she couldn't help herself. So, however much it grieved her heart, she hacked and cut away with her knife at the big beast till she got both his head and his hide off, and then she laid the hide up under the wall of rock, and put the copper leaf, and the silvern leaf, and the golden apple inside it.

So when she had done that, she went over to the pig-sty, but all the while she went she sobbed and wept. There she put on the wooden cloak, and so went up to the palace. When she came into the kitchen she begged for a place, and told them her name was Katie Woodencloak. Yes, the cook said she might have a place – she might have leave to be there in the scullery, and wash up, for the lassie who did that work before had just gone away.

"But as soon as you get weary of being here, you'll go your way too, I'll be bound."

No; she was sure she wouldn't do that.

So there she was, behaving so well, and washing up so handily. The Sunday after there were to be strange guests at the palace, so Katie asked if she might have leave to carry up water for the Prince's bath; but all the rest laughed at her, and said:

"What should you do there? Do you think the Prince will care to look at you, you who are such a fright!"

But she wouldn't give it up, and kept on begging and praying; and at last she got leave. So when she went up the stairs, her wooden cloak made such a clatter, the Prince came out and asked:

"Pray who are you?"

"Oh! I was just going to bring up water for your Royal Highness's bath", said Katie.

"Do you think now", said the Prince, "I'd have anything to do with the water you bring?" and with that he threw the water over her.

So she had to put up with that, but then she asked leave to go to church; well, she got that leave too, for the church lay close by. But, first of all, she went to the rock, and knocked on its face with the stick which stood there, just as the Bull had said. And straightway out came a man, who said:

"What's your will?"

So the Princess said she had got leave to go to church and hear the priest preach, but she had no clothes to go in. So he brought out a kirtle, which was as bright as the copper wood, and she got a horse and saddle beside. Now, when she got to the church she was so lovely and grand, all wondered who she could be, and scarce one of them listened to what the priest said, for they looked too much at her. As for the Prince, he fell so deep in love with her, he didn't take his eyes off her for a single moment.

So, as she went out of church, the Prince ran after her, and held the church door open for her; and so he got hold of one of her gloves, which was caught in the door. When she went away and mounted her horse, the Prince went up to her again, and asked whence she came.

"Oh! I'm from Bath", said Katie; and while the Prince took out the glove to give it to her, she said:

> Bright before and dark behind,
> Clouds come rolling on the wind;
> That this Prince may never see
> Where my good steed goes with me.

The Prince had never seen the like of that glove, and went about far and wide asking after the land whence the proud lady, who rode off without her glove, said she came; but there was no one who could tell where "Bath" lay.

Next Sunday some one had to go up to the Prince with a towel.

"Oh! may I have leave to go up with it?" said Katie.

"What's the good of your going?" said the others; "you saw how it fared with you last time."

But Katie wouldn't give in; she kept on begging and praying, till she got leave; and then she ran up the stairs, so that her wooden cloak made a great clatter. Out came the Prince, and when he saw it was Katie, he tore the towel out of her hand, and threw it into her face.

"Pack yourself off, you ugly Troll", he cried; "do you think I'd have a towel which you have touched with your smutty fingers?"

After that the Prince set off to church, and Katie begged for leave to go too. They all asked what business she had at church – she who had nothing to put on but that wooden cloak, which was so black and ugly. But Katie said the priest was such a brave man to preach, what he said did her so much good; and so she at last got leave. Now she went again to the rock and knocked, and so out came the man, and gave her a kirtle far finer than the first one; it was all covered with silver, and it shone like the silver wood; and she got besides a noble steed, with a saddle-cloth broidered with silver, and a silver bit.

So when the King's daughter got to the church, the folk were still standing about in the churchyard. And all wondered and wondered who she could be, and the Prince was soon on the spot, and came and wished to hold her horse for her while she got off. But she jumped down, and said there was no need, for her horse was so well broke, it stood still when she bid it, and came when she called it. So they all went into church; but there was scarce a soul that listened to what the priest said, for they looked at her a deal too much; and the Prince fell still deeper in love than the first time.

When the sermon was over, and she went out of church and was going to mount her horse, up came the Prince again, and asked her whence she came.

"Oh! I'm from Towelland", said the King's daughter; and as she said that, she dropped her riding-whip, and when the Prince stooped to pick it up, she said:

> Bright before and dark behind,
> Clouds come rolling on the wind;
> That this Prince may never see
> Where my good steed goes with me.

So away she was again; and the Prince couldn't tell what had become of her. He went about far and wide asking after the land whence she said she came, but there was no one who could tell him where it lay; and so the Prince had to make the best he could of it.

Next Sunday some one had to go up to the Prince with a comb. Katie begged for leave to go up with it, but the others put her in mind how she had fared the last time, and scolded her for wishing to go before the Prince – such a black and ugly fright as she was in her wooden cloak. But she wouldn't leave off asking till they let her go up to the Prince with his comb. So, when she came clattering up the stairs again, out came the Prince, and took the comb, and threw it at her, and bade her be off as fast as she could. After that the Prince went to church, and Katie begged for leave to go too. They asked again what business she had there, she who was so foul and black, and who had no clothes to show herself in. Might be the Prince or some one else would see her, and then both she and all the others would smart for it; but Katie said they had something else to do than to look at her; and she wouldn't leave off begging and praying till they gave her leave to go.

So the same thing happened now as had happened twice before. She went to the rock and knocked with the stick, and then the man came out and gave her a kirtle which was far grander than either of the others. It was almost all pure gold, and studded with diamonds; and she got besides a noble steed, with a gold broidered saddle-cloth and a golden bit.

Now when the King's daughter got to the church, there stood the priest and all the people in the churchyard waiting for her. Up came the Prince running, and wanted to hold her horse, but she jumped off, and said:

"No; thanks – there's no need, for my horse is so well broke, it stands still when I bid him."

So they all hastened into church, and the priest got into the pulpit, but no one listened to a word he said; for they all looked too much at her, and wondered whence she came; and the Prince, he was far deeper in love than either of the former times. He had no eyes, or ears, or sense for anything, but just to sit and stare at her.

So when the sermon was over, and the King's daughter was to go out of the church, the Prince had got a firkin of pitch poured out in the porch, that he might come and help her over it; but she didn't care a bit – she just put her foot right down into the midst of the pitch, and jumped across it; but then one of her golden shoes stuck fast in it, and as she got on her horse, up came the Prince running out of the church, and asked whence she came.

"I'm from Combland", said Katie. But when the Prince wanted to reach her the gold shoe, she said,

> *Bright before and dark behind,*
> *Clouds come rolling on the wind;*
> *That this Prince may never see*
> *Where my good steed goes with me.*

So the Prince couldn't tell still what had become of her, and he went about a weary time all over the world asking for "Combland"; but when no one could tell him where it lay, he ordered it to be given out everywhere that he would wed the woman whose foot could fit the gold shoe.

So many came of all sorts from all sides, fair and ugly alike; but there was no one who had so small a foot as to be able to get on the gold shoe. And after a long, long time, who should come but Katie's wicked stepmother, and her daughter, too, and her the gold shoe fitted; but ugly she was, and so loathly she looked, the Prince only kept his word sore against his will. Still they got ready the wedding-feast, and she was dressed up and decked out as a bride; but as they rode to church, a little bird sat upon a tree and sang:

> *A bit off her heel,*
> *And a bit off her toe;*
> *Katie Woodencloak's tiny shoe*
> *Is full of blood – that's all I know.*

And, sure enough, when they looked to it the bird told the truth, for blood gushed out of the shoe.

Then all the maids and women who were about the palace had to go up to try on the shoe, but there was none of them whom it would fit at all.

"But where's Katie Woodencloak?" asked the Prince, when all the rest had tried the shoe, for he understood the song of birds very well, and bore in mind what the little bird had said.

"Oh! she think of that!" said the rest; "it's no good her coming forward. Why, she's legs like a horse."

"Very true, I daresay", said the Prince; "but since all the others have tried, Katie may as well try too."

"Katie", he bawled out through the door; and Katie came trampling upstairs, and her wooden cloak clattered as if a whole regiment of dragoons were charging up.

"Now, you must try the shoe on, and be a Princess, you too," said the other maids, and laughed and made game of her.

So Katie took up the shoe, and put her foot into it like nothing, and threw off her wooden cloak; and so there she stood in her gold kirtle, and it shone so that the sunbeams glistened from her; and, lo! on her other foot she had the fellow to the gold shoe.

So when the Prince knew her again, he grew so glad, he ran up to her and threw his arms round her, and gave her a kiss; and when he heard she was a King's daughter, he got gladder still, and then came the wedding feast; and so,

Snip, snip, snover,
This story's over.

MOTHER HOLLE

There was once a widow who had two daughters – one of whom was pretty and industrious, whilst the other was ugly and idle. But she was much fonder of the ugly and idle one, because she was her own daughter; and the other, who was a step-daughter, was obliged to do all the work, and be the Cinderella of the house. Every day the poor girl had to sit by a well, in the highway, and spin and spin till her fingers bled.

Now it happened that one day the shuttle was marked with her blood, so she dipped it in the well, to wash the mark off; but it dropped out of her hand and fell to the bottom. She began to weep, and ran to her step-mother and told her of the mishap. But she scolded her sharply, and was so merciless as to say, "Since you have let the shuttle fall in, you must fetch it out again."

So the girl went back to the well, and did not know what to do; and in the sorrow of her heart she jumped into the well to get the shuttle. She lost her senses; and when she awoke and came to herself again, she was in a lovely meadow where the sun was shining and many thousands of flowers were growing. Along this meadow she went, and at last came to a baker's oven full of bread, and the bread cried out, "Oh, take me out! take me out! or I shall burn; I have been baked a long time!" So she went up to it, and took out all the loaves one after another with the bread-shovel. After that she went on till she came to a tree covered with apples, which called out to her, "Oh, shake me! shake me! we apples are all ripe!" So she shook the tree till the apples fell like rain, and went on shaking till they were all down, and when she had gathered them into a heap, she went on her way.

At last she came to a little house, out of which an old woman peeped; but she had such large teeth that the girl was frightened, and was about to run away.

But the old woman called out to her, "What are you afraid of, dear child? Stay with me; if you will do all the work in the house properly, you shall be the better for it. Only you must take care to make my bed well, and shake it thoroughly till the feathers fly – for then there is snow on the earth. I am Mother Holle.

As the old woman spoke so kindly to her, the girl took courage and agreed to enter her service. She attended to everything to the satisfaction of her mistress, and always shook her bed so vigorously that the feathers flew about like snow-flakes. So she had a pleasant life with her; never an angry word; and boiled or roast meat every day.

She stayed some time with Mother Holle, and then she became sad. At first she did not know what was the matter with her, but found at length that it was home-sickness: although she was many thousand times better off here than at home, still she had a longing to be there. At last she said to the old woman, "I have a longing for home; and however well off I am down here, I cannot stay any longer; I must go up again to my own people." Mother Holle said, "I am pleased that you long for your home again, and as you have served me so truly, I myself will take you up again." Thereupon she took her by the hand, and led her to a large door. The door was opened, and just as the maiden was standing beneath the doorway, a heavy shower of golden rain fell, and all the gold remained sticking to her, so that she was completely covered over with it.

"You shall have that because you have been so industrious," said Mother Holle, and at the same time she gave her back the shuttle which she had let fall into the well. Thereupon the door closed, and the maiden found herself up above upon the earth, not far from her mother's house.

And as she went into the yard the cock was standing by the well-side, and cried –

> *"Cock-a-doodle-doo!*
> *Your golden girl's come back to you!"*

So she went in to her mother, and as she arrived thus covered with gold, she was well received, both by her and her sister.

The girl told all that had happened to her; and as soon as the mother heard how she had come by so much wealth, she was very anxious to obtain the same good luck for the ugly and lazy daughter. She had to seat herself by the well and spin; and in order that her shuttle might be stained with blood, she stuck her hand into a thorn bush and pricked her finger. Then she threw her shuttle into the well, and jumped in after it.

She came, like the other, to the beautiful meadow and walked along the very same path. When she got to the oven the bread again cried, "Oh, take me out! take me out! or I shall burn; I have been baked a long time!" But the lazy thing answered, "As if I had any wish to make myself dirty?" and on she went. Soon she came to the apple tree, which cried, "Oh, shake me! shake me! we apples are all ripe!" But she answered, "I like that! one of you might fall on my head," and so went on.

When she came to Mother Holle's house she was not afraid, for she had already heard of her big teeth, and she hired herself to her immediately.

The first day she forced herself to work diligently, and obeyed Mother Holle when she told her to do anything, for she was thinking of all the gold that she would give her. But on the second day she began to be lazy, and on the third day still more so, and then she would not get up in the morning at all. Neither did she make Mother Holle's bed as she ought, and did not shake it so as to make the feathers fly up. Mother Holle was soon tired of this, and gave her notice to leave. The lazy girl was willing enough to go, and thought that now the golden rain would come. Mother Holle led her also to the great door; but while she was standing beneath it, instead of the gold a big kettleful of pitch was emptied over her. "That is the reward for your service," said Mother Holle, and shut the door.

So the lazy girl went home; but she was quite covered with pitch, and the cock by the well-side, as soon as he saw her, cried out –

> "Cock-a-doodle-doo!
> Your pitchy girl's come back to you!"

But the pitch stuck fast to her, and could not be got off as long as she lived.

EAST OF THE SUN AND WEST OF THE MOON

Once on a time there was a poor husbandman who had so many children that he hadn't much of either food or clothing to give them. Pretty children they all were, but the prettiest was the youngest daughter, who was so lovely there was no end to her loveliness.

So one day, 'twas on a Thursday evening late at the fall of the year, the weather was so wild and rough outside, and it was so cruelly dark, and rain fell and wind blew, till the walls of the cottage shook again. There they all sat round the fire, busy with this thing and that. But just then, all at once something gave three taps on the window-pane. Then the father went out to see what was the matter; and, when he got out of doors, what should he see but a great big White Bear.

"Good-evening to you!" said the White Bear.

"The same to you!" said the man.

"Will you give me your youngest daughter? If you will, I'll make you as rich as you are now poor," said the Bear.

Well, the man would not be at all sorry to be so rich; but still he thought he must have a bit of a talk with his daughter first; so he went in and told them how there was a great White Bear waiting outside, who had given his word to make them so rich if he could only have the youngest daughter.

The lassie said "No!" outright. Nothing could get her to say anything else; so the man went out and settled it with the White Bear that he should come again the next Thursday evening and get an answer. Meantime he talked his daughter over, and kept on telling her of all the riches they would get, and how well off she would be herself; and so at last she thought better of it, and washed and mended her rags, made herself as smart as she could, and was ready to start. I can't say her packing gave her much trouble.

Next Thursday evening came the White Bear to fetch her, and she got upon his back with her bundle, and off they went. So, when they had gone a bit of the way, the White Bear said:

"Are you afraid?"

"No," she wasn't.

"Well! mind and hold tight by my shaggy coat, and then there's nothing to fear," said the Bear.

So she rode a long, long way, till they came to a great steep hill. There, on the face of it, the White Bear gave a knock, and a door opened, and they came into a castle where there were many rooms all lit up; rooms gleaming with silver and gold; and there, too, was a table ready laid, and it was all as grand as grand could be. Then the White Bear gave her a silver bell; and when she wanted anything, she was only to ring it, and she would get it at once.

Well, after she had eaten and drunk, and evening wore on, she got sleepy after her journey, and thought she would like to go to bed, so she rang the bell; and she had scarce taken hold of it before she came into a chamber where there was a bed made, as fair and white as any one would wish to sleep in, with silken pillows and curtains and gold fringe. All that was in the room was gold or silver; but when she had gone to bed and put out the light, a man came and laid himself alongside her. That was the White Bear, who threw off his beast shape at night; but she never saw him, for he always came after she had put out the light, and before the day dawned he was up and off again. So things went on happily for a while, but at last she began to get silent and sorrowful; for there she went about all day alone, and she longed to go home to see her father and mother and brothers and sisters. So one day, when the White Bear asked what it was that she lacked, she said it was so dull and lonely there, and how she longed to go home to see her father and mother and brothers and sisters, and that was why she was so sad and sorrowful, because she couldn't get to them.

"Well, well!" said the Bear, "perhaps there's a cure for all this; but you must promise me one thing, not to talk alone with your mother, but only when the rest are by to hear; for she'll take you by the hand and try to lead you into a room alone to talk; but you must mind and not do that, else you'll bring bad luck on both of us."

So one Sunday the White Bear came and said, now they could set off to see her father and mother. Well, off they started, she sitting on his back; and they went far and long. At last they came to a grand house, and there her brothers and sisters were running about out of doors at play, and everything was so pretty, 'twas a joy to see.

"This is where your father and mother live now," said the White Bear; "but don't forget what I told you, else you'll make us both unlucky."

"No! bless her, she'd not forget;" – and when she had reached the house, the White Bear turned right about and left her.

Then, when she went in to see her father and mother, there was such joy, there was no end to it. None of them thought they could thank her enough for all she had done for them. Now, they had everything they wished, as good as good could be, and they all wanted to know how she got on where she lived.

Well, she said, it was very good to live where she did; she had all she wished. What she said beside I don't know, but I don't think any of them had the right end of the stick, or that they got much out of her. But so, in the afternoon, after they had done dinner, all happened as the White Bear had said. Her mother wanted to talk with her alone in her bedroom; but she minded what the White Bear had said, and wouldn't go upstairs.

"Oh! what we have to talk about will keep!" she said, and put her mother off. But, somehow or other, her mother got round her at last, and she had to tell her the whole story. So she said, how every night when she had gone to bed a man came and lay down beside her as soon as she had put out the light; and how she never saw him, because he was always up and away before the morning dawned; and how she went about woeful and sorrowing, for she thought she should so like to see him; and how all day long she walked about there alone; and how dull and dreary and lonesome it was.

"My!" said her mother; "it may well be a Troll you slept with! But now I'll teach you a lesson how to set eyes on him. I'll give you a bit of candle, which you can carry home in your bosom; just light that while he is asleep, but take care not to drop the tallow on him."

Yes! she took the candle and hid it in her bosom, and as night drew on, the White Bear came and fetched her away.

But when they had gone a bit of the way, the White Bear asked if all hadn't happened as he had said.

"Well, she couldn't say it hadn't."

"Now, mind," said he, "if you have listened to your mother's advice, you have brought bad luck on us both, and then, all that has passed between us will be as nothing."

"No," she said, "she hadn't listened to her mother's advice."

So when she reached home, and had gone to bed, it was the old story over again. There came a man and lay down beside her; but at dead of night, when she heard he slept, she got up and struck a light, lit the candle, and let the light shine on him, and so she saw that he was the loveliest Prince one ever set eyes on, and she fell so deep in love with him on the spot, that she thought she couldn't live if she didn't give him a kiss there and then. And so she did; but as she kissed him, she dropped three hot drops of tallow on his shirt, and he woke up.

"What have you done?" he cried; "now you have made us both unlucky, for had you held out only this one year, I had been freed. For I have a step-mother who has bewitched me, so that I am a White Bear by day, and a Man by night. But now all ties are snapt between us; now I must set off from you to her. She lives in a Castle which stands East of the Sun and West of the Moon, and there, too, is a Princess, with a nose three ells long, and she's the wife I must have now."

She wept and took it ill, but there was no help for it; go he must.

Then she asked if she mightn't go with him.

No, she mightn't.

"Tell me the way, then," she said, "and I'll search you out; that surely I may get leave to do."

"Yes," she might do that, he said; "but there was no way to that place. It lay East of the Sun and West of the Moon, and thither she'd never find her way."

So next morning, when she woke up, both Prince and castle were gone, and then she lay on a little green patch, in the midst of the gloomy thick wood, and by her side lay the same bundle of rags she had brought with her from her old home.

So when she had rubbed the sleep out of her eyes, and wept till she was tired, she set out on her way, and walked many, many days, till she came to a lofty crag. Under it sat an old hag, and played with a gold apple which she tossed about. Here the lassie asked if she knew the way to the Prince, who lived with his step-mother in the Castle, that lay East of the Sun and West of the Moon, and who was to marry the Princess with a nose three ells long.

"How did you come to know about him?" asked the old hag; "but maybe you are the lassie who ought to have had him?"

Yes, she was.

"So, so; it's you, is it?" said the old hag. "Well, all I know about him is, that he lives in the castle that lies East of the Sun and West of the Moon, and thither you'll come, late or never; but still you may have the loan of my horse, and on him you can ride to my next neighbour. Maybe she'll be able to tell you; and when you get there, just give the horse a switch under the left ear, and beg him to be off home; and, stay, this gold apple you may take with you."

So she got upon the horse, and rode a long, long time, till she came to another crag, under which sat another old hag, with a gold carding-comb. Here the lassie asked if she knew the way to the castle that lay East of the Sun and West of the Moon, and she answered, like the first old hag, that she knew nothing about it, except it was east of the sun and west of the moon.

"And thither you'll come, late or never, but you shall have the loan of my horse to my next neighbour; maybe she'll tell you all about it; and when you get there, just switch the horse under the left ear, and beg him to be off home."

And this old hag gave her the golden carding-comb; it might be she'd find some use for it, she said. So the lassie got up on the horse, and rode a far, far way, and a weary time; and so at last she came to another great crag, under which sat another old hag, spinning with a golden spinning-wheel. Her, too, she asked if she knew the way to the Prince, and where the castle was that lay East of the Sun and West of the Moon. So it was the same thing over again.

"Maybe it's you who ought to have had the Prince?" said the old hag.

Yes, it was.

But she, too, didn't know the way a bit better than the other two. "East of the sun and west of the moon it was," she knew – that was all.

"And thither you'll come, late or never; but I'll lend you my horse, and then I think you'd best ride to the East Wind and ask him; maybe he knows those parts, and can blow you thither. But when you get to him, you need only give the horse a switch under the left ear, and he'll trot home of himself."

And so, too, she gave her the gold spinning-wheel. "Maybe you'll find a use for it," said the old hag.

Then on she rode many many days, a weary time, before she got to the East Wind's house, but at last she did reach it, and then she asked the East Wind if he could tell her the way to the Prince who dwelt east of the sun and west of the moon. Yes, the East Wind had often heard tell of it, the Prince and the castle, but he couldn't tell the way, for he had never blown so far.

"But, if you will, I'll go with you to my brother the West Wind, maybe he knows, for he's much stronger. So, if you will just get on my back, I'll carry you thither."

Yes, she got on his back, and I should just think they went briskly along.

So when they got there, they went into the West Wind's house, and the East Wind said the lassie he had brought was the one who ought to have had the Prince who lived in the castle East of the Sun and West of the Moon; and so she had set out to seek him, and how he had come with her, and would be glad to know if the West Wind knew how to get to the castle.

"Nay," said the West Wind, "so far I've never blown; but if you will, I'll go with you to our brother the South Wind, for he's much stronger than either of us, and he has flapped his wings far and wide. Maybe he'll tell you. You can get on my back, and I'll carry you to him."

Yes! she got on his back, and so they travelled to the South Wind, and weren't so very long on the way, I should think.

When they got there, the West Wind asked him if he could tell her the way to the castle that lay East of the Sun and West of the Moon, for it was she who ought to have had the Prince who lived there.

"You don't say so! That's she, is it?" said the South Wind.

"Well, I have blustered about in most places in my time, but so far have I never blown; but if you will, I'll take you to my brother the North Wind; he is the oldest and strongest of the whole lot of us, and if he don't know where it is, you'll never find any one in the world to tell you. You can get on my back, and I'll carry you thither."

Yes! she got on his back, and away he went from his house at a fine rate. And this time, too, she wasn't long on her way.

So when they got to the North Wind's house, he was so wild and cross, cold puffs came from him a long way off.

"BLAST YOU BOTH, WHAT DO YOU WANT?" he roared out to them ever so far off, so that it struck them with an icy shiver.

"Well," said the South Wind, "you needn't be so foul-mouthed, for here I am, your brother, the South Wind, and here is the lassie who ought to have had the Prince who dwells in the castle that lies East of the Sun and West of the Moon, and now she wants to ask you if you ever were there, and can tell her the way, for she would be so glad to find him again."

"YES, I KNOW WELL ENOUGH WHERE IT IS," said the North Wind; "once in my life I blew an aspen-leaf thither, but, I was so tired I couldn't blow a puff for ever so many days, after. But if you really wish to go thither, and aren't afraid to come along with me, I'll take you on my back and see if I can blow you thither."

Yes! with all her heart; she must and would get thither if it were possible in any way; and as for fear, however madly he went, she wouldn't be at all afraid.

"Very well, then," said the North Wind, "but you must sleep here tonight, for we must have the whole day before us, if we're to get thither at all."

Early next morning the North Wind woke her, and puffed himself up, and blew himself out, and made himself so stout and big, 'twas gruesome to look at him; and so off they went high up through the air, as if they would never stop till they got to the world's end.

Down here below there was such a storm; it threw down long tracts of wood and many houses, and when it swept over the great sea, ships foundered by hundreds.

So they tore on and on – no one can believe how far they went – and all the while they still went over the sea, and the North Wind got more and more weary, and so out of breath he could scarce bring out a puff, and his wings drooped and drooped, till at last he sunk so low that the crests of the waves dashed over his heels.

"Are you afraid?" said the North Wind.

"No!" she wasn't.

But they weren't very far from land; and the North Wind had still so much strength left in him that he managed to throw her up on the shore under the windows of the castle which lay East of the Sun and West of the Moon; but then he was so weak and worn out, he had to stay there and rest many days before he could get home again.

Next morning the lassie sat down under the castle window, and began to play with the gold apple; and the first person she saw was the Long-nose who was to have the Prince.

"What do you want for your gold apple, you lassie?" said the Long-nose, and threw up the window.

"It's not for sale, for gold or money," said the lassie.

"If it's not for sale for gold or money, what is it that you will sell it for? You may name your own price," said the Princess.

"Well! if I may get to the Prince, who lives here, and be with him tonight, you shall have it," said the lassie whom the North Wind had brought.

Yes! she might; that could be done. So the Princess got the gold apple; but when the lassie came up to the Prince's bed-room at night he was fast asleep; she called him and shook him, and between whiles she wept sore; but all she could do she couldn't wake him up. Next morning, as soon as day broke, came the Princess with the long nose, and drove her out again.

So in the daytime she sat down under the castle windows and began to card with her carding-comb, and the same thing happened. The Princess asked what she wanted for it; and she said it wasn't for sale for gold or money, but if she might get leave to go up to the Prince and be with him that night, the Princess should have it. But when she went up she found him fast asleep again, and all she called, and all she shook, and wept, and prayed, she couldn't get life into him; and as soon as the first gray peep of day came, then came the Princess with the long nose, and chased her out again.

So, in the daytime, the lassie sat down outside under the castle window, and began to spin with her golden spinning-wheel, and that, too, the Princess with the long nose wanted to have. So she threw up the window and asked what she wanted for it. The lassie said, as she had said twice before, it wasn't for sale for gold or money; but if she might go up to the Prince who was there, and be with him alone that night, she might have it.

Yes! she might do that and welcome. But now you must know there were some Christian folk who had been carried off thither, and as they sat in their room, which was next the Prince, they had heard how a woman had been in there, and wept and prayed, and called to him two nights running, and they told that to the Prince.

That evening, when the Princess came with her sleepy drink, the Prince made as if he drank, but threw it over his shoulder, for he could guess it was a sleepy drink. So, when the lassie came in, she found the Prince wide awake; and then she told him the whole story how she had come thither.

"Ah," said the Prince, "you've just come in the very nick of time, for tomorrow is to be our wedding-day; but now I won't have the Long-nose, and you are the only woman in the world who can set me free. I'll say I want to see what my wife is fit for, and beg her to wash the shirt which has the three spots of tallow on it; she'll say yes, for she doesn't know 'tis you who put them there; but that's a work only for Christian folk, and not for such a pack of Trolls, and so I'll say that I won't have any other for my bride than the woman who can wash them out, and ask you to do it."

So there was great joy and love between them all that night. But next day, when the wedding was to be, the Prince said:

"First of all, I'd like to see what my bride is fit for."

"Yes!" said the step-mother, with all her heart.

"Well," said the Prince, "I've got a fine shirt which I'd like for my wedding shirt, but somehow or other it has got three spots of tallow on it, which I must have washed out; and I have sworn never to take any other bride than the woman who's able to do that. If she can't, she's not worth having."

Well, that was no great thing they said, so they agreed, and she with the long-nose began to wash away as hard as she could, but the more she rubbed and scrubbed, the bigger the spots grew.

"Ah!" said the old hag, her mother, "you can't wash; let me try."

But she hadn't long taken the shirt in hand before it got far worse than ever, and with all her rubbing, and wringing, and scrubbing, the spots grew bigger and blacker, and the darker and uglier was the shirt.

Then all the other Trolls began to wash, but the longer it lasted, the blacker and uglier the shirt grew, till at last it was as black all over as if it had been up the chimney.

"Ah!" said the Prince, "you're none of you worth a straw; you can't wash. Why there, outside, sits a beggar lassie, I'll be bound she knows how to wash better than the whole lot of you. COME IN, LASSIE!" he shouted.

Well, in she came.

"Can you wash this shirt clean, lassie you?" said he.

"I don't know," she said, "but I think I can."

And almost before she had taken it and dipped it in the water, it was as white as driven snow, and whiter still.

"Yes; you are the lassie for me," said the Prince.

At that the old hag flew into such a rage, she burst on the spot, and the Princess with the long nose after her, and the whole pack of Trolls after her – at least I've never heard a word about them since.

As for the Prince and Princess, they set free all the poor Christian folk who had been carried off and shut up there; and they took with them all the silver and gold, and flitted away as far as they could from the Castle that lay East of the Sun and West of the Moon.

THE EMPEROR'S NEW SUIT

Many, **many** years ago lived an emperor, who thought so much of new clothes that he spent all his money in order to obtain them; his only ambition was to be always well dressed. He did not care for his soldiers, and the theatre did not amuse him; the only thing, in fact, he thought anything of was to drive out and show a new suit of clothes. He had a coat for every hour of the day; and as one would say of a king "He is in his cabinet," so one could say of him, "The emperor is in his dressing-room."

The great city where he resided was very gay; every day many strangers from all parts of the globe arrived. One day two swindlers came to this city; they made people believe that they were weavers, and declared they could manufacture the finest cloth to be imagined. Their colours and patterns, they said, were not only exceptionally beautiful, but the clothes made of their material possessed the wonderful quality of being invisible to any man who was unfit for his office or unpardonably stupid.

"That must be wonderful cloth," thought the emperor. "If I were to be dressed in a suit made of this cloth I should be able to find out which men in my empire were unfit for their places, and I could distinguish the clever from the stupid. I must have this cloth woven for me without delay." And he gave a large sum of money to the swindlers, in advance, that they should set to work without any loss of time. They set up two looms, and pretended to be very hard at work, but they did nothing whatever on the looms. They asked for the finest silk and the most precious gold-cloth; all they got they did away with, and worked at the empty looms till late at night.

"I should very much like to know how they are getting on with the cloth," thought the emperor. But he felt rather uneasy when he remembered that he who was not fit for his office could not see it. Personally, he was of opinion that he had nothing to fear, yet he thought it advisable to send somebody else first to see how matters stood. Everybody in the town knew what a remarkable quality the stuff possessed, and all were anxious to see how bad or stupid their neighbours were.

"I shall send my honest old minister to the weavers," thought the emperor. "He can judge best how the stuff looks, for he is intelligent, and nobody understands his office better than he."

The good old minister went into the room where the swindlers sat before the empty looms. "Heaven preserve us!" he thought, and opened his eyes wide, "I cannot see anything at all," but he did not say so. Both swindlers requested him to come near, and asked him if he did not admire the exquisite pattern and the beautiful colours, pointing to the empty looms. The poor old minister tried his very best, but he could see nothing, for there was nothing to be seen. "Oh dear," he thought, "can I be so stupid? I should never have thought so, and nobody must know it! Is it possible that I am not fit for my office? No, no, I cannot say that I was unable to see the cloth."

"Now, have you got nothing to say?" said one of the swindlers, while he pretended to be busily weaving.

"Oh, it is very pretty, exceedingly beautiful," replied the old minister looking through his glasses. "What a beautiful pattern, what brilliant colours! I shall tell the emperor that I like the cloth very much."

"We are pleased to hear that," said the two weavers, and described to him the colours and explained the curious pattern. The old minister listened attentively, that he might relate to the emperor what they said; and so he did.

Now the swindlers asked for more money, silk and gold-cloth, which they required for weaving. They kept everything for themselves, and not a thread came near the loom, but they continued, as hitherto, to work at the empty looms.

Soon afterwards the emperor sent another honest courtier to the weavers to see how they were getting on, and if the cloth was nearly finished. Like the old minister, he looked and looked but could see nothing, as there was nothing to be seen.

"Is it not a beautiful piece of cloth?" asked the two swindlers, showing and explaining the magnificent pattern, which, however, did not exist.

"I am not stupid," said the man. "It is therefore my good appointment for which I am not fit. It is very strange, but I must not let any one know it;" and he praised the cloth, which he did not see, and expressed his joy at the beautiful colours and the fine pattern. "It is very excellent," he said to the emperor.

Everybody in the whole town talked about the precious cloth. At last the emperor wished to see it himself, while it was still on the loom. With a number of courtiers, including the two who had already been there, he went to the two clever swindlers, who now worked as hard as they could, but without using any thread.

"Is it not magnificent?" said the two old statesmen who had been there before. "Your Majesty must admire the colours and the pattern." And then they pointed to the empty looms, for they imagined the others could see the cloth.

"What is this?" thought the emperor, "I do not see anything at all. That is terrible! Am I stupid? Am I unfit to be emperor? That would indeed be the most dreadful thing that could happen to me."

"Really," he said, turning to the weavers, "your cloth has our most gracious approval;" and nodding contentedly he looked at the empty loom, for he did not like to say that he saw nothing. All his attendants, who were with him, looked and looked, and although they could not see anything more than the others, they said, like the emperor, "It is very beautiful." And all advised him to wear the new magnificent clothes at a great procession which was soon to take place. "It is magnificent, beautiful, excellent," one heard them say; everybody seemed to be delighted, and the emperor appointed the two swindlers "Imperial Court weavers."

The whole night previous to the day on which the procession was to take place, the swindlers pretended to work, and burned more than sixteen candles. People should see that they were busy to finish the emperor's new suit. They pretended to take the cloth from the loom, and worked about in the air with big scissors, and sewed with needles without thread, and said at last: "The emperor's new suit is ready now."

The emperor and all his barons then came to the hall; the swindlers held their arms up as if they held something in their hands and said: "These are the trousers!" "This is the coat!" and "Here is the cloak!" and so on. "They are all as light as a cobweb, and one must feel as if one had nothing at all upon the body; but that is just the beauty of them."

"Indeed!" said all the courtiers; but they could not see anything, for there was nothing to be seen.

"Does it please your Majesty now to graciously undress," said the swindlers, "that we may assist your Majesty in putting on the new suit before the large looking-glass?"

The emperor undressed, and the swindlers pretended to put the new suit upon him, one piece after another; and the emperor looked at himself in the glass from every side.

"How well they look! How well they fit!" said all. "What a beautiful pattern! What fine colours! That is a magnificent suit of clothes!"

The master of the ceremonies announced that the bearers of the canopy, which was to be carried in the procession, were ready.

"I am ready," said the emperor. "Does not my suit fit me marvellously?" Then he turned once more to the looking-glass, that people should think he admired his garments.

The chamberlains, who were to carry the train, stretched their hands to the ground as if they lifted up a train, and pretended to hold something in their hands; they did not like people to know that they could not see anything.

The emperor marched in the procession under the beautiful canopy, and all who saw him in the street and out of the windows exclaimed: "Indeed, the emperor's new suit is incomparable! What a long train he has! How well it fits him!" Nobody wished to let others know he saw nothing, for then he would have been unfit for his office or too stupid. Never emperor's clothes were more admired.

"But he has nothing on at all," said a little child at last. "Good heavens! listen to the voice of an innocent child," said the father, and one whispered to the other what the child had said. "But he has nothing on at all," cried at last the whole people. That made a deep impression upon the emperor, for it seemed to him that they were right; but he thought to himself, "Now I must bear up to the end." And the chamberlains walked with still greater dignity, as if they carried the train which did not exist.

THE MASTER-THIEF

One day an old man and his wife were sitting in front of a miserable house resting a while from their work. Suddenly a splendid carriage with four black horses came driving up, and a richly-dressed man descended from it. The peasant stood up, went to the great man, and asked what he wanted, and in what way he could be useful to him?

The stranger stretched out his hand to the old man, and said, "I want nothing but to enjoy for once a country dish; cook me some potatoes, in the way you always have them, and then I will sit down at your table and eat them with pleasure." The peasant smiled and said, "You are a count or a prince, or perhaps even a duke; noble gentlemen often have such fancies, but you shall have your wish." The wife went into the kitchen, and began to wash and rub the potatoes, and to make them into balls, as they are eaten by the country-folks. Whilst she was busy with this work, the peasant said to the stranger, "Come into my garden with me for a while, I have still something to do there." He had dug some holes in the garden, and now wanted to plant some trees in them. "Have you no children," asked the stranger, "who could help you with your work?" "No," answered the peasant, "I had a son, it is true, but it is long since he went out into the world. He was a ne'er-do-well; sharp, and knowing, but he would learn nothing and was full of bad tricks, at last he ran away from me, and since then I have heard nothing of him."

The old man took a young tree, put it in a hole, drove in a post beside it, and when he had shovelled in some earth and had trampled it firmly down, he tied the stem of the tree above, below, and in the middle, fast to the post by a rope of straw. "But tell me," said the stranger, "why you don't tie that crooked knotted tree, which is lying in the corner there, bent down almost to the ground, to a post also that it may grow straight, as well as these?" The old man smiled and said, "Sir, you speak according to your knowledge, it is easy to see that you are not familiar with gardening. That tree there is old, and misshapen, no one can make it straight now. Trees must be trained while they are young." "That is how it was with your son," said the stranger, "if you had trained him while he was still young, he would not have run away; now he too must have grown hard and misshapen." "Truly it is a long time since he went away," replied the old man, "he must have changed." "Would you know him again if he were to come to you?" asked the stranger. "Hardly by his face," replied the peasant, "but he has a mark about him, a birth-mark on his shoulder, that looks like a bean." When he had said that the stranger pulled off his coat, bared his shoulder, and showed the peasant the bean. "Good God!" cried the old man, "Thou art really my son!" and love for his child stirred in his heart. "But," he added, "how canst thou be my son, thou hast become a great lord and livest in wealth and luxury? How hast thou contrived to do that?" "Ah, father," answered the son, "the young tree was bound to no post and has grown crooked, now it is too old, it will never be straight again. How have I got all that? I have become a thief, but do not be alarmed, I am a master-thief. For me there are neither locks nor bolts, whatsoever I desire is mine. Do not imagine that I steal like a common thief, I only take some of the superfluity of the rich. Poor people are safe, I would rather give to them than take anything from them. It is the same with anything which I can have without trouble, cunning and dexterity I never touch it." "Alas, my son," said the father, "it still does not please me, a thief is still a thief, I tell thee it will end badly." He took him to his mother, and when she heard that was her son, she wept for joy, but when he told her that he had become a master-thief, two streams flowed down over her face. At length she said, "Even if he has become a thief, he is still my son, and my eyes have beheld him once more." They sat down to table, and once again he ate with his parents the wretched food which he had not eaten for so long. The father said, "If our Lord, the count up there in the castle, learns who thou art, and what trade thou followest, he will not take thee in his arms and cradle thee in them as he did when he held thee at the font, but will cause thee to swing from a halter." "Be easy, father, he will do me no harm, for I understand my trade. I will go to him myself this very day." When evening drew near, the master-thief seated himself in his carriage, and drove to the castle. The count received him civilly, for he took him for a distinguished man. When, however, the stranger made himself known, the count turned pale and was quite silent for some time. At length he said, "Thou art my godson, and on that account mercy shall take the place of justice, and I will deal leniently with thee. Since thou pridest thyself on being a master-thief, I will put thy art to the proof, but if thou dost not stand the test, thou must marry the rope-maker's daughter, and the croaking of the raven must be thy music on the occasion." "Lord count," answered the master-thief, "Think of three things, as difficult as you like, and if I do not perform your tasks, do with me what you will." The count reflected for some minutes, and then said, "Well, then, in the first place, thou shalt steal the horse I keep for my own riding, out of the stable; in the next, thou shalt steal the sheet from beneath the bodies of my wife and myself when we are asleep, without our observing it, and the wedding-ring of my wife as well; thirdly and lastly, thou shalt steal away out of the church, the parson and clerk. Mark what I am saying, for thy life depends on it."

The master-thief went to the nearest town; there he bought the clothes of an old peasant woman, and put them on. Then he stained his face brown, and painted wrinkles on it as well, so that no one could have recognized him. Then he filled a small cask with old Hungary wine in which was mixed a powerful sleeping-drink. He put the cask in a basket, which he took on his back, and walked with slow and tottering steps to the count's castle. It was already dark when he arrived. He sat down on a stone in the court-yard and began to cough, like an asthmatic old woman, and to rub his hands as if he were cold. In front of the door of the stable some soldiers were lying round a fire; one of them observed the woman, and called out to her, "Come nearer, old mother, and warm thyself beside us. After all, thou hast no bed for the night, and must take one where thou canst find it." The old woman tottered up to them, begged them to lift the basket from her back, and sat down beside them at the fire. "What hast thou got in thy little cask, old lady?" asked one. "A good mouthful of wine," she answered. "I live by trade, for money and fair words I am quite ready to let you have a glass." "Let us have it here, then," said the soldier, and when he had tasted one glass he said, "When wine is good, I like another glass," and had another poured out for himself, and the rest followed his example. "Hallo, comrades," cried one of them to those who were in the stable, "here is an old goody who has wine that is as old as herself; take a draught, it will warm your stomachs far better than our fire." The old woman carried her cask into the stable. One of the soldiers had seated himself on the saddled riding-horse, another held its bridle in his hand, a third had laid hold of its tail. She poured out as much as they wanted until the spring ran dry. It was not long before the bridle fell from the hand of the one, and he fell down and began to snore, the other left hold of the tail, lay down and snored still louder. The one who was sitting in the saddle, did remain sitting, but bent his head almost down to the horse's neck, and slept and blew with his mouth like the bellows of a forge. The soldiers outside had already been asleep for a long time, and were lying on the ground motionless, as if dead. When the master-thief saw that he had succeeded, he gave the first a rope in his hand instead of the bridle, and the other who had been holding the tail, a wisp of straw, but what was he to do with the one who was sitting on the horse's back? He did not want to throw him down, for he might have awakened and have uttered a cry. He had a good idea, he unbuckled the girths of the saddle, tied a couple of ropes which were hanging to a ring on the wall fast to the saddle, and drew the sleeping rider up into the air on it, then he twisted the rope round the posts, and made it fast. He soon unloosed the horse from the chain, but if he had ridden over the stony pavement of the yard they would have heard the noise in the castle. So he wrapped the horse's hoofs in old rags, led him carefully out, leapt upon him, and galloped off.

When day broke, the master galloped to the castle on the stolen horse. The count had just got up, and was looking out of the window. "Good morning, Sir Count," he cried to him, "here is the horse, which I have got safely out of the stable! Just look, how beautifully your soldiers are lying there sleeping; and if you will but go into the stable, you will see how comfortable your watchers have made it for themselves." The count could not help laughing, then he said, "For once thou hast succeeded, but things won't go so well the second time, and I warn thee that if thou comest before me as a thief, I will handle thee as I would a thief." When the countess went to bed that night, she closed her hand with the wedding-ring tightly together, and the count said, "All the doors are locked and bolted, I will keep awake and wait for the thief, but if he gets in by the window, I will shoot him." The master-thief, however, went in the dark to the gallows, cut a poor sinner who was hanging there down from the halter, and carried him on his back to the castle. Then he set a ladder up to the bedroom, put the dead body on his shoulders, and began to climb up. When he had got so high that the head of the dead man showed at the window, the count, who was watching in his bed, fired a pistol at him, and immediately the master let the poor sinner fall down, and hid himself in one corner. The night was sufficiently lighted by the moon, for the master to see distinctly how the count got out of the window on to the ladder, came down, carried the dead body into the garden, and began to dig a hole in which to lay it. "Now," thought the thief, "the favourable moment has come," stole nimbly out of his corner, and climbed up the ladder straight into the countess's bedroom. "Dear wife," he began in the count's voice, "the thief is dead, but, after all, he is my godson, and has been more of a scape-grace than a villain. I will not put him to open shame; besides, I am sorry for the parents. I will bury him myself before daybreak, in the garden that the thing may not be known, so give me the sheet, I will wrap up the body in it, and bury him as a dog burries things by scratching." The countess gave him the sheet. "I tell you what," continued the thief, "I have a fit of magnanimity on me, give me the ring too, – the unhappy man risked his life for it, so he may take it with him into his grave." She would not gainsay the count, and although she did it unwillingly she drew the ring from her finger, and gave it to him. The thief made off with both these things, and reached home safely before the count in the garden had finished his work of burying.

What a long face the count did pull when the master came next morning, and brought him the sheet and the ring. "Art thou a wizard?" said he, "Who has fetched thee out of the grave in which I myself laid thee, and brought thee to life again?" "You did not bury me," said the thief, "but the poor sinner on the gallows," and he told him exactly how everything had happened, and the count was forced to own to him that he was a clever, crafty thief. "But thou hast not reached the end yet," he added, "thou hast still to perform the third task, and if thou dost not succeed in that, all is of no use." The master smiled and returned no answer. When night had fallen he went with a long sack on his back, a bundle under his arms, and a lantern in his hand to the village-church. In the sack he had some crabs, and in the bundle short wax-candles. He sat down in the churchyard, took out a crab, and stuck a wax-candle on his back. Then he lighted the little light, put the crab on the ground, and let it creep about. He took a second out of the sack, and treated it in the same way, and so on until the last was out of the sack. Hereupon he put on a long black garment that looked like a monk's cowl, and stuck a gray beard on his chin. When at last he was quite unrecognizable, he took the sack in which the crabs had been, went into the church, and ascended the pulpit. The clock in the tower was just striking twelve; when the last stroke had sounded, he cried with a loud and piercing voice, "Hearken, sinful men, the end of all things has come! The last day is at hand! Hearken! Hearken! Whosoever wishes to go to heaven with me must creep into the sack. I am Peter, who opens and shuts the gate of heaven. Behold how the dead outside there in the churchyard, are wandering about collecting their bones. Come, come, and creep into the sack; the world is about to be destroyed!" The cry echoed through the whole village. The parson and clerk who lived nearest to the church, heard it first, and when they saw the lights which were moving about the churchyard, they observed that something unusual was going on, and went into the church. They listened to the sermon for a while, and then the clerk nudged the parson and said, "It would not be amiss if we were to use the opportunity together, and before the dawning of the last day, find an easy way of getting to heaven." "To tell the truth," answered the parson, "that is what I myself have been thinking, so if you are inclined, we will set out on our way." "Yes," answered the clerk, "but you, the pastor, have the precedence, I will follow." So the parson went first, and ascended the pulpit where the master opened his sack. The parson crept in first, and then the clerk. The master immediately tied up the sack tightly, seized it by the middle, and dragged it down the pulpit-steps, and whenever the heads of the two fools bumped against the steps, he cried, "We are going over the mountains." Then he drew them through the village in the same way, and when they were passing through puddles, he cried, "Now we are going through wet clouds." And when at last he was dragging them up the steps of the castle, he cried, "Now we are on the steps of heaven, and will soon be in the outer court." When he had got to the top, he pushed the sack into the pigeon-house, and when the pigeons fluttered about, he said, "Hark how glad the angels are, and how they are flapping their wings!" Then he bolted the door upon them, and went away.

Next morning he went to the count, and told him that he had performed the third task also, and had carried the parson and clerk out of the church. "Where hast thou left them?" asked the lord. "They are lying upstairs in a sack in the pigeon-house, and imagine that they are in heaven." The count went up himself, and convinced himself that the master had told the truth. When he had delivered the parson and clerk from their captivity, he said, "Thou art an arch-thief, and hast won thy wager. For once thou escapest with a whole skin, but see that thou leavest my land, for if ever thou settest foot on it again, thou may'st count on thy elevation to the gallows." The arch-thief took leave of his parents, once more went forth into the wide world, and no one has ever heard of him since.

THE ICELANDIC SORCERESSES

"**T**ell me," said Katla, a handsome and lively widow, to Gunlaugar, an accomplished and gallant young warrior, "tell me why thou goest so oft to Mahfahlida? Is it to caress an old woman?"

"Thine own age, Katla," answered the youth inconsiderately, "might prevent thy making that of Geirrida a subject of reproach."

"I little deemed," replied the offended matron, "that we were on an equality in that particular – but thou, who supposest that Geirrida is the sole source of knowledge, mayst find that there are others who equal her in science."

It happened in the course of the following winter that Gunlaugar, in company with Oddo, the son of Katla, had renewed one of those visits to Geirrida with which Katla had upbraided him.

"Thou shalt not depart tonight," said the sage matron; "evil spirits are abroad, and thy bad destiny predominates."

"We are two in company," answered Gunlaugar, "and have therefore nothing to fear."

"Oddo," replied Geirrida, "will be of no aid to thee; but go, since thou wilt go, and pay the penalty of thy own rashness."

In their way they visited the rival matron, and Gunlaugar was invited to remain in her house that night. This he declined, and, passing forward alone, was next morning found lying before the gate of his father Thorbiorn, severely wounded and deprived of his judgment. Various causes were assigned for this disaster; but Oddo, asserting that they had parted in anger that evening from Geirrida, insisted that his companion must have sustained the injury through her sorcery. Geirrida was accordingly cited to the popular assembly and accused of witchcraft. But twelve witnesses, or compurgators, having asserted upon their oath the innocence of the accused party, Geirrida was honourably freed from the accusation brought against her. Her acquittal did not terminate the rivalry between the two sorceresses, for, Geirrida belonging to the family of Kiliakan, and Katla to that of the pontiff Snorro, the animosity which still subsisted between these septs became awakened by the quarrel.

It chanced that Thorbiorn, called Digri (or the corpulent), one of the family of Snorro, had some horses which fed in the mountain pastures, near to those of Thorarin, called the Black, the son of the enchantress Geirrida. But when autumn arrived, and the horses were to be withdrawn from the mountains and housed for the winter, those of Thorbiorn could nowhere be found, and Oddo, the son of Katla, being sent to consult a wizard, brought back a dubious answer, which seemed to indicate that they had been stolen by Thorarin. Thorbiorn, with Oddo and a party of armed followers, immediately set forth for Mahfahlida, the dwelling of Geirrida and her son Thorarin. Arrived before the gate, they demanded permission to search for the horses which were missing. This Thorarin refused, alleging that neither was the search demanded duly authorised by law, nor were the proper witnesses cited to be present, nor did Thorbiorn offer any sufficient pledge of security when claiming the exercise of so hazardous a privilege. Thorbiorn replied, that as Thorarin declined to permit a search, he must be held as admitting his guilt; and constituting for that purpose a temporary court of justice, by choosing out six judges, he formally accused Thorarin of theft before the gate of his own house. At this the patience of Geirrida forsook her.

"Well," said she to her son Thorarin, "is it said of thee that thou art more a woman than a man, or thou wouldst not bear these intolerable affronts."

Thorarin, fired at the reproach, rushed forth with his servants and guests; a skirmish soon disturbed the legal process which had been instituted, and one or two of both parties were wounded and slain before the wife of Thorarin and the female attendants could separate the fray by flinging their mantles over the weapons of the combatants.

Thorbiorn and his party retreating, Thorarin proceeded to examine the field of battle. Alas! among the reliques of the fight was a bloody hand too slight and fair to belong to any of the combatants. It was that of his wife Ada, who had met this misfortune in her attempts to separate the foes. Incensed to the uttermost, Thorarin threw aside his constitutional moderation, and, mounting on horseback, with his allies and followers, pursued the hostile party, and overtook them in a hay-field, where they had halted to repose their horses, and to exult over the damage they had done to Thorarin. At this moment he assailed them with such fury that he slew Thorbiorn upon the spot, and killed several of his attendants, although Oddo, the son of Katla, escaped free from wounds, having been dressed by his mother in an invulnerable garment. After this action, more blood being shed than usual in an Icelandic engagement, Thorarin returned to Mahfahlida, and, being questioned by his mother concerning the events of the skirmish, he answered in the improvisatory and enigmatical poetry of his age and country –

> *"From me the foul reproach be far,*
> *With which a female waked the war,*
> *From me, who shunned not in the fray*
> *Through foemen fierce to hew my way*
> *(Since meet it is the eagle's brood*
> *On the fresh corpse should find their food);*
> *Then spared I not, in fighting field,*

> With stalwart hand my sword to wield;
> And well may claim at Odin's shrine
> The praise that waits this deed of mine."

To which effusion Geirrida answered –

"Do these verses imply the death of Thorbiorn?"

And Thorarin, alluding to the legal process which Thorbiorn had instituted against him, resumed his song –

> "Sharp bit the sword beneath the hood
> Of him whose zeal the cause pursued,
> And ruddy flowed the stream of death,
> Ere the grim brand resumed the sheath;
> Now on the buckler of the slain
> The raven sits, his draught to drain,
> For gore-drenched is his visage bold,
> That hither came his courts to hold."

As the consequence of this slaughter was likely to be a prosecution at the instance of the pontiff Snorro, Thorarin had now recourse to his allies and kindred, of whom the most powerful were Arnkill, his maternal uncle, and Verimond, who readily premised their aid both in the field and in the Comitia, or popular meeting, in spring, before which it was to be presumed Snorro would indict Thorarin for the slaughter of his kinsman. Arnkill could not, however, forbear asking his nephew how he had so far lost his usual command of temper. He replied in verse –

> "Till then, the master of my mood,
> Men called me gentle, mild, and good;

> *But yon fierce dame's sharp tongue might wake*
> *In wintry den the frozen snake."*

While Thorarin spent the winter with his uncle Arnkill, he received information from his mother Geirrida that Oddo, son of her old rival Katla, was the person who had cut off the hand of his wife Ada, and that he gloried in the fact. Thorarin and Arnkill determined on instant vengeance, and, travelling rapidly, surprised the house of Katla. The undismayed sorceress, on hearing them approach, commanded her son to sit close beside her, and when the assailants entered they only beheld Katla, spinning coarse yarn from what seemed a large distaff, with her female domestics seated around her.

"My son," she said, "is absent on a journey;" and Thorarin and Arnkill, having searched the house in vain, were obliged to depart with this answer. They had not, however, gone far before the well-known skill of Katla, in optical delusion occurred to them, and they resolved on a second and stricter search. Upon their return they found Katla in the outer apartment, who seemed to be shearing the hair of a tame kid, but was in reality cutting the locks of her son Oddo. Entering the inner room, they found the large distaff flung carelessly upon a bench. They returned yet a third time, and a third delusion was prepared for them; for Katla had given her son the appearance of a hog, which seemed to grovel upon the heap of ashes. Arnkill now seized and split the distaff, which he had at first suspected, upon which Kalta tauntingly observed, that if their visits had been frequent that evening, they could not be said to be altogether ineffectual, since they had destroyed a distaff. They were accordingly returning completely baffled, when Geirrida met them, and upbraided them with carelessness in searching for their enemy.

"Return yet again," she said, "and I will accompany you."

Katla's maidens, still upon the watch, announced to her the return of the hostile party, their number augmented by one who wore a blue mantle.

"Alas!" cried Katla, "it is the sorceress Geirrida, against whom spells will be of no avail."

Immediately rising from the raised and boarded seat which she occupied, she concealed Oddo beneath it, and covered it with cushions as before, on which she stretched herself complaining of indisposition. Upon the entrance of the hostile party, Geirrida, without speaking a word, flung aside her mantle, took out a piece of sealskin, in which she wrapped up Katla's head, and commanded that she should be held by some of the attendants, while the others broke open the boarded space, beneath which Oddo lay concealed, seized upon him, bound him, and led him away captive with his mother. Next morning Oddo was hanged, and Katla stoned to death; but not until she had confessed that, through her sorcery, she had occasioned the disaster of Gunlaugar, which first led the way to these feuds.

TALES OF TROLLS & GIANTS

Lying in wait beneath his bridge, the Troll in 'The Three Billy Goats Gruff' is not so much a character as a symbol. Ugly, outlandish and frighteningly fierce, he embodies the sort of destructive impulses that surge in our subconscious, ready to break the surface and upset our lives at any time. The Vikings never got to read the psychological theories of Sigmund Freud (1856–1939), but they understood the darker side of human nature. They also knew about life and the disagreeable surprises it could spring.

But they also appreciated that a vividly imagined monster or giant – the more bloodthirsty the better – could lend a welcome frisson to any tale. A troll with three, five or seven heads – especially if he's obligingly easy for a hero to outwit, and then dispatch with slapstick violence – makes for enjoyable entertainment every time. The monsters in these stories can be cartoonish creations, as comically inept as they are grotesque.

Trolls and giants in Nordic myth serve a paradoxical purpose, then.

Though emblems of evil, they underline the triumph of good.

THE THREE BILLY-GOATS GRUFF

Once on a time there were three Billy-goats, who were to go up to the hill-side to make themselves fat, and the name of all three was "Gruff".

On the way up was a bridge over a burn they had to cross; and under the bridge lived a great ugly Troll, with eyes as big as saucers, and a nose as long as a poker.

So first of all came the youngest billy-goat Gruff to cross the bridge.

"Trip, trap; trip, trap!" went the bridge.

"WHO'S THAT tripping over my bridge?" roared the Troll.

"Oh! it is only I, the tiniest billy-goat Gruff; and I'm going up to the hill-side to make myself fat", said the billy-goat, with such a small voice.

"Now, I'm coming to gobble you up", said the Troll.

"Oh, no! pray don't take me. I'm too little, that I am", said the billy-goat; "wait a bit till the second billy-goat Gruff comes, he's much bigger."

"Well! be off with you", said the Troll.

A little while after came the second billy-goat Gruff to cross the bridge.

"TRIP, TRAP! TRIP, TRAP! TRIP, TRAP!" went the bridge.

"WHO'S THAT tripping over my bridge?" roared the Troll.

"Oh! it's the second billy-goat Gruff, and I'm going up to the hill-side to make myself fat", said the billy-goat, who hadn't such a small voice.

"Now, I'm coming to gobble you up", said the Troll.

"Oh, no! don't take me, wait a little till the big billy-goat Gruff comes, he's much bigger."

"Very well! be off with you", said the Troll.

But just then up came the big billy-goat Gruff.

"TRIP, TRAP! TRIP, TRAP! TRIP, TRAP!" went the bridge, for the billy-goat was so heavy that the bridge creaked and groaned under him.

"WHO'S THAT tramping over my bridge?" roared the Troll.

"IT'S I! THE BIG BILLY-GOAT GRUFF", said the billy-goat, who had an ugly hoarse voice of his own.

"Now, I'm coming to gobble you up", roared the Troll.

> Well, come along! I've got two spears,
> And I'll poke your eyeballs out at your ears;
> I've got besides two curling-stones,
> And I'll crush you to bits, body and bones.

That was what the big billy-goat said; and so he flew at the Troll and poked his eyes out with his horns, and crushed him to bits, body and bones, and tossed him out into the burn, and after that he went up to the hill-side. There the billy-goats got so fat they were scarce able to walk home again; and if the fat hasn't fallen off them, why they're still fat; and so:

> Snip, snap, snout,
> This tale's told out.

SORIA MORIA CASTLE

There was once upon a time a couple of folks who had a son called Halvor. Ever since he had been a little boy he had been unwilling to do any work, and had just sat raking about among the ashes. His parents sent him away to learn several things, but Halvor stayed nowhere, for when he had been gone two or three days he always ran away from his master, hurried off home, and sat down in the chimney corner to grub among the ashes again.

One day, however, a sea captain came and asked Halvor if he hadn't a fancy to come with him and go to sea, and behold foreign lands. And Halvor had a fancy for that, so he was not long in getting ready.

How long they sailed I have no idea, but after a long, long time there was a terrible storm, and when it was over and all had become calm again, they knew not where they were, for they had been driven away to a strange coast of which none of them had any knowledge.

As there was no wind at all they lay there becalmed, and Halvor asked the skipper to give him leave to go on shore to look about him, for he would much rather do that than lie there and sleep.

"Dost thou think that thou art fit to go where people can see thee?" said the skipper; "thou hast no clothes but those rags thou art going about in!"

Halvor still begged for leave, and at last got it, but he was to come back at once if the wind began to rise.

So he went on shore, and it was a delightful country; whithersoever he went there were wide plains with fields and meadows, but as for people, there were none to be seen. The wind began to rise, but Halvor thought that he had not seen enough yet, and that he would like to walk about a little longer, to try if he could not meet somebody. So after a while he came to a great highway, which was so smooth that an egg might have been rolled along it without breaking. Halvor followed this, and when evening drew near he saw a big castle far away in the distance, and there were lights in it. So as he had now been walking the whole day and had not brought anything to eat away with him, he was frightfully hungry. Nevertheless, the nearer he came to the castle the more afraid he was.

A fire was burning in the castle, and Halvor went into the kitchen, which was more magnificent than any kitchen he had ever yet beheld. There were vessels of gold and silver, but not one human being was to be seen. When Halvor had stood there for some time, and no one had come out, he went in and opened a door, and inside a Princess was sitting at her wheel spinning.

"Nay!" she cried, "can Christian folk dare to come hither? But the best thing that you can do is to go away again, for if not the Troll will devour you. A Troll with three heads lives here."

"I should have been just as well pleased if he had had four heads more, for I should have enjoyed seeing the fellow," said the youth; "and I won't go away, for I have done no harm, but you must give me something to eat, for I am frightfully hungry."

When Halvor had eaten his fill, the Princess told him to try if he could wield the sword which was hanging on the wall, but he could not wield it, nor could he even lift it up.

"Well, then, you must take a drink out of that bottle which is hanging by its side, for that's what the Troll does whenever he goes out and wants to use the sword," said the Princess.

Halvor took a draught, and in a moment he was able to swing the sword about with perfect ease. And now he thought it was high time for the Troll to make his appearance, and at that very moment he came, panting for breath.

Halvor got behind the door.

"Hutetu!" said the Troll as he put his head in at the door. "It smells just as if there were Christian man's blood here!"

"Yes, you shall learn that there is!" said Halvor, and cut off all his heads.

The Princess was so rejoiced to be free that she danced and sang, but then she remembered her sisters, and said: "If my sisters were but free too!"

"Where are they?" asked Halvor.

So she told him where they were. One of them had been taken away by a Troll to his castle, which was six miles off, and the other had been carried off to a castle which was nine miles farther off still.

"But now," said she, "you must first help me to get this dead body away from here."

Halvor was so strong that he cleared everything away, and made all clean and tidy very quickly. So then they ate and drank, and were happy, and next morning he set off in the grey light of dawn. He gave himself no rest, but walked or ran the livelong day. When he came in sight of the castle he was again just a little afraid. It was much more splendid than the other, but here too there was not a human being to be seen. So Halvor went into the kitchen, and did not linger there either, but went straight in.

"Nay! do Christian folk dare to come here?" cried the second Princess. "I know not how long it is since I myself came, but during all that time I have never seen a Christian man. It will be better for you to depart at once, for a Troll lives here who has six heads."

"No, I shall not go," said Halvor; "even if he had six more I would not."

"He will swallow you up alive," said the Princess.

But she spoke to no purpose, for Halvor would not go; he was not afraid of the Troll, but he wanted some meat and drink, for he was hungry after his journey. So she gave him as much as he would have, and then she once more tried to make him go away.

"No," said Halvor, "I will not go, for I have not done anything wrong, and I have no reason to be afraid."

"He won't ask any questions about that," said the Princess, "for he will take you without leave or right; but as you will not go, try if you can wield that sword which the Troll uses in battle."

He could not brandish the sword; so the Princess said that he was to take a draught from the flask which hung by its side, and when he had done that he could wield the sword.

Soon afterwards the Troll came, and he was so large and stout that he was forced to go sideways to get through the door. When the Troll got his first head in he cried: "Hutetu! It smells of a Christian man's blood here!"

With that Halvor cut off the first head, and so on with all the rest. The Princess was now exceedingly delighted, but then she remembered her sisters, and wished that they too were free. Halvor thought that might be managed, and wanted to set off immediately; but first he had to help the Princess to remove the Troll's body, so it was not until morning that he set forth on his way.

It was a long way to the castle, and he both walked and ran to get there in time. Late in the evening he caught sight of it, and it was very much more magnificent than either of the others. And this time he was not in the least afraid, but went into the kitchen, and then straight on inside the castle. There a Princess was sitting, who was so beautiful that there was never anyone to equal her. She too said what the others had said, that no Christian folk had ever been there since she had come, and entreated him to go away again, or else the Troll would swallow him up alive. The Troll had nine heads, she told him.

"Yes, and if he had nine added to the nine, and then nine more still, I would not go away," said Halvor, and went and stood by the stove.

The Princess begged him very prettily to go lest the Troll should devour him; but Halvor said, "Let him come when he will."

So she gave him the Troll's sword, and bade him take a drink from the flask to enable him to wield it.

At that same moment the Troll came, breathing hard, and he was ever so much bigger and stouter than either of the others, and he too was forced to go sideways to get in through the door.

"Hutetu! what a smell of Christian blood there is here!" said he.

Then Halvor cut off the first head, and after that the others, but the last was the toughest of them all, and it was the hardest work that Halvor had ever done to get it off, but he still believed that he would have strength enough to do it.

And now all the Princesses came to the castle, and were together again, and they were happier than they had ever been in their lives; and they were delighted with Halvor, and he with them, and he was to choose the one he liked best; but of the three sisters the youngest loved him best.

But Halvor went about and was so strange and so mournful and quiet that the Princesses asked what it was that he longed for, and if he did not like to be with them. He said that he did like to be with them, for they had enough to live on, and he was very comfortable there; but he longed to go home, for his father and mother were alive, and he had a great desire to see them again.

They thought that this might easily be done.

"You shall go and return in perfect safety if you will follow our advice," said the Princesses.

So he said that he would do nothing that they did not wish.

Then they dressed him so splendidly that he was like a King's son; and they put a ring on his finger, and it was one which would enable him to go there and back again by wishing, but they told him that he must not throw it away, or name their names; for if he did, all his magnificence would be at an end, and then he would never see them more.

"If I were but at home again, or if home were but here!" said Halvor, and no sooner had he wished this than it was granted. Halvor was standing outside his father and mother's cottage before he knew what he was about. The darkness of night was coming on, and when the father and mother saw such a splendid and stately stranger walk in, they were so startled that they both began to bow and curtsey.

Halvor then inquired if he could stay there and have lodging for the night. No, that he certainly could not. "We can give you no such accommodation," they said, "for we have none of the things that are needful when a great lord like you is to be entertained. It will be better for you to go up to the farm. It is not far off, you can see the chimney-pots from here, and there they have plenty of everything."

Halvor would not hear of that, he was absolutely determined to stay where he was; but the old folks stuck to what they had said, and told him that he was to go to the farm, where he could get both meat and drink, whereas they themselves had not even a chair to offer him.

"No," said Halvor, "I will not go up there till early tomorrow morning; let me stay here tonight. I can sit down on the hearth."

They could say nothing against that, so Halvor sat down on the hearth, and began to rake about among the ashes just as he had done before, when he lay there idling away his time.

They chattered much about many things, and told Halvor of this and of that, and at last he asked them if they had never had any child.

"Yes," they said; they had had a boy who was called Halvor, but they did not know where he had gone, and they could not even say whether he were dead or alive.

"Could I be he?" said Halvor.

"I should know him well enough," said the old woman rising. "Our Halvor was so idle and slothful that he never did anything at all, and he was so ragged that one hole ran into another all over his clothes. Such a fellow as he was could never turn into such a man as you are, sir."

In a short time the old woman had to go to the fireplace to stir the fire, and when the blaze lit up Halvor, as it used to do when he was at home raking up the ashes, she knew him again.

"Good Heavens! is that you, Halvor?" said she, and such great gladness fell on the old parents that there were no bounds to it. And now he had to relate everything that had befallen him, and the old woman was so delighted with him that she would take him up to the farm at once to show him to the girls who had formerly looked down on him so. She went there first, and Halvor followed her. When she got there she told them how Halvor had come home again, and now they should just see how magnificent he was. "He looks like a prince," she said.

"We shall see that he is just the same ragamuffin that he was before," said the girls, tossing their heads.

At that same moment Halvor entered, and the girls were so astonished that they left their kirtles lying in the chimney corner, and ran away in nothing but their petticoats. When they came in again they were so shamefaced that they hardly dared to look at Halvor, towards whom they had always been so proud and haughty before.

"Ay, ay! you have always thought that you were so pretty and dainty that no one was equal to you," said Halvor, "but you should just see the eldest Princess whom I set free. You look like herds-women compared with her, and the second Princess is also much prettier than you; but the youngest, who is my sweetheart, is more beautiful than either sun or moon. I wish to Heaven they were here, and then you would see them."

Scarcely had he said this before they were standing by his side, but then he was very sorrowful, for the words which they had said to him came to his mind.

Up at the farm a great feast was made ready for the Princesses, and much respect paid to them, but they would not stay there.

"We want to go down to your parents," they said to Halvor, "so we will go out and look about us."

He followed them out, and they came to a large pond outside the farmhouse. Very near the water there was a pretty green bank, and there the Princesses said they would sit down and while away an hour, for they thought that it would be pleasant to sit and look out over the water, they said.

There they sat down, and when they had sat for a short time the youngest Princess said, "I may as well comb your hair a little, Halvor."

So Halvor laid his head down on her lap, and she combed it, and it was not long before he fell asleep. Then she took her ring from him and put another in its place, and then she said to her sisters: "Hold me as I am holding you. I would that we were at Soria Moria Castle."

When Halvor awoke he knew that he had lost the Princesses, and began to weep and lament, and was so unhappy that he could not be comforted. In spite of all his father's and mother's entreaties, he would not stay, but bade them farewell, saying that he would never see them more, for if he did not find the Princess again he did not think it worth while to live.

He again had three hundred dollars, which he put into his pocket and went on his way. When he had walked some distance he met a man with a tolerably good horse. Halvor longed to buy it, and began to bargain with the man.

"Well, I have not exactly been thinking of selling him," said the man, "but if we could agree, perhaps—"

Halvor inquired how much he wanted to have for the horse.

"I did not give much for him, and he is not worth much; he is a capital horse to ride, but good for nothing at drawing; but he will always be able to carry your bag of provisions and you too, if you walk and ride by turns." At last they agreed about the price, and Halvor laid his bag on the horse, and sometimes he walked and sometimes he rode. In the evening he came to a green field, where stood a great tree, under which he seated himself. Then he let the horse loose and lay down to sleep, but before he did that he took his bag off the horse. At daybreak he set off again, for he did not feel as if he could take any rest. So he walked and rode the whole day, through a great wood where there were many green places which gleamed very prettily among the trees. He did not know where he was or whither he was going, but he never lingered longer in any place than was enough to let his horse get a little food when they came to one of these green spots, while he himself took out his bag of provisions.

So he walked and he rode, and it seemed to him that the wood would never come to an end. But on the evening of the second day he saw a light shining through the trees.

"If only there were some people up there I might warm myself and get something to eat," thought Halvor.

When he got to the place where the light had come from, he saw a wretched little cottage, and through a small pane of glass he saw a couple of old folks inside. They were very old, and as grey-headed as a pigeon, and the old woman had such a long nose that she sat in the chimney corner and used it to stir the fire.

"Good evening! good evening!" said the old hag; "but what errand have you that can bring you here? No Christian folk have been here for more than a hundred years."

So Halvor told her that he wanted to get to Soria Moria Castle, and inquired if she knew the way thither.

"No," said the old woman, "that I do not, but the Moon will be here presently, and I will ask her, and she will know. She can easily see it, for she shines on all things."

So when the Moon stood clear and bright above the tree-tops the old woman went out. "Moon! Moon!" she screamed. "Canst thou tell me the way to Soria Moria Castle?"

"No," said the Moon, "that I can't, for when I shone there, there was a cloud before me."

"Wait a little longer," said the old woman to Halvor, "for the West Wind will presently be here, and he will know it, for he breathes gently or blows into every corner."

"What! have you a horse too?" she said when she came in again. "Oh! let the poor creature loose in our bit of fenced-in pasture, and don't let it stand there starving at our very door. But won't you exchange him with me? We have a pair of old boots here with which you can go fifteen quarters of a mile at each step. You shall have them for the horse, and then you will be able to get sooner to Soria Moria Castle."

Halvor consented to this at once, and the old woman was so delighted with the horse that she was ready to dance. "For now I, too, shall be able to ride to church," she said. Halvor could take no rest, and wanted to set off immediately; but the old woman said that there was no need to hasten. "Lie down on the bench and sleep a little, for we have no bed to offer you," said she, "and I will watch for the coming of the West Wind."

Ere long came the West Wind, roaring so loud that the walls creaked.

The old woman went out and cried:

"West Wind! West Wind! Canst thou tell me the way to Soria Moria Castle? Here is one who would go thither."

"Yes, I know it well," said the West Wind. "I am just on my way there to dry the clothes for the wedding which is to take place. If he is fleet of foot he can go with me."

Out ran Halvor.

"You will have to make haste if you mean to go with me," said the West Wind; and away it went over hill and dale, and moor and morass, and Halvor had enough to do to keep up with it.

"Well, now I have no time to stay with you any longer," said the West Wind, "for I must first go and tear down a bit of spruce fir before I go to the bleaching-ground to dry the clothes; but just go along the side of the hill, and you will come to some girls who are standing there washing clothes, and then you will not have to walk far before you are at Soria Moria Castle."

Shortly afterwards Halvor came to the girls who were standing washing, and they asked him if he had seen anything of the West Wind, who was to come there to dry the clothes for the wedding.

"Yes," said Halvor, "he has only gone to break down a bit of spruce fir. It won't be long before he is here." And then he asked them the way to Soria Moria Castle. They put him in the right way, and when he came in front of the castle it was so full of horses and people that it swarmed with them. But Halvor was so ragged and torn with following the West Wind through bushes and bogs that he kept on one side, and would not go among the crowd until the last day, when the feast was to be held at noon.

So when, as was the usage and custom, all were to drink to the bride and the young girls who were present, the cup-bearer filled the cup for each in turn, both bride and bridegroom, and knights and servants, and at last, after a very long time, he came to Halvor. He drank their health, and then slipped the ring which the Princess had put on his finger when they were sitting by the waterside into the glass, and ordered the cup-bearer to carry the glass to the bride from him and greet her.

Then the Princess at once rose up from the table, and said, "Who is most worthy to have one of us – he who has delivered us from the Trolls or he who is sitting here as bridegroom?"

There could be but one opinion as to that, everyone thought, and when Halvor heard what they said he was not long in flinging off his beggar's rags and arraying himself as a bridegroom.

"Yes, he is the right one," cried the youngest Princess when she caught sight of him; so she flung the other out of the window and held her wedding with Halvor.

CHARCOAL NILS AND THE TROLL-WOMAN

In the old days there lived on a headland that juts out into the northwestern corner of Lake Rasval, in the neighborhood of the Linde mining-district, a charcoal-burner named Nils, generally known as Charcoal Nils. He let a farm-hand attend to his little plot of land, and he himself made his home in the forest, where he chopped wood in the summer and burned it to charcoal in the winter. Yet no matter how hard he struggled, his work was unblessed with reward, and no one ever spoke of him save as poor Charcoal Nils.

One day, when he was on the opposite shore of the lake, near the gloomy Harsberg, a strange woman came up to him, and asked whether he needed some one to help him with his charcoal burning.

"Yes, indeed," said he, "help would be welcome." So she began to gather blocks of wood and tree-trunks, more than Charcoal Nils could have dragged together with his horse, and by noon there was enough wood for a new kiln. When evening came, she asked the charcoal-burner whether he were satisfied with the day's work she had done, and if she were to come back the next day.

That suited the charcoal-burner perfectly, and she came back the next day and all the following ones. And when the kiln had been burned out she helped Nils clear it, and never before had he had such a quantity of charcoal, nor charcoal of so fine a quality.

So she became his wife and lived with him in the wood for three years. They had three children, yet this worried Nils but little, seeing that she looked after them, and they gave him no trouble.

But when the fourth year came, she grew more exacting, and insisted on going back to his home with him, and living with him there. Nils wished to hear nothing about this; yet since she was so useful to him in his charcoal-burning, he did not betray his feelings, and said he would think it over.

It happened one Sunday that he went to church – where he had not been for many years, and what he heard there brought up thoughts he had not known since the innocent days of his childhood. He began to wonder whether there were not some hocus-pocus about the charcoal-burning, and whether it were not due to the forest woman, who aided him so willingly.

Preoccupied with this and other thoughts, he forgot while returning to his kiln, that he had promised the strange woman at the very beginning, when she had first helped him, that, whenever he had been home and was returning to the kiln, he would rap three times with his ax against an old pine tree not far from it. On this occasion, as we have said, he forgot the sign, and as a result he saw something that nearly robbed him of his wits.

As he drew near the kiln, he saw it all aflame, and around it stood the three children and their mother, and they were clearing out the kiln. They were pulling down and putting out so that flames, smoke and ashes whirled sky-high, but instead of the spruce-branches that were generally used to put out the fire, *they had bushy tails which they dipped in the snow!*

When Charcoal Nils had looked on for a while, he slunk back to the old pine tree, and made its trunk echo to the sound of his three ax-strokes till one could hear them on the Harsberg. Then he went to the kiln, as though he had seen nothing, and all went on as before. The kiln was glowing with a handsome, even glow, and the tall woman was about and working as usual.

As soon as she saw Charcoal Nils, she came back with her pressing demand that he take her home to his little house, and that they live there.

"Yes, that shall come about," said Nils to console her, and turned back home to fetch a horse. But instead he went out on the headline of Kallernäs, on the eastern shore of Lake Rasval, where a wise man lived, and asked the latter what he should do.

The old man advised him to go home and hitch his horse to his charcoal-wagon, but to hitch the horse in such wise that there would be not a single loop either in the harness or traces. Then he was to mount the horse and ride back to the kiln without stopping, have the troll-woman and her children get into the wagon, and at once drive out on the ice with them.

The charcoal-burner did as the old man told him, saddled his horse, paying strict attention that there were no loops in saddle or bridle, rode across the ice through the wood to his kiln, and told the troll-woman and her children to get in. Then he quickly turned back through the wood, out on the ice, and there let his horse run as fast as he could. When he reached the middle of the lake, he saw a pack of wolves running along in the direction of Aboda-land, at the northern end of the lake, and heading for the ice. Then he tore the saddle-harness from the traces, so that the wagon with the troll-folk was left standing on the bare ice, and rode as fast as his horse could carry him for the opposite shore. When the trolls saw the wolves they began to scream.

"Turn back, turn back!" cried the mother. "And if you will not for my sake, then at least do so for the sake of Vipa (Peewee), your youngest daughter!" But Charcoal Nils rode for the shore without looking back. Then he heard the troll-woman calling on others for aid.

"Brother in the Harsberg, Sister in Stripa, Cousin in Ringfels; Take the loop and pull!"

"There is no loop to pull!" came the answer from deep within the Harsberg. "Then catch him at Harkallarn." "He is not riding in that direction." The reply came from Ringfels.

And indeed Charcoal Nils did not ride in that direction; but over stick and stone straight to his own home. Yet when he reached his own courtyard, the horse fell, and a shot from the trolls tore away a corner of the stable. Nils shortly after fell sick, and had to lie a-bed for a number of weeks. When he was well again he sold his forest land, and worked the little farm by the cottage until his death. So that was one occasion when the troll-folk came off second best.

ORIGIN OF TIIS LAKE

A troll had once taken up his abode near the village of Kund, in the high bank on which the church now stands, but when the people about there had become pious, and went constantly to church, the troll was dreadfully annoyed by their almost incessant ringing of bells in the steeple of the church. He was at last obliged, in consequence of it, to take his departure, for nothing has more contributed to the emigration of the troll-folk out of the country, than the increasing piety of the people, and their taking to bell-ringing. The troll of Kund accordingly quitted the country, and went over to Funen, where he lived for some time in peace and quiet. Now it chanced that a man who had lately settled in the town of Kund, coming to Funen on business, met this same troll on the road.

"Where do you live?" asked the troll.

Now there was nothing whatever about the troll unlike a man, so he answered him, as was the truth –

"I am from the town of Kund."

"So?" said the troll, "I don't know you then. And yet I think I know every man in Kund. Will you, however," said he, "be so kind as to take a letter for me back with you to Kund?"

The man, of course, said he had no objection.

The troll put a letter into his pocket and charged him strictly not to take it out until he came to Kund church. Then he was to throw it over the churchyard wall, and the person for whom it was intended would get it.

The troll then went away in great haste, and with him the letter went entirely out of the man's mind. But when he was come back to Zealand he sat down by the meadow where Tiis lake now is, and suddenly recollected the troll's letter. He felt a great desire to look at it at least, so he took it out of his pocket and sat a while with it in his hands, when suddenly there began to dribble a little water out of the seal. The letter now unfolded itself and the water came out faster and faster, and it was with the utmost difficulty the poor man was able to save his life, for the malicious troll had enclosed a whole lake in the letter.

The troll, it is plain, had thought to avenge himself on Kund church by destroying it in this manner, but God ordered it so that the lake chanced to run out in the great meadow where it now stands.

MINNIKIN

There was once upon a time a couple of needy folk who lived in a wretched hut, in which there was nothing but black want; so they had neither food to eat nor wood to burn. But if they had next to nothing of all else they had the blessing of God so far as children were concerned, and every year brought them one more. The man was not overpleased at this. He was always going about grumbling and growling, and saying that it seemed to him that there might be such a thing as having too many of these good gifts; so shortly before another baby was born he went away into the wood for some firewood, saying that he did not want to see the new child; he would hear him quite soon enough when he began to squall for some food.

As soon as this baby was born it began to look about the room. "Ah, my dear mother!" said he, "give me some of my brothers' old clothes, and food enough for a few days, and I will go out into the world and seek my fortune, for, so far as I can see, you have children enough."

"Heaven help thee, my son!" said the mother, "that will never do; thou art still far too little."

But the little creature was determined to do it, and begged and prayed so long that the mother was forced to let him have some old rags, and tie up a little food for him, and then gaily and happily he went out into the world.

But almost before he was out of the house another boy was born, and he too looked about him, and said, "Ah, my dear mother! give me some of my brothers" old clothes, and food for some days, and then I will go out into the world and find my twin brother, for you have children enough."

"Heaven help thee, little creature! thou art far too little for that," said the woman; "it would never do."

But she spoke to no purpose, for the boy begged and prayed until he had got some old rags and a bundle of provisions, and then he set out manfully into the world to find his twin brother.

When the younger had walked for some time he caught sight of his brother a short distance in front of him, and called to him and bade him to stop.

"Wait a minute," he said; "you are walking as if for a wager, but you ought to have stayed to see your younger brother before you hurried off into the world."

So the elder stood still and looked back, and when the younger had got up to him, and had told him that he was his brother, he said: "But now, let us sit down and see what kind of food our mother has given us," and that they did.

When they had walked on a little farther they came to a brook which ran through a green meadow, and there the younger said that they ought to christen each other. "As we had to make such haste, and had no time to do it at home, we may as well do it here," said he.

"What will you be called?" asked the elder.

"I will be called Minnikin," answered the second; "and you, what will you be called?"

"I will be called King Pippin," answered the elder.

They christened each other and then went onwards. When they had walked for some time they came to a crossway, and there they agreed to part, and each take his own road. This they did, but no sooner had they walked a short distance than they met again. So they parted once more, and each took his own road, but in a very short time the same thing happened again – they met each other before they were at all aware, and so it happened the third time also. Then they arranged with each other that each should choose his own quarter, and one should go east and the other west.

"But if ever you fall into any need or trouble," said the elder, "call me thrice, and I will come and help you; only you must not call me until you are in the utmost need."

"In that case we shall not see each other for some time," said Minnikin; so they bade farewell to each other, and Minnikin went east and King Pippin went west.

When Minnikin had walked a long way alone, he met an old, old crook-backed hag, who had only one eye. Minnikin stole it.

"Oh! oh!" cried the old hag, "what has become of my eye?"

"What will you give me to get your eye back?" said Minnikin.

"I will give thee a sword which is such a sword that it can conquer a whole army, let it be ever so great," replied the woman.

"Let me have it, then," said Minnikin.

The old hag gave him the sword, so she got her eye back. Then Minnikin went onwards, and when he had wandered on for some time he again met an old, old crook-backed hag, who had only one eye. Minnikin stole it before she was aware.

"Oh! oh! what has become of my eye?" cried the old hag.

"What will you give me to get your eye back?" said Minnikin.

"I will give thee a ship which can sail over fresh water and salt water, over high hills and deep dales," answered the old woman.

"Let me have it then," said Minnikin.

So the old woman gave him a little bit of a ship which was no bigger than he could put in his pocket, and then she got her eye back, and she went her way and Minnikin his. When he had walked on for a long time, he met for the third time an old, old crook-backed hag, who had only one eye. This eye also Minnikin stole, and when the woman screamed and lamented, and asked what had become of her eye, Minnikin said, "What will you give me to get your eye back?"

"I will give thee the art to brew a hundred lasts of malt in one brewing."

So, for teaching that art, the old hag got her eye back, and they both went away by different roads.

But when Minnikin had walked a short distance, it seemed to him that it might be worth while to see what his ship could do; so he took it out of his pocket, and first he put one foot into it, and then the other, and no sooner had he put one foot into the ship than it became much larger, and when he set the other foot into it, it grew as large as ships that sail on the sea.

Then Minnikin said: "Now go over fresh water and salt water, over high hills and deep dales, and do not stop until thou comest to the King's palace."

And in an instant the ship went away as swiftly as any bird in the air till it got just below the King's palace, and there it stood still.

From the windows of the King's palace many persons had seen Minnikin come sailing thither, and had stood to watch him; and they were all so astounded that they ran down to see what manner of man this could be who came sailing in a ship through the air. But while they were running down from the King's palace, Minnikin had got out of the ship and had put it in his pocket again; for the moment he got out of it, it once more became as small as it had been when he got it from the old woman, and those who came from the King's palace could see nothing but a ragged little boy who was standing down by the sea-shore. The King asked where he had come from, but the boy said he did not know, nor yet could he tell them how he had got there, but he begged very earnestly and prettily for a place in the King's palace. If there was nothing else for him to do, he said he would fetch wood and water for the kitchen-maid, and that he obtained leave to do.

When Minnikin went up to the King's palace he saw that everything there was hung with black both outside and inside, from the bottom to the top; so he asked the kitchen-maid what that meant.

"Oh, I will tell you that," answered the kitchen-maid. "The King's daughter was long ago promised away to three Trolls, and next Thursday evening one of them is to come to fetch her. Ritter Red has said that he will be able to set her free, but who knows whether he will be able to do it? so you may easily imagine what grief and distress we are in here."

So when Thursday evening came, Ritter Red accompanied the Princess to the sea-shore; for there she was to meet the Troll, and Ritter Red was to stay with her and protect her. He, however, was very unlikely to do the Troll much injury, for no sooner had the Princess seated herself by the sea-shore than Ritter Red climbed up into a great tree which was standing there, and hid himself as well as he could among the branches.

The Princess wept, and begged him most earnestly not to go and leave her; but Ritter Red did not concern himself about that. "It is better that one should die than two," said he.

In the meantime Minnikin begged the kitchen-maid very prettily to give him leave to go down to the strand for a short time.

"Oh, what could you do down at the strand?" said the kitchen-maid. "You have nothing to do there."

"Oh yes, my dear, just let me go," said Minnikin. "I should so like to go and amuse myself with the other children."

"Well, well, go then!" said the kitchen-maid, "but don't let me find you staying there over the time when the pan has to be set on the fire for supper, and the roast put on the spit; and mind you bring back a good big armful of wood for the kitchen."

Minnikin promised this, and ran down to the sea-shore.

Just as he got to the place where the King's daughter was sitting, the Troll came rushing up with a great whistling and whirring, and he was so big and stout that he was terrible to see, and he had five heads.

"Fire!" screeched the Troll.

"Fire yourself!" said Minnikin.

"Can you fight?" roared the Troll.

"If not, I can learn," said Minnikin.

So the Troll struck at him with a great thick iron bar which he had in his fist, till the sods flew five yards up into the air.

"Fie!" said Minnikin. "That was not much of a blow. Now you shall see one of mine."

So he grasped the sword which he had got from the old crook-backed woman, and slashed at the Troll so that all five heads went flying away over the sands.

When the Princess saw that she was delivered she was so delighted that she did not know what she was doing, and skipped and danced.

"Come and sleep a bit with your head in my lap," she said to Minnikin, and as he slept she put a golden dress on him.

But when Ritter Red saw that there was no longer any danger afoot, he lost no time in creeping down from the tree. He then threatened the Princess, until at length she was forced to promise to say that it was he who had rescued her, for he told her that if she did not he would kill her. Then he took the Troll's lungs and tongue and put them in his pocket-handkerchief, and led the Princess back to the King's palace; and whatsoever had been lacking to him in the way of honour before was lacking no longer, for the King did not know how to exalt him enough, and always set him on his own right hand at table.

As for Minnikin, first he went out on the Troll's ship and took a great quantity of gold and silver hoops away with him, and then he trotted back to the King's palace.

When the kitchen-maid caught sight of all this gold and silver she was quite amazed, and said: "My dear friend Minnikin, where have you got all that from?" for she was half afraid that he had not come by it honestly.

"Oh," answered Minnikin, "I have been home a while, and these hoops had fallen off some of our buckets, so I brought them away with me for you."

So when the kitchen-maid heard that they were for her, she asked no more questions about the matter. She thanked Minnikin, and everything was right again at once.

Next Thursday evening all went just the same, and everyone was full of grief and affliction, but Ritter Red said that he had been able to deliver the King's daughter from one Troll, so that he could very easily deliver her from another, and he led her down to the sea-shore. But he did not do much harm to this Troll either, for when the time came when the Troll might be expected, he said as he had said before: "It is better that one should die than two," and then climbed up into the tree again.

Minnikin once more begged the cook's leave to go down to the sea-shore for a short time.

"Oh, what can you do there?" said the cook.

"My dear, do let me go!" said Minnikin; "I should so like to go down there and amuse myself a little with the other children."

So this time also she said that he should have leave to go, but he must first promise that he would be back by the time the joint was turned and that he would bring a great armful of wood with him.

No sooner had Minnikin got down to the strand than the Troll came rushing along with a great whistling and whirring, and he was twice as big as the first Troll, and he had ten heads.

"Fire!" shrieked the Troll.

"Fire yourself!" said Minnikin.

"Can you fight?" roared the Troll.

"If not, I can learn," said Minnikin.

So the Troll struck at him with his iron club – which was still bigger than that which the first Troll had had – so that the earth flew ten yards up in the air.

"Fie!" said Minnikin. "That was not much of a blow. Now you shall see one of my blows."

Then he grasped his sword and struck at the Troll, so that all his ten heads danced away over the sands.

And again the King's daughter said to him, "Sleep a while on my lap," and while Minnikin lay there she drew some silver raiment over him.

As soon as Ritter Red saw that there was no longer any danger afoot, he crept down from the tree and threatened the Princess, until at last she was again forced to promise to say that it was he who had rescued her; after which he took the tongue and the lungs of the Troll and put them in his pocket-handkerchief, and then he conducted the Princess back to the palace. There was joy and gladness in the palace, as may be imagined, and the King did not know how to show enough honour and respect to Ritter Red.

Minnikin, however, took home with him an armful of gold and silver hoops from the Troll's ship. When he came back to the King's palace the kitchen-maid clapped her hands and wondered where he could have got all that gold and silver; but Minnikin answered that he had been home for a short time, and that it was only the hoops which had fallen off some pails, and that he had brought them away for the kitchen-maid.

When the third Thursday evening came, everything happened exactly as it had happened on the two former occasions. Everything in the King's palace was hung with black, and everyone was sorrowful and distressed; but Ritter Red said that he did not think that they had much reason to be afraid – he had delivered the King's daughter from two Trolls, so he could easily deliver her from the third as well.

He led her down to the strand, but when the time drew near for the Troll to come, he climbed up into the tree again and hid himself.

The Princess wept and entreated him to stay, but all to no purpose. He stuck to his old speech, "It is better that one life should be lost than two."

This evening also, Minnikin begged for leave to go down to the sea-shore.

"Oh, what can you do there?" answered the kitchen-maid.

However, he begged until at last he got leave to go, but he was forced to promise that he would be back again in the kitchen when the roast had to be turned.

Almost immediately after he had got down to the sea-shore the Troll came with a great whizzing and whirring, and he was much, much bigger than either of the two former ones, and he had fifteen heads.

"Fire!" roared the Troll.

"Fire yourself!" said Minnikin.

"Can you fight?" screamed the Troll.

"If not, I can learn," said Minnikin.

"I will teach you," yelled the Troll, and struck at him with his iron club so that the earth flew up fifteen yards high into the air.

"Fie!" said Minnikin. "That was not much of a blow. Now I will let you see one of my blows."

So saying he grasped his sword, and cut at the Troll in such a way that all his fifteen heads danced away over the sands.

Then the Princess was delivered, and she thanked Minnikin and blessed him for saving her.

"Sleep a while now on my lap," said she, and while he lay there she put a garment of brass upon him.

"But now, how shall we have it made known that it was you who saved me?" said the King's daughter.

"That I will tell you," answered Minnikin. "When Ritter Red has taken you home again, and given out that it was he who rescued you, he will, as you know, have you to wife, and half the kingdom. But when they ask you on your wedding-day whom you will have to be your cup-bearer, you must say, 'I will have the ragged boy who is in the kitchen, and carries wood and water for the kitchen-maid;' and when I am filling your cups for you, I will spill a drop upon his plate but none upon yours, and then he will be angry and strike me, and this will take place thrice. But the third time you must say, 'Shame on you thus to smite the beloved of mine heart. It is he who delivered me from the Troll, and he is the one whom I will have.'"

Then Minnikin ran back to the King's palace as he had done before, but first he went on board the Troll's ship and took a great quantity of gold and silver and other precious things, and out of these he once more gave to the kitchen-maid a whole armful of gold and silver hoops.

No sooner did Ritter Red see that all danger was over than he crept down from the tree, and threatened the King's daughter till he made her promise to say that he had rescued her. Then he conducted her back to the King's palace, and if honour enough had not been done him before it was certainly done now, for the King had no other thought than how to make much of the man who had saved his daughter from the three Trolls; and it was settled then that Ritter Red should marry her, and receive half the kingdom.

On the wedding-day, however, the Princess begged that she might have the little boy who was in the kitchen, and carried wood and water for the kitchen-maid, to fill the wine-cups at the wedding feast.

"Oh, what can you want with that dirty, ragged boy, in here?" said Ritter Red, but the Princess said that she insisted on having him as cup-bearer and would have no one else; and at last she got leave, and then everything was done as had been agreed on between the Princess and Minnikin. He spilt a drop on Ritter Red's plate but none upon hers, and each time that he did it Ritter Red fell into a rage and struck him. At the first blow all the ragged garments which he had worn in the kitchen fell from off Minnikin, at the second blow the brass garments fell off, and at the third the silver raiment, and there he stood in the golden raiment, which was so bright and splendid that light flashed from it.

Then the King's daughter said: "Shame on you thus to smite the beloved of my heart. It is he who delivered me from the Troll, and he is the one whom I will have."

Ritter Red swore that he was the man who had saved her, but the King said: "He who delivered my daughter must have some token in proof of it."

So Ritter Red ran off at once for his handkerchief with the lungs and tongue, and Minnikin went and brought all the gold and silver and precious things which he had taken out of the Trolls' ships; and they each of them laid these tokens before the King.

"He who has such precious things in gold and silver and diamonds," said the King, "must be the one who killed the Troll, for such things are not to be had anywhere else." So Ritter Red was thrown into the snake-pit, and Minnikin was to have the Princess, and half the kingdom.

One day the King went out walking with Minnikin, and Minnikin asked him if he had never had any other children.

"Yes," said the King, "I had another daughter, but the Troll carried her away because there was no one who could deliver her. You are going to have one daughter of mine, but if you can set free the other, who has been taken by the Troll, you shall willingly have her too, and the other half of the kingdom as well."

"I may as well make the attempt," said Minnikin, "but I must have an iron rope which is five hundred ells long, and then I must have five hundred men with me, and provisions for five weeks, for I have a long voyage before me."

So the King said he should have these things, but the King was afraid that he had no ship large enough to carry them all.

"But I have a ship of my own," said Minnikin, and he took the one which the old woman had given him out of his pocket. The King laughed at him and thought that it was only one of his jokes, but Minnikin begged him just to give him what he had asked for, and then he should see something. Then all that Minnikin had asked for was brought; and first he ordered them to lay the cable in the ship, but there was no one who was able to lift it, and there was only room for one or two men at a time in the little bit of a ship. Then Minnikin himself took hold of the cable, and laid one or two links of it into the ship, and as he threw the links into it the ship grew bigger and bigger, and at last it was so large that the cable, and the five hundred men, and provisions, and Minnikin himself, had room enough.

"Now go over fresh water and salt water, over hill and dale, and do not stop until thou comest to where the King's daughter is," said Minnikin to the ship, and off it went in a moment over land and water till the wind whistled and moaned all round about it.

When they had sailed thus a long, long way, the ship stopped short in the middle of the sea.

"Ah, now we have got there," said Minnikin, "but how we are to get back again is a very different thing."

Then he took the cable and tied one end of it round his body. "Now I must go to the bottom," he said, "but when I give a good jerk to the cable and want to come up again, you must all pull like one man, or there will be an end of all life both for you and for me." So saying he sprang into the water, and yellow bubbles rose up all around him. He sank lower and lower, and at last he came to the bottom. There he saw a large hill with a door in it, and in he went. When he had got inside he found the other Princess sitting sewing, but when she saw Minnikin she clapped her hands.

"Ah, heaven be praised!" she cried, "I have not seen a Christian man since I came here."

"I have come for you," said Minnikin.

"Alas! you will not be able to get me," said the King's daughter. "It is no use even to think of that; if the Troll catches sight of you he will take your life."

"You had better tell me about him," said Minnikin. "Where is he gone? It would be amusing to see him."

So the King's daughter told Minnikin that the Troll was out trying to get hold of someone who could brew a hundred lasts of malt at one brewing, for there was to be a feast at the Troll's, at which less than that would not be drunk.

"I can do that," said Minnikin.

"Ah! if only the Troll were not so quick-tempered I might have told him that," answered the Princess, "but he is so ill-natured that he will tear you to pieces, I fear, as soon as he comes in. But I will try to find some way of doing it. Can you hide yourself here in the cupboard? and then we will see what happens."

Minnikin did this, and almost before he had crept into the cupboard and hidden himself, came the Troll.

"Huf! What a smell of Christian man's blood!" said the Troll.

"Yes, a bird flew over the roof with a Christian man's bone in his bill, and let it fall down our chimney," answered the

Princess. "I made haste enough to get it away again, but it must be that which smells so, notwithstanding."

"Yes, it must be that," said the Troll.

Then the Princess asked if he had got hold of anyone who could brew a hundred lasts of malt at one brewing.

"No, there is no one who can do it," said the Troll.

"A short time since there was a man here who said he could do it," said the King's daughter.

"How clever you always are!" said the Troll. "How could you let him go away? You must have known that I was just wanting a man of that kind."

"Well, but I didn't let him go, after all," said the Princess; "but father is so quick-tempered, so I hid him in the cupboard, but if father has not found any one then the man is still here."

"Let him come in," said the Troll.

When Minnikin came, the Troll asked if it were true that he could brew a hundred lasts of malt at one brewing.

"Yes," said Minnikin, "it is."

"It is well then that I have lighted on thee," said the Troll. "Fall to work this very minute, but Heaven help thee if thou dost not brew the ale strong."

"Oh, it shall taste well," said Minnikin, and at once set himself to work to brew.

"But I must have more trolls to help to carry what is wanted," said Minnikin; "these that I have are good for nothing."

So he got more and so many that there was a swarm of them, and then the brewing went on. When the sweet-wort was ready they were all, as a matter of course, anxious to taste it, first the Troll himself and then the others; but Minnikin had brewed the wort so strong that they all fell down dead like so many flies as soon as they had drunk any of it. At last there was no one left but one wretched old hag who was lying behind the stove.

"Oh, poor old creature!" said Minnikin, "you shall have a taste of the wort too like the rest." So he went away and scooped up a little from the bottom of the brewing vat in a milk pan, and gave it to her, and then he was quit of the whole of them.

While Minnikin was now standing there looking about him, he cast his eye on a large chest. This he took and filled it with gold and silver, and then he tied the cable round himself and the Princess and the chest, and tugged at the rope with all his might, whereupon his men drew them up safe and sound.

As soon as Minnikin had got safely on his ship again, he said: "Now go over salt water and fresh water, over hill and dale, and do not stop until thou comest unto the King's palace." And in a moment the ship went off so fast that the yellow foam rose up all round about it.

When those who were in the King's palace saw the ship, they lost no time in going to meet him with song and music, and thus they marched up towards Minnikin with great rejoicings; but the gladdest of all was the King, for now he had got his other daughter back again.

But now Minnikin was not happy, for both the Princesses wanted to have him, and he wanted to have none other than the one whom he had first saved, and she was the younger. For this cause he was continually walking backwards and forwards, thinking how he could contrive to get her, and yet do nothing that was unkind to her sister. One day when he was walking about and thinking of this, it came into his mind that if he only had his brother, King Pippin, with him, who was so like himself that no one could distinguish the one from the other, he could let him have the elder Princess and half the kingdom; as for himself, he thought, the other half was quite enough. As soon as this thought occurred to him he went outside the palace and called for King Pippin, but no one came. So he called a second time, and a little louder, but no! still no one came. So Minnikin called for the third time, and with all his might, and there stood his brother by his side.

"I told you that you were not to call me unless you were in the utmost need," he said to Minnikin, "and there is not even so much as a midge here who can do you any harm!" and with that he gave Minnikin such a blow that he rolled over on the grass.

"Shame on you to strike me!" said Minnikin. "First have I won one Princess and half the kingdom, and then the other Princess and the other half of the kingdom; and now, when I was just thinking that I would give you one of the Princesses and one of the halves of the kingdom, do you think you have any reason to give me such a blow?"

When King Pippin heard that he begged his brother's pardon, and they were reconciled at once and became good friends.

"Now, as you know," said Minnikin, "we are so like each other that no one can tell one of us from the other; so just change clothes with me and go up to the palace, and then the Princesses will think that I am coming in, and the one who kisses you first shall be yours, and I will have the other." For he knew that the elder Princess was the stronger, so he could very well guess how things would go.

King Pippin at once agreed to this. He changed clothes with his brother, and went into the palace. When he entered the Princess's apartments they believed that he was Minnikin, and both of them ran up to him at once; but the elder, who was bigger and stronger, pushed her sister aside, and threw her arms round King Pippin's neck and kissed him; so he got her to wife, and Minnikin the younger sister. It will be easy to understand that two weddings took place, and they were so magnificent that they were heard of and talked about all over seven kingdoms.

THE GIANT WHO HAD NO HEART IN HIS BODY

Once on a time there was a king who had seven sons, and he loved them so much that he could never bear to be without them all at once, but one must always be with him. Now, when they were grown up, six were to set off to woo, but as for the youngest, his father kept him at home, and the others were to bring back a princess for him to the palace. So the king gave the six the finest clothes you ever set eyes on, so fine that the light gleamed from them a long way off, and each had his horse, which cost many, many hundred dollars, and so they set off. Now, when they had been to many palaces, and seen many princesses, at last they came to a king who had six daughters; such lovely king's daughters they had never seen, and so they fell to wooing them, each one, and when they had got them for sweethearts, they set off home again, but they quite forgot that they were to bring back with them a sweetheart for Boots, their brother, who stayed at home, for they were over head and ears in love with their own sweethearts.

But when they had gone a good bit on their way, they passed close by a steep hill-side, like a wall, where the giant's house was, and there the giant came out, and set his eyes upon them, and turned them all into stone, princes and princesses and all. Now the king waited and waited for his six sons, but the more he waited, the longer they stayed away; so he fell into great trouble, and said he should never know what it was to be glad again.

"And if I had not you left", he said to Boots, "I would live no longer, so full of sorrow am I for the loss of your brothers."

"Well, but now I've been thinking to ask your leave to set out and find them again; that's what I'm thinking of", said Boots.

"Nay, nay!" said his father; "that leave you shall never get, for then you would stay away too."

But Boots had set his heart upon it; go he would; and he begged and prayed so long that the king was forced to let him go. Now, you must know the king had no other horse to give Boots but an old broken-down jade, for his six other sons and their train had carried off all his horses; but Boots did not care a pin for that, he sprang up on his sorry-old-steed.

"Farewell, father", said he; "I'll come back, never fear, and like enough I shall bring my six brothers back with me"; and with that he rode off.

So, when he had ridden a while, he came to a Raven, which lay in the road and flapped its wings, and was not able to get out of the way, it was so starved.

"Oh, dear friend", said the Raven, "give me a little food, and I'll help you again at your utmost need."

"I haven't much food", said the Prince, "and I don't see how you'll ever be able to help me much; but still I can spare you a little. I see you want it."

So he gave the raven some of the food he had brought with him.

Now, when he had gone a bit further, he came to a brook, and in the brook lay a great Salmon, which had got upon a dry place and dashed itself about, and could not get into the water again.

"Oh, dear friend", said the Salmon to the Prince; "shove me out into the water again, and I'll help you again at your utmost need."

"Well!" said the Prince, "the help you'll give me will not be great, I daresay, but it's a pity you should lie there and choke"; and with that he shot the fish out into the stream again.

After that he went a long, long way, and there met him a Wolf, which was so famished that it lay and crawled along the road on its belly.

"Dear friend, do let me have your horse", said the Wolf; "I'm so hungry the wind whistles through my ribs; I've had nothing to eat these two years."

"No", said Boots, "this will never do; "first I came to a raven, and I was forced to give him my food; next I came to a salmon, and him I had to help into the water again; and now you will have my horse. It can't be done, that it can't, for then I should have nothing to ride on."

"Nay, dear friend, but you can help me", said Graylegs the wolf; "you can ride upon my back, and I'll help you again in your utmost need."

"Well! the help I shall get from you will not be great, I'll be bound", said the Prince; "but you may take my horse, since you are in such need."

So when the wolf had eaten the horse, Boots took the bit and put it into the wolf's jaw, and laid the saddle on his back; and now the wolf was so strong, after what he had got inside, that he set off with the Prince like nothing. So fast he had never ridden before.

"When we have gone a bit farther", said Graylegs; "I'll show you the Giant's house."

So after a while they came to it.

"See, here is the Giant's house", said the Wolf; "and see, here are your six brothers, whom the Giant has turned into stone; and see here are their six brides, and away yonder is the door, and in at that door you must go."

"Nay, but I daren't go in", said the Prince; "he'll take my life."

"No! no!" said the Wolf; "when you get in you'll find a Princess, and she'll tell you what to do to make an end of the Giant. Only mind and do as she bids you."

Well! Boots went in, but, truth to say, he was very much afraid. When he came in the Giant was away, but in one of the rooms sat the Princess, just as the wolf had said, and so lovely a princess Boots had never yet set eyes on.

"Oh! heaven help you! whence have you come?" said the Princess, as she saw him; "it will surely be your death. No one can make an end of the Giant who lives here, for he has no heart in his body."

"Well! well!" said Boots; "but now that I am here, I may as well try what I can do with him; and I will see if I can't free my brothers, who are standing turned to stone out of doors; and you, too, I will try to save, that I will."

"Well, if you must, you must", said the Princess; "and so let us see if we can't hit on a plan. Just creep under the bed yonder, and mind and listen to what he and I talk about. But, pray, do lie as still as a mouse."

So he crept under the bed, and he had scarce got well underneath it, before the Giant came.

"Ha!" roared the Giant, "what a smell of Christian blood there is in the house!"

"Yes, I know there is", said the Princess, "for there came a magpie flying with a man's bone, and let it fall down the chimney. I made all the haste I could to get it out, but all one can do, the smell doesn't go off so soon."

So the Giant said no more about it, and when night came, they went to bed. After they had lain awhile, the Princess said:

"There is one thing I'd be so glad to ask you about, if I only dared."

"What thing is that?" asked the Giant.

"Only where it is you keep your heart, since you don't carry it about you", said the Princess.

"Ah! that's a thing you've no business to ask about; but if you must know, it lies under the door-sill", said the Giant.

"Ho! ho!" said Boots to himself under the bed, "then we'll soon see if we can't find it."

Next morning the Giant got up cruelly early, and strode off to the wood; but he was hardly out of the house before Boots and the Princess set to work to look under the door-sill for his heart; but the more they dug, and the more they hunted, the more they couldn't find it.

"He has baulked us this time", said the Princess, "but we'll try him once more."

So she picked all the prettiest flowers she could find, and strewed them over the door-sill, which they had laid in its right place again; and when the time came for the Giant to come home again, Boots crept under the bed. Just as he was well under, back came the Giant.

Snuff – snuff, went the Giant's nose. "My eyes and limbs, what a smell of Christian blood there is in here", said he.

"I know there is", said the Princess, "for there came a magpie flying with a man's bone in his bill, and let it fall down the chimney. I made as much haste as I could to get it out, but I daresay it's that you smell."

So the Giant held his peace, and said no more about it. A little while after, he asked who it was that had strewed flowers about the door-sill.

"Oh, I, of course", said the Princess.

"And, pray, what's the meaning of all this?" said the Giant.

"Ah!" said the Princess, "I'm so fond of you that I couldn't help strewing them, when I knew that your heart lay under there."

"You don't say so", said the Giant; "but after all it doesn't lie there at all."

So when they went to bed again in the evening, the Princess asked the Giant again where his heart was, for she said she would so like to know.

"Well", said the Giant, "if you must know, it lies away yonder in the cupboard against the wall."

"So, so!" thought Boots and the Princess; "then we'll soon try to find it."

Next morning the Giant was away early, and strode off to the wood, and so soon as he was gone Boots and the Princess were in the cupboard hunting for his heart, but the more they sought for it, the less they found it.

"Well", said the Princess, "we'll just try him once more."

So she decked out the cupboard with flowers and garlands, and when the time came for the Giant to come home, Boots crept under the bed again.

Then back came the Giant.

Snuff-snuff! "My eyes and limbs, what a smell of Christian blood there is in here!"

"I know there is", said the Princess; "for a little while since there came a magpie flying with a man's bone in his bill, and let it fall down the chimney. I made all the haste I could to get it out of the house again; but after all my pains, I daresay it's that you smell."

When the Giant heard that, he said no more about it; but a little while after, he saw how the cupboard was all decked about with flowers and garlands; so he asked who it was that had done that? Who could it be but the Princess.

"And, pray, what's the meaning of all this tom-foolery?" asked the Giant.

"Oh, I'm so fond of you, I couldn't help doing it when I knew that your heart lay there", said the Princess.

"How can you be so silly as to believe any such thing?" said the Giant.

"Oh yes; how can I help believing it, when you say it", said the Princess.

"You're a goose", said the Giant; "where my heart is, you will never come."

"Well", said the Princess;" but for all that, 'twould be such a pleasure to know where it really lies."

Then the poor Giant could hold out no longer, but was forced to say:

"Far, far away in a lake lies an island; on that island stands a church; in that church is a well; in that well swims a duck; in that duck there is an egg, and in that egg there lies my heart, – you darling!"

In the morning early, while it was still grey dawn, the Giant strode off to the wood.

"Yes! now I must set off too", said Boots; "if I only knew how to find the way." He took a long, long farewell of the Princess, and when he got out of the Giant's door, there stood the Wolf waiting for him. So Boots told him all that had happened inside the house, and said now he wished to ride to the well in the church, if he only knew the way. So the Wolf bade him jump on his back, he'd soon find the way; and away they went, till the wind whistled after them, over hedge and field, over hill and dale. After they had travelled many, many days, they came at last to the lake. Then the Prince did not know how to get over it, but the Wolf bade him only not be afraid, but stick on, and so he jumped into the lake with the Prince on his back, and swam over to the island. So they came to the church; but the church keys hung high, high up on the top of the tower, and at first the Prince did not know how to get them down.

"You must call on the raven", said the Wolf.

So the Prince called on the raven, and in a trice the raven came, and flew up and fetched the keys, and so the Prince got into the church. But when he came to the well, there lay the duck, and swam about backwards and forwards, just as the Giant had said. So the Prince stood and coaxed it and coaxed it, till it came to him, and he grasped it in his hand; but just as he lifted it up from the water the duck dropped the egg into the well, and then Boots was beside himself to know how to get it out again.

"Well, now you must call on the salmon to be sure", said the Wolf; and the king's son called on the salmon, and the salmon came and fetched up the egg from the bottom of the well.

Then the Wolf told him to squeeze the egg, and as soon as ever he squeezed it the Giant screamed out.

"Squeeze it again", said the Wolf; and when the Prince did so, the Giant screamed still more piteously, and begged and prayed so prettily to be spared, saying he would do all that the Prince wished if he would only not squeeze his heart in two.

"Tell him, if he will restore to life again your six brothers and their brides, whom he has turned to stone, you will spare his life", said the Wolf. Yes, the Giant was ready to do that, and he turned the six brothers into king's sons again, and their brides into king's daughters.

"Now, squeeze the egg in two", said the Wolf. So Boots squeezed the egg to pieces, and the Giant burst at once.

Now, when he had made an end of the Giant, Boots rode back again on the wolf to the Giant's house, and there stood all his six brothers alive and merry, with their brides. Then Boots went into the hill-side after his bride, and so they all set off home again to their father's house. And you may fancy how glad the old king was when he saw all his seven sons come back, each with his bride – "But the loveliest bride of all is the bride of Boots, after all", said the king, "and he shall sit uppermost at the table, with her by his side."

So he sent out, and called a great wedding-feast, and the mirth was both loud and long, and if they have not done feasting, why, they are still at it.

FINN, THE GIANT, AND THE MINSTER OF LUND

There stands in the university town of Schonen, the town of Lund, the seat of the first archbishopric in all Scandinavia, a stately Romanic minster, with a large, handsome crypt beneath the choir. The opinion is universal that the minster will never be altogether finished, but that something will always be lacking about the structure. The reason is said to be as follows:

When St. Lawrence came to Lund to preach the Gospel, he wanted to build a church; but did not know how he was to obtain the means to do so.

While he was cudgelling his brains about it, a giant came to him and offered to build the church on condition that St. Lawrence tell him his name before the church was completed. But should St. Lawrence be unable to do so, the giant was to receive either the sun, the moon or St. Lawrence's eyes. The saint agreed to his proposal.

The building of the church made rapid progress, and ere long it was nearly finished. St. Lawrence thought ruefully about his prospects, for he did not know the giant's name; yet at the same time he did not relish losing his eyes. And it happened that while he was walking without the town, much concerned about the outcome of the affair, he grew weary, and sat down on a hill to rest. As he sat there he heard a child crying within the hill, and a woman's voice began to sing:

> "Sleep, sleep, my baby dear,
> Tomorrow your father, Finn, will be here;
> Then sun and moon you shall have from the skies
> To play with, or else St. Lawrence's eyes."

When St. Lawrence heard that he was happy; for now he knew the giant's name. He ran back quickly to town, and went to the church. There sat the giant on the roof, just about to set the last stone in place, when at that very moment the saint called out:

> "Finn, Finn,
> *Take care how you put the stone in!*"

Then the giant flung the stone from him, full of rage, said that the church should never be finished, and with that he disappeared. Since then something has always been missing from the church.

Others say that the giant and his wife rushed down into the crypt in their rage, and each seizing a column were about to tear down the church, when they were turned into stone, and may be seen to this day standing beside the columns they had grasped

KNÖS

Once upon a time there was a poor widow, who found an egg under a pile of brush as she was gathering kindlings in the forest. She took it and placed it under a goose, and when the goose had hatched it, a little boy slipped out of the shell. The widow had him baptized Knös, and such a lad was a rarity; for when no more than five years old he was grown, and taller than the tallest man. And he ate in proportion, for he would swallow a whole batch of bread at a single sitting, and at last the poor widow had to go to the commissioners for the relief of the poor in order to get food for him. But the town authorities said she must apprentice the boy at a trade, for he was big enough and strong enough to earn his own keep.

So Knös was apprenticed to a smith for three years. For his pay he asked a suit of clothes and a sword each year: a sword of five hundredweights the first year, one of ten hundredweights the second year, and one of fifteen hundredweights the third year. But after he had been in the smithy only a few days, the smith was glad to give him all three suits and all three swords at once; for he smashed all his iron and steel to bits.

Knös received his suits and swords, went to a knight's estate, and hired himself out as a serving-man. Once he was told to go to the forest to gather firewood with the rest of the men, but sat at the table eating long after the others had driven off and when he had at last satisfied his hunger and was ready to start, he saw the two young oxen he was to drive waiting for him. But he let them stand and went into the forest, seized the two largest trees growing there, tore them out by the roots, took one tree under each arm, and carried them back to the estate. And he got there long before the rest, for they had to chop down the trees, saw them up and load them on the carts.

On the following day Knös had to thresh. First he hunted up the largest stone he could find, and rolled it around on the grain, so that all the corn was loosened from the ears. Then he had to separate the grain from the chaff. So he made a hole in each side of the roof of the barn, and stood outside the barn and blew, and the chaff and straw flew out into the yard, and the corn remained lying in a heap on the floor. His master happened to come along, laid a ladder against the barn, climbed up and looked down into one of the holes. But Knös was still blowing, and the wind caught his master, and he fell down and was nearly killed on the stone pavement of the court.

"He's a dangerous fellow," thought his master. It would be a good thing to be rid of him, otherwise he might do away with all of them; and besides, he ate so that it was all one could do to keep him fed. So he called Knös in, and paid him his wages for the full year, on condition that he leave. Knös agreed, but said he must first be decently provisioned for his journey.

So he was allowed to go into the store-house himself, and there he hoisted a flitch of bacon on each shoulder, slid a batch of bread under each arm, and took leave. But his master loosed the vicious bull on him. Knös, however, grasped him by the horns, and flung him over his shoulder, and thus he went off. Then he came to a thicket where he slaughtered the bull, roasted him and ate him together with a batch of bread. And when he had done this he had about taken the edge off his hunger.

Then he came to the king's court, where great sorrow reigned because, once upon a time, when the king was sailing out at sea, a sea troll had called up a terrible tempest, so that the ship was about to sink. In order to escape with his life, the king had to promise the sea troll to give him whatever first came his way when he reached shore. The king thought his hunting dog would be the first to come running to meet him, as usual; but instead his three young daughters came rowing out to meet him in a boat. This filled the king with grief, and he vowed that whoever delivered his daughters should have one of them for a bride, whichever one he might choose. But the only man who seemed to want to earn the reward was a tailor, named Red Peter.

Knös was given a place at the king's court, and his duty was to help the cook. But he asked to be let off on the day the troll was to come and carry away the oldest princess, and they were glad to let him go; for when he had to rinse the dishes he broke the king's vessels of gold and silver; and when he was told to bring firewood, he brought in a whole wagon-load at once, so that the doors flew from their hinges.

The princess stood on the sea-shore and wept and wrung her hands; for she could see what she had to expect. Nor did she have much confidence in Red Peter, who sat on a willow-stump, with a rusty old sabre in his hand. Then Knös came and tried to comfort the princess as well as he knew how, and asked her whether she would comb his hair. Yes, he might lay his head in her lap, and she combed his hair. Suddenly there was a dreadful roaring out at sea. It was the troll who was coming along, and he had five heads. Red Peter was so frightened that he rolled off his willow-stump. "Knös, is that you?" cried the troll. "Yes," said Knös. "Haul me up on the shore!" said the troll. "Pay out the cable!" said Knös. Then he hauled the troll ashore; but he had his sword of five hundredweights at his side, and with it he chopped off all five of the troll's heads, and the princess was free. But when Knös had gone off, Red Peter put his sabre to the breast of the princess, and told her he would kill her unless she said he was her deliverer.

Then came the turn of the second princess. Once more Red Peter sat on the willow-stump with his rusty sabre, and Knös asking to be let off for the day, went to the sea-shore and begged the princess to comb his hair, which she did. Then along came the troll, and this time he had ten heads. "Knös, is that you?" asked the troll. "Yes," said Knös. "Haul me ashore!" said the troll. "Pay out the cable!" said Knös. And this time Knös had his sword of ten hundredweights at his side, and he cut off all ten of the troll's heads. And so the second princess was freed. But Red Peter held his sabre at the princess' breast, and forced her to say that he had delivered her.

Now it was the turn of the youngest princess. When it was time for the troll to come, Red Peter was sitting on his willow-stump, and Knös came and begged the princess to comb his hair, and she did so. This time the troll had fifteen heads.

"Knös, is that you?" asked the troll. "Yes," said Knös. "Haul me ashore!" said the troll. "Pay out the cable," said Knös. Knös had his sword of fifteen hundredweights at his side, and with it he cut off all the troll's heads. But the fifteen hundredweights were half-an-ounce short, and the heads grew on again, and the troll took the princess, and carried her off with him.

One day as Knös was going along, he met a man carrying a church on his back. "You are a strong man, you are!" said Knös. "No, I am not strong," said he, "but Knös at the king's court, he is strong; for he can take steel and iron, and weld them together with his hands as though they were clay." "Well, I'm the man of whom you are speaking," said Knös, "come, let us travel together." And so they wandered on.

Then they met a man who carried a mountain of stone on his back. "You are strong, you are!" said Knös. "No, I'm not strong," said the man with the mountain of stone, "but Knös at the king's court, he is strong; for he can weld together steel and iron with his hands as though they were clay."

"Well, I am that Knös, come let us travel together," said Knös. So all three of them traveled along together. Knös took them for a sea-trip; but I think they had to leave the church and the hill of stone ashore. While they were sailing they grew thirsty, and lay alongside an island, and there on the island stood a castle, to which they decided to go and ask for a drink. Now this was the very castle in which the troll lived.

First the man with the church went, and when he entered the castle, there sat the troll with the princess on his lap, and she was very sad. He asked for something to drink. "Help yourself, the goblet is on the table!" said the troll. But he got nothing to drink, for though he could move the goblet from its place, he could not raise it.

Then the man with the hill of stone went into the castle and asked for a drink. "Help yourself, the goblet is on the table!" said the troll. And he got nothing to drink either, for though he could move the goblet from its place, he could not raise it.

Then Knös himself went into the castle, and the princess was full of joy and leaped down from the troll's lap when she saw it was he. Knös asked for a drink. "Help yourself," said the troll, "the goblet is on the table!" And Knös took the goblet and emptied it at a single draught. Then he hit the troll across the head with the goblet, so that he rolled from the chair and died.

Knös took the princess back to the royal palace, and O, how happy every one was! The other princesses recognized Knös again, for they had woven silk ribbons into his hair when they had combed it; but he could only marry one of the princesses, whichever one he preferred, so he chose the youngest. And when the king died, Knös inherited the kingdom.

As for Red Peter, he had to go into the nail-barrel.

And now you know all that I know.

TALES OF WIND, SNOW & SEA

A thousand years after the first longships struck their way across the high Atlantic swell, Hans Christian Andersen's 'Little Match-Seller' struggled through a city's icy winter streets. No one knew better than the Vikings did the raw power of the snow and wind and rain: the elements are an elemental force in Nordic myth.

Father Weatherbeard, who rides the winds ('I am at home both in the north and south and the east and the west...'), is as sinister as any troll. The parents who entrust their son to him – he promises to train him up as his apprentice – find he's nothing like as quick to give him back. As for the Sea Queen, in 'First Born, First Wed', she may be happy enough to save the stricken mariner – but she demands that he hand over his young son in return.

Human life has always hung by a thread and mythology everywhere is aware of our fragility, but the Vikings were unusually – perhaps uniquely – vulnerable. Countless lives have been lost to wind and waves in every generation in what are still seafaring nations.

FARMER WEATHERBEARD

T here was once upon a time a man and a woman who had an only son, and he was called Jack. The woman thought that it was his duty to go out to service, and told her husband that he was to take him somewhere.

"You must get him such a good place that he will become master of all masters," she said, and then she put some food and a roll of tobacco into a bag for them.

Well, they went to a great many masters, but all said that they could make the lad as good as they were themselves, but better than that they could not make him. When the man came home to the old woman with this answer, she said, "I shall be equally well pleased whatever you do with him; but this I do say, that you are to have him made a master over all masters." Then she once more put some food and a roll of tobacco into the bag, and the man and his son had to set out again.

When they had walked some distance they got upon the ice, and there they met a man in a carriage who was driving a black horse.

"Where are you going?" he said.

"I have to go and get my son apprenticed to someone who will be able to teach him a trade, for my old woman comes of such well-to-do folk that she insists on his being taught to be master of all masters," said the man.

"We are not ill met, then," said the man who was driving, "for I am the kind of man who can do that, and I am just looking out for such an apprentice. Get up behind with you," he said to the boy, and off the horse went with them straight up into the air.

"No, no, wait a little!" screamed the father of the boy. "I ought to know what your name is and where you live."

"Oh, I am at home both in the north and the south and the east and the west, and I am called Farmer Weatherbeard," said the master. "You may come here again in a year's time, and then I will tell you if the lad suits me." And then they set off again and were gone.

When the man got home the old woman inquired what had become of the son.

"Ah! Heaven only knows what has become of him!" said the man. "They went up aloft." And then he told her what had happened.

But when the woman heard that, and found that the man did not at all know either when their son would be out of his apprentice-ship, or where he had gone, she packed him off again to find out, and gave him a bag of food and a roll of tobacco to take away with him.

When he had walked for some time he came to a great wood, and it stretched before him all day long as he went on, and when night began to fall he saw a great light, and went towards it. After a long, long time he came to a small hut at the foot of a rock, outside which an old woman was standing drawing water up from a well with her nose, it was so long.

"Good-evening, mother," said the man.

"Good-evening to you too," said the old woman. "No one has called me mother this hundred years."

"Can I lodge here tonight?" said the man.

"No," said the old woman. But the man took out his roll of tobacco, lighted a little of it, and then gave her a whiff. Then she was so delighted that she began to dance, and thus the man got leave to stay the night there. It was not long before he asked about Farmer Weatherbeard.

She said that she knew nothing about him, but that she ruled over all the four-footed beasts, and some of them might know him. So she gathered them all together by blowing a whistle which she had, and questioned them, but there was not one of them which knew anything about Farmer Weatherbeard.

"Well," said the old woman, "there are three of us sisters; it may be that one of the other two knows where he is to be found. You shall have the loan of my horse and carriage, and then you will get there by night; but her house is three hundred miles off, go the nearest way you will."

The man set out and got there at night. When he arrived, this old woman also was standing drawing water out of the well with her nose.

"Good-evening, mother," said the man.

"Good-evening to you," said the old woman. "No one has ever called me mother this hundred years."

"Can I lodge here tonight?" said the man.

"No," said the old woman.

Then he took out the roll of tobacco, took a whiff, and gave the old woman some snuff on the back of her hand. Then she was so delighted that she began to dance, and the man got leave to stay all night. It was not long before he began to ask about Farmer Weatherbeard.

She knew nothing about him, but she ruled over all the fishes, she said, and perhaps some of them might know something. So she gathered them all together by blowing a whistle which she had, and questioned them, but there was not one of them which knew anything about Farmer Weatherbeard.

"Well," said the old woman, "I have another sister; perhaps she may know something about him. She lives six hundred miles off, but you shall have my horse and carriage, and then you will get there by nightfall."

So the man set off and he got there by nightfall. The old woman was standing raking the fire, and she was doing it with her nose, so long it was.

"Good-evening, mother," said the man.

"Good-evening to you," said the old woman. "No one has called me mother this hundred years."

"Can I lodge here tonight?" said the man.

"No," said the old woman. But the man pulled out his roll of tobacco again, and filled his pipe with some of it, and gave the old woman enough snuff to cover the back of her hand. Then she was so delighted that she began to dance, and the man got leave to stay in her house. It was not long before he asked about Farmer Weatherbeard. She knew nothing at all about him, she said, but she governed all the birds; and she gathered them together with her whistle. When she questioned them all, the eagle was not there, but it came soon afterwards, and when asked, it said that it had just come from Farmer Weatherbeard's. Then the old woman said that it was to guide the man to him. But the eagle would have something to eat first, and then it wanted to wait until the next day, for it was so tired with the long journey that it was scarcely able to rise from the earth.

When the eagle had had plenty of food and rest, the old woman plucked a feather out of its tail, and set the man in the feather's place, and then the bird flew away with him, but they did not get to Farmer Weatherbeard's before midnight.

When they got there the Eagle said: "There are a great many dead bodies lying outside the door, but you must not concern yourself about them. The people who are inside the house are all so sound asleep that it will not be easy to awake them; but you must go straight to the table-drawer, and take out three bits of bread, and if you hear anyone snoring, pluck three feathers from his head; he will not waken for that."

The man did this; when he had got the bits of bread he first plucked out one feather.

"Oof!" screamed Farmer Weatherbeard.

So the man plucked out another, and then Farmer Weatherbeard shrieked "Oof!" again; but when the man had plucked the third, Farmer Weatherbeard screamed so loudly that the man thought that brick and mortar would be rent in twain, but for all that he went on sleeping. And now the Eagle told the man what he was to do next, and he did it. He went to the stable door, and there he stumbled against a hard stone, which he picked up, and beneath it lay three splinters of wood, which he also picked up. He knocked at the stable door and it opened at once. He threw down the three little bits of bread and a hare came out and ate them. He caught the hare. Then the Eagle told him to pluck three feathers out of its tail, and put in the hare, the stone, the splinters of wood and himself instead of them, and then he would be able to carry them all home.

When the Eagle had flown a long way it alighted on a stone.

"Do you see anything?" it asked.

"Yes; I see a flock of crows coming flying after us," said the man.

"Then we shall do well to fly on a little farther," said the Eagle, and off it set.

In a short time it asked again, "Do you see anything now?"

"Yes; now the crows are close behind us," said the man.

"Then throw down the three feathers which you plucked out of his head," said the Eagle.

So the man did this, and no sooner had he flung them down than the feathers became a flock of ravens, which chased the crows home again. Then the Eagle flew on much farther with the man, but at length it alighted on a stone for a while.

"Do you see anything?" it said.

"I am not quite certain," said the man, "but I think I see something coming in the far distance."

"Then we shall do well to fly on a little farther," said the Eagle, and away it went.

"Do you see anything now?" it said, after some time had gone by.

"Yes; now they are close behind us," said the man.

"Then throw down the splinters of wood which you took from beneath the gray stone by the stable door," said the Eagle. The man did this, and no sooner had he flung them down than they grew up into a great thick wood, and Farmer Weatherbeard had to go home for an axe to cut his way through it. So the Eagle flew on a long, long way, but then it grew tired and sat down on a fir tree.

"Do you see anything?" it asked.

"Yes; I am not quite certain," said the man, "but I think I can catch a glimpse of something far, far away."

"Then we shall do well to fly on a little farther," said the Eagle, and it set off again.

"Do you see anything now?" it said after some time had gone by.

"Yes; he is close behind us now," said the man.

"Then you must fling down the great stone which you took away from the stable door," said the Eagle.

The man did so, and it turned into a great high mountain of stone, which Farmer Weatherbeard had to break his way through before he could follow them. But when he had got to the middle of the mountain he broke one of his legs, so he had to go home to get it put right.

While he was doing this the Eagle flew off to the man's home with him, and with the hare, and when they had got home the man went to the churchyard, and had some Christian earth laid upon the hare, and then it turned into his son Jack.

When the time came for the fair the youth turned himself into a light-coloured horse, and bade his father go to the market with him. "If anyone should come who wants to buy me," said he, "you are to tell him that you want a hundred dollars for me; but you must not forget to take off the halter, for if you do I shall never be able to get away from Farmer Weatherbeard, for he is the man who will come and bargain for me."

And thus it happened. A horse-dealer came who had a great fancy to bargain for the horse, and the man got a hundred dollars for it, but when the bargain was made, and Jack's father had got the money, the horse-dealer wanted to have the halter.

"That was no part of our bargain," said the man, "and the halter you shall not have, for I have other horses which I shall have to sell."

So each of them went his way. But the horse dealer had not got very far with Jack before he resumed his own form again, and when the man got home he was sitting on the bench by the stove.

The next day he changed himself into a brown horse and told his father that he was to set off to market with him. "If a man should come who wants to buy me," said Jack, "you are to tell him that you want two hundred dollars, for that he will give, and treat you besides; but whatsoever you drink, and whatsoever you do, don't forget to take the halter off me, or you will never see me more."

And thus it happened. The man got his two hundred dollars for the horse, and was treated as well, and when they parted from each other it was just as much as he could do to remember to take off the halter. But the buyer had not got far on his way before the youth took his own form again, and when the man reached home Jack was already sitting on the bench by the stove.

On the third day all happened in the same way. The youth changed himself into a great black horse, and told his father that if a man came and offered him three hundred dollars, and treated him well and handsomely into the bargain, he was to sell him, but whatsoever he did, or how much soever he drank, he must not forget to take off the halter, or else he himself would never get away from Farmer Weatherbeard as long as he lived.

"No," said the man, "I will not forget."

When he got to the market, he received the three hundred dollars, but Farmer Weatherbeard treated him so handsomely that he quite forgot to take off the halter; so Farmer Weatherbeard went away with the horse.

When he had got some distance he had to go into an inn to get some more brandy; so he set a barrel full of red-hot nails under his horse's nose, and a trough filled with oats beneath its tail, and then he tied the halter fast to a hook and went away into the inn. So the horse stood there stamping, and kicking, and snorting, and rearing, and out came a girl who thought it a sin and a shame to treat a horse so ill.

"Ah, poor creature, what a master you must have to treat you thus!" she said, and pushed the halter off the hook so that the horse might turn round and eat the oats.

"I am here!" shrieked Farmer Weatherbeard, rushing out of doors. But the horse had already shaken off the halter and flung himself into a goose-pond, where he changed himself into a little fish. Farmer Weatherbeard went after him, and changed himself into a great pike. So Jack turned himself into a dove, and Farmer Weatherbeard turned himself into a hawk, and flew after the dove and struck it. But a Princess was standing at a window in the King's palace watching the struggle.

"If thou didst but know as much as I know, thou wouldst fly in to me through the window," said the Princess to the dove.

So the dove came flying in through the window and changed itself into Jack again, and told her all as it had happened.

"Change thyself into a gold ring, and set thyself on my finger," said the Princess.

"No, that will not do," said Jack, "for then Farmer Weatherbeard will make the King fall sick, and there will be no one who can make him well again before Farmer Weatherbeard comes and cures him, and for that he will demand the gold ring."

"I will say that it was my mother's, and that I will not part with it," said the Princess.

So Jack changed himself into a gold ring, and set himself on the Princess's finger, and Farmer Weatherbeard could not get at him there. But then all that the youth had foretold came to pass.

The King became ill, and there was no doctor who could cure him till Farmer Weatherbeard arrived, and he demanded the ring which was on the Princess's finger as a reward.

So the King sent a messenger to the Princess for the ring. She, however, refused to part with it, because she had inherited it from her mother. When the King was informed of this he fell into a rage, and said that he would have the ring, let her have inherited it from whom she might.

"Well, it's of no use to be angry about it," said the Princess, "for I can't get it off. If you want the ring you will have to take the finger too!"

"I will try, and then the ring will very soon come off," said Farmer Weatherbeard.

"No, thank you, I will try myself," said the Princess, and she went away to the fireplace and put some ashes on the ring.

So the ring came off and was lost among the ashes.

Farmer Weatherbeard changed himself into a hare, which scratched and scraped about in the fireplace after the ring until the ashes were up to its ears. But Jack changed himself into a fox, and bit the hare's head off, and if Farmer Weatherbeard was possessed by the evil one all was now over with him.

THE THREE PRINCESSES OF WHITELAND

There was once upon a time a fisherman, who lived hard by a palace and fished for the King's table. One day he was out fishing, but caught nothing at all. Let him do what he might with rod and line, there was never even so much as a sprat on his hook; but when the day was well nigh over, a head rose up out of the water, and said: "If you will give me what your wife shows you when you go home, you shall catch fish enough."

So the man said "Yes" in a moment, and then he caught fish in plenty; but when he got home at night, and his wife showed him a baby which had just been born, and fell a-weeping and wailing when he told her of the promise which he had given, he was very unhappy.

All this was soon told to the King up at the palace, and when he heard what sorrow the woman was in, and the reason of it, he said that he himself would take the child and see if he could not save it. The baby was a boy, and the King took him at once and brought him up as his own son until the lad grew up. Then one day he begged to have leave to go out with his father to fish; he had a strong desire to do this, he said. The King was very unwilling to permit it, but at last the lad got leave. He stayed with his father, and all went prosperously and well with them the whole day, until they came back to land in the evening. Then the lad found that he had lost his pocket-handkerchief, and would go out in the boat after it; but no sooner had he got into the boat than it began to move off with him so quickly that the water foamed all round about, and all that the lad did to keep the boat back with the oars was done to no purpose, for it went on and on the whole night through, and at last he came to a white strand that lay far, far away. There he landed, and when he had walked on for some distance he met an old man with a long white beard.

"What is the name of this country?" said the youth.

"Whiteland," answered the man, and then he begged the youth to tell him whence he came and what he was going to do, and the youth did so.

"Well, then," said the man, "if you walk on farther along the seashore here, you will come to three princesses who are standing in the earth so that their heads alone are out of it. Then the first of them will call you – she is the eldest – and will beg you very prettily to come to her and help her, and the second will do the same, but you must not go near either of them. Hurry past, as if you neither saw nor heard them; but you shall go to the third and do what she bids you; it will bring you good fortune."

When the youth came to the first princess, she called to him and begged him to come to her very prettily, but he walked on as if he did not even see her, and he passed by the second in the same way, but he went up to the third.

"If thou wilt do what I tell thee, thou shalt choose among us three," said the Princess.

So the lad said that he was most willing, and she told him that three Trolls had planted them all three there in the earth, but that formerly they had dwelt in the castle which he could see at some distance in the wood.

"Now," she said, "thou shalt go into the castle, and let the Trolls beat thee one night for each of us, and if thou canst but endure that, thou wilt set us free."

"Yes," answered the lad, "I will certainly try to do so."

"When thou goest in," continued the Princess, "two lions will stand by the doorway, but if thou only goest straight between them they will do thee no harm; go straight forward into a small dark chamber; there thou shalt lie down. Then the Troll will come and beat thee, but thou shalt take the flask which is hanging on the wall, and anoint thyself wheresoever he has wounded thee, after which thou shalt be as well as before. Then lay hold of the sword which is hanging by the side of the flask, and smite the Troll dead."

So he did what the Princess had told him. He walked straight in between the lions just as if he did not see them, and then into the small chamber, and lay down on the bed.

The first night a Troll came with three heads and three rods, and beat the lad most unmercifully; but he held out until the Troll was done with him, and then he took the flask and rubbed himself. Having done this, he grasped the sword and smote the Troll dead.

In the morning when he went to the sea-shore the Princesses were out of the earth as far as their waists.

The next night everything happened in the same way, but the Troll who came then had six heads and six rods, and he beat him much more severely than the first had done but when the lad went out of doors next morning, the Princesses were out of the earth as far as their knees.

On the third night a Troll came who had nine heads and nine rods, and he struck the lad and flogged him so long, that at last he swooned away; so the Troll took him up and flung him against the wall, and this made the flask of ointment fall down, and it splashed all over him, and he became as strong as ever again.

Then, without loss of time, he grasped the sword and struck the Troll dead, and in the morning when he went out of the castle the Princesses were standing there entirely out of the earth. So he took the youngest for his Queen, and lived with her very happily for a long time.

At last, however, he took a fancy to go home for a short time to see his parents. His Queen did not like this, but when his longing grew so great that he told her he must and would go, she said to him:

"One thing shalt thou promise me, and that is, to do what thy father bids thee, but not what thy mother bids thee," and this he promised.

So she gave him a ring, which enabled him who wore it to obtain two wishes.

He wished himself at home, and instantly found himself there; but his parents were so amazed at the splendour of his apparel that their wonder never ceased.

When he had been at home for some days his mother wanted him to go up to the palace, to show the King what a great man he had become.

The father said, "No; he must not do that, for if he does we shall have no more delight in him this time" but he spoke in vain, for the mother begged and prayed until at last he went.

When he arrived there he was more splendid, both in raiment and in all else, than the other King, who did not like it, and said:

"Well, you can see what kind of Queen mine is, but I can't see yours. I do not believe you have such a pretty Queen as I have."

"Would to heaven she were standing here, and then you would be able to see!" said the young King, and in an instant she was standing there.

But she was very sorrowful, and said to him, "Why didst thou not remember my words, and listen only to what thy father said? Now must I go home again at once, and thou hast wasted both thy wishes."

Then she tied a ring in his hair, which had her name upon it, and wished herself at home again.

And now the young King was deeply afflicted, and day out and day in went about thinking of naught else but how to get back again to his Queen. "I will try to see if there is any place where I can learn how to find Whiteland," he thought, and journeyed forth out into the world.

When he had gone some distance he came to a mountain, where he met a man who was Lord over all the beasts in the forest – for they all came to him when he blew a horn which he had. So the King asked where Whiteland was.

"I do not know that," he answered, "but I will ask my beasts." Then he blew his horn and inquired whether any of them knew where Whiteland lay, but there was not one who knew that.

So the man gave him a pair of snow shoes. "When you have these on," he said, "you will come to my brother, who lives hundreds of miles from here; he is Lord over all the birds in the air – ask him. When you have got there, just turn the shoes so that the toes point this way, and then they will come home again of their own accord."

When the King arrived there he turned the shoes as the Lord of the beasts had bidden him, and they went back.

And now he once more asked after Whiteland, and the man summoned all the birds together, and inquired if any of them knew where Whiteland lay. No, none knew this. Long after the others there came an old eagle. He had been absent ten whole years, but he too knew no more than the rest.

"Well, well," said the man, "then you shall have the loan of a pair of snow shoes of mine. If you wear them you will get to my brother, who lives hundreds of miles from here. He is Lord of all the fish in the sea – you can ask him. But do not forget to turn the shoes round."

The King thanked him, put on the shoes, and when he had got to him who was Lord of all the fish in the sea, he turned the snow shoes round, and back they went just as the others had gone, and he asked once more where Whiteland was.

The man called the fish together with his horn, but none of them knew anything about it. At last came an old, old pike, which he had great difficulty in bringing home to him.

When he asked the pike, it said, "Yes, Whiteland is well known to me, for I have been cook there these ten years. Tomorrow morning I have to go back there, for now the Queen, whose King is staying away, is to marry some one else."

"If that be the case I will give you a piece of advice," said the man. "Not far from here on a moor stand three brothers, who have stood there a hundred years fighting for a hat, a cloak, and a pair of boots; if any one has these three things he can make himself invisible, and if he desires to go to any place, he has but to wish and he is there. You may tell them that you have a desire to try these things, and then you will be able to decide which of the men is to have them."

So the King thanked him and went, and did what he had said.

"What is this that you are standing fighting about for ever and ever?" said he to the brothers; "let me make a trial of these things, and then I will judge between you."

They willingly consented to this, but when he had got the hat, the cloak, and the boots, he said, "Next time we meet you shall have my decision," and hereupon he wished himself away.

While he was going quickly through the air he fell in with the North Wind.

"And where may you be going?" said the North Wind.

"To Whiteland," said the King, and then he related what had happened to him.

"Well," said the North Wind, "you can easily go a little quicker than I can, for I have to puff and blow into every corner; but when you get there, place yourself on the stairs by the side of the door, and then I will come blustering in as if I wanted to blow down the whole castle, and when the Prince who is to have your Queen comes out to see what is astir, just take him by the throat and fling him out, and then I will try to carry him away from court."

As the North Wind had said, so did the King. He stood on the stairs, and when the North Wind came howling and roaring, and caught the roof and walls of the castle till they shook again, the Prince went out to see what was the matter; but as soon as he came the King took him by the neck and flung him out, and then the North Wind laid hold of him and carried him off. And when he was rid of him the King went into the castle. At first the Queen did not know him, because he had grown so thin and pale from having travelled so long and so sorrowfully; but when she saw her ring she was heartily glad, and then the rightful wedding was held, and held in such a way that it was talked about far and wide.

WHY THE SEA IS SALT

Once on a time, but it was a long, long time ago, there were two brothers, one rich and one poor. Now, one Christmas eve, the poor one hadn't so much as a crumb in the house, either of meat or bread, so he went to his brother to ask him for something to keep Christmas with, in God's name. It was not the first time his brother had been forced to help him, and you may fancy he wasn't very glad to see his face, but he said:

"If you will do what I ask you to do, I'll give you a whole flitch of bacon."

So the poor brother said he would do anything, and was full of thanks.

"Well, here is the flitch", said the rich brother, "and now go straight to Hell."

"What I have given my word to do, I must stick to", said the other; so he took the flitch and set off. He walked the whole day, and at dusk he came to a place where he saw a very bright light.

"Maybe this is the place", said the man to himself. So he turned aside, and the first thing he saw was an old, old man, with a long white beard, who stood in an outhouse, hewing wood for the Christmas fire.

"Good even", said the man with the flitch.

"The same to you; whither are you going so late?" said the man.

"Oh! I'm going to Hell, if I only knew the right way", answered the poor man.

"Well, you're not far wrong, for this is Hell", said the old man; "when you get inside they will be all for buying your flitch, for meat is scarce in Hell; but mind, you don't sell it unless you get the hand-quern which stands behind the door for it. When you come out, I'll teach you how to handle the quern, for it's good to grind almost anything."

So the man with the flitch thanked the other for his good advice, and gave a great knock at the Devil's door.

When he got in, everything went just as the old man had said. All the devils, great and small, came swarming up to him like ants round an anthill, and each tried to outbid the other for the flitch.

"Well!" said the man, "by rights my old dame and I ought to have this flitch for our Christmas dinner; but since you have all set your hearts on it, I suppose I must give it up to you; but if I sell it at all, I'll have for it that quern behind the door yonder."

At first the Devil wouldn't hear of such a bargain, and chaffered and haggled with the man; but he stuck to what he said, and at last the Devil had to part with his quern. When the man got out into the yard, he asked the old woodcutter how he was to handle the quern; and after he had learned how to use it, he thanked the old man and went off home as fast as he could, but still the clock had struck twelve on Christmas eve before he reached his own door.

"Wherever in the world have you been?" said his old dame, "here have I sat hour after hour waiting and watching, without so much as two sticks to lay together under the Christmas brose."

"Oh!" said the man, "I couldn't get back before, for I had to go a long way first for one thing, and then for another; but now you shall see what you shall see."

So he put the quern on the table, and bade it first of all grind lights, then a table-cloth, then meat, then ale, and so on till they had got everything that was nice for Christmas fare. He had only to speak the word, and the quern ground out what he wanted. The old dame stood by blessing her stars, and kept on asking where he had got this wonderful quern, but he wouldn't tell her.

"It's all one where I got it from; you see the quern is a good one, and the mill-stream never freezes, that's enough."

So he ground meat and drink and dainties enough to last out till Twelfth Day, and on the third day he asked all his friends and kin to his house, and gave a great feast. Now, when his rich brother saw all that was on the table, and all that was behind in the larder, he grew quite spiteful and wild, for he couldn't bear that his brother should have anything.

"'Twas only on Christmas eve", he said to the rest, "he was in such straits, that he came and asked for a morsel of food in God's name, and now he gives a feast as if he were count or king"; and he turned to his brother and said:

"But whence, in Hell's name, have you got all this wealth?"

"From behind the door", answered the owner of the quern, for he didn't care to let the cat out of the bag. But later on the evening, when he had got a drop too much, he could keep his secret no longer, and brought out the quern and said:

"There, you see what has gotten me all this wealth"; and so he made the quern grind all kind of things. When his brother saw it, he set his heart on having the quern, and, after a deal of coaxing, he got it; but he had to pay three hundred dollars for it, and his brother bargained to keep it till hay-harvest, for he thought, if I keep it till then, I can make it grind meat and drink that will last for years. So you may fancy the quern didn't grow rusty for want of work, and when hay-harvest came, the rich brother got it, but the other took care not to teach him how to handle it.

It was evening when the rich brother got the quern home, and next morning he told his wife to go out into the hay-field and toss, while the mowers cut the grass, and he would stay at home and get the dinner ready. So, when dinner-time drew near, he put the quern on the kitchen table and said:

"Grind herrings and broth, and grind them good and fast."

So the quern began to grind herrings and broth; first of all, all the dishes full, then all the tubs full, and so on till the kitchen floor was quite covered. Then the man twisted and twirled at the quern to get it to stop, but for all his twisting and fingering the quern went on grinding, and in a little while the broth rose so high that the man was like to drown. So he threw open the kitchen door and ran into the parlour, but it wasn't long before the quern had ground the parlour full too, and it was only at the risk of his life that the man could get hold of the latch of the house door through the stream of broth. When he got the door open, he ran out and set off down the road, with the stream of herrings and broth at his heels, roaring like a waterfall over the whole farm. Now, his old dame, who was in the field tossing hay, thought it a long time to dinner, and at last she said:

"Well! though the master doesn't call us home, we may as well go. Maybe he finds it hard work to boil the broth, and will be glad of my help."

The men were willing enough, so they sauntered homewards; but just as they had got a little way up the hill, what should they meet but herrings, and broth, and bread, all running and dashing, and splashing together in a stream, and the master himself running before them for his life, and as he passed them he bawled out:

"Would to heaven each of you had a hundred throats! but take care you're not drowned in the broth."

Away he went, as though the Evil One were at his heels, to his brother's house, and begged him for God's sake to take back the quern that instant; for, said he:

"If it grinds only one hour more, the whole parish will be swallowed up by herrings and broth."

But his brother wouldn't hear of taking it back till the other paid him down three hundred dollars more.

So the poor brother got both the money and the quern, and it wasn't long before he set up a farmhouse far finer than the one in which his brother lived, and with the quern he ground so much gold that he covered it with plates of gold; and as the farm lay by the sea-side, the golden house gleamed and glistened far away over the sea. All who sailed by put ashore to see the rich man in the golden house, and to see the wonderful quern, the fame of which spread far and wide, till there was nobody who hadn't heard tell of it.

So one day there came a skipper who wanted to see the quern; and the first thing he asked was if it could grind salt.

"Grind salt!" said the owner; "I should just think it could. It can grind anything."

When the skipper heard that, he said he must have the quern, cost what it would; for if he only had it, he thought he should be rid of his long voyages across stormy seas for a lading of salt. Well, at first the man wouldn't hear of parting with the quern; but the skipper begged and prayed so hard, that at last he let him have it, but he had to pay many, many thousand dollars for it. Now, when the skipper had got the quern on his back, he soon made off with it, for he was afraid lest the man should change his mind; so he had no time to ask how to handle the quern, but got on board his ship as fast as he could, and set sail. When he had sailed a good way off, he brought the quern on deck and said:

"Grind salt, and grind both good and fast."

Well, the quern began to grind salt so that it poured out like water; and when the skipper had got the ship full, he wished to stop the quern, but whichever way he turned it, and however much he tried, it was no good; the quern kept grinding on, and the heap of salt grew higher and higher, and at last down sank the ship.

There lies the quern at the bottom of the sea, and grinds away at this very day, and that's why the sea is salt.

THE LITTLE MATCH-SELLER

It was terribly cold and nearly dark on the last evening of the old year, and the snow was falling fast. In the cold and the darkness, a poor little girl, with bare head and naked feet, roamed through the streets. It is true she had on a pair of slippers when she left home, but they were not of much use. They were very large, so large, indeed, that they had belonged to her mother, and the poor little creature had lost them in running across the street to avoid two carriages that were rolling along at a terrible rate. One of the slippers she could not find, and a boy seized upon the other and ran away with it, saying that he could use it as a cradle, when he had children of his own. So the little girl went on with her little naked feet, which were quite red and blue with the cold. In an old apron she carried a number of matches, and had a bundle of them in her hands. No one had bought anything of her the whole day, nor had any one given here even a penny. Shivering with cold and hunger, she crept along; poor little child, she looked the picture of misery. The snowflakes fell on her long, fair hair, which hung in curls on her shoulders, but she regarded them not.

Lights were shining from every window, and there was a savory smell of roast goose, for it was New Year's Eve – yes, she remembered that. In a corner, between two houses, one of which projected beyond the other, she sank down and huddled herself together. She had drawn her little feet under her, but she could not keep off the cold; and she dared not go home, for she had sold no matches, and could not take home even a penny of money. Her father would certainly beat her; besides, it was almost as cold at home as here, for they had only the roof to cover them, through which the wind howled, although the largest holes had been stopped up with straw and rags. Her little hands were almost frozen with the cold. Ah! perhaps a burning match might be some good, if she could draw it from the bundle and strike it against the wall, just to warm her fingers. She drew one out – "scratch!" how it sputtered as it burnt! It gave a warm, bright light, like a little candle, as she held her hand over it. It was really a wonderful light. It seemed to the little girl that she was sitting by a large iron stove, with polished brass feet and a brass ornament. How the fire burned! and seemed so beautifully warm that the child stretched out her feet as if to warm them, when, lo! the flame of the match went out, the stove vanished, and she had only the remains of the half-burnt match in her hand.

She rubbed another match on the wall. It burst into a flame, and where its light fell upon the wall it became as transparent as a veil, and she could see into the room. The table was covered with a snowy white table-cloth, on which stood a splendid dinner service, and a steaming roast goose, stuffed with apples and dried plums. And what was still more wonderful, the goose jumped down from the dish and waddled across the floor, with a knife and fork in its breast, to the little girl. Then the match went out, and there remained nothing but the thick, damp, cold wall before her.

She lighted another match, and then she found herself sitting under a beautiful Christmas tree. It was larger and more beautifully decorated than the one which she had seen through the glass door at the rich merchant's. Thousands of tapers were burning upon the green branches, and colored pictures, like those she had seen in the show-windows, looked down upon it all. The little one stretched out her hand towards them, and the match went out.

The Christmas lights rose higher and higher, till they looked to her like the stars in the sky. Then she saw a star fall, leaving behind it a bright streak of fire. "Some one is dying," thought the little girl, for her old grandmother, the only one who had ever loved her, and who was now dead, had told her that when a star falls, a soul was going up to God.

She again rubbed a match on the wall, and the light shone round her; in the brightness stood her old grandmother, clear and shining, yet mild and loving in her appearance. "Grandmother," cried the little one, "O take me with you; I know you will go away when the match burns out; you will vanish like the warm stove, the roast goose, and the large, glorious Christmas tree." And she made haste to light the whole bundle of matches, for she wished to keep her grandmother there. And the matches glowed with a light that was brighter than the noon-day, and her grandmother had never appeared so large or so beautiful. She took the little girl in her arms, and they both flew upwards in brightness and joy far above the earth, where there was neither cold nor hunger nor pain, for they were with God.

In the dawn of morning there lay the poor little one, with pale cheeks and smiling mouth, leaning against the wall; she had been frozen to death on the last evening of the year; and the New Year's sun rose and shone upon a little corpse! The child still sat, in the stiffness of death, holding the matches in her hand, one bundle of which was burnt. "She tried to warm herself," said some. No one imagined what beautiful things she had seen, nor into what glory she had entered with her grandmother, on New Year's Day.

FIRST BORN, FIRST WED

Once upon a time there was a king who had a three-year old son, and was obliged to go to war against another king. Then, when his ships sailed home again after he had gained a splendid victory, a storm broke out and his whole fleet was near sinking. But the king vowed he would sacrifice to the sea-queen the first male creature that came to meet him when he reached land and entered his capital. Thereby the whole fleet reached the harbor in safety. But the five-year old prince, who had not seen his father for the past two years, and who was delighted with the thunder of the cannon as the ships came in, secretly slipped away from his attendants, and ran to the landing; and when the king came ashore he was the first to cast himself into his arms, weeping with joy. The king was frightened when he thought of the sea-queen; but he thought that, after all, the prince was only a child, and at any rate he could sacrifice the next person to step up to him after the prince. But from that time on no one could make a successful sea-trip, and the people began to murmur because the king had not kept the promise he had made the sea-queen. But the king and queen never allowed the prince out without a great escort, and he was never permitted to enter a ship, for all his desire to do so.

After a few years they gradually forgot the sea-queen, and when the prince was ten years old, a little brother came to join him. Not long after the older of the princes was out walking with his tutor and several other gentlemen. And when they reached the end of the royal gardens by the sea-shore – it was a summer's day, unusually clear – they were suddenly enveloped by a thick cloud, which disappeared as swiftly as it had come. And when it vanished, the prince was no longer there; nor did he return, to the great sorrow of the king, the queen and the whole country. In the meantime the young prince who was now the sole heir to the crown and kingdom grew up; and when he was sixteen, they began to think of finding a wife for him. For the old king and queen wished to see him marry the daughter of some powerful monarch to whom they were allied, before they died. With this in view, letters were written and embassies sent out to the most distant countries.

While these negotiations were being conducted, it began to be said that the sea-shore was haunted; various people had heard cries, and several who had walked by the sea-shore late in the evening had fallen ill. At length no one ventured to go there after eleven at night, because a voice kept crying from out at sea: "First born, first wed!" And when some one did venture nearer he did so at the risk of his life. At last these complaints came to the king's ear; he called together his council, and it was decided to question a wise woman, who had already foretold many mysterious happenings, which had all taken place exactly as she had said they would. When the wise woman was brought before the king she said it was the prince who had been taken into the sea who was calling, and that they would have to find him a bride, young, beautiful, and belonging to one of the noblest families of the land, and she must be no less than fifteen and no more than seventeen years old. That seemed a serious difficulty; for no one wished to give their daughter to a sea-king.

Yet, when there was no end to the cries and the commotion, the wise woman said, that first it might be well to build a little house by the sea, perhaps then the turmoil might die away. At any rate, she said, no phantoms would haunt the place while the building was in progress. Hence no more than four workmen need be employed, and they might first prepare a site, then lay the stone foundation, and finally erect the small house, comprising no more than two pleasant, handsome rooms, one behind the other, and a good floor. The house was carefully erected, and the royal architect himself had to superintend the work, so that everything might be done as well as possible. And while the building was going on, there were no mysterious noises, and every one could travel peacefully along the sea-shore. For that reason the four workmen did not hurry with their work; yet not one of them could stay away for a day, because when they did the tumult along the shore would begin again, and one could hear the cries: "First born, first wed!" When the little house was finally completed, the best carpenters came and worked in it, then painters and other craftsmen, and at last it was furnished, because when the work stopped for no more than a single day the cries were heard again by night. The rooms were fitted out as sumptuously as possible, and a great mirror was hung in the drawing-room. According to the instructions of the wise woman, it was hung in such wise that from the bed in the bedroom, even though one's face were turned to the wall, one could still see who stepped over the threshold into the drawing-room; for the door between each room was always to stand open.

When all was finished, and the little house had been arranged with regal splendor, the cries of "First born, first wed!" again began to sound from the shore. And it was found necessary, though all were unwilling, to follow the wise woman's counsel, and choose three of the loveliest maidens between the ages of fifteen and seventeen, belonging to the first families of the land. They were to be taken to the castle, said the wise woman, and to be treated like ladies of the blood royal, and one after another they were to be sent to the little house by the sea-shore; for should one of them find favor in the eyes of the sea-prince, then the commotion and turmoil would surely cease. In the meantime the negotiations for the marriage of the younger prince were continued, and the bride selected for him was soon expected to arrive. So the girls were also chosen for the sea-prince. The three chosen, as well as their parents, were quite inconsolable over their fate; even the fact that they were to be treated like princesses did not console them; yet had they not yielded it would have been all the worse for them and for the whole land. The first girl destined to sleep in the sea-palace was the oldest, and when she sought out the wise woman, and asked her advice, the latter said she should lie down in the handsome bed; but should turn her face to the wall, and under no circumstances turn around curiously, and try and see what was going on. She had only the right to behold what she saw reflected in the mirror in the drawing-room as she lay with her face to the wall. At ten o'clock that night the royal sea-bride was led with great pomp to the little house.

Her relatives and the court said farewell to her with many tears, left her before eleven, locked the door on the outside, and took the keys with them to the castle. The wise woman was also there, consoled the people, and assured them that if the maiden only forbore to speak, and did not turn around, she would come out in the morning fresh and blooming. The poor girl prayed and wept until she grew sleepy; but toward twelve o'clock the outer door suddenly opened, and then the door of the drawing-room. She was startled and filled with fear when, her face turned toward the wall, she saw in the great mirror, how a tall, well-built youth entered, from whose garments the water ran in streams to the floor. He shook himself as though freezing, and said "Uh hu!" Then he went to the window, and there laid down an unusually large and handsome apple, and hung a bottle in the casement. Next he stepped to the bed, bent over the sleeping girl and looked at her, strode up and down a few times, shaking the water from his clothes and saying "Uh hu!" Then he went back to the bed, undressed hurriedly, lay down and fell asleep. The poor girl, had not been sleeping; but had only closed her eyes when the prince bent over her. Now she was glad to think he was fast asleep, and forgot the wise woman's warning not to turn around. Her curiosity got the better of her, and she wanted to find out if this were a real human being. She turned around softly, lest she wake him; but just as she sat up quietly in bed, in order to take a good look at her neighbor, he swiftly seized her right hand, hewed it off, and flung it under the bed. Then he at once lay down and fell asleep again. As soon as it was day, he rose, dressed without casting even a glance at the bed, took the bottle and the apple from the window, went hastily out and locked the door after him. One can imagine how the poor girl suffered in the meantime, and when her friends and relatives came to fetch her they found her weeping and robbed of her hand. She was brought to the castle and the wise woman sent for, and overwhelmed with bitter reproaches. But she said that if the maiden had not turned around, and had overcome her curiosity, she would not have lost her hand. They were to treat her as though she were really and truly a princess; but that it would be as much as her life were worth to allow her to return to the neighborhood of the little house.

The two girls were all the more discouraged by this mishap, and thought themselves condemned to death, though the wise woman consoled them as well as she knew how. The second promised her faithfully not to turn around; yet it happened with her as it had with the first. The prince came in at twelve o'clock dripping, shook himself so that the water flew about, said "Uh hu!" went to the window, laid down the beautiful apple, hung up the bottle, came into the bedroom, bent over the bed, strode up and down a few times, said "Uh hu!" hastily undressed, and at once fell asleep. Her curiosity gained the upper hand, and when she made sure that he was sleeping soundly, she carefully turned around in order to look at him. But he seized her right hand, hewed it off and cast it under the bed, and then laid down again and slept on. At dawn he rose, dressed without casting a glance at the bed, took the apple and the bottle, went out and locked the door after him. When her friends and relatives came to fetch the girl in the morning, they found her weeping and without a right hand. She was taken to the castle, where she found herself just as little welcome as her predecessor, and the wise woman insisted that the girl must have turned around, though at first she denied it absolutely.

Then the youngest, sweetest and loveliest of the three maidens had to go to the sea-castle amid the mourning of the entire court. The wise woman accompanied her, and implored her not to turn around; since there was no other means of protection against the spell.

The maiden promised to heed her warning, and said that she would pray God to help her if she were plagued with curiosity. All happened as before: the prince came on the stroke of twelve, dripping wet, said "Uh hu!" shook himself, laid the apple on the window, hung up the bottle, went into the bedroom, bent over the bed, strode up and down for a few times, said "Uh hu!" undressed, and at once fell asleep. The poor girl was half-dead with fear and terror, and prayed and struggled against her curiosity till at length she fell asleep, and did not awake until the prince rose and dressed. He stepped up to the bed, bent over it for a moment, went out, turned at the door and took the bottle and the apple, and then locked the door after him. In the morning the entire court, the girl's parents and the wise woman came to fetch her. She came to meet them weeping with joy, and was conducted to the castle in triumph and with joy indescribable. The king and queen embraced her, and she was paid the same honors destined for the princess who was to arrive in the course of the next few days to marry the heir to the throne. Now the maiden had to sleep every night in the little house by the strand, and every evening the prince came in with his apple and his bottle, and every morning went away at dawn. But it seemed to her that each succeeding evening and morning he looked at her a little longer; though she, always silent, timid, and turned toward the wall, did not dare see more than her mirror showed her of his coming and going. But the two other girls, who had lost their hands, and who now no longer lived in the castle, were jealous of the honor shown the youngest, and threatened to have her done away with if she did not restore their hands. The maiden went weeping to the wise woman; and the latter said that when the prince had lain down as usual she should say – keeping her face turned toward the wall:

> *"The maidens twain will see me slain, or*
> *else have back their hands again!"*

But she was to offer no further information nor say another word. With a beating heart the poor girl waited until the prince came, and when he had bent over the bed longer than usual, sighed, then hastily undressed and lain down, the maiden said, quivering and trembling:

*"The maidens twain will see me slain, or
else have back their hands again!"*

The prince at once replied: "Take the hands – they are lying under the bed – and the bottle hanging in the window, and pour some of the contents of the bottle on their arms and hands, join them together, bind them up, take away the bandages in three days' time and the hands will have been healed!" The maiden made no reply and fell asleep. In the morning the prince rose as usual, stepped over to the bed several times and looked at her from its foot; but she did not dare look up, and closed her eyes. He sighed, took his apple; but left the bottle, and went. When the maiden rose she did as he had told her, and in three days' time removed the bandages, and the girls' hands were well and whole.

Now the foreign princess arrived and the wedding was to be celebrated as soon as possible. Yet she was not fitted out with any more magnificence than the bride of the sea-prince, and both were equally honored by the king and court. This annoyed the two other girls, and they again threatened to have the youngest done away with if she did not let them taste the apple which the prince always brought with him. Again the maiden sought the advice of the wise woman, in whom she had confidence. And that night, when the prince had lain down, she said:

*"The maidens twain will see me slain, or
else your apple they would gain!"*

Then the prince said: "Take the apple lying in the window, and when you go out, lay it on the ground and follow wherever it may roll. And when it stops, pick as many apples as you wish, and return the same way you came." The maiden made no reply, and fell asleep. On the following morning it seemed harder than ever for the prince to resolve to go away. He appeared excited and restless, sighed often, bent over the maiden several times, went into the living room, then turned around and looked at her once more. Finally, when the sun rose, he hurried out and locked the door after him. When the maiden rose, she could not help weeping, for she had really begun to love the prince.

Then she took the apple, and when she was outside the door, laid it on the ground, and it rolled and rolled, and she followed it, a long, long way, to a region unknown to her. There she came to a high garden wall, over which hung the branches of trees, loaded with beautiful fruit. Finally she reached a great portal, adorned with gold and splendid ornaments, which opened of its own accord as the apple rolled up to it. And the apple rolled through the portal and the maiden followed it into the garden, which was the most beautiful she ever had seen. The apple rolled over to a low-growing tree weighed with the most magnificent apples, and there it stopped. The maiden picked all that her silken apron would hold, and turned to see from which direction she had come, and where the portal stood through which she would have to pass on her way back. But the garden was so lovely that she felt like enjoying its charms a while longer, and without thinking of the prince's words, she touched the apple with her foot, and it began to roll again. Suddenly the portal closed with a great crash. Then the maiden was much frightened, and regretted having done what had been forbidden her; yet now she could not get out, and was compelled to follow the apple once more. It rolled far into the beautiful garden and stopped at a little fireplace, where stood two kettles of water, one small, the other large. There was a great fire burning under the large kettle; but only a weak fire beneath the smaller one. Now when the apple stopped there the maiden did not know what to do. Then it occurred to her to scrape away the fire beneath the large kettle and thrust it under the little one; and soon the kettle over the small fire began to boil and the kettle over the large one simmered down. But she could not stay there. And since she had already disobeyed the order given her, she expected to die, nothing less, and was quite resigned to do so, because she had lost all hope of winning the prince.

So she gave the apple another push, and it rolled into a meadow in the middle of the garden, and there lay two little children, asleep, with the hot sun beating straight down upon them. The maiden felt sorry for the children, and she took her apron and laid it over them to protect them from the sun, and only kept the apples she could put in her little basket. But she could not stay here either, so again she touched the apple, and it rolled on and before she knew it the girl found herself by the sea-shore. There, under a shady tree lay the prince asleep; while beside him sat the sea-queen. Both rose when the maiden drew near, and the prince looked at her with alarm and tenderness in his flashing eyes. Then he leaped into the sea, and the white foam closed over him. But the sea-queen was enraged and seized the girl, who thought that her last moment had struck, and begged for a merciful death. The sea-queen looked at her, and asked her who had given her permission to pass beyond the apple tree. The maiden confessed her disobedience, and said that she had done so without meaning any harm, whereupon the sea-queen said she would see how she had conducted herself and punish her accordingly. Thereupon the sea-queen gave the apple a push, and it rolled back through the portal to the apple tree. The sea-queen saw that the apple tree was uninjured, again pushed the apple and it rolled on to the little fireplace. But when the sea-queen saw the small kettle boiling furiously, while the large one was growing cold, she became very angry, seized the girl's arm savagely and rising to her full height, asked: "What have you dared do here? How dared you take the fire from under my kettle and put it under your own?" The maiden did not know that she had done anything wrong, and said that she did not know why. Then the sea-queen replied: "The large kettle signified the love between the prince and myself; the small one the love between the prince and you. Since you have taken the fire from under my kettle and laid it under your own, the prince is now violently in love with you, while his love for me is well-nigh extinguished. "Look," she cried, angrily, "now my kettle has stopped boiling altogether, and yours is boiling over! But I will see what other harm you have done and punish you accordingly." And the sea-queen again pushed the apple with her foot, and it rolled to the sleeping children, who had been covered with the apron. Then the sea-queen said: "Did you do that?" "Yes," replied the maiden, weeping, "but I meant no harm. I covered the little ones with my apron so that the sun might not burn down on them so fiercely, and I left with them the apples I could not put in my basket." The sea-queen said: "This deed and your truthfulness are your salvation. I see that you have a kind heart. These children belong to me and to the prince; but since he now loves you more than he does me, I will resign him to you. Go back to the castle and there say what I tell you: that your wedding with my prince is to be celebrated at the same time as that of his younger brother. And all your jewels, your ornaments, your wedding-dress and your bridal chair, are to be exactly like those of the other princess. From the moment on that the priest blesses the prince and yourself I have no further power over him. But since I have seen to it that he has all the qualities which adorn a ruler, I demand that he be made the heir to his father's kingdom; for he is the oldest son. The younger prince may rule over the kingdom which his bride brings him. All this you must tell them, for only under these conditions will I release the prince. And when you are arrayed in your bridal finery, come to me here, without anyone's knowledge, so that I may see how they have adorned you. Here is the apple which will show you the way without any one being able to tell where you go." With that the sea-queen parted from her, and gave the apple a push. It rolled out of the garden and to the castle, where the maiden, with mingled joy and terror, delivered the sea-queen's message to the king, and told him what she demanded for the prince. The king gladly promised all that was desired, and great preparations were at once made for the double wedding. Two bridal chairs were set up side by side, two wedding gowns, and two sets of jewels exactly similar were made ready. When the maiden had been dressed in her bridal finery she pretended to have forgotten something, which she had to fetch from a lower floor, went downstairs with her apple, and laid it on the ground. It at once rolled to the spot by the sea-shore where she had found the sea-queen and the prince, and where the sea-queen was now awaiting her. "It is well that you have come," said the sea-queen, "for the slightest disobedience would have meant misfortune for you! But how do you look? Are you dressed just as the princess is? And has the princess no better clothes or jewels?" The maiden answered timidly, that they were dressed exactly alike. Then the sea-queen tore her gown from her body, unclasped the jewels from her hair and flinging them on the ground cried: "Is that the way the bride of my prince should look! Since I have given him to you I will give you my bridal outfit as well." And with that she raised up a sod beneath the great tree, and a shrine adorned with gold and precious stones appeared, from which she drew out her bridal outfit, which fitted the maiden as though made for her. And it was so costly and so covered with gems that the maiden was almost blinded by its radiance. The crown, too, glowed with light, and was set with the most wonderful emeralds, and all was magnificent beyond what any princess had ever worn. "Now," said the sea-queen, when she had finished adorning the maiden, "now go back to the castle, and show them how I was dressed when I wedded the prince. All this I give as a free gift to you and your descendants; but you must always conduct yourself so that the prince will be content with you, and you must make his happiness your first thought all your life long."

This the maiden promised, with honest tears, and the sea-queen bade her go. When she was again in the castle, all were astonished at the beauty and costliness of her dress and jewels, in comparison to which those of the other princess were as nothing. The treasures of the whole kingdom would not have sufficed to pay for such a bridal outfit. And none any longer dared envy the lovely maiden, for never had a princess brought a richer bridal dower into the country. Now all went in solemn procession to the church, and the priests stood before the bridal chairs with their books open, and waited for the prince who, according to the sea-queen's word, would not come until the blessing was to be spoken. They waited impatiently, and the king finally told one of the greatest nobles to seat himself in the bridal chair in the prince's place, which he did. But the very moment the priest began to pray, the two wings of the church portal quickly flew open, and a tall, strong, handsome man with flashing eyes, royally clad, came in, stepped up to the bridal chair, thrust his proxy out so hastily that he nearly fell, and cried: "This is my place! Now, priest, speak the blessing!" While the blessing was spoken the prince became quiet again, and then greeted his parents and the whole court with joy, and before all embraced his wife, who now for the first time ventured to take a good look at him. Thenceforward the prince was like any other human being, and in the end he inherited his father's kingdom, and became a great and world-renowned ruler, beloved by his subjects, and adored by his wife. They lived long and happily, and their descendants are still the rulers of the land over which he reigned.

TALES OF THE NISSE &
OTHER SMALL FOLK

A **wonderful** array of little people – nisses, dwarfs and goblins – are to be found in Nordic myth. They're mostly benign, but can be crotchety and bear a grudge. Their precise functions can vary: nisses often lend a hand with household tasks and farmwork.

Obviously a throwback to a former time in that modern science doesn't recognize such beings, the nisse belongs to a former age more literally as well. Traditionally, he (he's always male) was the surviving soul of the first man to live in a particular house and work its land, so he stands for continuity, providing a living link between the generations.

These beings may be strange, but the weirdest thing about them is the matter-of-factness with which their presence is accepted – in a tale like Hans Andersen's 'The Goblin and the Huckster', for example. Here a 'goblin' stays in a pedlar's home in the city 'because at Christmas he always had a large dish full of jam, with a great piece of butter in the middle'. The supernatural was never more mundane.

TALES OF THE NISSES

The **Nis** is the same being that is called Kobold in Germany, and Brownie in Scotland. He is in Denmark and Norway also called Nisse god Dreng (Nissè good lad), and in Sweden, Tomtegubbe (the old man of the house).

He is of the dwarf family, and resembles them in appearance, and, like them, has the command of money, and the same dislike to noise and tumult.

His usual dress is grey, with a pointed red cap, but on Michaelmas-day he wears a round hat like those of the peasants.

No farmhouse goes on well without there is a Nis in it, and well is it for the maids and the men when they are in favour with him. They may go to their beds and give themselves no trouble about their work, and yet in the morning the maids will find the kitchen swept up, and water brought in; and the men will find the horses in the stable well cleaned and curried, and perhaps a supply of corn cribbed for them from the neighbours' barns.

There was a Nis in a house in Jutland. He every evening got his groute at the regular time, and he, in return, used to help both the men and the maids, and looked to the interest of the master of the house in every respect.

There came one time a mischievous boy to live at service in this house, and his great delight was, whenever he got an opportunity, to give the Nis all the annoyance in his power.

Late one evening, when everything was quiet in the house, the Nis took his little wooden dish, and was just going to eat his supper, when he perceived that the boy had put the butter at the bottom and had concealed it, in hopes that he might eat the groute first, and then find the butter when all the groute was gone. He accordingly set about thinking how he might repay the boy in kind. After pondering a little he went up into the loft where a man and the boy were lying asleep in the same bed. The Nis whisked off the bed clothes, and when he saw the little boy by the tall man, he said –

"Short and long don't match," and with this word he took the boy by the legs and dragged him down to the man's feet. He then went up to the head of the bed, and –

"Short and long don't match," said he again, and then he dragged the boy up to the man's head. Do what he would he could not succeed in making the boy as long as the man, but persisted in dragging him up and down in the bed, and continued at this work the whole night long till it was broad daylight.

By this time he was well tired, so he crept up on the window stool, and sat with his legs dangling down into the yard. The house-dog – for all dogs have a great enmity to the Nis – as soon as he saw him began to bark at him, which afforded him much amusement, as the dog could not get up to him. So he put down first one leg and then the other, and teased the dog, saying –

"Look at my little leg. Look at my little leg!"

In the meantime the boy had awoke, and had stolen up behind him, and, while the Nis was least thinking of it, and was going on with his, "Look at my little leg," the boy tumbled him down into the yard to the dog, crying out at the same time –

"Look at the whole of him now!"

* * *

There lived a man in Thyrsting, in Jutland, who had a Nis in his barn. This Nis used to attend to his cattle, and at night he would steal fodder for them from the neighbours, so that this farmer had the best fed and most thriving cattle in the country.

One time the boy went along with the Nis to Fugleriis to steal corn. The Nis took as much as he thought he could well carry, but the boy was more covetous, and said –

"Oh! take more. Sure, we can rest now and then!"

"Rest!" said the Nis. "Rest! and what is rest?"

"Do what I tell you," replied the boy. "Take more, and we shall find rest when we get out of this."

The Nis took more, and they went away with it, but when they came to the lands of Thyrsting, the Nis grew tired, and then the boy said to him –

"Here now is rest!" and they both sat down on the side of a little hill.

"If I had known," said the Nis, as they sat. "If I had known that rest was so good, I'd have carried off all that was in the barn."

It happened, some time after, that the boy and the Nis were no longer friends, and as the Nis was sitting one day in the granary-window with his legs hanging out into the yard, the boy ran at him and tumbled him back into the granary. The Nis was revenged on him that very night, for when the boy was gone to bed he stole down to where he was lying and carried him as he was into the yard. Then he laid two pieces of wood across the well and put him lying on them, expecting that when he awoke he would fall, from the fright, into the well and be drowned. He was, however, disappointed, for the boy came off without injury.

* * *

There was a man who lived in the town of Tirup who had a very handsome white mare. This mare had for many years belonged to the same family, and there was a Nis attached to her who brought luck to the place.

This Nis was so fond of the mare that he could hardly endure to let them put her to any kind of work, and he used to come himself every night and feed her of the best; and as for this purpose he usually brought a superfluity of corn, both thrashed and in the straw, from the neighbours' barns, all the rest of the cattle enjoyed the advantage, and they were all kept in exceedingly good condition.

It happened at last that the farmhouse passed into the hands of a new owner, who refused to put any faith in what they told him about the mare, so the luck speedily left the place, and went after the mare to a poor neighbour who had bought her. Within five days after his purchase, the poor farmer began to find his circumstances gradually improving, while the income of the other, day after day, fell away and diminished at such a rate that he was hard set to make both ends meet.

If now the man who had got the mare had only known how to be quiet and enjoy the good times that were come upon him, he and his children and his children's children after him would have been in flourishing circumstances till this very day. But when he saw the quantity of corn that came every night to his barn, he could not resist his desire to get a sight of the Nis. So he concealed himself one evening at nightfall in the stable, and as soon as it was midnight he saw how the Nis came from his neighbour's barn and brought a sack full of corn with him. It was now unavoidable that the Nis should get a sight of the man who was watching, so he, with evident marks of grief, gave the mare her food for the last time, cleaned and dressed her to the best of his ability, and when he had done, turned round to where the man was lying, and bid him farewell.

From that day forward the circumstances of both the neighbours were on an equality, for each now kept his own.

THE GOBLIN AND THE HUCKSTER

There was once a regular student, who lived in a garret, and had no possessions. And there was also a regular huckster, to whom the house belonged, and who occupied the ground floor. A goblin lived with the huckster, because at Christmas he always had a large dish full of jam, with a great piece of butter in the middle. The huckster could afford this; and therefore the goblin remained with the huckster, which was very cunning of him.

One evening the student came into the shop through the back door to buy candles and cheese for himself, he had no one to send, and therefore he came himself; he obtained what he wished, and then the huckster and his wife nodded good evening to him, and she was a woman who could do more than merely nod, for she had usually plenty to say for herself. The student nodded in return as he turned to leave, then suddenly stopped, and began reading the piece of paper in which the cheese was wrapped. It was a leaf torn out of an old book, a book that ought not to have been torn up, for it was full of poetry.

"Yonder lies some more of the same sort," said the huckster: "I gave an old woman a few coffee berries for it; you shall have the rest for sixpence, if you will."

"Indeed I will," said the student; "give me the book instead of the cheese; I can eat my bread and butter without cheese. It would be a sin to tear up a book like this. You are a clever man; and a practical man; but you understand no more about poetry than that cask yonder."

This was a very rude speech, especially against the cask; but the huckster and the student both laughed, for it was only said in fun. But the goblin felt very angry that any man should venture to say such things to a huckster who was a householder and sold the best butter. As soon as it was night, and the shop closed, and every one in bed except the student, the goblin stepped softly into the bedroom where the huckster's wife slept, and took away her tongue, which of course, she did not then want. Whatever object in the room he placed his tongue upon immediately received voice and speech, and was able to express its thoughts and feelings as readily as the lady herself could do. It could only be used by one object at a time, which was a good thing, as a number speaking at once would have caused great confusion. The goblin laid the tongue upon the cask, in which lay a quantity of old newspapers.

"Is it really true," he asked, "that you do not know what poetry is?"

"Of course I know," replied the cask: "poetry is something that always stand in the corner of a newspaper, and is sometimes cut out; and I may venture to affirm that I have more of it in me than the student has, and I am only a poor tub of the huckster's."

Then the goblin placed the tongue on the coffee mill; and how it did go to be sure! Then he put it on the butter tub and the cash box, and they all expressed the same opinion as the waste-paper tub; and a majority must always be respected.

"Now I shall go and tell the student," said the goblin; and with these words he went quietly up the back stairs to the garret where the student lived. He had a candle burning still, and the goblin peeped through the keyhole and saw that he was reading in the torn book, which he had brought out of the shop. But how light the room was! From the book shot forth a ray of light which grew broad and full, like the stem of a tree, from which bright rays spread upward and over the student's head. Each leaf was fresh, and each flower was like a beautiful female head; some with dark and sparkling eyes, and others with eyes that were wonderfully blue and clear. The fruit gleamed like stars, and the room was filled with sounds of beautiful music. The little goblin had never imagined, much less seen or heard of, any sight so glorious as this. He stood still on tiptoe, peeping in, till the light went out in the garret. The student no doubt had blown out his candle and gone to bed; but the little goblin remained standing there nevertheless, and listening to the music which still sounded on, soft and beautiful, a sweet cradle-song for the student, who had lain down to rest.

"This is a wonderful place," said the goblin; "I never expected such a thing. I should like to stay here with the student;" and the little man thought it over, for he was a sensible little spirit. At last he sighed, "but the student has no jam!" So he went down stairs again into the huckster's shop, and it was a good thing he got back when he did, for the cask had almost worn out the lady's tongue; he had given a description of all that he contained on one side, and was just about to turn himself over to the other side to describe what was there, when the goblin entered and restored the tongue to the lady. But from that time forward, the whole shop, from the cash box down to the pinewood logs, formed their opinions from that of the cask; and they all had such confidence in him, and treated him with so much respect, that when the huckster read the criticisms on theatricals and art of an evening, they fancied it must all come from the cask.

But after what he had seen, the goblin could no longer sit and listen quietly to the wisdom and understanding down stairs; so, as soon as the evening light glimmered in the garret, he took courage, for it seemed to him as if the rays of light were strong cables, drawing him up, and obliging him to go and peep through the keyhole; and, while there, a feeling of vastness came over him such as we experience by the ever-moving sea, when the storm breaks forth; and it brought tears into his eyes. He did not himself know why he wept, yet a kind of pleasant feeling mingled with his tears. "How wonderfully glorious it would be to sit with the student under such a tree;" but that was out of the question, he must be content to look through the keyhole, and be thankful for even that.

There he stood on the old landing, with the autumn wind blowing down upon him through the trap-door. It was very cold; but the little creature did not really feel it, till the light in the garret went out, and the tones of music died away. Then how he shivered, and crept down stairs again to his warm corner, where it felt home-like and comfortable. And when Christmas came again, and brought the dish of jam and the great lump of butter, he liked the huckster best of all.

Soon after, in the middle of the night, the goblin was awoke by a terrible noise and knocking against the window shutters and the house doors, and by the sound of the watchman's horn; for a great fire had broken out, and the whole street appeared full of flames. Was it in their house, or a neighbor's? No one could tell, for terror had seized upon all. The huckster's wife was so bewildered that she took her gold earrings out of her ears and put them in her pocket, that she might save something at least. The huckster ran to get his business papers, and the servant resolved to save her blue silk mantle, which she had managed to buy. Each wished to keep the best things they had. The goblin had the same wish; for, with one spring, he was up stairs and in the student's room, whom he found standing by the open window, and looking quite calmly at the fire, which was raging at the house of a neighbor opposite. The goblin caught up the wonderful book which lay on the table, and popped it into his red cap, which he held tightly with both hands. The greatest treasure in the house was saved; and he ran away with it to the roof, and seated himself on the chimney. The flames of the burning house opposite illuminated him as he sat, both hands pressed tightly over his cap, in which the treasure lay; and then he found out what feelings really reigned in his heart, and knew exactly which way they tended. And yet, when the fire was extinguished, and the goblin again began to reflect, he hesitated, and said at last, "I must divide myself between the two; I cannot quite give up the huckster, because of the jam."

And this is a representation of human nature. We are like the goblin; we all go to visit the huckster "because of the jam."

THE DWARFS' BANQUET

There lived in Norway, not far from the city of Drontheim, a powerful man who was blessed with all the goods of fortune. A part of the surrounding country was his property, numerous herds fed on his pastures, and a great retinue and a crowd of servants adorned his mansion. He had an only daughter, called Aslog, the fame of whose beauty spread far and wide. The greatest men of the country sought her, but all were alike unsuccessful in their suit, and he who had come full of confidence and joy, rode away home silent and melancholy. Her father, who thought his daughter delayed her choice only to select, forbore to interfere, and exulted in her prudence, but when at length the richest and noblest tried their fortune with as little success as the rest, he grew angry and called his daughter, and said to her –

"Hitherto I have left you to your free choice, but since I see that you reject all without any distinction, and the very best of your suitors seems not good enough for you, I will keep measures no longer with you. What! shall my family become extinct, and my inheritance pass away into the hands of strangers? I will break your stubborn spirit. I give you now till the festival of the great winter-night. Make your choice by that time, or prepare to accept him whom I shall fix on."

Aslog loved a youth named Orm, handsome as he was brave and noble. She loved him with her whole soul, and she would sooner die than bestow her hand on another. But Orm was poor, and poverty compelled him to serve in the mansion of her father. Aslog's partiality for him was kept a secret, for her father's pride of power and wealth was such that he would never have given his consent to a union with so humble a man.

When Aslog saw the darkness of his countenance, and heard his angry words, she turned pale as death, for she knew his temper, and doubted not that he would put his threats into execution. Without uttering a word in reply, she retired to her chamber, and thought deeply but in vain how to avert the dark storm that hung over her. The great festival approached nearer and nearer, and her anguish increased every day.

At last the lovers resolved on flight.

"I know," said Orm, "a secure place where we may remain undiscovered until we find an opportunity of quitting the country."

At night, when all were asleep, Orm led the trembling Aslog over the snow and ice-fields away to the mountains. The moon and the stars, sparkling still brighter in the cold winter's night, lighted them on their way. They had under their arms a few articles of dress and some skins of animals, which were all they could carry. They ascended the mountains the whole night long till they reached a lonely spot enclosed with lofty rocks. Here Orm conducted the weary Aslog into a cave, the low and narrow entrance to which was hardly perceptible, but it soon enlarged to a great hall, reaching deep into the mountain. He kindled a fire, and they now, reposing on their skins, sat in the deepest solitude far away from all the world.

Orm was the first who had discovered this cave, which is shown to this very day, and as no one knew anything of it, they were safe from the pursuit of Aslog's father. They passed the whole winter in this retirement. Orm used to go a-hunting, and Aslog stayed at home in the cave, minded the fire, and prepared the necessary food. Frequently did she mount the points of the rocks, but her eyes wandered as far as they could reach only over glittering snow-fields.

The spring now came on: the woods were green, the meadows pat on their various colours, and Aslog could but rarely, and with circumspection, venture to leave the cave. One evening Orm came in with the intelligence that he had recognised her father's servants in the distance, and that he could hardly have been unobserved by them whose eyes were as good as his own.

"They will surround this place," continued he, "and never rest till they have found us. We must quit our retreat then without a minute's delay."

They accordingly descended on the other side of the mountain, and reached the strand, where they fortunately found a boat. Orm shoved off, and the boat drove into the open sea. They had escaped their pursuers, but they were now exposed to dangers of another kind. Whither should they turn themselves? They could not venture to land, for Aslog's father was lord of the whole coast, and they would infallibly fall into his hands. Nothing then remained for them but to commit their bark to the wind and waves. They drove along the entire night. At break of day the coast had disappeared, and they saw nothing but the sky above, the sea beneath, and the waves that rose and fell. They had not brought one morsel of food with them, and thirst and hunger began now to torment them. Three days did they toss about in this state of misery, and Aslog, faint and exhausted, saw nothing but certain death before her.

At length, on the evening of the third day, they discovered an island of tolerable magnitude, and surrounded by a number of smaller ones. Orm immediately steered for it, but just as he came near to it there suddenly arose a violent wind, and the sea rolled higher and higher against him. He turned about with a view of approaching it on another side, but with no better success. His vessel, as often as he approached the island, was driven back as if by an invisible power.

"Lord God!" cried he, and blessed himself and looked on poor Aslog, who seemed to be dying of weakness before his eyes.

Scarcely had the exclamation passed his lips when the storm ceased, the waves subsided, and the vessel came to the shore without encountering any hindrance. Orm jumped out on the beach. Some mussels that he found upon the strand strengthened and revived the exhausted Aslog so that she was soon able to leave the boat.

The island was overgrown with low dwarf shrubs, and seemed to be uninhabited; but when they had got about the middle of it, they discovered a house reaching but a little above the ground, and appearing to be half under the surface of the earth. In the hope of meeting human beings and assistance, the wanderers approached it. They listened if they could hear any noise, but the most perfect silence reigned there. Orm at length opened the door, and with his companion walked in; but what was their surprise to find everything regulated and arranged as if for inhabitants, yet not a single living creature visible. The fire was burning on the hearth in the middle of the room, and a kettle with fish hung on it, apparently only waiting for some one to take it off and eat. The beds were made and ready to receive their weary tenants. Orm and Aslog stood for some time dubious, and looked on with a certain degree of awe, but at last, overcome with hunger, they took up the food and ate. When they had satisfied their appetites, and still in the last beams of the setting sun, which now streamed over the island far and wide, discovered no human being, they gave way to weariness, and laid themselves in the beds to which they had been so long strangers.

They had expected to be awakened in the night by the owners of the house on their return home, but their expectation was not fulfilled. They slept undisturbed till the morning sun shone in upon them. No one appeared on any of the following days, and it seemed as if some invisible power had made ready the house for their reception. They spent the whole summer in perfect happiness. They were, to be sure, solitary, yet they did not miss mankind. The wild birds' eggs and the fish they caught yielded them provisions in abundance.

When autumn came, Aslog presented Orm with a son. In the midst of their joy at his appearance they were surprised by a wonderful apparition. The door opened on a sudden, and an old woman stepped in. She had on her a handsome blue dress. There was something proud, but at the same time strange and surprising in her appearance.

"Do not be afraid," said she, "at my unexpected appearance. I am the owner of this house, and I thank you for the clean and neat state in which you have kept it, and for the good order in which I find everything with you. I would willingly have come sooner, but I had no power to do so, till this little heathen (pointing to the new-born babe) was come to the light. Now I have free access. Only, fetch no priest from the mainland to christen it, or I must depart again. If you will in this matter comply with my wishes, you may not only continue to live here, but all the good that ever you can wish for I will cause you. Whatever you take in hand shall prosper. Good luck shall follow you wherever you go; but break this condition, and depend upon it that misfortune after misfortune will come on you, and even on this child will I avenge myself. If you want anything, or are in danger, you have only to pronounce my name three times, and I will appear and lend you assistance. I am of the race of the old giants, and my name is Guru. But beware of uttering in my presence the name of him whom no giant may hear of, and never venture to make the sign of the cross, or to cut it on beam or on board of the house. You may dwell in this house the whole year long, only be so good as to give it up to me on Yule evening, when the sun is at the lowest, as then we celebrate our great festival, and then only are we permitted to be merry. At least, if you should not be willing to go out of the house, keep yourselves up in the loft as quiet as possible the whole day long, and, as you value your lives, do not look down into the room until midnight is past. After that you may take possession of everything again."

When the old woman had thus spoken she vanished, and Aslog and Orm, now at ease respecting their situation, lived, without any disturbance, content and happy. Orm never made a cast of his net without getting a plentiful draught. He never shot an arrow from his bow that missed its aim. In short, whatever they took in hand, were it ever so trifling, evidently prospered.

When Christmas came, they cleaned up the house in the best manner, set everything in order, kindled a fire on the hearth, and, as the twilight approached, they went up to the loft, where they remained quiet and still. At length it grew dark. They thought they heard a sound of flying and labouring in the air, such as the swans make in the winter-time. There was a hole in the roof over the fireplace which might be opened or shut either to let in the light from above or to afford a free passage for the smoke. Orm lifted up the lid, which was covered with a skin, and put out his head, but what a wonderful sight then presented itself to his eyes! The little islands around were all lit up with countless blue lights, which moved about without ceasing, jumped up and down, then skipped down to the shore, assembled together, and now came nearer and nearer to the large island where Orm and Aslog lived. At last they reached it and arranged themselves in a circle around a large stone not far from the shore, and which Orm well knew. What was his surprise when he saw that the stone had now completely assumed the form of a man, though of a monstrous and gigantic one! He could clearly perceive that the little blue lights were borne by dwarfs, whose pale clay-coloured faces, with their huge noses and red eyes, disfigured, too, by birds' bills and owls' eyes, were supported by misshapen bodies. They tottered and wobbled about here and there, so that they seemed to be, at the same time, merry and in pain. Suddenly the circle opened, the little ones retired on each side, and Guru, who was now much enlarged and of as immense a size as the stone, advanced with gigantic steps. She threw both her arms about the stone image, which immediately began to receive life and motion. As soon as the first sign of motion showed itself the little ones began, with wonderful capers and grimaces, a song, or, to speak more properly, a howl, with which the whole island resounded and seemed to tremble. Orm, quite terrified, drew in his head, and he and Aslog remained in the dark, so still that they hardly ventured to draw their breath.

The procession moved on towards the house, as might be clearly perceived by the nearer approach of the shouting and crying. They were now all come in, and, light and active, the dwarfs jumped about on the benches, and heavy and loud sounded, at intervals, the steps of the giants. Orm and his wife heard them covering the table, and the clattering of the plates, and the shouts of joy with which they celebrated their banquet. When it was over, and it drew near to midnight, they began to dance to that ravishing fairy air which charms the mind into such sweet confusion, and which some have heard in the rocky glens, and learned by listening to the underground musicians. As soon as Aslog caught the sound of the air she felt an irresistible longing to see the dance, nor was Orm able to keep her back.

"Let me look," said she, "or my heart will burst."

She took her child and placed herself at the extreme end of the loft whence, without being observed, she could see all that passed. Long did she gaze, without taking off her eyes for an instant, on the dance, on the bold and wonderful springs of the little creatures who seemed to float in the air and not so much as to touch the ground, while the ravishing melody of the elves filled her whole soul. The child, meanwhile, which lay in her arms, grew sleepy and drew its breath heavily, and without ever thinking of the promise she had given to the old woman, she made, as is usual, the sign of the cross over the mouth of the child, and said –

"Christ bless you, my babe!"

The instant she had spoken the word there was raised a horrible, piercing cry. The spirits tumbled head over heels out at the door, with terrible crushing and crowding, their lights went out, and in a few minutes the whole house was clear of them and left desolate. Orm and Aslog, frightened to death, hid themselves in the most retired nook in the house. They did not venture to stir till daybreak, and not till the sun shone through the hole in the roof down on the fireplace did they feel courage enough to descend from the loft.

The table remained still covered as the underground people had left it. All their vessels, which were of silver, and manufactured in the most beautiful manner, were upon it. In the middle of the room there stood upon the ground a huge copper kettle half-full of sweet mead, and, by the side of it, a drinking-horn of pure gold. In the corner lay against the wall a stringed instrument not unlike a dulcimer, which, as people believe, the giantesses used to play on. They gazed on what was before them full of admiration, but without venturing to lay their hands on anything; but great and fearful was their amazement when, on turning about, they saw sitting at the table an immense figure, which Orm instantly recognised as the giant whom Guru had animated by her embrace. He was now a cold and hard stone. While they were standing gazing on it, Guru herself entered the room in her giant form. She wept so bitterly that the tears trickled down on the ground. It was long ere her sobbing permitted her to utter a single word. At length she spoke –

"Great affliction have you brought on me, and henceforth must I weep while I live. I know you have not done this with evil intentions, and therefore I forgive you, though it were a trifle for me to crush the whole house like an eggshell over your heads."

"Alas!" cried she, "my husband, whom I love more than myself, there he sits petrified for ever. Never again will he open his eyes! Three hundred years lived I with my father on the island of Kunnan, happy in the innocence of youth, as the fairest among the giant maidens. Mighty heroes sued for my hand. The sea around that island is still filled with the rocky fragments which they hurled against each other in their combats. Andfind won the victory, and I plighted myself to him; but ere I was married came the detestable Odin into the country, who overcame my father, and drove us all from the island. My father and sisters fled to the mountains, and since that time my eyes have beheld them no more. Andfind and I saved ourselves on this island, where we for a long time lived in peace and quiet, and thought it would never be interrupted. Destiny, which no one escapes, had determined it otherwise. Oluf came from Britain. They called him the Holy, and Andfind instantly found that his voyage would be inauspicious to the giants. When he heard how Oluf's ship rushed through the waves, he went down to the strand and blew the sea against him with all his strength. The waves swelled up like mountains, but Oluf was still more mighty than he. His ship flew unchecked through the billows like an arrow from a bow. He steered direct for our island. When the ship was so near that Andfind thought he could reach it with his hands, he grasped at the fore-part with his right hand, and was about to drag it down to the bottom, as he had often done with other ships. Then Oluf, the terrible Oluf, stepped forward, and, crossing his hands over each other, he cried with a loud voice –

"'Stand there as a stone till the last day!' and in the same instant my unhappy husband became a mass of rock. The ship went on unimpeded, and ran direct against the mountain, which it cut through, separating from it the little island which lies yonder."

"Ever since my happiness has been annihilated, and lonely and melancholy have I passed my life. On Yule eve alone can petrified giants receive back their life, for the space of seven hours, if one of their race embraces them, and is, at the same time, willing to sacrifice a hundred years of his own life. Seldom does a giant do that. I loved my husband too well not to bring him back cheerfully to life, every time that I could do it, even at the highest price, and never would I reckon how often I had done it that I might not know when the time came when I myself should share his fate, and, at the moment I threw my arms around him, become the same as he. Alas! now even this comfort is taken from me. I can never more by any embrace awake him, since he has heard the name which I dare not utter, and never again will he see the light till the dawn of the last day shall bring it."

"Now I go hence! You will never again behold me! All that is here in the house I give you! My dulcimer alone will I keep. Let no one venture to fix his habitation on the little islands which lie around here. There dwell the little underground ones whom you saw at the festival, and I will protect them as long as I live."

With these words Guru vanished. The next spring Orm took the golden horn and the silver ware to Drontheim where no one knew him. The value of the things was so great that he was able to purchase everything a wealthy man desires. He loaded his ship with his purchases, and returned to the island, where he spent many years in unalloyed happiness, and Aslog's father was soon reconciled to his wealthy son-in-law.

The stone image remained sitting in the house. No human power was able to move it. So hard was the stone that hammer and axe flew in pieces without making the slightest impression upon it. The giant sat there till a holy man came to the island, who, with one single word, removed him back to his former station, where he stands to this hour. The copper kettle, which the underground people left behind them, was preserved as a memorial upon the island, which bears the name of House Island to the present day.

SNOWDROP

It was the middle of winter, when the broad flakes of snow were falling around, that the queen of a country many thousand miles off sat working at her window. The frame of the window was made of fine black ebony, and as she sat looking out upon the snow, she pricked her finger, and three drops of blood fell upon it. Then she gazed thoughtfully upon the red drops that sprinkled the white snow, and said, "Would that my little daughter may be as white as that snow, as red as that blood, and as black as this ebony windowframe!" And so the little girl really did grow up; her skin was as white as snow, her cheeks as rosy as the blood, and her hair as black as ebony; and she was called Snowdrop.

But this queen died; and the king soon married another wife, who became queen, and was very beautiful, but so vain that she could not bear to think that anyone could be handsomer than she was. She had a fairy looking-glass, to which she used to go, and then she would gaze upon herself in it, and say:

> "Tell me, glass, tell me true!
> Of all the ladies in the land,
> Who is fairest, tell me, who?"

And the glass had always answered:

> "Thou, queen, art the fairest in all the land."

But Snowdrop grew more and more beautiful; and when she was seven years old she was as bright as the day, and fairer than the queen herself. Then the glass one day answered the queen, when she went to look in it as usual:

> "Thou, queen, art fair, and beauteous to see,
> But Snowdrop is lovelier far than thee!"

When she heard this she turned pale with rage and envy, and called to one of her servants, and said, "Take Snowdrop away into the wide wood, that I may never see her any more." Then the servant led her away; but his heart melted when Snowdrop begged him to spare her life, and he said, "I will not hurt you, thou pretty child." So he left her by herself; and though he thought it most likely that the wild beasts would tear her in pieces, he felt as if a great weight were taken off his heart when he had made up his mind not to kill her but to leave her to her fate, with the chance of someone finding and saving her.

Then poor Snowdrop wandered along through the wood in great fear; and the wild beasts roared about her, but none did her any harm. In the evening she came to a cottage among the hills, and went in to rest, for her little feet would carry her no further. Everything was spruce and neat in the cottage: on the table was spread a white cloth, and there were seven little plates, seven little loaves, and seven little glasses with wine in them; and seven knives and forks laid in order; and by the wall stood seven little beds. As she was very hungry, she picked a little piece of each loaf and drank a very little wine out of each glass; and after that she thought she would lie down and rest. So she tried all the little beds; but one was too long, and another was too short, till at last the seventh suited her: and there she laid herself down and went to sleep.

By and by in came the masters of the cottage. Now they were seven little dwarfs, that lived among the mountains, and dug and searched for gold. They lighted up their seven lamps, and saw at once that all was not right. The first said, "Who has been sitting on my stool?" The second, "Who has been eating off my plate?" The third, "Who has been picking my bread?" The fourth, "Who has been meddling with my spoon?" The fifth, "Who has been handling my fork?" The sixth, "Who has been cutting with my knife?" The seventh, "Who has been drinking my wine?" Then the first looked round and said, "Who has been lying on my bed?" And the rest came running to him, and everyone cried out that somebody had been upon his bed. But the seventh saw Snowdrop, and called all his brethren to come and see her; and they cried out with wonder and astonishment and brought their lamps to look at her, and said, "Good heavens! what a lovely child she is!" And they were very glad to see her, and took care not to wake her; and the seventh dwarf slept an hour with each of the other dwarfs in turn, till the night was gone.

In the morning Snowdrop told them all her story; and they pitied her, and said if she would keep all things in order, and cook and wash and knit and spin for them, she might stay where she was, and they would take good care of her. Then they went out all day long to their work, seeking for gold and silver in the mountains: but Snowdrop was left at home; and they warned her, and said, "The queen will soon find out where you are, so take care and let no one in."

But the queen, now that she thought Snowdrop was dead, believed that she must be the handsomest lady in the land; and she went to her glass and said:

> "Tell me, glass, tell me true!
> Of all the ladies in the land,
> Who is fairest, tell me, who?"

And the glass answered:

> "Thou, queen, art the fairest in all this land:
> But over the hills, in the greenwood shade,
> Where the seven dwarfs their dwelling have made,
> There Snowdrop is hiding her head; and she
> Is lovelier far, O queen! than thee."

Then the queen was very much frightened; for she knew that the glass always spoke the truth, and was sure that the servant had betrayed her. And she could not bear to think that anyone lived who was more beautiful than she was; so she dressed herself up as an old pedlar, and went her way over the hills, to the place where the dwarfs dwelt. Then she knocked at the door, and cried, "Fine wares to sell!" Snowdrop looked out at the window, and said, "Good day, good woman! what have you to sell?" "Good wares, fine wares," said she; "laces and bobbins of all colours." "I will let the old lady in; she seems to be a very good sort of body," thought Snowdrop, as she ran down and unbolted the door. "Bless me!" said the old woman, "how badly your stays are laced! Let me lace them up with one of my nice new laces." Snowdrop did not dream of any mischief; so she stood before the old woman; but she set to work so nimbly, and pulled the lace so tight, that Snowdrop"s breath was stopped, and she fell down as if she were dead. "There's an end to all thy beauty," said the spiteful queen, and went away home.

In the evening the seven dwarfs came home; and I need not say how grieved they were to see their faithful Snowdrop stretched out upon the ground, as if she was quite dead. However, they lifted her up, and when they found what ailed her, they cut the lace; and in a little time she began to breathe, and very soon came to life again. Then they said, "The old woman was the queen herself; take care another time, and let no one in when we are away."

When the queen got home, she went straight to her glass, and spoke to it as before; but to her great grief it still said:

> "Thou, queen, art the fairest in all this land:
> But over the hills, in the greenwood shade,
> Where the seven dwarfs their dwelling have made,
> There Snowdrop is hiding her head; and she
> Is lovelier far, O queen! than thee."

Then the blood ran cold in her heart with spite and malice, to see that Snowdrop still lived; and she dressed herself up again, but in quite another dress from the one she wore before, and took with her a poisoned comb. When she reached the dwarfs' cottage, she knocked at the door, and cried, "Fine wares to sell!" But Snowdrop said, "I dare not let anyone in." Then the queen said, "Only look at my beautiful combs!" and gave her the poisoned one. And it looked so pretty, that she took it up and put it into her hair to try it; but the moment it touched her head, the poison was so powerful that she fell down senseless. "There you may lie," said the queen, and went her way. But by good luck the dwarfs came in very early that evening; and when they saw Snowdrop lying on the ground, they thought what had happened, and soon found the poisoned comb. And when they took it away she got well, and told them all that had passed; and they warned her once more not to open the door to anyone.

Meantime the queen went home to her glass, and shook with rage when she read the very same answer as before; and she said, "Snowdrop shall die, if it cost me my life." So she went by herself into her chamber, and got ready a poisoned apple: the outside looked very rosy and tempting, but whoever tasted it was sure to die. Then she dressed herself up as a peasant's wife, and travelled over the hills to the dwarfs' cottage, and knocked at the door; but Snowdrop put her head out of the window and said, "I dare not let anyone in, for the dwarfs have told me not." "Do as you please," said the old woman, "but at any rate take this pretty apple; I will give it you." "No," said Snowdrop, "I dare not take it." "You silly girl!" answered the other, "what are you afraid of? Do you think it is poisoned? Come! do you eat one part, and I will eat the other." Now the apple was so made up that one side was good, though the other side was poisoned. Then Snowdrop was much tempted to taste, for the apple looked so very nice; and when she saw the old woman eat, she could wait no longer. But she had scarcely put the piece into her mouth, when she fell down dead upon the ground. "This time nothing will save thee," said the queen; and she went home to her glass, and at last it said:

> *"Thou, queen, art the fairest of all the fair."*

And then her wicked heart was glad, and as happy as such a heart could be.

When evening came, and the dwarfs had gone home, they found Snowdrop lying on the ground: no breath came from her lips, and they were afraid that she was quite dead. They lifted her up, and combed her hair, and washed her face with wine and water; but all was in vain, for the little girl seemed quite dead. So they laid her down upon a bier, and all seven watched and bewailed her three whole days; and then they thought they would bury her: but her cheeks were still rosy; and her face looked just as it did while she was alive; so they said, "We will never bury her in the cold ground." And they made a coffin of glass, so that they might still look at her, and wrote upon it in golden letters what her name was, and that she was a king's daughter. And the coffin was set among the hills, and one of the dwarfs always sat by it and watched. And the birds of the air came too, and bemoaned Snowdrop; and first of all came an owl, and then a raven, and at last a dove, and sat by her side.

And thus Snowdrop lay for a long, long time, and still only looked as though she was asleep; for she was even now as white as snow, and as red as blood, and as black as ebony. At last a prince came and called at the dwarfs' house; and he saw Snowdrop, and read what was written in golden letters. Then he offered the dwarfs money, and prayed and besought them to let him take her away; but they said, "We will not part with her for all the gold in the world." At last, however, they had pity on him, and gave him the coffin; but the moment he lifted it up to carry it home with him, the piece of apple fell from between her lips, and Snowdrop awoke, and said, "Where am I?" And the prince said, "Thou art quite safe with me."

Then he told her all that had happened, and said, "I love you far better than all the world; so come with me to my father's palace, and you shall be my wife." And Snowdrop consented, and went home with the prince; and everything was got ready with great pomp and splendour for their wedding.

To the feast was asked, among the rest, Snowdrop's old enemy the queen; and as she was dressing herself in fine rich clothes, she looked in the glass and said:

> "Tell me, glass, tell me true!
> Of all the ladies in the land,
> Who is fairest, tell me, who?"

And the glass answered:

> "Thou, lady, art loveliest here, I ween
> But lovelier far is the new-made queen."

When she heard this she started with rage; but her envy and curiosity were so great, that she could not help setting out to see the bride. And when she got there, and saw that it was no other than Snowdrop, who, as she thought, had been dead a long while, she choked with rage, and fell down and died: but Snowdrop and the prince lived and reigned happily over that land many, many years; and sometimes they went up into the mountains, and paid a visit to the little dwarfs, who had been so kind to Snowdrop in her time of need.

THE LOST BELL

A shepherd's boy, belonging to Patzig, about half a mile from Bergen, where there are great numbers of underground people in the hills, found one morning a little silver bell on the green heath among the giants' graves, and fastened it on him. It happened to be the bell belonging to the cap of one of the little brown ones, who had lost it while he was dancing, and did not immediately miss it or observe that it was no longer tinkling in his cap. He had gone down into the hill without his bell, and, having discovered his loss, was filled with melancholy, for the worst thing that can befall the underground people is to lose their cap, or their shoes; but even to lose the bell from their caps, or the buckle from their belts, is no trifle to them. Whoever loses his bell must pass some sleepless nights, for not a wink of sleep can he get till he has recovered it.

The little fellow was in the greatest trouble, and looked and searched about everywhere. But how could he learn who had the bell? for only on a very few days in the year may they come up to daylight, nor can they then appear in their true form. He had turned himself into every form of birds, beasts, and men, and he had sung and groaned and lamented about his bell, but not the slightest tidings or trace of tidings had he been able to get. Most unfortunately for him, the shepherd's boy had left Patzig the very day he found the little bell, and he was now keeping sheep at Unrich, near Gingst, so that it was not till many a day after, and then by mere chance, that the little underground fellow recovered his bell, and with it his peace of mind.

He had thought it not unlikely that a raven, or a crow, or a jackdaw, or a magpie, had found his bell, and from its thievish disposition, which attracts it to anything bright and shining, had carried it into its nest. With this thought he turned himself into a beautiful little bird, and searched all the nests in the island, and he'd sang before all kinds of birds to see if they had found what he had lost, and could restore to him his sleep. He had, however, been able to learn nothing from the birds. As he now, one evening, was flying over the waters of Ralov and the fields of Unrich, the shepherd's boy, whose name was John Schlagenteufel (Smite-devil), happened to be keeping his sheep there at the very time. Several of the sheep had bells about their necks, and they tinkled merrily when the boy's dog set them trotting. The little bird who was flying over them thought of his bell, and sang in a melancholy tone –

> "Little bell, little bell,
> Little ram as well,
> You, too, little sheep,
> If you've my tingle too,
> No sheep's so rich as you,
> My rest you keep."

The boy looked up and listened to this strange song which came out of the sky, and saw the pretty bird, which seemed to him still more strange.

"If one," said he to himself, "had but that bird that's singing up there, so plain that one of us could hardly match him! What can he mean by that wonderful song? The whole of it is, it must be a feathered witch. My rams have only pinchbeck bells, he calls them rich cattle; but I have a silver bell, and he sings nothing about me."

With these words he began to fumble in his pocket, took out his bell, and rang it.

The bird in the air instantly saw what it was, and rejoiced beyond measure. He vanished in a second, flew behind the nearest bush, alighted, and drew off his speckled feather dress, and turned himself into an old woman dressed in tattered clothes. The old dame, well supplied with sighs and groans, tottered across the field to the shepherd-boy, who was still ringing his bell and wondering what was become of the beautiful bird. She cleared her throat, and coughing, bid him a kind good evening, and asked him which was the way to Bergen. Pretending then that she had just seen the little bell, she exclaimed –

"Well now, what a charming pretty little bell! Well, in all my life, I never beheld anything more beautiful. Hark ye, my son, will you sell me that bell? What may be the price of it? I have a little grandson at home, and such a nice plaything as it would make for him!"

"No," replied the boy, quite short; "the bell is not for sale. It is a bell that there is not such another bell in the whole world. I have only to give it a little tinkle, and my sheep run of themselves wherever I would have them go. And what a delightful sound it has! Only listen, mother," said he, ringing it; "is there any weariness in the world that can hold out against this bell? I can ring with it away the longest time, so that it will be gone in a second."

The old woman thought to herself –

"We will see if he can hold out against bright shining money," and she took out no less than three silver dollars and offered them to him, but he still replied –

"No, I will not sell the bell."

She then offered him five dollars.

"The bell is still mine," said he.

She stretched out her hand full of ducats. He replied this third time –

"Gold is dirt, and does not ring."

The old dame then shifted her ground, and turned the discourse another way. She grew mysterious, and began to entice him by talking of secret arts and of charms by which his cattle might be made to thrive prodigiously, relating to him all kinds of wonders of them. It was then the young shepherd began to long, and he lent a willing ear to her tales.

The end of the matter was, that she said to him –

"Hark ye, my child, give me your bell; and see, here is a white stick for you," said she, taking out a little white stick which had Adam and Eve very ingeniously cut upon it as they were feeding their flocks in the Garden, with the fattest sheep and lambs dancing before them. There, too, was the shepherd David, as he stood up with his sling against the giant Goliath. "I will give you," said the woman, "this stick for the bell, and as long as you drive the cattle with it they will be sure to thrive. With this you will become a rich shepherd. Your wethers will be always fat a month sooner than the wethers of other shepherds, and every one of your sheep will have two pounds of wool more than others, and yet no one will ever be able to see it on them."

The old woman handed him the stick. So mysterious was her gesture, and so strange and bewitching her smile, that the lad was at once in her power. He grasped eagerly at the stick, gave her his hand, and cried –

"Done! strike hands! The bell for the stick!"

Cheerfully the old woman took the bell for the stick, and departed like a light breeze over the field and the heath. He saw her vanish, and she seemed to float away before his eyes like a mist, and to go off with a slight whiz and whistle that made the shepherd's hair stand on end.

The underground one, however, who, in the shape of an old woman, had wheedled him out of his bell, had not deceived him. For the underground people dare not lie, but must ever keep their word – a breach of it being followed by their sudden change into the shape of toads, snakes, dunghill beetles, wolves, and apes, forms in which they wander about, objects of fear and aversion, for a long course of years before they are freed. They have, therefore, naturally a great dread of lying. John Schlagenteufel gave close attention and made trial of his new shepherd's staff, and he soon found that the old woman had told him the truth, for his flocks and his work, and all the labour of his hands, prospered with him, and he had wonderful luck, so that there was not a sheep-owner or head shepherd but was desirous of having him in his employment.

It was not long, however, that he remained an underling. Before he was eighteen years of age he had got his own flocks, and in the course of a few years was the richest sheep-master in the whole island of Bergen. At last he was able to buy a knight's estate for himself, and that estate was Grabitz, close by Rambin, which now belongs to the Lords of Sunde. My father knew him there, and how from a shepherd's boy he became a nobleman. He always conducted himself like a prudent, honest, and pious man, who had a good word for every one. He brought up his sons like gentlemen, and his daughters like ladies, some of whom are still alive, and accounted people of great consequence.

Well may people who hear such stories wish that they had met with such an adventure, and had found a little silver bell which the underground people had lost!

A GLOSSARY OF MYTH & FOLKLORE

Aaru Heavenly paradise where the blessed went after death.

Ab Heart or mind.

Abiku (Yoruba) Person predestined to die. Also known as ogbanje.

Absál Nurse to Saláman, who died after their brief love affair.

Achilles The son of Peleus and the sea-nymph Thetis, who distinguished himself in the Trojan War. He was made almost immortal by his mother, who dipped him in the River Styx, and he was invincible except for a portion of his heel which remained out of the water.

Acropolis Citadel in a Greek city.

Adad-Ea Ferryman to Ut-Napishtim, who carried Gilgamesh to visit his ancestor.

Adapa Son of Ea and a wise sage.

Adar God of the sun, who is worshipped primarily in Nippur.

Aditi Sky goddess and mother of the gods.

Adityas Vishnu, children of Aditi, including Indra, Mitra, Rudra, Tvashtar, Varuna and Vishnu.

Aeneas The son of Anchises and the goddess Aphrodite, reared by a nymph. He led the Dardanian troops in the Trojan War According to legend, he became the founder of Rome.

Aengus Óg Son of Dagda and Boann (a woman said to have given the Boyne river its name), Aengus is the Irish god of love whose stronghold is reputed to have been at New Grange. The famous tale 'Dream of Aengus' tells of how he fell in love with a maiden he had dreamt of. He eventually discovered that she was to be found at the Lake of the Dragon's Mouth in Co. Tipperary, but that she lived every alternate year in the form of a swan. Aengus plunges into the lake transforming himself also into the shape of a swan. Then the two fly back together to his palace on the Boyne where they live out their days as guardians of would-be lovers.

Aesir Northern gods who made their home in Asgard; there are twelve in number.

Afrásiyáb Son of Poshang, king of Túrán, who led an army against the ruling shah Nauder. Afrásiyáb became ruler of Persia on defeating Nauder.

Afterlife Life after death or paradise, reached only by the process of preserving the body from decay through embalming and preparing it for reincarnation.

Agamemnon A famous King of Mycenae. He married Helen of Sparta's sister Clytemnestra. When Paris abducted Helen, beginning the Trojan War, Menelaus called on Agamemnon to raise the Greek troops. He had to sacrifice his daughter Iphigenia in order to get a fair wind to travel to Troy.

Agastya A rishi (sage). Leads hermits to Rama.

Agemo (Yoruba) A chameleon who aided Olorun in outwitting Olokun, who was angry at him for letting Obatala create life on her lands without her permission. Agemo outwitted Olokun by changing colour, letting her think that he and Olorun were better cloth dyers than she was. She admitted defeat and there was peace between the gods once again.

Aghasur A dragon sent by Kans to destroy Krishna.

Aghríras Son of Poshang and brother of Afrásiyáb, who was killed by his brother.

Agni The god of fire.

Agora Greek marketplace.

Ahura-Mazda Supreme god of the Persians, god of the sky. Similar to the Hindu god Varuna.

Ajax Ajax of Locris was another warrior at Troy. When Troy was captured, he committed the ultimate sacrilege by seizing Cassandra from her sanctuary with the Palladium.

Ajax Ajax the Greater was the bravest, after Achilles, of all warriors at Troy, fighting Hector in single combat and distinguishing himself in the Battle of the Ships. He was not chosen as the bravest warrior and eventually went mad.

Aje (Igbo) Goddess of the earth and the underworld.

Aje (Yoruba) Goddess of the River Niger, daughter of Yemoja.

Akhet Season of the year when the River Nile traditionally flooded.

Akkadian Person of the first Mesopotamian empire, centred in Akkad.

Akwán Diw An evil spirit who appeared as a wild ass in the court of Kai-khosráu. Rustem fought and defeated the demon, presenting its head to Kai-khosráu.

Alba Irish word for Scotland.

Alberich King of the dwarfs.

Alcinous King of the Phaeacians.

Alf-heim Home of the elves, ruled by Frey.

All Hallowmass All Saints' Day.

Allfather Another name for Odin; Yggdrasill was created by Allfather.

Alsvider Steed of the moon (Mani) chariot.

Alsvin Steed of the sun (Sol) chariot.

Amado Outer panelling of a dwelling, usually made of wood.

Ama-no-uzume Goddess of the dawn, meditation and the arts, who showed courage when faced with a giant who scared the other deities, including Ninigi. Also known as Uzume.

Amaterasu Goddess of the sun and daughter of Izanagi after Izanami's death; she became ruler of the High Plains of Heaven on her father's withdrawal from the world. Sister of Tsuki-yomi and Susanoo.

Ambalika Daughter of the king of Benares.

Ambika Daughter of the king of Benares.

Ambrosia Food of the gods.

Amemet Eater of the dead, monster who devoured the souls of the unworthy.

Amen Original creator deity.

Amen-Ra A being created from the fusion of Ra and Osiris. He champions the poor and those in trouble. Similar to the Greek god Zeus.

Ananda Disciple of Buddha.

Anansi One of the most popular African animal myths, Anansi the spider is a clever and shrewd character who outwits his fellow animals to get his own way. He is an entertaining but morally dubious character. Many African countries tell Anansi stories.

Ananta Thousand-headed snake that sprang from Balarama's mouth, Vishnu's attendant, serpent of infinite time.

Andhrímnir Cook at Valhalla.

Andvaranaut Ring of Andvari, the King of the dwarfs.

Angada Son of Vali, one of the monkey host.

Anger-Chamber Room designated for an angry queen.

Angurboda Loki's first wife, and the mother of Hel, Fenris and Jormungander.

Aniruddha Son of Pradyumna.

Anjana Mother of Hanuman.

Anunnaki Great spirits or gods of Earth.

Ansar God of the sky and father of Ea and Anu. Brother-husband to Kishar. Also known as Anshar or Asshur.

Anshumat A mighty chariot fighter.

Anu God of the sky and lord of heaven, son of Ansar and Kishar.

Anubis Guider of souls and ruler of the underworld before Osiris;

he was one of the divinities who brought Osiris back to life. He is portrayed as a canid, African wolf or jackal.

Apep Serpent and emblem of chaos.

Apollo One of the twelve Olympian gods, son of Zeus and Leto. He is attributed with being the god of plague, music, song and prophecy.

Apsaras Dancing girls of Indra's court and heavenly nymphs.

Apsu Primeval domain of fresh water, originally part of Tiawath with whom he mated to have Mummu. The term is also used for the abyss from which creation came.

Aquila The divine eagle.

Arachne A Lydian woman with great skill in weaving. She was challenged in a competition by the jealous Athene who destroyed her work and when she killed herself, turned her into a spider destined to weave until eternity.

Aralu Goddess of the underworld, also known as Eres-ki-Gal. Married to Nergal.

Ares God of War, 'gold-changer of corpses', and the son of Zeus and Hera.

Argonauts Heroes who sailed with Jason on the ship Argo to fetch the golden fleece from Colchis.

Ariki A high chief, a leader, a master, a lord.

Arjuna The third of the Pandavas.

Aroha Affection, love.

Artemis The virgin goddess of the chase, attributed with being the moon goddess and the primitive mother-goddess. She was daughter of Zeus and Leto.

Arundhati The Northern Crown.

Asamanja Son of Sagara.

Asclepius God of healing who often took the form of a snake. He is the son of Apollo by Coronis.

Asgard Home of the gods, at one root of Yggdrasill.

Ashvatthaman Son of Drona.

Ashvins Twin horsemen, sons of the sun, benevolent gods and related to the divine.

Ashwapati Uncle of Bharata and Satrughna.

Asipû Wizard.

Asopus The god of the River Asopus.

Assagai Spear, usually made from hardwood tipped with iron and used in battle.

Astrolabe Instrument for making astronomical measurements.

Asuras Titans, demons, and enemies of the gods possessing magical powers.

Atef crown White crown made up of the Hedjet, the white crown of Upper Egypt, and red feathers.

Atem The first creator-deity, he is also thought to be the finisher of the world. Also known as Tem.

Athene Virgin warrior-goddess, born from the forehead of Zeus when he swallowed his wife Metis. Plays a key role in the travels of Odysseus, and Perseus.

Atlatl Spear-thrower.

Atua A supernatural being, a god.

Atua-toko A small carved stick, the symbol of the god whom it represents. It was stuck in the ground whilst holding incantations to its presiding god.

Augeas King of Elis, one of the Argonauts.

Augsburg Tyr's city.

Avalon Legendary island where Excalibur was created and where Arthur went to recover from his wounds. It is said he will return from Avalon one day to reclaim his kingdom.

Ba Dead person or soul. Also known as ka.

Bairn Little child, also called bairnie.

Balarama Brother of Krishna.

Balder Son of Frigga; his murder causes Ragnarok. Also spelled as Baldur.

Bali Brother of Sugriva and one of the five great monkeys in the Ramayana.

Balor The evil, one-eyed King of the Fomorians and also grandfather of Lugh of the Long Arm. It was prophesied that Balor would one day be slain by his own grandson so he locked his daughter away on a remote island where he intended that she would never fall pregnant. But Cian, father of Lugh, managed to reach the island disguised as a woman, and Balor's daughter eventually bore him a child. During the second battle of Mag Tured (or Moytura), Balor was killed by Lugh who slung a stone into his giant eye.

Ban King of Benwick, father of Lancelot and brother of King Bors.

Bannock Flat loaf of bread, typically of oat or barley, usually cooked on a griddle.

Banshee Mythical spirit, usually female, who bears tales of imminent death. They often deliver the news by wailing or keening outside homes. Also known as bean sí.

Bard Traditionally a storyteller, poet or music composer whose work often focused on legends.

Barû Seer.

Basswood Any of several North American linden trees with a soft light-coloured wood.

Bastet Goddess of love, fertility and sex and a solar deity. She is often portrayed with the head of a cat.

Bateta (Yoruba) The first human, created alongside Hanna by the Toad and reshaped into human form by the Moon.

Bau Goddess of humankind and the sick, and known as the 'divine physician'. Daughter of Anu.

Bawn Fortified enclosure surrounding a castle.

Beaver Largest rodent in the United States of America, held in high esteem by the native American people. Although a land mammal, it spends a great deal of time in water and has a dense waterproof fur coat to protect it from harsh weather conditions.

Behula Daughter of Saha.

Bel Name for the god En-lil, the word Is also used as a title meaning 'lord'.

Belus Deity who helped form the heavens and earth and created animals and celestial beings. Similar to Zeus in Greek mythology.

Benten Goddess of the sea and one of the Seven Divinities of Luck. Also referred to as the goddess of love, beauty and eloquence and as being the personification of wisdom.

Bere Barley.

Berossus Priest of Bel who wrote a history of Babylon.

Berserker Norse warrior who fights with a frenzied rage.

Bestla Giant mother of Aesir's mortal element.

Bhadra A mighty elephant.

Bhagavati Shiva's wife, also known as Parvati.

Bhagiratha Son of Dilipa.

Bharadhwaja Father of Drona and a hermit.

Bharata One of Dasharatha's four sons.

Bhaumasur A demon, slain by Krishna.

Bhima The second of the Pandavas.

Bhimasha King of Rajagriha and disciple of Buddha.

Bier Frame on which a coffin or dead body is placed before being carried to the grave.

Bifrost Rainbow bridge presided over by Heimdall.

Big-Belly One of Ravana's monsters.

Bilskirnir Thor's palace.

Bodach The term means 'old man'. The Highlanders believed that the Bodach crept down chimneys in order to steal naughty children. In other territories, he was a spirit who warned of death.

Bodkin Large, blunt needle used for threading strips of cloth or tape through cloth; short pointed dagger or blade.

Boer Person of Dutch origin who settled in southern Africa in the late seventeenth century. The term means 'farmer'. Boer people are often called Afrikaners.

Bogle Ghost or phantom; goblin-like creature.

Boliaun Ragwort, a weed with ragged leaves.

Book of the Dead Book for the dead, thought to be written by Thoth, texts from which were written on papyrus and buried with the dead, or carved on the walls of tombs, pyramids or sarcophagi.

Bors King of Gaul and brother of King Ban.

Bothy Small cottage or hut.

Brahma Creator of the world, mythical origin of colour (caste).

Brahmadatta King of Benares.

Brahman Member of the highest Hindu caste, traditionally a priest.

Bran In Scottish legend, Bran is the great hunting hound of Fionn Mac Chumail. In Irish mythology, he is a great hero.

Branstock Giant oak tree in the Volsung's hall; Odin placed a sword in it and challenged the guests of a wedding to withdraw it.

Brave Young warrior of native American descent, sometimes also referred to as a 'buck'.

Bree Thin broth or soup.

Breidablik Balder's palace.

Brigit Scottish saint or spirit associated with the coming of spring.

Brisingamen Freyia's necklace.

Britomartis A Cretan goddess, also known as Dictynna.

Brocéliande Legendary enchanted forest and the supposed burial place of Merlin.

Brokki Dwarf who makes a deal with Loki, and who makes Miolnir, Draupnir and Gulinbursti.

Brollachan A shapeless spirit of unknown origin. One of the most frightening in Scottish mythology, it spoke only two words, 'Myself' and 'Thyself', taking the shape of whatever it sat upon.

Brownie A household spirit or creature which took the form of a small man (usually hideously ugly) who undertakes household chores, and mill or farm work, in exchange for a bowl of milk.

Brugh Borough or town.

Brunhilde A Valkyrie found by Sigurd.

Buddha Founder of buddhism, Gautama, avatar of Vishnu in Hinduism.

Buddhism Buddhism arrived in China in the first century BC via the silk trading route from India and Central Asia. Its founder was Guatama Siddhartha (the Buddha), a religious teacher in northern India. Buddhist doctrine declared that by destroying the causes of all suffering, mankind could attain perfect enlightenment. The religion encouraged a new respect for all living things and brought with it the idea of reincarnation; i.e. that the soul returns to the earth after death in another form, dictated by the individual's behaviour in his previous life. By the fourth century, Buddhism was the dominant religion in China, retaining its powerful influence over the nation until the mid-ninth century.

Buffalo A type of wild ox, once widely scattered over the Great Plains of North America. Also known as a 'bison', the buffalo was an important food source for the Indian tribes and its hide was also used in the construction of tepees and to make clothing. The buffalo was also sometimes revered as a totem animal, i.e. venerated as a direct ancestor of the tribesmen, and its skull used in ceremonial fashion.

Bull of Apis Sacred bull, thought to be the son of Hathor.

Bulu Sacrificial rite.

Bundles, sacred These bundles contained various venerated objects of the tribe, believed to have supernatural powers. Custody or ownership of the bundle was never lightly entered upon, but involved the learning of endless songs and ritual dances.

Bushel Unit of measurement, usually used for agricultural products or food.

Bushi Warrior.

Byre Barn for keeping cattle.

Byrny Coat of mail.

Cacique King or prince.

Cailleach Bheur A witch with a blue face who represents winter. When she is reborn each autumn, snow falls. She is mother of the god of youth (Angus mac Og).

Calabash Gourd from the calabash tree, commonly used as a bottle.

Calchas The seer of Mycenae who accompanied the Greek fleet to Troy. It was his prophecy which stated that Troy would never be taken without the aid of Achilles.

Calpulli Village house, or group or clan of families.

Calumet Ceremonial pipe used by the north American Indians.

Calypso A nymph who lived on the island of Ogygia.

Camaxtli Tlascalan god of war and the chase, similar to Huitzilopochtli.

Camelot King Arthur's castle and centre of his realm.

Caoineag A banshee.

Caravanserai Traveller's inn, traditionally found in Asia or North Africa.

Carle Term for a man, often old; peasant.

Cat A black cat has great mythological significance, is often the bearer of bad luck, a symbol of black magic, and the familiar of a witch. Cats were also the totem for many tribes.

Cath Sith A fairy cat who was believed to be a witch transformed.

Cazi Magical person or influence.

Ceasg A Scottish mermaid with the body of a maiden and the tail of a salmon.

Ceilidh Party.

Cerberus The three-headed dog who guarded the entrance to the Underworld.

Chalchiuhtlicue Goddess of water and the sick or newborn, and wife of Tlaloc. She is often symbolized as a small frog.

Changeling A fairy substitute-child left by fairies in place of a human child they have stolen.

Channa Guatama's charioteer.

Chaos A state from which the universe was created – caused by fire and ice meeting.

Charon The ferryman of the dead who carries souls across the River Styx to Hades.

Charybdis See Scylla and Charybdis.

Chicomecohuatl Chief goddess of maize and one of a group of deities called Centeotl, who care for all aspects of agriculture.

Chicomoztoc Legendary mountain and place of origin of the Aztecs. The name means 'seven caves'.

Chinawezi Primordial serpent.

Chinvat Bridge Bridge of the Gatherer, which the souls of the righteous cross to reach Mount Alborz or the world of the dead. Unworthy beings who try to cross Chinvat Bridge fall or are dragged into a place of eternal punishment.

Chitambaram Sacred city of Shiva's dance.

Chrysaor Son of Poseidon and Medusa, born from the severed neck of Medusa when Perseus beheaded her.

Chryseis Daughter of Chryses who was taken by Agamemnon in the battle of Troy.

Chullasubhadda Wife of Buddha-elect (Sumedha).

Chunda A good smith who entertains Buddha.

Churl Mean or unkind person.

Circe An enchantress and the daughter of Helius. She lived on the island of Aeaea with the power to change men to beasts.

Citlalpol The Mexican name for Venus, or the Great Star, and one of the only stars they worshipped. Also known as Tlauizcalpantecutli, or Lord of the Dawn.

Cleobis and Biton Two men of Argos who dragged the wagon carrying their mother, priestess of Hera, from Argos to the sanctuary.

Clio Muse of history and prophecy.

Clytemnestra Daughter of Tyndareus, sister of Helen, who married Agamemnon but deserted him when he sacrificed Iphigenia, their daughter, at the beginning of the Trojan War.

Coatepetl Mythical mountain, known as the 'serpent mountain'.

Coatl Serpent.

Coatlicue Earth mother and celestial goddess, she gave birth to Huitzilopochtli and his sister, Coyolxauhqui, and the moon and stars.

Codex Ancient book, often a list with pages folded into a zigzag pattern.

Confucius (Kong Fuzi) Regarded as China's greatest sage and ethical teacher, Confucius (551–479 BC) was not especially revered during his lifetime and had a small following of some three thousand people. After the Burning of the Books in 213 BC, interest in his philosophies became widespread. Confucius believed that mankind was essentially good, but argued for a highly structured society, presided over by a strong central government which would set the highest moral standards. The individual's sense of duty and obligation, he argued, would play a vital role in maintaining a well-run state.

Coracle Small, round boat, similar to a canoe. Also known as curragh or currach.

Coyolxauhqui Goddess of the moon and sister to Huitzilopochtli, she was decapitated by her brother after trying to kill their mother.

Creel Large basket made of wicker, usually used for fish.

Crodhmara Fairy cattle.

Cronan Musical humming, thought to resemble a cat purring or the drone of bagpipes.

Crow Usually associated with battle and death, but many mythological figures take this form.

Cu Sith A great fairy dog, usually green and oversized.

Cubit Ancient measurement, equal to the approximate length of a forearm.

Cuculain Irish warrior and hero. Also known as Cuchulainn.

Cutty Girl.

Cyclopes One-eyed giants who were imprisoned in Tartarus by Uranus and Cronus, but released by Zeus, for whom they made thunderbolts. Also a tribe of pastoralists who live without laws, and on, whenever possible, human flesh.

Daedalus Descendant of the Athenian King Erechtheus and son of Eupalamus. He killed his nephew and apprentice. Famed for constructing the labyrinth to house the Minotaur, in which he was later imprisoned. He constructed wings for himself and his son to make their escape.

Dagda One of the principal gods of the Tuatha De Danann, the father and chief, the Celtic equivalent of Zeus. He was the god reputed to have led the People of Dana in their successful conquest of the Fir Bolg.

Dagon God of fish and fertility; he is sometimes described as a sea-monster or chthonic god.

Daikoku God of wealth and one of the gods of luck.

Daimyō Powerful lord or magnate.

Daksha The chief Prajapati.

Dana Also known as Danu, a goddess worshipped from antiquity by the Celts and considered to be the ancestor of the Tuatha De Danann.

Danae Daughter of Acrisius, King of Argos. Acrisius trapped her in a cave when he was warned that his grandson would be the cause of his ultimate death. Zeus came to her and Perseus was born.

Danaids The fifty daughters of Danaus of Argos, by ten mothers.

Daoine Sidhe The people of the Hollow Hills, or Otherworld.

Dardanus Son of Zeus and Electra, daughter of Atlas.

Dasharatha A Manu amongst men, King of Koshala, father of Santa.

Deianeira Daughter of Oeneus, who married Heracles after he won her in a battle with the River Achelous.

Deirdre A beautiful woman doomed to cause the deaths of three Irish heroes and bring war to the whole country. After a soothsayer prophesied her fate, Deidre's father hid her away from the world to prevent it. However, fate finds its way and the events come to pass before Deidre eventually commits suicide to remain with her love.

Demeter Goddess of agriculture and nutrition, whose name means earth mother. She is the mother of Persephone.

Demophoon Son of King Celeus of Eleusis, who was nursed by Demeter and then dropped in the fire when she tried to make him immortal.

Dervish Member of a religious order, often Sufi, known for their wild dancing and whirling.

Desire The god of love.

Deva A god other than the supreme God.

Devadatta Buddha's cousin, plots evil against Buddha.

Dhrishtadyumna Twin brother of Draupadi, slays Drona.

Dibarra God of plague. Also a demonic character or evil spirit.

Dik-dik Dwarf antelope native to eastern and southern Africa.

Dilipa Son of Anshumat, father of Bhagiratha.

Dionysus The god of wine, vegetation and the life force, and of ecstasy. He was considered to be outside the Greek pantheon, and generally thought to have begun life as a mortal.

Dioscuri Castor and Polydeuces, the twin sons of Zeus and Leda, who are important deities.

Distaff Tool used when spinning which holds the wool or flax and keeps the fibres from tangling.

Divan Privy council.

Divots Turfs.

Dog The dog is a symbol of humanity, and usually has a role helping the hero of the myth or legend. Fionn's Bran and Grey Dog are two examples of wild beasts transformed to become invaluable servants.

Dōshin Government official.

Dossal Ornamental altar cloth.

Doughty Persistent and brave person.

Dragon Important animal in Japanese culture, symbolizing power, wealth, luck and success.

Draiglin' Hogney Ogre.

Draupadi Daughter of Drupada.

Draupnir Odin's famous ring, fashioned by Brokki.

Drona A Brahma, son of the great sage Bharadwaja.

Druid An ancient order of Celtic priests held in high esteem who flourished in the pre-Christian era. The word 'druid' is derived from an ancient Celtic one meaning 'very knowledgeable'. These individuals were believed to have mystical powers and in ancient Irish literature possess the ability to conjure up magical charms, to create tempests, to curse and debilitate their enemies and to perform as soothsayers to the royal courts.

Drupada King of the Panchalas.

Dryads Nymphs of the trees.

Dun A stronghold or royal abode surrounded by an earthen wall.

Durga Goddess, wife of Shiva.

Durk Knife. Also spelled as dirk.

Duryodhana One of Drona's pupils.

Dvalin Dwarf visited by Loki; also the name for the stag on Yggdrasill.

Dwarfie Stone Prehistoric tomb or boulder.

Dwarfs Fairies and black elves are called dwarfs.

Dwarkanath The Lord of Dwaraka; Krishna.

Dyumatsena King of the Shalwas and father of Satyavan.

Ea God of water, light and wisdom, and one of the creator deities. He brought arts and civilization to humankind. Also known as Oannes and Nudimmud.

Eabani Hero originally created by Aruru to defeat Gilgamesh, the two became friends and destroyed Khumbaba together. He personifies the natural world.

Each Uisge The mythical water-horse which haunts lochs and appears in various forms.

Ebisu One of the gods of luck. He is also the god of labour and fishermen.

Echo A nymph who was punished by Hera for her endless stories told to distract Hera from Zeus's infidelity.

Ector King Arthur's foster father, who raised Arthur to protect him.

Edda Collection of prose and poetic myths and stories from the Norsemen.

Eight Immortals Three of these are reputed to be historical: Han Chung-li, born in Shaanxi, who rose to become a Marshal of the Empire in 21 BC. Chang Kuo-Lao, who lived in the seventh to eighth century AD, and Lü Tung-pin, who was born in AD 755.

Einheriear Odin's guests at Valhalla.

Eisa Loki' daughter.

Ekake (Ibani) Person of great intelligence, which means 'tortoise'. Also known as Mbai (Igbo).

Ekalavya Son of the king of the Nishadas.

Electra Daughter of Agamemnon and Clytemnestra.

Eleusis A town in which the cult of Demeter is centred.

Elf Sigmund is buried by an elf; there are light and dark elves (the latter called dwarfs).

Elokos (Central African) Imps of dwarf-demons who eat human flesh.

Elpenor The youngest of Odysseus's crew who fell from the roof of Circe's house on Aeaea and visited with Odysseus at Hades.

Elysium The home of the blessed dead.

Emain Macha The capital of ancient Ulster.

Emma Dai-o King of hell and judge of the dead.

En-lil God of the lower world, storms and mist, who held sway over the ghostly animistic spirits, which at his bidding might pose as the friends or enemies of men. Also known as Bel.

Eos Goddess of the dawn and sister of the sun and moon.

Erichthonius A child born of the semen spilled when Hephaestus tried to rape Athene on the Acropolis.

Eridu The home of Ea and one of the two major cities of Babylonian civilization.

Erin Term for Ireland, originally spelled Éirinn.

Erirogho Magical mixture made from the ashes of the dead.

Eros God of Love, the son of Aphrodite.

Erpa Hereditary chief.

Erysichthon A Thessalian who cut down a grove sacred to Demeter, who punished him with eternal hunger.

Eshu (Yoruba) God of mischief. He also tests people's characters and controls law enforcement.

Eteocles Son of Oedipus.

Eumaeus Swineherd of Odysseus's family at Ithaca.

Euphemus A son of Poseidon who could walk on water. He sailed with the Argonauts.

Europa Daughter of King Agenor of Tyre, who was taken by Zeus to Crete.

Eurydice A Thracian nymph married to Orpheus.

Excalibur The magical sword given to Arthur by the Lady of the Lake. In some versions of the myths, Excalibur is also the sword that the young Arthur pulls from the stone to become king.

Fabulist Person who composes or tells fables.

Fafnir Shape-changer who kills his father and becomes a dragon to guard the family jewels. Slain by Sigurd.

Fairy The word is derived from 'Fays' which means Fates. They are immortal, with the gift of prophecy and of music, and their role changes according to the origin of the myth. They were often considered to be little people, with enormous propensity for mischief, but they are central to many myths and legends, with important powers.

Faro (Mali, Guinea) God of the sky.

Fates In Greek mythology, daughters of Zeus and Themis, who spin the thread of a mortal's life and cut it when his time is due. Called Norns in Viking mythology.

Fenris A wild wolf, who is the son of Loki. He roams the earth after Ragnarok.

Ferhad Sculptor who fell in love with Shireen, the wife of Khosru, and undertook a seemingly impossible task to clear a passage through the mountain of Beysitoun and join the rivers in return for winning Shireen's hand.

Fialar Red cock of Valhalla.

Fianna/Fenians The word 'fianna' was used in early times to describe young warrior-hunters. These youths evolved under the leadership of Finn Mac Cumaill as a highly skilled band of military men who took up service with various kings throughout Ireland.

Filheim Land of mist, at the end of one of Yggdrasill's roots.

Fingal Another name for Fionn Mac Chumail, used after MacPherson's Ossian in the eighteenth century.

Fionn Mac Chumail Irish and Scottish warrior, with great powers of fairness and wisdom. He is known not for physical strength but for knowledge, sense of justice, generosity and canny instinct. He had two hounds, which were later discovered to be his nephews transformed. He became head of the Fianna, or Féinn, fighting the enemies of Ireland and Scotland. He was the father of Oisin (also called Ossian, or other derivatives), and father or grandfather of Osgar.

Fir Bolg One of the ancient, pre-Gaelic peoples of Ireland who were reputed to have worshipped the god Bulga, meaning god of lighting. They are thought to have colonized Ireland around 1970 BC, after the death of Nemed and to have reigned for a short period of thirty-seven years before their defeat by the Tuatha De Danann.

Fir Chlis Nimble men or merry dancers, who are the souls of fallen angels.

Flitch Side of salted and cured bacon.

Folkvang Freyia's palace.

Fomorians A race of monstrous beings, popularly conceived as sea-pirates with some supernatural characteristics who opposed the earliest settlers in Ireland, including the Nemedians and the Tuatha De Danann.

Frey Comes to Asgard with Freyia as a hostage following the war between the Aesir and the Vanir.

Freyia Comes to Asgard with Frey as a hostage following the war between the Aesir and the Vanir. Goddess of beauty and love.

Frigga Odin's wife and mother of gods; she is goddess of the earth.

Fuath Evil spirits which lived in or near the water.

Fulla Frigga's maidservant.

Furies Creatures born from the blood of Cronus, guarding the greatest sinners of the Underworld. Their power lay in their ability to drive mortals mad. Snakes writhed in their hair and around their waists.

Furoshiki Cloths used to wrap things.

Gae Bolg Cuchulainn alone learned the use of this weapon from the woman-warrior, Scathach and with it he slew his own son Connla and his closest friend, Ferdia. Gae Bolg translates as 'harpoon-like javelin' and the deadly weapon was reported to have been created by Bulga, the god of lighting.

Gaea Goddess of Earth, born from Chaos, and the mother of Uranus and Pontus. Also spelled as Gaia.

Gage Object of value presented to a challenger to symbolize good faith.

Galahad Knight of the Round Table, who took up the search for the Holy Grail. Son of Lancelot, Galahad is considered the purest and most perfect knight.

Galatea Daughter of Nereus and Doris, a sea-nymph loved by Polyphemus, the Cyclops.

Gandhari Mother of Duryodhana.

Gandharvas Demi-gods and musicians.

Gandjharva Musical ministrants of the upper air.

Ganesha Elephant-headed god of scribes and son of Shiva.

Ganges Sacred river personified by the goddess Ganga, wife of Shiva and daughter of the mount Himalaya.

Gareth of Orkney King Arthur's nephew and knight of the Round Table.

Garm Hel's hound.

Garuda King of the birds and mount Vishnu, the divine bird, attendant of Narayana.

Gautama Son of Suddhodana and also known as Siddhartha.

Gawain Nephew of King Arthur and knight of the Round Table, he is best known for his adventure with the Green Knight, who challenges one of Arthur's knights to cut off his head, but only if he agrees to be beheaded in turn in a year and a day, if the Green Knight survives. Gawain beheads the Green Knight, who simply replaces his head. At the appointed time, they meet, and the Green Knight swings his axe but merely nicks Gawain's skin instead of beheading him.

Geisha Performance artist or entertainer, usually female.

Geri Odin's wolf.

Ghommid (Yoruba) Term for mythological creatures such as goblins or ogres.

Giallar Bridge in Filheim.

Giallarhorn Heimdall's trumpet – the final call signifies Ragnarok.

Giants In Greek mythology, a race of beings born from Gaea, grown from the blood that dropped from the castrated Uranus. Usually represent evil in Viking mythology.

Gilgamesh King of Erech known as a half-human, half-god hero similar to the Greek Heracles, and often listed with the gods. He is the personification of the sun and is protected by the god Shamash, who in some texts is described as his father. He is also portrayed as an evil tyrant at times.

Gillie Someone who works for a Scottish chief, usually as an attendant or servant; guide for fishing or hunting parties.

Gladheim Where the twelve deities of Asgard hold their thrones. Also called Gladsheim.

Gled Bird of prey.

Golden Fleece Fleece of the ram sent by Poseidon to substitute for Phrixus when his father was going to sacrifice him. The Argonauts went in search of the fleece.

Goodman Man of the house.

Goodwife Woman of the house.

Gopis Lovers of the young Krishna and milkmaids.

Gorgon One of the three sisters, including Medusa, whose frightening looks could turn mortals to stone.

Graces Daughters of Aphrodite by Zeus.

Gramercy Expression of surprise or strong feeling.

Great Head The Iroquois Indians believed in the existence of a curious being known as Great Head, a creature with an enormous head poised on slender legs.

Great Spirit The name given to the Creator of all life, as well as the term used to describe the omnipotent force of the Creator existing in every living thing.

Great-Flank One of Ravana's monsters.

Green Knight A knight dressed all in green and with green hair and skin who challenged one of Arthur's knights to strike him a blow with an axe and that, if he survived, he would return to behead the knight in a year and a day. He turned out to be Lord Bertilak and was under an enchantment cast by Morgan le Fay to test Arthur's knights.

Gruagach Mythical creature, often a giant or ogre similar to a wild man of the woods. The term can also refer to other mythical creatures such as brownies or fairies. As a brownie, he is usually dressed in red or green as opposed to the traditional brown. He has great power to enchant the hapless, or to help mortals who are worthy (usually heroes). He often appears to challenge a boy-hero, during his period of education.

Gudea High priest of Lagash, known to be a patron of the arts and a writer himself.

Guebre Religion founded by Zoroaster, the Persian prophet.

Gugumatz Creator god who, with Huracan, formed the sky, earth and everything on it.

Guha King of Nishadha.

Guidewife Woman.

Guinevere Wife of King Arthur; she is often portrayed as a virtuous lady and wife, but is perhaps best known for having a love affair with Lancelot, one of Arthur's friends and knights of the Round Table. Her name is also spelled Guenever.

Gulistan *Rose Garden*, written by the poet Sa'di

Gungnir Odin's spear, made of Yggdrasill wood, and the tip fashioned by Dvalin.

Gylfi A wandering king to whom the Eddas are narrated.

Haab Mayan solar calendar that consisted of eighteen twenty-day months.

Hades One of the three sons of Cronus; brother of Poseidon and Zeus. Hades is King of the Underworld, which is also known as the House of Hades.

Haere-mai Maori phrase meaning 'come here, welcome.'

Haere-mai-ra, me o tatou mate Maori phrase meaning 'come here, that I may sorrow with you.'

Haere-ra Maori phrase meaning 'goodbye, go, farewell.'

Haji Muslim pilgrim who has been to Mecca.

Hakama Traditional Japanese clothing, worn on the bottom half of the body.

Hanuman General of the monkey people.

Harakiri Suicide, usually by cutting or stabbing the abdomen. Also known as seppuku.

Hari-Hara Shiva and Vishnu as one god.

Harmonia Daughter of Ares and Aphrodite, wife of Cadmus.

Hatamoto High-ranking samurai.

Hathor Great cosmic mother and patroness of lovers. She is portrayed as a cow.

Hati The wolf who pursues the sun and moon.

Hatshepsut Second female pharaoh.

Hauberk Armour to protect the neck and shoulders, sometimes a full-length coat of mail.

Hector Eldest son of King Priam who defended Troy from the Greeks. He was killed by Achilles.

Hecuba The second wife of Priam, King of Troy. She was turned into a dog after Troy was lost.

Heimdall White god who guards the Bifrost bridge.

Hel Goddess of death and Loki's daughter. Also known as Hela.

Helen Daughter of Leda and Tyndareus, King of Sparta, and the most beautiful woman in the world. She was responsible for starting the Trojan War.

Heliopolis City in modern-day Cairo, known as the City of the Sun and the central place of worship of Ra. Also known as Anu.

Helius The sun, son of Hyperion and Theia.

Henwife Witch.

Hephaestus or **Hephaistos** The Smith of Heaven.

Hera A Mycenaean palace goddess, married to Zeus.

Heracles An important Greek hero, the son of Zeus and Alcmena. His name means 'Glory of Hera'. He performed twelve labours for King Eurystheus, and later became a god.

Hermes The conductor of souls of the dead to Hades, and god of trickery and of trade. He acts as messenger to the gods.

Hermod Son of Frigga and Odin who travelled to see Hel in order to reclaim Balder for Asgard.

Hero and Leander Hero was a priestess of Aphrodite, loved by Leander, a young man of Abydos. He drowned trying to see her.

Hestia Goddess of the hearth, daughter of Cronus and Rhea.

Hieroglyphs Type of writing that combines symbols and pictures, usually cut into tombs or rocks, or written on papyrus.

Himalaya Great mountain and range, father of Parvati.

Hiordis Wife of Sigmund and mother of Sigurd.

Hoderi A fisher and son of Okuninushi.

Hodur Balder's blind twin; known as the personification of darkness.

Hoenir Also called Vili; produced the first humans with Odin and Loki, and was one of the triad responsible for the creation of the world.

Hōichi the Earless A biwa hōshi, a blind storyteller who played the biwa or lute. Also a priest.

Holger Danske Legendary Viking warrior who is thought to never die. He sleeps until he is needed by his people and then he will rise to protect them.

Homayi Phoenix.

Hoodie Mythical creature which often appears as a crow.

Hoori A hunter and son of Okuninushi.

Horus God of the sky and kinship, son of Isis and Osiris. He captained the boat that carried Ra across the sky. He is depicted with the head of a falcon.

Hotei One of the gods of luck. He also personifies humour and contentment.

Houlet Owl.

Houri Beautiful virgin from paradise.

Hrim-faxi Steed of the night.

Hubris Presumptuous behaviour which causes the wrath of the gods to be brought on to mortals.

Hueytozoztli Festival dedicated to Tlaloc and, at times, Chicomecohuatl or other deities. Also the fourth month of the Aztec calendar.

Hugin Odin's raven.

Huitzilopochtli God of war and the sun, also connected with the summer and crops; one of the principal Aztec deities. He was born a full-grown adult to save his mother, Coatlicue, from the jealousy of his sister, Coyolxauhqui, who tried to kill Coatlicue. The Mars of the Aztec gods. In some origin stories he is one of four offspring of Ometeotl and Omecihuatl.

Hurley A traditional Irish game played with sticks and balls, quite similar to hockey.

Hurons A tribe of Iroquois stock, originally one people with the Iroquois.

Huveane (Pedi, Venda) Creator of humankind, who made a baby from clay into which he breathed life. He is known as the High God or Great God. He is also known as a trickster god.

Hymir Giant who fishes with Thor and is drowned by him.

Iambe Daughter of Pan and Echo, servant to King Celeus of Eleusis and Metaeira.

Icarus Son of Daedalus, who plunged to his death after escaping from the labyrinth.

Ichneumon Mongoose.

Idunn Guardian of the youth-giving apples.

Ifa (Yoruba) God of wisdom and divination. Also the term for a Yoruban religion.

Ife (Yoruba) The place Obatala first arrived on Earth and took for his home.

Igigi Great spirits or gods of Heaven and the sky.

Igraine Wife of the duke of Tintagel, enemy of Uther Pendragon, who marries Uther when her first husband dies. She is King Arthur's mother.

Ile (Yoruba) Goddess of the earth.

Imhetep High priest and wise sage. He is sometimes thought to be the son of Ptah.

Imam Person who leads prayers in a mosque.

Imana (Banyarwanda) Creator or sky god.

In The male principle who, joined with Yo, the female side, brought about creation and the first gods. In and Yo correspond to the Chinese Yang and Yin.

Inari God of rice, fertility, agriculture and, later, the fox god. Inari has both good and evil attributes but is often presented as an evil trickster.

Indra The King of Heaven.

Indrajit Son of Ravana.

Indrasen Daughter of Nala and Damayanti.

Indrasena Son of Nala and Damayanti.

Inundation Annual flooding of the River Nile.

Iphigenia The eldest daughter of Agamemnon and Clytemnestra who was sacrificed to appease Artemis and obtain a fair wind for Troy.

Iris Messenger of the gods who took the form of a rainbow.

Iseult Princess of Ireland and niece of the Morholt. She falls in love with Tristan after consuming a love potion but is forced to marry King Mark of Cornwall.

Ishtar Goddess of love, beauty, justice and war, especially in Ninevah, and earth mother who symbolizes fertility. Married to Tammuz, she is similar to the Greek goddess Aphrodite. Ishtar is sometimes known as Innana or Irnina.

Isis Goddess of the Nile and the moon, sister-wife of Osiris. She and her son, Horus, are sometimes thought of in a similar way to Mary and Jesus. She was one of the most worshipped female

Egyptian deities and was instrumental in returning Osiris to life after he was killed by his brother, Set.

Istakbál Deputation of warriors.

Izanagi Deity and brother-husband to Izanami, who together created the Japanese islands from the Floating Bridge of Heaven. Their offspring populated Japan.

Izanami Deity and sister-wife of Izanagi, creator of Japan. Their children include Amaterasu, Tsuki-yomi and Susanoo.

Jade It was believed that jade emerged from the mountains as a liquid which then solidified after ten thousand years to become a precious hard stone, green in colour. If the correct herbs were added to it, it could return to its liquid state and when swallowed increase the individual's chances of immortality.

Jambavan A noble monkey.

Jason Son of Aeson, King of Iolcus and leader of the voyage of the Argonauts.

Jatayu King of all the eagle-tribes.

Jesseraunt Flexible coat of armour or mail.

Jimmo Legendary first emperor of Japan. He is thought to be descended from Hoori, while other tales claim him to be descended from Amaterasu through her grandson, Ninigi.

Jizo God of little children and the god who calms the troubled sea.

Jord Daughter of Nott; wife of Odin.

Jormungander The world serpent; son of Loki. Legends tell that when his tail is removed from his mouth, Ragnarok has arrived.

Jorō Geisha who also worked as a prostitute.

Jotunheim Home of the giants.

Ju Ju tree Deciduous tree that produces edible fruit.

Jurasindhu A rakshasa, father-in-law of Kans.

Jyeshtha Goddess of bad luck.

Ka Life power or soul. Also known as ba.

Kai-káús Son of Kai-kobád. He led an army to invade Mázinderán, home of the demon-sorcerers, after being persuaded by a demon. Known for his ambitious schemes, he later tried to reach Heaven by trapping eagles to fly him there on his throne.

Kaikeyi Mother of Bharata, one of Dasharatha's three wives.

Kai-khosrau Son of Saiawúsh, who killed Afrásiyáb in revenge for the death of his father.

Kai-kobád Descendant of Feridún, he was selected by Zál to lead an army against Afrásiyáb. Their powerful army, led by Zál and Rustem, drove back Afrásiyáb's army, who then agreed to peace.

Kailyard Kitchen garden or small plot, usually used for growing vegetables.

Kali The Black, wife of Shiva.

Kalindi Daughter of the sun, wife of Krishna.

Kaliya A poisonous hydra that lived in the jamna.

Kalki Incarnation of Vishnu yet to come.

Kalnagini Serpent who kills Lakshmindara.

Kal-Purush The Time-man, Bengali name for Orion.

Kaluda A disciple of Buddha.

Kalunga-ngombe (Mbundu) Death, also depicted as the king of the netherworld.

Kama God of desire.

Kamadeva Desire, the god of love.

Kami Spirits, deities or forces of nature.

Kamund Lasso.

Kans King of Mathura, son of Ugrasena and Pavandrekha.

Kanva Father of Shakuntala.

Kappa River goblin with the body of a tortoise and the head of an ape. Kappa love to challenge human beings to single combat.

Karakia Invocation, ceremony, prayer.

Karna Pupil of Drona.

Kaross Blanket or rug, also worn as a traditional garment. It is often made from the skins of animals which have been sewn together.

Kasbu A period of twenty-four hours.

Kashyapa One of Dasharatha's counsellors.

Kauravas or Kurus Sons of Dhritarashtra, pupils of Drona.

Kaushalya Mother of Rama, one of Dasharatha's three wives.

Kay Son of Ector and adopted brother to King Arthur, he becomes one of Arthur's knights of the Round Table.

Keb God of the earth and father of Osiris and Isis, married to Nut. Keb is identified with Kronos, the Greek god of time.

Kehua Spirit, ghost.

Kelpie Another word for each uisge, the water-horse.

Ken Know.

Keres Black-winged demons or daughters of the night.

Keshini Wife of Sagara.

Khalif Leader.

Khara Younger brother of Ravana.

Khepera God who represents the rising sun. He is portrayed as a scarab. Also known as Nebertcher.

Kher-heb Priest and magician who officiated over rituals and ceremonies.

Khnemu God of the source of the Nile and one of the original Egyptian deities. He is thought to be the creator of children and of other gods. He is portrayed as a ram.

Khosru King and husband to Shireen, daughter of Maurice, the Greek Emperor. He was murdered by his own son, who wanted his kingdom and his wife.

Khumbaba Monster and guardian of the goddess Irnina, a form of the goddess Ishtar. Khumbaba is likened to the Greek gorgon.

Kia-ora Welcome, good luck. A greeting.

Kiboko Hippopotamus.

Kikinu Soul.

Kimbanda (Mbundu) Doctor.

Kimono Traditional Japanese clothing, similar to a robe.

King Arthur Legendary king of Britain who plucked the magical sword from the stone, marking him as the heir of Uther Pendragon and 'true king' of Britain. He and his knights of the Round Table defended Britain from the Saxons and had many adventures, including searching for the Holy Grail. Finally wounded in battle, he left Britain for the mythical Avalon, vowing to one day return to reclaim his kingdom.

Kingu Tiawath's husband, a god and warrior who she promised would rule Heaven once he helped her defeat the 'gods of light'. He was killed by Merodach who used his blood to make clay, from which he formed the first humans. In some tales, Kingu is Tiawath's son as well as her consort.

Kinnaras Human birds with musical instruments under their wings.

Kinyamkela (Zaramo) Ghost of a child.

Kirk Church, usually a term for Church of Scotland churches.

Kirtle One-piece garment, similar to a tunic, which was worn by men or women.

Kis Solar deity, usually depicted as an eagle.

Kishar Earth mother and sister-wife to Anshar.

Kist Trunk or large chest.

Kitamba (Mbundu) Chief who made his whole village go into mourning when his head-wife, Queen Muhongo, died. He also pledged that no one should speak or eat until she was returned to him.

Knowe Knoll or hillock.

Kojiki One of two myth-histories of Japan, along with the *Nihon Shoki*.

Ko-no-Hana Goddess of Mount Fuji, princess and wife of Ninigi.

Kore 'Maiden', another name for Persephone.

Kraal Traditional rural African village, usually consisting of huts surrounded by a fence or wall. Also an animal enclosure.

Krishna The Dark one, worshipped as an incarnation of Vishnu.

Kui-see Edible root.

Kumara Son of Shiva and Paravati, slays demon Taraka.

Kumbha-karna Ravana's brother.

Kunti Mother of the Pandavas.

Kura Red. The sacred colour of the Maori.

Kusha or Kusi One of Sita's two sons.

Kvasir Clever warrior and colleague of Odin. He was responsible for finally outwitting Loki.

Kwannon Goddess of mercy.

Labyrinth A prison built at Knossos for the Minotaur by Daedalus.

Lady of the Lake Enchantress who presents Arthur with Excalibur.

Laertes King of Ithaca and father of Odysseus.

Laestrygonians Savage giants encountered by Odysseus on his travels.

Laili In love with Majnun but unable to marry him, she was given to the prince, Ibn Salam, to marry. When he died, she escaped and found Majnun, but they could not be legally married. The couple died of grief and were buried together. Also known as Laila.

Laird Person who owns a significant estate in Scotland.

Lakshmana Brother of Rama and his companion in exile.

Lakshmi Consort of Vishnu and a goddess of beauty and good fortune.

Lakshmindara Son of Chand resurrected by Manasa Devi.

Lancelot Knight of the Round Table. Lancelot was raised by the Lady of the Lake. While he went on many quests, he is perhaps best known for his affair with Guinevere, King Arthur's wife.

Land of Light One of the names for the realm of the fairies. If a piece of metal welded by human hands is put in the doorway to their land, the door cannot close. The door to this realm is only open at night, and usually at a full moon.

Lang syne The days of old.

Lao Tzu (Laozi) The ancient Taoist philosopher thought to have been born in 571 BC a contemporary of Confucius with whom, it is said, he discussed the tenets of Tao. Lao Tzu was an advocate of simple rural existence and looked to the Yellow Emperor and Shun as models of efficient government. His philosophies were recorded in the Tao Te Ching. Legends surrounding his birth suggest that he emerged from the left-hand side of his mother's body, with white hair and a long white beard, after a confinement lasting eighty years.

Laocoon A Trojan wiseman who predicted that the wooden horse contained Greek soldiers.

Laomedon The King of Troy who hired Apollo and Poseidon to build the impregnable walls of Troy.

Lava Son of Sita.

Leda Daughter of the King of Aetolia, who married Tyndareus. Helen and Clytemnestra were her daughters.

Legba (Dahomey) Youngest offspring of Mawu-Lisa. He was given the gift of all languages. It was through him that humans could converse with the gods.

Leman Lover.

Leprechaun Mythical creature from Irish folk tales who often appears as a mischievous and sometimes drunken old man.

Lethe One of the four rivers of the Underworld, also called the River of Forgetfulness.

Lif The female survivor of Ragnarok.

Lifthrasir The male survivor of Ragnarok.

Lil Demon.

Liongo (Swahili) Warrior and hero.

Lofty mountain Home of Ahura-Mazda.

Logi Utgard-loki's cook.

Loki God of fire and mischief-maker of Asgard; he eventually brings about Ragnarok. Also spelled as Loptur.

Lotus-Eaters A race of people who live a dazed, drugged existence, the result of eating the lotus flower.

Ma'at State of order meaning truth, order or justice. Personified by the goddess Ma'at, who was Thoth's consort.

Macha There are thought to be several different Machas who appear in quite a number of ancient Irish stories. For the purposes of this book, however, the Macha referred to is the wife of Crunnchu. The story unfolds that after her husband had boasted of her great athletic ability to the King, she was subsequently forced to run against his horses in spite of the fact that she was heavily pregnant. Macha died giving birth to her twin babies and with her dying breath she cursed Ulster for nine generations, proclaiming that it would suffer the weakness of a woman in childbirth in times of great stress. This curse had its most disastrous effect when Medb of Connacht invaded Ulster with her great army.

Machi-bugyō Senior official or magistrate, usually samurai.

Macuilxochitl God of art, dance and games, and the patron of luck in gaming. His name means 'source of flowers' or 'prince of flowers'. Also known as Xochipilli, meaning 'five-flower'.

Madake Weapon used for whipping, made of bamboo.

Maduma Taro tuber.

Mag Muirthemne Cuchulainn's inheritance. A plain extending from River Boyne to the mountain range of Cualgne, close to Emain Macha in Ulster.

Magni Thor's son.

Mahaparshwa One of Ravana's generals.

Maharaksha Son of Khara, slain at Lanka.

Mahasubhadda Wife of Buddha-select (Sumedha).

Majnun Son of a chief, who fell in love with Laili and followed her tribe through the desert, becoming mad with love until they were briefly reunited before dying.

Makaras Mythical fish-reptiles of the sea.

Makoma (Senna) Folk hero who defeated five mighty giants.

Mana Power, authority, prestige, influence, sanctity, luck.

Manasa Devi Goddess of snakes, daughter of Shiva by a mortal woman.

Manasha Goddess of snakes.

Mandavya Daughter of Kushadhwaja.

Man-Devourer One of Ravana's monsters.

Mandodari Wife of Ravana.

Mandrake Poisonous plant from the nightshade family which has hallucinogenic and hypnotic qualities if ingested. Its roots resemble the human form and it has supposedly magical qualities.

Mani The moon.

Manitto Broad term used to describe the supernatural or a potent spirit among the Algonquins, the Iroquois and the Sioux.

Man-Slayer One of Ravana's counsellors.

Manthara Kaikeyi's evil nurse, who plots Rama's ruin.

Mantle Cloak or shawl.

Manu Lawgiver.

Manu Mythical mountain on which the sun sets.

Mara The evil one, tempts Gautama.

Markandeya One of Dasharatha's counsellors.

Mashu Mountain of the Sunset, which lies between Earth and the underworld. Guarded by scorpion-men.

Matali Sakra's charioteer.

Mawu-Lisa (Dahomey) Twin offspring of Nana Baluka. Mawu (female) and Lisa (male) are often joined to form one being. Their own offspring populated the world.

Mbai (Igbo) Person of great intelligence, also known as Ekake (Ibani), which means 'tortoise'.

Medea Witch and priestess of Hecate, daughter of Aeetes and sister of Circe. She helped Jason in his quest for the Golden Fleece.

Medusa One of the three Gorgons whose head had the power to turn onlookers to stone.

Melpomene One of the muses, and mother of the Sirens.

Menaka One of the most beautiful dancers in Heaven.

Menat Amulet, usually worn for protection.

Mendicant Beggar.

Menelaus King of Sparta, brother of Agamemnon. Married Helen and called war against Troy when she eloped with Paris.

Menthu Lord of Thebes and god of war. He is portrayed as a hawk or falcon.

Mere-pounamu A native weapon made of a rare green stone.

Merlin Wizard and advisor to King Arthur. He is thought to be the son of a human female and an incubus (male demon). He brought about Arthur's birth and ascension to king, then acted as his mentor.

Merodach God who battled Tiawath and defeated her by cutting out her heart and dividing her corpse into two pieces. He used these pieces to divide the upper and lower waters once controlled by Tiawath, making a dwelling for the gods of light. He also created humankind. Also known as Marduk.

Merrow Mythical mermaid-like creature, often depicted with an enchanted cap called a cohuleen driuth which allows it to travel between land and the depths of the sea. Also known as murúch.

Metaneira Wife of Celeus, King of Eleusis, who hired Demeter in disguise as her nurse.

Metztli Goddess of the moon, her name means 'lady of the night'. Also known as Yohualtictl.

Michabo Also known as Manobozho, or the Great Hare, the principal deity of the Algonquins, maker and preserver of the earth, sun and moon.

Mictlan God of the dead and ruler of the underworld. He was married to Mictecaciuatl and is often represented as a bat. He is also the Aztec lord of Hades. Also known as Mictlantecutli. Mictlan is also the name for the underworld.

Midgard Dwelling place of humans (Earth).

Midsummer A time when fairies dance and claim human victims.

Mihrab Father of Rúdábeh and descendant of Zohák, the serpent-king.

Milesians A group of iron-age invaders led by the sons of Mil, who arrived in Ireland from Spain around 500 BC and overcame the Tuatha De Danann.

Mimir God of the ocean. His head guards a well; reincarnated after Ragnarok.

Minos King of Crete, son of Zeus and Europa. He was considered to have been the ruler of a sea empire.

Minotaur A creature born of the union between Pasiphae and a Cretan Bull.

Minúchihr King who lives to be one hundred and twenty years old. Father of Nauder.

Miolnir *See* Mjolnir.

Mithra God of the sun and light in Iran, protector of truth and guardian of pastures and cattle. Alo known as Mitra in Hindu mythology and Mithras in Roman mythology.

Mixcoatl God of the chase or the hunt. Sometimes depicted as the god of air and thunder, he introduced fire to humankind. His name means 'cloud serpent'.

Mjolnir Hammer belonging to the Norse god of thunder, which is used as a fearsome weapon which always returns to Thor's hand, and as an instrument of consecration.

Mnoatia Forest spirits.

Moccasins One-piece shoes made of soft leather, especially deerskin.

Modi Thor's son.

Moly A magical plant given to Odysseus by Hermes as protection against Circe's powers.

Montezuma Great emperor who consolidated the Aztec Empire.

Mordred Bastard son of King Arthur and Morgawse, Queen of Orkney, who, unknown to Arthur, was his half-sister. Mordred becomes one of King Arthur's knights of the Round Table before betraying and fatally wounding Arthur, causing him to leave Britain for Avalon.

Morgan le Fay Enchantress and half-sister to King Arthur, Morgan was an apprentice of Merlin's. She is generally depicted as benevolent, yet did pit herself against Arthur and his knights on occasion. She escorts Arthur on his final journey to Avalon. Also known as Morgain le Fay.

Morholt The Knight sent to Cornwall to force King Mark to pay tribute to Ireland. He is killed by Tristan.

Morongoe the brave (Lesotho) Man who was turned into a snake by evil spirits because Tau was jealous that he had married the beautiful Mokete, the chief's daughter. Morongoe was returned to human form after his son, Tsietse, returned him to their family.

Mosima (Bapedi) The underworld or abyss.

Mount Fuji Highest mountain in Japan, on the island of Honshū.

Mount Kunlun This mountain features in many Chinese legends as the home of the great emperors on Earth. It is written in the *Shanghaijing* (*The Classic of Mountains and Seas*) that this towering structure measured no less than 3300 miles in circumference and 4000 miles in height. It acted both as a central pillar to support the heavens, and as a gateway between Heaven and Earth.

Moving Finger Expression for taking responsibility for one's life and actions, which cannot be undone.

Moytura Translated as the 'Plain of Weeping', Mag Tured, or Moytura, was where the Tuatha De Danann fought two of their most significant battles.

Mua An old-time Polynesian god.

Muezzin Person who performs the Muslim call to prayer.

Mugalana A disciple of Buddha.

Muilearteach The Cailleach Bheur of the water, who appears as a witch or a sea-serpent. On land she grew larger and stronger by fire.

Mul-lil God of Nippur, who took the form of a gazelle.

Muloyi Sorcerer, also called mulaki, murozi, ndozi or ndoki.

Mummu Son of Tiawath and Apsu. He formed a trinity with them to battle the gods. Also known as Moumis. In some tales, Mummu is also Merodach, who eventually destroyed Tiawath.

Munin Odin's raven.

Murile (Chaga) Man who dug up a taro tuber that resembled his baby brother, which turned into a living boy. His mother killed the baby when she saw Murile was starving himself to feed it.

Murtough Mac Erca King who ruled Ireland when many of its people – including his wife and family – were converting to Christianity. He remained a pagan.

Muses Goddesses of poetry and song, daughters of Zeus and Mnemosyne.

Musha Expression, often of surprise.

Muskrat North American beaver-like, amphibious rodent.

Muspell Home of fire, and the fire-giants.

Mwidzilo Taboo which, if broken, can cause death.

Nabu God of writing and wisdom. Also known as Nebo. Thought to be the son of Merodach.

Nahua Ancient Mexicans.

Nakula Pandava twin skilled in horsemanship.

Nala One of the monkey host, son of Vishvakarma.

Nana Baluka (Dahomey) Mother of all creation. She gave birth to an androgynous being with two faces. The female face was Mawu, who controlled the night and lands to the west. The male face was Lisa and he controlled the day and the east.

Nanahuatl Also known as Nanauatzin. Presided over skin diseases and known as Leprous, which in Nahua meant 'divine'.

Nandi Shiva's bull.

Nanna Balder's wife.

Nannar God of the moon and patron of the city of Ur.

Naram-Sin Son or ancestor of Sargon and king of the Four Zones or Quarters of Babylon.

Narcissus Son of the River Cephisus. He fell in love with himself and died as a result.

Narve Son of Loki.

Nataraja Manifestation of Shiva, Lord of the Dance.

Natron Preservative used in embalming, mined from the Natron Valley in Egypt.

Nauder Son of Minúchihr, who became king on his death and was tyrannical and hated until Sám begged him to follow in the footsteps of his ancestors.

Nausicaa Daughter of Alcinous, King of Phaeacia, who fell in love with Odysseus.

Nebuchadnezzar Famous king of Babylon. Also known as Nebuchadrezzar.

Necromancy Communicating with the dead.

Nectar Drink of the gods.

Neith Goddess of hunting, fate and war. Neith is sometimes known as the creator of the universe.

Nemesis Goddess of retribution and daughter of night.

Neoptolemus Son of Achilles and Deidameia, he came to Troy at the end of the war to wear his father's armour. He sacrificed Polyxena at the tomb of Achilles.

Nephthys Goddess of the air, night and the dead. Sister of Isis and sister-wife to Seth, she is also the mother of Anubis.

Nereids Sea-nymphs who are the daughters of Nereus and Doris. Thetis, mother of Achilles, was a Nereid.

Nergal God of death and patron god of Cuthah, which was often known as a burial place. He is also known as the god of fire. Married to Aralu, the goddess of the underworld.

Nestor Wise King of Pylus, who led the ships to Troy with Agamemnon and Menelaus.

Neta Daughter of Shiva, friend of Manasa.

Ngai (Gikuyu) Creator god.

Ngaka (Lesotho) Witch doctor.

Niflheim The underworld In Norse mythology, ruled over by Hel.

Night Daughter of Norvi.

Nikumbha One of Ravana's generals.

Nila One of the monkey host, son of Agni.

Nin-Girsu God of fertility and war, patron god of Girsu. Also known as Shul-gur.

Ninigi Grandson of Amaterasu, Ninigi came to Earth bringing rice and order to found the Imperial family. He is known as the August Grandchild.

Niord God of the sea; marries Skadi.

Nippur The home of En-lil and one of the two major cities of Babylonian civilization.

Nirig God of war and storms, and son of Bel. Also known as Enu-Restu.

Nirvana Transcendent state and the final goal of Buddhism.

Nis Mythological creature, similar to a brownie or goblin, usually harmless or even friendly, but can be easily offended. They are often associated with Christmas or the winter solstice.

Noatun Niord's home.

Noisy-Throat One of Ravana's counsellors.

Noondah (Zanzibar) Cannibalistic cat which attacked and killed animals and humans.

Norns The fates and protectors of Yggdrasill. Many believe them to be the same as the Valkyries.

Norvi Father of the night.

Nott Goddess of night.

Nsasak bird Small bird who became chief of all small birds after winning a competition to go without food for seven days. The

Nsasak bird beat the Odudu bird by sneaking out of his home to feed.

Nü Wa The Goddess Nü Wa, who in some versions of the Creation myths is the sole creator of mankind, and in other tales is associated with the God Fu Xi, also a great benefactor of the human race. Some accounts represent Fu Xi as the brother of Nü Wa, but others describe the pair as lovers who lie together to create the very first human beings. Fu Xi is also considered to be the first of the Chinese emperors of mythical times who reigned from 2953 to 2838 BC.

Nuada The first king of the Tuatha De Danann in Ireland, who lost an arm in the first battle of Moytura against the Fomorians. He became known as 'Nuada of the Silver Hand' when Diancecht, the great physician of the Tuatha De Danann, replaced his hand with a silver one after the battle.

Nunda (Swahili, East Africa) Slayer that took the form of a cat and grew so big that it consumed everyone in the town except the sultan's wife, who locked herself away. Her son, Mohammed, killed Nunda and cut open its leg, setting free everyone Nunda had eaten.

Nut Goddess of the sky, stars and astronomy. Sister-wife of Keb and mother of Osiris, Isis, Set and Nephthys. She often appears in the form of a cow.

Nyame (Ashanti) God of the sky, who sees and knows everything.

Nymphs Minor female deities associated with particular parts of the land and sea.

Obassi Osaw (Ekoi) Creator god with his twin, Obassi Nsi. Originally, Obassi Osaw ruled the skies while Obassi Nsi ruled the Earth.

Obatala (Yoruba) Creator of humankind. He climbed down a golden chain from the sky to the earth, then a watery abyss, and formed land and humankind. When Olorun heard of his success, he created the sun for Obatala and his creations.

Oberon Fairy king.

Odin Allfather and king of all gods, he is known for travelling the nine worlds in disguise and recognized only by his single eye; dies at Ragnarok.

Oduduwa (Yoruba) Divine king of Ile-Ife, the holy city of Yoruba.

Odur Freyia's husband.

Odysseus Greek hero, son of Laertes and Anticleia, who was renowned for his cunning, the master behind the victory at Troy, and known for his long voyage home.

Oedipus Son of Leius, King of Thebes and Jocasta. Became King of Thebes and married his mother.

Ogdoad Group of eight deities who were formed into four male-female couples who joined to create the gods and the world.

Ogham One of the earliest known forms of Irish writing, originally used to inscribe upright pillar stones.

Oiran Courtesan.

Oisin Also called Ossian (particularly by James Macpherson who wrote a set of Gaelic Romances about this character, supposedly garnered from oral tradition). Ossian was the son of Fionn and Sadbh, and had various brothers, according to different legends. He was a man of great wisdom, became immortal for many centuries, but in the end he became mad.

Ojibwe Another name for the Chippewa, a tribe of Algonquin stock.

Okuninushi Deity and descendant of Susanoo, who married Suseri-hime, Susanoo's daughter, without his consent. Susanoo tried to kill him many times but did not succeed and eventually forgave Okuninushi. He is sometimes thought to be the son or grandson of Susanoo.

Olokun (Yoruba) Most powerful goddess who ruled the seas and marshes. When Obatala created Earth in her domain, other gods began to divide it up between them. Angered at their presumption, she caused a great flood to destroy the land.

Olorun (Yoruba) Supreme god and ruler of the sky. He sees and controls everything, but others, such as Obatala, carry out the work for him. Also known as Olodumare.

Olympia Zeus's home in Elis.

Olympus The highest mountain in Greece and the ancient home of the gods.

Omecihuatl Female half of the first being, combined with Ometeotl. Together they are the lords of duality or lords of the two sexes. Also known as Ometecutli and Omeciuatl or Tonacatecutli and Tonacaciuatl. Their offspring were Xipe Totec, Huitzilopochtli, Quetzalcoatl and Tezcatlipoca.

Ometeotl Male half of the first being, combined with Omecihuatl.

Ometochtli Collective name for the pulque-gods or drink-gods. These gods were often associated with rabbits as they were thought to be senseless creatures.

Onygate Anyway.

Opening the Mouth Ceremony in which mummies or statues were prayed over and anointed with incense before their mouths were opened, allowing them to eat and drink in the afterlife.

Oracle The response of a god or priest to a request for advice – also a prophecy; the place where such advice was sought; the person or thing from whom such advice was sought.

Oranyan (Yoruba) Youngest grandson of King Oduduwa, who later became king himself.

Orestes Son of Agamemnon and Clytemnestra who escaped following Agamemnon's murder to King Strophius. He later returned to Argos to murder his mother and avenge the death of his father.

Orpheus Thracian singer and poet, son of Oeagrus and a Muse. Married Eurydice and when she died tried to retrieve her from the Underworld.

Orunmila (Yoruba) Eldest son of Olorun, he helped Obatala create land and humanity, which he then rescued after Olokun flooded the lands. He has the power to see the future.

Osiris God of fertility, the afterlife and death. Thought to be the first of the pharaohs. He was murdered by his brother, Set, after which he was conjured back to life by Isis, Anubis and others before becoming lord of the afterworld. Married to Isis, who was also his sister.

Otherworld The world of deities and spirits, also known as the Land of Promise, or the Land of Eternal Youth, a place of everlasting life where all earthly dreams come to be fulfilled.

Owuo (Krachi, West Africa) Giant who personifies death. He causes a person to die every time he blinks his eye.

Palamedes Hero of Nauplia, believed to have created part of the ancient Greek alphabet. He tricked Odysseus into joining the fleet setting out for Troy by placing the infant Telemachus in the path of his plough.

Palermo Stone Stone carved with hieroglyphs, which came from the Royal Annals of ancient Egypt and contains a list of the kings of Egypt from the first to the early fifth dynasties.

Palfrey Docile and light horse, often used by women.

Palladium Wooden image of Athene, created by her as a monument to her friend Pallas who she accidentally killed. While in Troy it protected the city from invaders.

Pallas Athene's best friend, whom she killed.

Pan God of Arcadia, half-goat and half-man. Son of Hermes. He is connected with fertility, masturbation and sexual drive. He is also associated with music, particularly his pipes, and with laughter.

Pan Gu Some ancient writers suggest that this God is the offspring of the opposing forces of nature, the yin and the yang. The yin (female) is associated with the cold and darkness of the earth, while the yang (male) is associated with the sun and the warmth of the heavens. 'Pan' means 'shell of an egg' and 'Gu' means 'to secure' or 'to achieve'. Pan Gu came into existence so that he might create order from chaos.

Pandareus Cretan King killed by the gods for stealing the shrine of Zeus.

Pandavas Alternative name for sons of Pandu, pupils of Drona.

Pandora The first woman, created by the gods, to punish man for Prometheus's theft of fire. Her dowry was a box full of powerful evil.

Papyrus Paper-like material made from the pith of the papyrus plant, first manufactured in Egypt. Used as a type of paper as well as for making mats, rope and sandals.

Paramahamsa The supreme swan.

Parashurama Human incarnation of Vishnu, 'Rama with an axe'.

Paris Handsome son of Priam and Hecuba of Troy, who was left for dead on Mount Ida but raised by shepherds. Was reclaimed by his family, then brought them shame and caused the Trojan War by eloping with Helen.

Parsa Holy man. Also known as a zahid.

Parvati Consort of Shiva and daughter of Himalaya.

Passion Wife of desire.

Pavanarekha Wife of Ugrasena, mother of Kans.

Peerie Folk Fairy or little folk.

Pegasus The winged horse born from the severed neck of Medusa.

Peggin Wooden vessel with a handle, often shaped like a tub and used for drinking.

Peleus Father of Achilles. He married Antigone, caused her death, and then became King of Phthia. Saved from death himself by Jason and the Argonauts. Married Thetis, a sea nymph.

Penelope The long-suffering but equally clever wife of Odysseus who managed to keep at bay suitors who longed for Ithaca while Odysseus was at the Trojan War and on his ten-year voyage home.

Pentangle Pentagram or five-pointed star.

Pentecost Christian festival held on the seventh Sunday after Easter. It celebrates the holy spirit descending on the disciples after Jesus's ascension.

Percivale Knight of the Round Table and original seeker of the Holy Grail.

Persephone Daughter of Zeus and Demeter who was raped by Hades and forced to live in the Underworld as his queen for three months of every year.

Perseus Son of Danae, who was made pregnant by Zeus. He fought the Gorgons and brought home the head of Medusa. He eventually founded the city of Mycenae and married Andromeda.

Pesh Kef Spooned blade used in the Opening the Mouth ceremony.

Phaeacia The Kingdom of Alcinous on which Odysseus landed after a shipwreck which claimed the last of his men as he left Calypso's island.

Pharaoh King or ruler of Egypt.

Philoctetes Malian hero, son of Poeas, received Heracles's bow and arrows as a gift when he lit the great hero's pyre on Mount Oeta. He was involved in the last part of the Trojan War, killing Paris.

Philtre Magic potion, usually a love potion.

Pibroch Bagpipe music.

Pintura Native manuscript or painting.

Pipiltin Noble class of the Aztecs.

Pismire Ant.

Piu-piu Short mat made from flax leaves and neatly decorated.

Po Gloom, darkness, the lower world.

Polyphemus A Cyclops, but a son of Poseidon. He fell in love with Galatea, but she spurned him. He was blinded by Odysseus.

Polyxena Daughter of Priam and Hecuba of Troy. She was sacrificed on the grave of Achilles by Neoptolemus.

Pooka Mythical creature with the ability to shapeshift. Often appears as a horse, but also as a bull, dog or in human form, and has the ability to talk. Also known as púca.

Popol Vuh Sacred 'book of counsel' of the Quiché or K'iche' Maya people.

Poseidon God of the sea, and of sweet waters. Also the god of earthquakes. His is brother to Zeus and Hades, who divided the earth between them.

Pradyumna Son of Krishna and Rukmini.

Prahasta (Long-Hand) One of Ravana's generals.

Prajapati Creator of the universe, father of the gods, demons and all creatures, later known as Brahma.

Priam King of Troy, married to Hecuba, who bore him Hector, Paris, Helenus, Cassandra, Polyxena, Deiphobus and Troilus. He was murdered by Neoptolemus.

Pritha Mother of Karna and of the Pandavas.

Prithivi Consort of Dyaus and goddess of the earth.

Proetus King of Argos, son of Abas.

Prometheus A Titan, son of Iapetus and Themus. He was champion of mortal men, which he created from clay. He stole fire from the gods and was universally hated by them.

Prose Edda Collection of Norse myths and poems, thought to have been compiled in the 1200s by Icelandic historian Snorri Sturluson.

Proteus The old man of the sea who watched Poseidon's seals.

Psyche A beautiful nymph who was the secret wife of Eros, against the wishes of his mother Aphrodite, who sent Psyche to perform many tasks in hope of causing her death. She eventually married Eros and was allowed to become partly immortal.

Ptah Creator god and deity of Memphis who was married to Sekhmet. Ptah built the boats to carry the souls of the dead to the afterlife.

Puddock Frog.

Pulque Alcoholic drink made from fermented agave.

Purusha The cosmic man, he was sacrificed and his dismembered body became all the parts of the cosmos, including the four classes of society.

Purvey To provide or supply.

Pushkara Nala's brother.

Pushpaka Rama's chariot.

Putana A rakshasi.

Pygmalion A sculptor who was so lonely he carved a statue of a beautiful woman, and eventually fell in love with it. Aphrodite brought the image to life.

Quauhtli Eagle.

Quern Hand mill used for grinding corn.

Quetzalcoatl Deity and god of wind. He is represented as a feathered or plumed serpent and is usually a wise and benevolent god. Offspring of Ometeotl and Omecihuatl, he is also known as Kukulkan.

Ra God of the sun, ruling male deity of Egypt whose name means 'sole creator'.

Radha The principal mistress of Krishna.

Ragnarok The end of the world.

Rahula Son of Siddhartha and Yashodhara.

Raiden God of thunder. He traditionally has a fierce and demonic appearance.

Rakshasas Demons and devils.

Ram of Mendes Sacred symbol of fatherhood and fertility.

Rama or **Ramachandra** A prince and hero of the Ramayana, worshipped as an incarnation of Vishnu.

Ra-Molo (Lesotho) Father of fire, a chief who ruled by fear. When trying to kill his brother, Tau the lion, he was turned into a monster with the head of a sheep and the body of a snake.

Rangatira Chief, warrior, gentleman.

Regin A blacksmith who educated Sigurd.

Reinga The spirit land, the home of the dead.

Reservations Tracts of land allocated to the native American people by the United States Government with the purpose of bringing the many separate tribes under state control.

Rewati Daughter of Raja, marries Balarama.

Rhadha Wife of Adiratha, a gopi of Brindaban and lover of Krishna.

Rhea Mother of the Olympian gods. Cronus ate each of her children, but she concealed Zeus and gave Cronus a swaddled rock in his place.

Rill Small stream.

Rimu (Chaga) Monster known to feed off human flesh, which sometimes takes the form of a werewolf.

Rishis Sacrificial priests associated with the devas in Swarga.

Rituparna King of Ayodhya.

Rohini The wife of Vasudeva, mother of Balarama and Subhadra, and carer of the young Krishna. Another Rohini is a goddess and consort of Chandra.

Rōnin Samurai whose master had died or fallen out of favour.

Rubáiyát Collection of poems written by Omar Khayyám.

Rúdábeh Wife of Zál and mother of Rustem.

Rudra Lord of Beasts and disease, later evolved into Shiva.

Rukma Rukmini's eldest brother.

Rustem Son of Zál and Rúdábeh, he was a brave and mighty warrior who undertook seven labours to travel to Mázinderán to rescue Kai-káús. Once there, he defeated the White Demon and rescued Kai-káús. He rode the fabled stallion Rakhsh and is also known as Rustam.

Ryō Traditional gold currency.

Sabdh Mother of Ossian, or Oisin.

Sabitu Goddess of the sea.

Sagara King of Ayodhya.

Sahadeva Pandava twin skilled in swordsmanship.

Sahib diwan Lord high treasurer or chief royal executive.

Saiawúsh Son of Kai-káús, who was put through trial by fire when Sudaveh, Kai-káús's wife, told him that Saiawúsh had taken advantage of her. His innocence was proven when the fire did not harm him. He was eventually killed by Afrásiyáb.

Saithe Blessed.

Sajara (Mali) God of rainbows. He takes the form of a multi-coloured serpent.

Sake Japanese rice wine.

Sakuni Cousin of Duryodhana.

Salam Greeting or salutation.

Saláman Son of the Shah of Yunan, who fell in love with Absál, his nurse. She died after they had a brief love affair and he returned to his father.

Salmali tree Cotton tree.

Salmon A symbol of great wisdom, around which many Scottish legends revolve.

Sám Mighty warrior who fought and won many battles. Father of Zál and grandfather to Rustem.

Sambu Son of Krishna.

Sampati Elder brother of Jatayu.

Samurai Noblemen who were part of the military in medieval Japan.

Sanehat Member of the royal bodyguard.

Sango (Yoruba) God of war and thunder.

Sangu (Mozambique) Goddess who protects pregnant women, depicted as a hippopotamus.

Santa Daughter of Dasharatha.

Sarapis Composite deity of Apis and Osiris, sometimes known as Serapis. Thought to be created to unify Greek and Egyptian citizens under the Greek pharaoh Ptolemy.

Sarasvati The tongue of Rama.

Sarcophagus Stone coffin.

Sargon of Akkad Raised by Akki, a husbandman, after being hidden at birth. Sargon became King of Assyria and a great hero. He founded the first library in Babylon. Similar to King Arthur or Perseus.

Sarsar Harsh, whistling wind.

Sasabonsam (Ashanti) Forest ogre.

Sassun Scottish word for England.

Sati Daughter of Daksha and Prasuti, first wife of Shiva.

Satrughna One of Dasharatha's four sons.

Satyavan Truth speaker, husband of Savitri.

Satyavati A fisher-maid, wife of Bhishma's father, Shamtanu.

Satyrs Elemental spirits which took great pleasure in chasing nymphs. They had horns, a hairy body and cloven hooves.

Saumanasa A mighty elephant.

Scamander River running across the Trojan plain, and father of Teucer.

Scarab Dung beetle, often used as a symbol of the immortal human soul and regeneration.

Scylla and Charybdis Scylla was a monster who lived on a rock of the same name in the Straits of Messina, devouring sailors. Charybdis was a whirlpool in the Straits which was supposedly inhabited by the hateful daughter of Poseidon.

Seal Often believed that seals were fallen angels. Many families are descended from seals, some of which had webbed hands or feet. Some seals were the children of sea-kings who had become enchanted (selkies).

Seelie-Court The court of the Fairies, who travelled around their realm. They were usually fair to humans, doling out punishment that was morally sound, but they were quick to avenge insults to fairies.

Segu (Swahili, East Africa) Guide who informs humans where honey can be found.

Sekhmet Solar deity who led the pharaohs in war. She is goddess of healing and was sent by Ra to destroy humanity when people turned against the sun god. She is portrayed with the head of a lion.

Selene Moon-goddess, daughter of Hyperion and Theia. She was seduced by Pan, but loved Endymion.

Selkie Mythical creature which is seal-like when in water but can shed its skin to take on human form when on land.

Seneschal Steward of a royal or noble household.

Sensei Teacher.

Seriyut A disciple of Buddha.

Sessrymnir Freyia's home.

Set God of chaos and evil, brother of Osiris, who killed him by tricking him into getting into a chest, which he then threw in the Nile, before cutting Osiris's body into fourteen separate pieces. Also known as Seth.

Sgeulachd Stories.

Shah Nameh *The Book of Kings* written by Ferdowski, one of the world's longest epic poems, which describes the mythology and history of the Persian Empire.

Shaikh Respected religious man.

Shaivas or Shaivites Worshippers of Shiva.

Shakti Power or wife of a god and Shiva's consort as his feminine aspect.

Shaman Also known as the 'Medicine Men' of Indian tribes, it was the shaman's role to cultivate communication with the spirit world. They were endowed with knowledge of all healing herbs, and learned to diagnose and cure disease. They could foretell the future, find lost property and had power over animals, plants and stones.

Shamash God of the sun and protector of Gilgamesh, the great Babylonian hero. Known as the son of Sin, the moon god, he is also portrayed as a judge of good and evil.

Shamtanu Father of Bhishma.

Shankara A great magician, friend of Chand Sadagar.

Shashti The Sixth, goddess who protects children and women in childbirth.

Sheen Beautiful and enchanted woman who casts a spell on Murtough, King of Ireland, causing him to fall in love with her and cast out his family. He dies at her hands, half burned and half drowned, but she then dies of grief as she returns his love. Sheen is known by many names, including Storm, Sigh and Rough Wind.

Shesh A serpent that takes human birth through Devaki.

Shi-en Fairy dwelling.

Shinto Indigenous religion of Japan, from the pre-sixth century to the present day.

Shireen Married to Khosru. Her beauty meant that she was desired by many, including Khosru's own son by his previous marriage. She killed herself rather than give in to her stepson.

Shitala The Cool One and goddess of smallpox.

Shiva One of the two great gods of post-Vedic Hinduism with Vishnu.

Shogun Military ruler or overlord.

Shoji Sliding door, usually a lattice screen of paper.

Shu God of the air and half of the first divine couple created by Atem. Brother and husband to Tefnut, father to Keb and Nut.

Shubistán Household.

Shudra One of the four fundamental colours (caste).

Shuttle Part of a machine used for spinning cloth, used for passing weft threads between warp threads.

Siddhas Musical ministrants of the upper air.

Sif Thor's wife; known for her beautiful hair.

Sigi Son of Odin.

Sigmund Warrior able to pull the sword from Branstock in the Volsung's hall.

Signy Volsung's daughter.

Sigurd Son of Sigmund, and bearer of his sword. Slays Fafnir the dragon.

Sigyn Loki's faithful wife.

Símúrgh Griffin, an animal with the body of a lion and the head and wings of an eagle. Known to hold great wisdom. Also called a symurgh.

Sin God of the moon, worshipped primarily in Ur.

Sindri Dwarf who worked with Brokki to fashion gifts for the gods; commissioned by Loki.

Sirens Sea nymphs who are half-bird, half-woman, whose song lures hapless sailors to their death.

Sisyphus King of Ephrya and a trickster who outwitted Autolycus. He was one of the greatest sinners in Hades.

Sita Daughter of the earth, adopted by Janaka, wife of Rama.

Skadi Goddess of winter and the wife of Niord for a short time.

Skanda Six-headed son of Shiva and a warrior god.

Skraeling Person native to Canada and Greenland. The name was given to them by Viking settlers and can be translated as 'barbarian'.

Skrymir Giant who battled against Thor.

Sleipnir Odin's steed.

Sluagh The host of the dead, seen fighting in the sky and heard by mortals.

Smote Struck with a heavy blow.

Sohráb Son of Rustem and Tahmineh, Sohráb was slain in battle by his own father, who killed him by mistake.

Sol The sun-maiden.

Soma A god and a drug, the elixir of life.

Somerled Lord of the Isles, and legendary ancestor of the Clan MacDonald.

Soothsayer Someone with the ability to predict or see the future, by the use of magic, special knowledge or intuition. Known as seanagal in Scottish myths.

Squaw North American Indian married woman.

Squint-Eye One of Ramana's monsters.

Squire Shield- or armour-bearer of a knight.

Srutakirti Daughter of Kushadhwaja.

Stirabout Porridge made by stirring oatmeal into boiling milk or water.

Stone Giants A malignant race of stone beings whom the Iroquois believed invaded Indian territory, threatening the Confederation of the Five Nations. These fierce and hostile creatures lived off human flesh and were intent on exterminating the human race.

Stoorworm A great water monster which frequented lochs. When it thrust its great body from the sea, it could engulf islands and whole ships. Its appearance prophesied devastation.

Stot Bullock.

Styx River in Arcadia and one of the four rivers in the Underworld. Charon ferried dead souls across it into Hades, and Achilles was dipped into it to make him immortal.

Subrahmanian Son of Shiva, a mountain deity.

Sugriva The chief of the five great monkeys in the Ramayana.

Sukanya The wife of Chyavana.

Suman Son of Asamanja.

Sumantra A noble Brahman.

Sumati Wife of Sagara.

Sumedha A righteous Brahman who dwelt in the city of Amara.

Sumitra One of Dasharatha's three wives, mother of Lakshmana and Satrughna.

Suniti Mother of Dhruva.

Suparshwa One of Ravana's counsellors.

Supranakha A rakshasi, sister of Ravana.

Surabhi The wish-bestowing cow.

Surcoat Loose robe, traditionally worn over armour.

Surtr Fire-giant who eventually destroys the world at Ragnarok.

Surya God of the sun.

Susanoo God of the storm. He is depicted as a contradictory character with both good and bad characteristics. He was banished from Heaven after trying to kill his sister, Amaterasu.

Sushena A monkey chief.

Svasud Father of summer.

Swarga An Olympian paradise, where all wishes and desires are gratified.

Sweating A ritual customarily associated with spiritual purification and prayer practised by most tribes throughout North America prior to sacred ceremonies or vision quests. Steam was produced within a 'sweat lodge', a low, dome-shaped hut, by sprinkling water on heated stones.

Syrinx An Arcadian nymph who was the object of Pan's love.

Tablet of Destinies Cuneiform clay tablet on which the fates were written. Tiawath had given this to Kingu, but it was taken by Merodach when he defeated them. The storm god Zu later stole it for himself.

Taiaha A weapon made of wood.

Tailtiu One of the most famous royal residences of ancient Ireland. Possibly also a goddess linked to this site.

Tall One of Ravana's counsellors.

Tammuz Solar deity of Eridu who, with Gishzida, guards the gates of Heaven. Protector of Anu.

Tamsil Example or guidance.

Tangi Funeral, dirge. Assembly to cry over the dead.

Taniwha Sea monster, water spirit.

Tantalus Son of Zeus who told the secrets of the gods to mortals and stole their nectar and ambrosia. He was condemned to eternal torture in Hades, where he was tempted by food and water but allowed to partake of neither.

Taoism Taoism (or Daoism) came into being at roughly the same time as Confucianism, although its tenets were radically different and were largely founded on the philosophies of Lao Tzu (Laozi). While Confucius argued for a system of state discipline, Taoism strongly favoured self-discipline and looked upon nature as the architect of essential laws. A newer form of Taoism evolved after the Burning of the Books, placing great emphasis on spirit worship and pacification of the gods.

Tapu Sacred, supernatural possession of power. Involves spiritual rules and restrictions.

Tara Also known as Temair, the Hill of Tara was the popular seat of the ancient High-Kings of Ireland from the earliest times to the sixth century. Located in Co. Meath, it was also the place where great noblemen and chieftains congregated during wartime, or for significant events.

Tara Sugriva's wife.

Tartarus Dark region, below Hades.

Tau (Lesotho) Brother to Ra-Molo, depicted as a lion.

Taua War party.

Tefnut Goddess of water and rain. Married to Shu, who was also her brother. She, like Sekhmet, is portrayed with the head of a lion. Also known as Tefenet.

Telegonus Son of Odysseus and Circe. He was allegedly responsible for his father's death.

Telemachus Son of Odysseus and Penelope who was aided by Athene in helping his mother to keep away the suitors in Odysseus's absence.

Temu The evening form of Ra, the Sun God.

Tengu Goblin or gnome, often depicted as bird-like. A powerful fighter with weapons.

Tenochtitlán Capital city of the Aztecs, founded around AD 1350 and the site of the 'Great Temple'. Now Mexico City.

Teo-Amoxtli Divine book.

Teocalli Great temple built in Tenochtitlán, now Mexico City.

Teotleco Festival of the Coming of the Gods; also the twelfth month of the Aztec calendar.

Tepee A conical-shaped dwelling constructed of buffalo hide stretched over lodge-poles. Mostly used by native American tribes living on the plains.

Tepeyollotl God of caves, desert places and earthquakes, whose name means 'heart of the mountain'. He is depicted as a jaguar, often leaping at the sun. Also known as Tepeolotlec.

Tepitoton Household gods.

Tereus King of Daulis who married Procne, daughter of Pandion King of Athens. He fell in love with Philomela, raped her and cut out her tongue.

Tezcatlipoca Supreme deity and Lord of the Smoking Mirror. He was also patron of royalty and warriors. Invented human sacrifice to the gods. Offspring of Ometeotl and Omecihuatl, he is known as the Jupiter of the Aztec gods.

Thalia Muse of pastoral poetry and comedy.

Theia Goddess of many names, and mother of the sun.

Theseus Son of King Aegeus of Athens. A cycle of legends has been woven around his travels and life.

Thetis Chief of the Nereids loved by both Zeus and Poseidon. They married her to a mortal, Peleus, and their child was Achilles. She tried to make him immortal by dipping him in the River Styx.

Thialfi Thor's servant, taken when his peasant father unwittingly harms Thor's goat.

Thiassi Giant and father of Skadi, he tricked Loki into bringing Idunn to him. Thrymheim is his kingdom.

Thomas the Rhymer Also called 'True Thomas', he was Thomas of Ercledoune, who lived in the thirteenth century. He met with the Queen of Elfland, and visited her country, was given clothes and a tongue that could tell no lie. He was also given the gift of prophecy, and many of his predictions were proven true.

Thor God of thunder and of war (with Tyr). Known for his huge size, and red hair and beard. Carries the hammer Miolnir. Slays Jormungander at Ragnarok.

Thoth God of the moon. Invented the arts and sciences and regulated the seasons. He is portrayed with the head of an ibis or a baboon.

Three-Heads One of Ravana's monsters.

Thrud Thor's daughter.

Thrudheim Thor's realm. Also called Thrudvang.

Thunder-Tooth Leader of the rakshasas at the siege of Lanka.

Tiawath Primeval dark ocean or abyss, Tiawath is also a monster and evil deity of the deep. She took the form of a dragon or sea serpent and battled the gods of light for supremacy over all living beings. She was eventually defeated by Merodach, who used her body to create Heaven and Earth.

Tiglath-Pileser I King of Assyria, who made it a leading power for centuries.

Tiki   First man created, a figure carved of wood, or other representation of man.

Tirawa   The name given to the Great Creator (see Great Spirit) by the Pawnee tribe who believed that four direct paths led from his house in the sky to the four semi-cardinal points: north-east, north-west, south-east and south-west.

Tiresias   A Theban who was given the gift of prophecy by Zeus. He was blinded for seeing Athene bathing. He continued to use his prophetic talents after his death, advising Odysseus.

Tirfing   Sword made by dwarves which was cursed to kill every time it was drawn, be the cause of three great atrocities, and kill Suaforlami (Odin's grandson), for whom it was made.

Tisamenus   Son of Orestes, who inherited the Kingdom of Argos and Sparta.

Titania   Queen of the fairies.

Tlaloc   God of rain and fertility, so important to the people, because he ensured a good harvest, that the Aztec heaven or paradise was named Tlalocan in his honour.

Tlazolteotl   Goddess of ordure, filth and vice. Also known as the earth-goddess or Tlaelquani, meaning 'filth-eater'. She acted as a confessor of sins or wrongdoings.

Tohu-mate   Omen of death.

Tohunga   A priest; a possessor of supernatural powers.

Toltec   Civilization that preceded the Aztecs.

Tomahawk   Hatchet with a stone or iron head used in war or hunting.

Tonalamatl   Record of the Aztec calendar, which was recorded in books made from bark paper.

Tonalpohualli   Aztec calendar composed of twenty thirteen-day weeks called trecenas.

Totec Solar deity known as Our Great Chief.

Totemism System of belief in which people share a relationship with a spirit animal or natural being with whom they interact. Examples include Ea, who is represented by a fish.

Toxilmolpilia The binding up of the years.

Tristan Nephew of King Mark of Cornwall, who travels to Ireland to bring Iseult back to marry his uncle. On the way, he and Iseult consume a love potion and fall madly in love before their story ends tragically.

Triton A sea-god, and son of Poseidon and Amphitrite. He led the Argonauts to the sea from Lake Tritonis.

Trojan War War waged by the Greeks against Troy, in order to reclaim Menelaus's wife Helen, who had eloped with the Trojan prince Paris. Many important heroes took part, and form the basis of many legends and myths.

Troll Unfriendly mythological creature of varying size and strength. Usually dwells in mountainous areas, among rocks or caves.

Truage Tribute or pledge of peace or truth, usually made on payment of a tax.

Tsuki-yomi God of the moon, brother of Amaterasu and Susanoo.

Tuat The other world or land of the dead.

Tupuna Ancestor.

Tvashtar Craftsman of the gods.

Tyndareus King of Sparta, perhaps the son of Perseus's daughter Grogphone. Expelled from Sparta but restored by Heracles. Married Leda and fathered Helen and Clytemnestra, among others.

Tyr Son of Frigga and the god of war (with Thor). Eventually kills Garm at Ragnarok.

Tzompantli Pyramid of Skulls.

Uayeb The five unlucky days of the Mayan calendar, which were believed to be when demons from the underworld could reach Earth. People would often avoid leaving their houses on uayeb days.

Ubaaner Magician, whose name meant 'splitter of stones', who created a wax crocodile that came to life to swallow up the man who was trying to seduce his wife.

Uile Bheist Mythical creature, usually some form of wild beast.

Uisneach A hill formation between Mullingar and Athlone said to mark the centre of Ireland.

uKqili (Zulu) Creator god.

Uller God of winter, whom Skadi eventually marries.

Ulster Cycle Compilation of folk tales and legends telling of the Ulaids, people from the northeast of Ireland, now named Ulster. Also known as the *Uliad Cycle*, it is one of four Irish cycles of mythology.

Unseelie Court An unholy court comprising a kind of fairies, antagonistic to humans. They took the form of a kind of Sluagh, and shot humans and animals with elf-shots.

Urd One of the Norns.

Urien King of Gore, husband of Morgan le Fey and father to Yvain.

Urmila Second daughter of Janaka.

Usha Wife of Aniruddha, daughter of Vanasur.

Ushas Goddess of the dawn.

Utgard-loki King of the giants. Tricked Thor.

Uther Pendragon King of England in sub-Roman Britain; father of King Arthur.

Utixo (Hottentot) Creator god.

Ut-Napishtim Ancestor of Gilgamesh, whom Gilgamesh sought out to discover how to prevent death. Similar to Noah in that he was sent a vision warning him of a great deluge. He built an ark in seven days, filling it with his family, possessions and all kinds of animals.

Uz Deity symbolized by a goat.

Vach Goddess of speech.

Vajrahanu One of Ravana's generals.

Vala Another name for Norns.

Valfreya Another name for Freyia.

Valhalla Odin's hall for the celebrated dead warriors chosen by the Valkyries.

Vali The cruel brother of Sugriva, dethroned by Rama.

Valkyries Odin's attendants, led by Freyia. Chose dead warriors to live at Valhalla. Also spelled as Valkyrs.

Vamadeva One of Dasharatha's priests.

Vanaheim Home of the Vanir.

Vanir Race of gods in conflict with the Aesir; they are gods of the sea and wind.

Varuna Ancient god of the sky and cosmos, later, god of the waters.

Vasishtha One of Dasharatha's priests.

Vassal Person under the protection of a feudal lord.

Vasudev Descendant of Yadu, husband of Rohini and Devaki, father of Krishna.

Vasudeva A name of Narayana or Vishnu.

Vavasor Vassal or tenant of a baron or lord who himself has vassals.

Vedic Mantras, hymns.

Vernandi One of the Norns.

Vichitravirya Bhishma's half-brother.

Vidar Slays Fenris.

Vidura Friend of the Pandavas.

Vigrid The plain where the final battle is held.

Vijaya Karna's bow.

Vikramaditya A king identified with Chandragupta II.

Vintail Moveable front of a helmet.

Virabhadra A demon that sprang from Shiva's lock of hair.

Viradha A fierce rakshasa, seizes Sita, slain by Rama.

Virupaksha The elephant who bears the whole world.

Vishnu The Preserver, Vedic sun-god and one of the two great gods of post-Vedic Hinduism.

Vision Quest A sacred ceremony undergone by Native Americans to establish communication with the spirit set to direct them in life. The quest lasted up to four days and nights and was preceded by a period of solitary fasting and prayer.

Vivasvat The sun.

Vizier High-ranking official or adviser. Also known as vizir or vazir.

Volsung Family of great warriors about whom a great saga was spun.

Vrishadarbha King of Benares.

Vrishasena Son of Karna, slain by Arjuna.

Vyasa Chief of the royal chaplains.

Wairua Spirit, soul.

Wanjiru (Kikuyu) Maiden who was sacrificed by her village to appease the gods and make it rain after years of drought.

Weighing of the heart Procedure carried out after death to assess whether the deceased was free from sin. If the deceased's heart weighed less than the feather of Ma'at, they would join Osiris in the Fields of Peace.

Whare Hut made of fern stems tied together with flax and vines, and roofed in with raupo (reeds).

White Demon Protector of Mázinderán. He prevented Kai-káús and his army from invading.

Withy Thin twig or branch which is very flexible and strong.

Wolverine Large mammal of the musteline family with dark, very thick, water-resistant fur, inhabiting the forests of North America and Eurasia.

Wroth Angry.

Wyrd One of the Norns.

Xanthus & Balius Horses of Achilles, immortal offspring of Zephyrus the west wind. A gift to Achilles's father Peleus.

Xipe Totec High priest and son of Ometeotl and Omecihuatl. Also known as the god of the seasons.

Xiupohualli Solar year, composed of eighteen twenty-day months. Also spelt Xiuhpōhualli.

Yadu A prince of the Lunar dynasty.

Yakshas Same as rakshasas.

Yakunin Government official.

Yama God of Death, king of the dead and son of the sun.

Yamato Take Legendary warrior and prince. Also known as Yamato Takeru.

Yashiki Residence or estate, usually of a daimyō.

Yasoda Wife of Nand.

Yemaya (Yoruba) Wife of Obatala.

Yemoja (Yoruba) Goddess of water and protector of women.

Yggdrasill The World Ash, holding up the Nine Worlds. Does not fall at Ragnarok.

Ymir Giant created from fire and ice; his body created the world.

Yo The female principle who, joined with In, the male side, brought about creation and the first gods. In and Yo correspond to the Chinese Yang and Yin.

Yomi The underworld.

Yudhishthira The eldest of the Pandavas, a great soldier.

Yuki-Onna The Snow-Bride or Lady of the Snow, who represents death.

Yvain Son of Morgan le Fay and knight of the Round Table, who goes on chivalric quests with a lion he rescued from a dragon.

Zahid Holy man.

Zál Son of Sám, who was born with pure white hair. Sám abandoned Zál, who was raised by the Símúrgh, or griffins. Zal became a great warrior, second only to his son, Rustem. Also known as Ním-rúz and Dustán.

Zephyr Gentle breeze.

Zeus King of gods, god of sky, weather, thunder, lightning, home, hearth and hospitality. He plays an important role as the voice of justice, arbitrator between man and gods, and among them. Married to Hera, but lover of dozens of others.

Zohák Serpent-king and figure of evil. Father of Mihrab.

Zu God of the storm, who took the form of a huge bird. Similar to the Persian símúrgh.

Zukin Head covering.